THEY STOOD GAZING DOWN AT THE POOL.

"I suppose you knew Mr. Tyler's first wife," Lora Tyler said to Rebecca.

The young black girl moved back, keeping her gaze from the shimmering pool as if she shrank from looking at it. "Yes'm," she finally said. "A real nice lady she was. That was a sorry thing that happened, ma'am."

Lora walked down the bank to the edge of the water. "They say it's very deep out there."

"I reckon that's right." The girl turned suddenly, showing her first sign of emotion. "Mrs. Tyler, this is a bad place. If you want to rest, we can go a mite higher up the hill."

Lora moved closer to the pond. "Miss Virginia's death must have been a tragic thing for everyone," she said thoughtfully. "But it was an accident, wasn't it?"

The girl watched her, wide-eyed for a moment.

"Wasn't it an accident?" Lora repeated.

Rebecca did not answer.

The girl backed away and started to run up the hill, as if some demon from the pool pursued her.

The
QUICKSILVER POOL

Phyllis A. Whitney

FAWCETT CREST • NEW YORK

THE QUICKSILVER POOL

THIS BOOK CONTAINS THE COMPLETE TEXT OF
THE ORIGINAL HARDCOVER EDITION.

Published by Fawcett Crest Books, a unit of CBS Publications,
the Consumer Publishing Division of CBS Inc., by arrangement
with Meredith Press.

ISBN: 0-449-23983-7

Printed in the United States of America

27   26   25   24   23   22   21   20   19

The

QUICKSILVER
POOL

I

ONE BRIGHT SMILE shone among more sober faces in the ferry crowd that evening as a tall young woman in her early thirties walked proudly aboard beside her husband in Union blue. To have your captain home for Christmas—that was cause for joy, and Serena Lord revealed her feelings in the look of love she turned upon him.

They hurried through the lower precincts, which smelled strongly of cigar smoke and horses, and mounted the stairs to the draughty upper cabin. Here they found a seat not too far from the circle of warmth cast by a glowing stove, and Edgar Lord seated his wife, hoops and all, with a slightly military flourish before he took his place beside her.

Serena was a handsome woman, far from stingily built, though she carried her buxom quality well, thanks to her height and good-sized bones. Beneath the peak of her green bonnet rusty red hair shone in the light of kerosene lamps, and there was a saucy sprinkling of reddish freckles across her nose. But it was her eyes that made you look twice— warm and brown and alive with interest. Even now as she sat with her hand tucked through the crook of her husband's arm, as if she could not let him go for a moment, her lively gaze found time to note other passengers, so that she might smile and bow to those she recognized, speculate about those who were strangers.

Paddle wheels churned the waters of New York harbor to a froth and black smoke studded with sparks poured from tall stacks as the ferry pulled away from the Whitehall slip for the last trip of the evening to Staten Island. There was the usual sprinkling of uniforms among the passengers and the all too frequent evidence of wounds or crippling.

As the war wound along through its second year uniforms had begun to look less spruce, the brass of buttons had tarnished a bit and the expression of men in blue had grown more grim. No one talked these days of licking the foolish South in a hurry. Though Christmas was only two weeks off,

New York had been unable to whip itself into a festive spirit. With the disaster of Fredericksburg so recently upon them, the hospitals so full and the prospect of victory doubtful and distant, it was difficult to stir up any semblance of holiday joy.

A few moments after the boat left the slip Serena noted with recognition a soldier who leaned on a single crutch, swinging himself painfully toward a bench not far distant in the center of the cabin. At his side moved a slightly built girl in a brown mantle and drab brown bonnet. The man's cheeks were hollowed, his blue eyes sunken, but there was still the mark of extraordinary good looks upon him. Dark brown hair grew thickly back from a brow which belonged more to a man of thought than of action. Remembering him in a happier role, pity rose in Serena.

"Don't look now," she whispered to her husband, "but in a moment . . . there, she's helping him down. Edgar, that's Wade Tyler!"

Edgar nodded gravely. "You wrote that he'd been wounded. He looks ill too. Is he just coming home?"

"He must be," Serena said, her gaze flicking away, then swiftly back so that she could study the girl. "I saw his mother only yesterday, but she said nothing about his returning. And I asked about him too. But then, that's like the old lady. Do you suppose he's brought home a new wife?"

"Why not?" Edgar smiled at his wife's familiar flaring of curiosity. "The sooner he forgets Virginia the better."

"I'm sorry for the girl then," said Serena firmly. "Going into a gloomy old house with a woman who is an invalid, to say nothing of that difficult little boy. Edgar, do you suppose we could go over and speak to them? After all, I grew up with Wade. It seems discourteous not to greet him and—"

"Let him be," said her husband gently. "He looks worn out. This is no time for neighborly chatter. If they need help when we dock, we'll go speak to them then."

Serena had to be satisfied with that. She tightened her hand in an affectionate squeeze upon her husband's arm and gave all her attention to him for a few moments. But her curious interest soon turned again to the girl and she speculated silently.

Wade's companion was a thin, rather drab little thing. Her brown mantle looked shabby and her hoops were unfashionably small. The strings of her bonnet, though neatly tied, were frayed. Well, Mrs. Tyler would change all that. She would never tolerate shabbiness in her son's wife. Not with

8

her exalted opinion of the Cowles-Tyler position to uphold.

"Virginia was so pretty," Serena mused. "I wonder what he could have seen in this girl. She's brown as a winter berry and as plain. I wonder if he's got himself another meek one."

Edgar chuckled. "You women! And especially you, my dear. It must always be hard to guess what any man sees in another girl. But since you're going to pay no attention to me until your curiosity is satisfied, let me tell you about her."

It was an old game they used to play—making up stories about people they did not know. Serena's brown eyes sparkled and she hung on his words.

"I doubt that she has married him for his money," Edgar went on. "She doesn't seem that sort, even though wealth is obviously not a part of her world. So it must be love."

Serena nodded. "The girls always fell in love with the Tyler charm—all except me. That's the way it was with his father before him. Though he was a different sort—that one."

"I think," Edgar went on, "that she is not meek. If you'll note—there's a set to her chin, a certain firmness of mouth. I'd like to see her smile—she might surprise us."

But the girl with Wade Tyler did not smile. Now and then she glanced solicitously at the man beside her, but she did not touch him. Her hands lay quietly in her lap, as tanned as her face, the gold wedding band their only ornament. They were square, sturdy hands, the nails short and broken—not the well-kept hands of a lady.

Wade winced, apparently at a twinge of pain from his leg, and she bent toward him anxiously. Serena could not hear her words, but the girl evidently persuaded him to stretch out on the empty seat, to sleep if he could and rest his wounded leg. His cavalry uniform, with its lieutenant's insignia, was far shabbier than Edgar's and had been patched in several places. He stretched out willingly and seemed to fall at once into exhausted slumber. His wife bent over him for a moment, touched his forehead lightly, as if to reassure herself that he had not fever, and then sat back in her seat, her dark eyes looking straight ahead unseeingly, as if she were hardly aware of those about her.

"Jemmy Tyler needs a mother," Serena murmured softly. "If it weren't for Adam I don't know what he'd do these days. Adam's been fine with the boys."

"How is Adam?" Edgar asked.

Serena considered for a moment. Her brother had been released from Libby Prison in an exchange only two months before and it was still too early to say how he was. He needed

9

to recover his strength and there were still fever bouts. He'd always had a wry twist of mind and now he sometimes seemed very bitter. But he had been wonderful with her own two boys, and especially kind to Jemmy Tyler. Before she could find words to answer her husband, the girl in shabby brown suddenly rose and walked toward the ladies' cabin. Serena saw her chance. She waited no more than forty seconds, then excused herself to her husband, who nodded in amused understanding, and followed the girl into the cabin.

Here there was red upholstery, curtains of red rep and a watery mirror. To her satisfaction, Serena saw that they had the place to themselves. The younger woman had taken off her bonnet and was smoothing down dark brown wings of hair drawn over her ears from a center part. At the back of her neck a snood held a thick, lustrous coil and her fingers worked absently at a more secure pinning. She paid no attention to Serena's entrance, but continued to stare at her image in the wavery glass as if she looked at some person she did not know and about whom she was curious.

Serena coughed gently and when that attracted no attention, she stepped to the girl's side and frankly held out her hand.

"Good evening," she said. "I am Serena Lord, Mrs. Edgar Lord. I would like to welcome you to Staten Island. My husband and I are neighbors of the Tylers, just along the lane."

The girl threw her a startled look, then seemed to gain reassurance from Serena's warm smile, and gave her small, rough hand into the older woman's clasp.

"Thank you," she said. "It is nice to meet a neighbor so quickly. I am Lora Blair. That is"—color darkened her cheeks —"that is, I'm Lora Blair *Tyler* now. I keep forgetting."

Serena's laugh was warm as her smile. "I know! I can remember doing that myself in the beginning. Of course you realize I followed you in here deliberately because I was curious about whether Wade was bringing home a new wife. I'm glad he is."

Unexpectedly the girl smiled, and Edgar had been right. Her teeth were whitely even, her lips generous, and the smile lighted her face to prettiness. She would never be a beauty, but when the dark weight of worry and weariness lifted, there was a bright look of youth about her that was appealing. Serena's ready heart was touched.

"You must come to see us very soon," she said.

The smile faded and the look of doubt returned to cloud

the young face. "I'd love to—but my husband—well, you see . . ."

Serena nodded. "Don't let him mope in that old house, my dear. Or if he will not come out, then run away to visit me yourself. Any time you are lonely. Or if anything should go wrong. Not that it will, of course," she added hastily.

Lora Tyler bowed and turned gravely back to the mirror. Serena had the feeling that while the girl had warmed to her for an instant, she had as quickly forgotten she was there. Without further speech Serena slipped out of the cabin and went back to her husband.

"Forgive me, Edgar," she told him contritely. "I simply had to greet that poor, lonely little thing."

"Of course," he said. "I'd love you less if you weren't ready to take every lost kitten to your heart. But now you are to forget her and attend only to me."

Her hand was upon his arm again. "I have never for a moment stopped attending to you. Edgar, I wonder if she knows about Morgan Channing?"

Edgar sighed in mock resignation. "What does it matter? The fascinating Mrs. Channing spends most of her time abroad these days, does she not?"

"She's coming home," Serena said. "They're opening up the big house and when I saw Ambrose the other day he told me she was due any time now. None of us who knew Morgan and Wade in the old days is likely to forget that stormy affair."

"I think it hardly matters now," Edgar repeated. "All that belongs to the past before he married Virginia. And now we will talk about no one but you."

Back in the ladies' cabin, Lora Blair Tyler tied the frayed ribbons of her bonnet and stared at her own somber reflection. Already she had forgotten Serena, returning to the treadmill of her concern. Had she made the right move in this step she had taken? Or had she done a dangerous, wicked thing that would bring disaster upon Wade as well as herself? It was so hard to know. Nothing was clear and simple any more. She turned away and went back into the wavering lamplight of the main cabin.

A glance assured her that Wade still slept in complete oblivion, in spite of the vibration of the boat, and she did not for the moment return to his side. Restlessness drove her and she walked toward the front of the ferry to glass windows where she could look out at the water. December cold seeped in upon her through the cracks and she drew her brown

11

mantle more closely about her, pulled neatly darned gloves over her hands. She had lived too long on the rim of the South and her blood was thin. But the cold woke her, drove lethargy from her veins, and she peered ahead anxiously toward the dark mound that rose out there across the black waters of the harbor. It was a mound sprinkled with pinpoints of yellow light and she knew it must be the island. What lay ahead of her there she could not tell, but she straightened her shoulders, knowing she must face without faltering this life she had chosen.

Yet, even as she accepted this, a name flashed unbidden through her mind as it had so often in these last months. "Martin," she thought. "Oh, Martin!"

The ringing of his name in her mind carried her back to that October day in Pineville when she had stood in the kitchen of her father's house washing dishes after the noon meal. She had been thinking of him then too, and she had not even started at the sound of shots, though they meant skirmishes again on the edge of town, perhaps in the very streets. Pineville was on the border, neither wholly North nor South, and many a time since Sumter blue uniforms or gray had marched its streets.

To Doc Blair it made no difference what color a soldier wore if he were wounded or in need. Her father's great hatred was for war itself, for its wicked wastefulness of life. All his long working years had been spent in saving life and he boiled with anger against governments which valued it so little. She was glad he had dropped into heavy sleep in the darkened parlor that afternoon. He took so little time for rest these days.

Her hands in soapy water, she had returned to thoughts of Martin. They would have been married on his next leave. A leave that now would never come. He had died of wounds in Kentucky some two months before and she still could not believe it. No one she had ever known had been so gaily, so vitally alive as Martin. The little that had been carefree in her own life had vanished with his dying. Nothing mattered to her now except her father.

The rattle of shots sounded in the very street outside the house, but she was at the back and only hoped dully that her father might not hear, that no one would be hurt, that no new panes would be broken. It was not until she heard the front door open that she snatched up a towel to dry her hands and ran into the front hall.

The door stood ajar and Doc was running down the

steps into sunlight when she called after him, while a rider-
less horse screamed in the street.

Her father snapped at her over his shoulder, "Feller by the
front gate. Needs me!" and on he went.

She looked up and down the street in fright and saw the
handful of cavalry, heard again the ugly rattle of shots. Shots
not intended for the town's citizenry, but playing no favorites
if the wrong man got in the way. Even as she stood helpless
in the doorway, the damp towel twisted in her hands, she
saw her father crumple, saw the familiar crimson seeping
against his white shirt.

He was coughing when she reached him, the bright, betraying bubbles on his lips. She bent above him and he
clutched at her, choking out words.

"Feller needs help. Never . . . mind . . . me. Get . . .
him . . ."

He sagged in her arms and the crimson spread against her
white apron. She knew. She had seen men die before. And
as suddenly as this. No tears came because what was happening could not be. Her father was needed so badly—by
others as well as herself. Doc Blair had always considered
God his good friend, and surely He would not reward a life
of faithful service by an act such as this. But apparently He
had and Lora could only hold her father numbly against
her heart while the warm October sun beat upon her head
and there was a galloping in the street.

A voice shouted at her suddenly, angrily. "Gawd's sake,
ma'am, get in the house! Y'lost y'senses?"

She looked up dully to note without interest that the boy
on the prancing horse wore gray. The wounded horse
screamed again and the Confederate soldier hesitated, perhaps
counting the waste of good ammunition, then leaned from
his saddle to put a bullet through the beast's head. A moment later he was gone and the horse lay quivering in the
dust. Near at hand someone moaned in pain.

"Go get him," Doc had said. But why should she? If it
had not been for that sprawled heap of blue out there in
the dusty road her father would not have thrown away his
own life, wasted it so cruelly. She held him closer against her
heart, but in her mind he seemed to speak to her sternly
from the dimness into which he had gone. "It *is* wasted if
that boy dies too. I came out to save him, Lorie. Now you
go do it."

She knew him so well.

Gently she lowered him to the grass beside the path and

got shakily to her feet. The heap of blue in the road had turned into a man with a thick shock of tumbled brown hair and eyes that looked at her in agony as she stepped into the street.

It was a good thing she had worked hard all her life, was strong, for all her small size. Her sturdy hands raised him beneath the armpits, dragged him through the gate. There was blood against his shoulder, more upon his left thigh. He cried out in pain just once and after that bit his lips and did not hinder her.

The steps were hardest to manage, but she got him up them and into the parlor. This would not be the first time it had served as hospital and a cot stood ready. He roused himself then, on good arm and leg, and fell onto it, fainting with pain. She went to work at once in ways her father had taught her. Scissors first, to cut away clinging strands of blue, then warm water. . . .

She worked like a machine, without thought, without sympathy for the man on the cot, without feeling for herself. Part of her remembered that her father lay in the yard, untended in the bright sun. But she knew he would not care. Not so long as she did his bidding.

October . . . how long ago. Now it was nearly Christmas.

The ferry had cut its speed and through the spray-dotted glass before her Lora saw the nearness of lights, of land. She went quickly back to the man who lay stretched asleep on the bench where she had left him. As she bent over him she wondered if he would look up and call her "Virginia" as he had done so many times in his long fever and delirium.

A moment of panic swept through her, of sudden intense consciousness. What had she done in marrying Wade Tyler? She knew far better than he that he loved not her, but only his lost Virginia. Knew too, in all honesty, that she did not love him, except in a way of tenderness and pity that she would have felt toward any helpless being.

Then he opened his eyes, smiled at her and she was herself again, strong and sure. This was what mattered. Only this.

When Edgar Lord and Serena came to offer their help in leaving the ferry, she was grateful to them. She had liked Serena at once and it was a relief that she need not deal with the entire problem of getting Wade and their bundles off the boat by herself.

Wade shook hands with Edgar cheerfully and flashed his winning smile at Serena. Then he swung himself up on his single crutch while Edgar reached for Doc's old carpetbag.

14

"Good to see you both," Wade said. "But we'll be all right. If Peter hasn't followed instructions to meet this boat I'll wring his skinny old neck when I get my hands on him."

"That's the spirit," Edgar said. Nevertheless, he and Serena stayed close by until Peter himself—a lanky fellow with a wide grin—came to greet them. He touched his cap to Lora and gave her a quick look before he turned his attention to Wade and the problem of helping him into the carriage.

"Your mother's waiting, Mr. Wade," he said when they were settled and he had tucked the buffalo robe around them.

"I would suspect as much," said Wade dryly. Under the thick fur his hand found Lora's, held it tight, and she knew he was not wholly confident of the coming meeting with his mother.

II

STEAM from the breath of the horses smoked in the frosty air and there was a jangle of harness as they stamped the ground restlessly. From his seat Peter flapped the reins and the carriage turned onto the rutty, frozen ground of the road. Lamps from hacks and other carriages shone in the gloom near the landing, but Lora had already lost sight of the Lords.

As the Tyler carriage followed a course which ran parallel with the long, dark ridge of hills, Wade gestured toward the hillside.

"Do you see those three clusters of lights up there above us? That's where Dogwood Lane curves around and makes a loop. The lights on the lower right are those of our house, the ones farther on along the hill are at the Lords'."

There were many more lights shining in the Lord windows and to Lora's eyes their welcome seemed somehow warm and bright. The fewer lights at the Tylers' had a spare, cold look. There she went again with her ready imaginings, she chided herself, and turned her attention to higher lights on the hill far above.

"I see you have other neighbors. Who lives in the house on the hilltop?" she asked.

Wade's fingers slackened about her own, and she sensed withdrawal as he spoke. "The name is Channing. We do not care for their society."

15

She put the matter by as having no particular interest for her at the moment. It was not the neighbors who concerned her, but the woman who waited for her son to bring home his new wife.

Lora had exchanged several letters with Wade's mother in the days of his illness. She had written to her at once when she found the address among his papers and Mrs. Tyler had replied, sending money, asking that no expense be spared in the care of her son. But there had been no one to care for him except Lora herself, for Pineville had no second doctor and there was no nearby Union hospital to which he could be moved, or encampment to which she could appeal. She had written to his company, but the letter had been delayed and there was no answer until she no longer needed their help.

The superficial shoulder wound healed quickly and cleanly, but the state of his leg had frightened her. She knew about the horrors of amputation if gangrene set in. But somehow, miraculously, the leg was healing in its own way, though it would be long months before it would carry his weight without aid.

The letters from Mrs. Tyler had been curt and faintly imperious, but Lora had sensed her anxiety and had written fully and warmly in return. She learned that Mrs. Tyler could not come to her son because she was bound to a wheel-chair existence. Later, during Wade's convalescence, Lora had asked about Mrs. Tyler's injury and he had told her briefly that his mother had fallen downstairs some years before.

In the long days when she had fought death away from her patient, Lora's own capacity to feel pain had returned and with it had come tenderness and pity for Wade. That the girl he called for through his fever was the wife who had died a year before, she was quick to discern, and the fact that he too had suffered a loss drew them more closely together. Wade's need of her, the way he began to cling to her and take some cheer from her presence, had increased the tenderness of her own feeling toward him, though at the same time she had shrunk a little within herself as she sensed what might be happening.

While there was never any time when she sought to dream Wade into Martin's place, that was what he was plainly doing with her and his memory of Virginia. He seemed to take joy in finding new resemblances between her own gentleness

16

with him and the gentle ways of Virginia. Lora had struggled against this for a time—insisting that she was *not* Virginia, and not like Virginia, that it was dangerous for him to build such a likeness in his mind. But when he clung to her in desperate need, she could not chide him.

The silence in the carriage had grown heavy and she wrenched herself back to the demands of the present. The horses were walking now, as they climbed the steepening road toward the crest of the hill.

She reached again for Wade's left hand beneath the fur robe. As her fingers touched it she felt through her thin gloves the jagged scar that marked palm and back where something had pierced it long ago.

"You must be anxious to see Jemmy," she said. "As anxious as I am to meet him. I suppose he'll be waiting at the door to greet you."

She felt him stir beside her as he drew his hand from beneath the robe. "Jemmy is not given to demonstrative action, Lora. He is a strange child, as I've tried to make you understand. Not at all like his mother. It may be that he will disappoint you."

"He will not," she asserted firmly. "I've told you about the little brother who died a few years after my mother. Jemmy is going to take his place. Besides, you'll remember that I've been a schoolmarm for the last few years, and I like little boys."

Wade said nothing. He had leaned back against the seat and she knew he was weary to the point of exhaustion. The miserably long ride on the jerky train, with its frequent stops, had been hard to endure. She must be quiet now, let him gather his forces against the encounter ahead.

She felt that it had been wrong not to write his mother of their marriage until just before they left home. There had been no time for Amanda Tyler to answer. But that was the way Wade had wished it. Last night and today they had stayed at the St. Nicholas Hotel in New York, and Wade had sent a message to the island for Peter to meet the last ferry tonight. But he had rested badly at the hotel and the intended respite had not helped him.

She sighed and her breath misted the air within the carriage. How strange to be going as a bride to her husband's home in so cheerless a manner as this. All her plans with Martin had been full of laughter and teasing and gaiety. He had grown up across the street, always known to her, pulling her pigtails when she was little, kissing her under the mistletoe

17

at Christmas time a few years later. How long ago it all seemed to her twenty-two years. Martin had still been a boy when he had gone to fight for the Union cause, and somehow her girlhood had gone with him. Already she felt that she was older than Martin had ever been and that perhaps he would not recognize her now. She felt older even than Wade, who was her senior by seven years.

The horses were turning, the carriage wheels bumping over a driveway, and Wade awoke from his uneasy doze with a start. A moment later they had come to a halt before a flight of porch steps and Peter had dismounted from his seat to open the carriage door. Lora got out quickly and while Peter helped Wade, she stood looking up at the tall, frowning house before her. Candlelight flickered in the hallway, and there was a lamp in the window of a front room upstairs, but that was all. There were no parlor lights in evidence. The frowning aspect, she decided, was due to peaked eaves and a narrowness of architecture. It took a generously wide house to smile.

The door opened as she moved up the steps beside Wade and a bobbing little woman in a black dress and white apron, with a white mobcap on her head, appeared in the doorway. This, Lora knew, was Ellie, Peter's wife—both long in the service of Mrs. Tyler.

Ellie's smile was toothy but fond as she greeted Wade. Like her husband she had only a quick glance for her new mistress, as if she dared not look too closely until a higher jurisdiction sanctioned her interest.

"Your mother's waiting for ye, Mr. Wade. It's better you see her first afore ye go upstairs. Though your room's sparkling ready." She darted a look at Lora and added, "An' yours too, Miz Tyler."

Lora thanked her and stepped into the dimly lighted hall. It was a narrow hall, running past dark, closed doors on right and left, vanishing toward the rear of the house. At one side rose a steep, equally narrow staircase, with a dark-red runner mounting toward the second floor.

Since the hallway was too narrow to permit easy passage of two side by side when one swung a crutch, Lora stepped back for her husband to go ahead. She had a sudden reluctance to face the old woman who waited for them in the back parlor. Her gaze sought the stair landing and the railing above, half expecting to see the bright eyes of an eight-year-old boy peering down at her. But the upper hall was dark and there was no small boy watching for his father.

18

The stale chill of the unheated hallway penetrated to Lora's bones as the outside cold had not done, and she found her teeth chattering as she followed Wade. Ellie scuttled ahead to open the door and announced their coming with a bobbed curtsy to the woman who waited there.

"Come in, come in and shut the door!" commanded a voice that was firm of texture, with no quaver of age to mar its resonance.

Ellie gave Lora a nervous shove, giggled an apology, and shut herself promptly into the hall, leaving the others in the room. Lora was aware of a wave of heat and an odor of wintergreen, of firelight flickering on the ceiling and a lamp aglow on a round walnut table. Then Wade stepped to the side of his mother's chair and she could see for the first time the woman who sat there.

Amanda Tyler wore full black skirts without hoops; black relieved only by the round lace collar and cameo pin at her throat. She sat tall in her chair and one sensed a backbone that was well trained, even though her injured hip had betrayed her. Her hair was still brown, with only a streaking of gray at the temples, though she was well past sixty, and her eyes were remarkably blue and unfaded. There was no evidence of past beauty here, but the strength of will was plain. This was a woman accustomed to her own way, who held her own strong convictions.

She raised her hands to her son and as Wade bent gallantly to kiss them, Lora noted the flash of jewels against their whiteness. Here were beautiful, well-kept hands, betraying age in the blue tracery of veins, but cared for, nevertheless, and revealing a certain vanity on the part of their possessor. Lora had removed her mended gloves, but now she wished they still hid her own rough hands.

Wade turned to present her and she moved forward into the firelight to face sharp blue eyes and take the hand extended to her. It felt cold and dry in her own, like parchment that might crumple if she pressed it, but the strength of the thin fingers startled her.

"My wife, Lora," said Wade and she sensed the stirring of anxiety in him.

The old lady released her hand as if the touch of it displeased her, but her gaze did not waver.

"I shall want to know all about you, Lora," Mrs. Tyler said bluntly. "But that will keep for later. I can see that my son is weary. So now I will merely thank you for your kindness in caring for him. Though I still question your wisdom in trying to do it yourself."

"There wasn't anyone else, Mother," Wade said gently. "For a while the Confederates were between us and our own lines. If it were not for Lora I might not be here now."

"Then I am grateful indeed," said Mrs. Tyler, but her eyes remained cold. It was not necessary, she seemed to imply, to marry one's nurse out of gratitude.

Wade, however, seemed to have thrown off his first uneasiness over this meeting with his mother. The rosy firelight had lessened his pallor. It found bright highlights in the thick dark hair which he wore long above his collar in the fashion of the day. His somewhat ascetic good looks had not been impaired by his thinness and to Lora's eyes he looked at the moment like a portrait she had once seen of a famous English poet.

"It's good to be home, Mother," Wade said and touched her shoulder with the hand not engaged with his crutch.

No word had been spoken of his son and Lora could contain herself no longer.

"I'm very anxious to meet Jemmy," she said. "Has he gone to bed by now?"

Mrs. Tyler threw her a look which discouraged friendly interest. "He has indeed. Though this is Friday and a school day he had to stay home. All day long he refused to eat a bite and at dinner I insisted that he finish every scrap of his meal. I will not have such nonsense. But he has thrown it up since, disgracefully. Weak stomachs never ran in my family—this must be an inheritance from your father's side, Wade. At any rate, he should be asleep by now and I suggest that you do not disturb him."

A sapphire sparked blue fire as she reached her hand to a small bell on the table beside her. Its chime was silver-clear and hung vibrantly in the air for a second or two before fading. At once Ellie appeared, letting in a chill breath from the hallway.

The old woman nodded to her. "Will you show Mrs. Tyler to her room, please. You will have your old room, of course, Wade. And while you did not give us much time, Ellie tells me she has done her best with the rear guest room for Lora. I will say good night now, Lora. But perhaps, Wade, you will stay with me for a moment?"

"Of course, Mother," Wade said and smiled at Lora, who stood uneasy and hesitant, not knowing what was expected of her.

Mrs. Tyler gave her a nod of dismissal and Lora spoke a quick good night to Wade and went into the dim hallway. A candle in Ellie's hand lighted their way up the narrow staircase to the hall above.

"Your room's at the back on the left," Ellie explained. "Mr. Wade's is across the hall at the front. And that other front room is—was Miss Virginia's. Jemmy's room's right back here across from yours." She waved the candle toward the dark wood of a closed door.

"How is Jemmy?" Lora whispered.

Ellie shook her head. "He's been chucking up all evening. I think he does it on purpose. How an angel as sweet as his dear mother could have such a changeling for a son, I'm sure I don't—" She broke off, for the blank door had given way suddenly to a patch of lamplight and a small figure stood in the opening.

Jemmy Tyler was wearing a long flannel nightshirt that hung below his knees and his feet were bare on the cold floor. The dark shock of hair that tumbled over his forehead was like his father's, but there any resemblance ended. He had none of his father's good looks, though his eyes were dark blue and hauntingly intense.

"Good evening, Jemmy," Lora said quietly, making no move toward him.

Jemmy troubled with no amenities. "I know who you are," he announced directly. "But you're not my mother and I'm not going to do what my grandmother says."

Lora smiled at him. "What does your grandmother say you must do?"

There was no returning smile. "She says I'm to call you Mama. But I won't. Nobody can make me."

"Of course not," Lora said. "It would be foolish to call me Mama when I'm not, wouldn't it? Just as foolish as it would be if I called you Son."

Jeremy blinked astonishingly long lashes and shivered faintly.

"Goodness!" Lora cried. "It's cold out here. You'd better hop back in bed and wait for your father to come tuck you in. I think he'll be up in a moment."

There was wisdom in Jemmy's eyes that was greater than his eight years. "My father doesn't like me. And I don't like him." He turned and went back into his room, but before he could close the door Lora went quickly after him.

"All little boys say things like that sometimes. But they

21

aren't very sensible. Hop in bed and I'll tuck you in this time."

"I don't need to be tucked in," said Jemmy stiffly and crawled beneath the star-patterned quilt on his narrow bed.

"That's for you to decide," said Lora. "Would you like your lamp on or off?"

"Ellie said to leave it on while I'm being sick."

Lora's fingers touched the brass knob that would turn down the wick. "But you're through being sick for tonight, aren't you?"

He pulled the quilt up to his chin and thought about that solemnly. "It's funny, but I think maybe I am."

"Of course you are." The light dimmed and went out beneath her fingers and only Ellie's waiting candle in the hall pushed back the shadows in the small room. "You were only sick because I was coming. You were worried about what I might be like. But now you're not worried any more, so you'll go right to sleep."

"How do you know?" he challenged from the darkness of the bed.

"My father was a doctor," she told him. "He taught me lots of things about people who get sick. Good night, Jemmy."

He did not answer and she moved toward the door. But before she could close it, his voice stopped her again.

"What *am* I to call you?" he asked.

She hesitated, seeking for some answer that would satisfy him, but no happy choice came to mind.

"I'll have to think about that," she said. "Shall we talk about it tomorrow?"

"Tomorrow," he said, and she closed the door softly. At least she had given him something to ponder.

Ellie shook her head wonderingly. "I thought you'd have more trouble with him than that. He's a limb, that one."

"I like limbs," said Lora, and went through the door into her own room.

"Peter told me to fix a fire for you," Ellie said grudgingly. "Bathroom's right next door. Anything else you want?"

"Nothing, thank you," said Lora, and Ellie went away.

A bathroom! She had heard of houses that had whole rooms put aside for the purpose of bathing, but she had never been in one before. At home a tin tub in the kitchen had always served her needs.

She was glad to close the door behind her and be alone with her thoughts. How strange for husband and wife to have separate rooms, as was apparently the custom in this house. She felt no hurt, however, but only a faintly guilty sense of relief. She could not deny that it would be good to have a haven of her own to come to; a place where she could think her own thoughts without fear of betraying them to other eyes.

She stepped onto the oval rag rug before the fireplace and bent to warm cold fingers. Then, turning her back to the flames, she surveyed the little room. There were cheerful yellow nosegays in the wallpaper and a flowered yellow globe on the china lamp. Ruffled white curtains framed a window that looked out on the rear of the house, while at the side were long glass doors with outer shutters closed against the night. The battered trunk she had shipped north was nowhere to be seen, though she even looked for it beneath the high bed. Against one wall stood a huge wardrobe closet of mahogany and when she opened its creaking doors she found her few shabby garments lost in cavernous depths. The drawers of a mahogany dresser held the rest of her meager possessions.

A twinge of dismay pricked through her. She hated to think that strangers had handled her few belongings. Their shabbiness should have remained her own secret and she should have had their distribution left to herself. Mrs. Tyler, undoubtedly, had given orders that her trunk be unpacked.

The stairs creaked as someone climbed them and Lora waited, listening. Wade preferred to manage the climbing of steps himself and he was becoming fairly proficient in his use of a crutch. Nevertheless, his progress was painfully slow as he lifted himself stiff-legged from step to step. There came the long silence of a rest as he reached the top of the stairs. Then she heard his own door open and close. The house was quiet again.

She wondered if she should go to him. But if he had wanted to see her he would have come here to her room. His mother had put a strangeness between them—she had sensed it downstairs. And there was no telling what had transpired between those two after she had been somewhat curtly dismissed.

Weariness swept through her and she returned to the fire to undress. For once she braided her long hair without brushing it and crawled limply beneath the covers. The plump feather bed enveloped her body, soothing her physical being. But her mind would not cease its scurrying from one thought to another.

Mrs. Tyler, plainly, was ready to dislike her. Wade was still weak and it was not fair to submit him to any tug of war between them. She must try her best to please this old lady with the beautiful hands and strong will, and spare Wade any friction.

The dying fire muttered to itself as it crumbled into ash, but otherwise the house, the hillside, seemed utterly still. Only the distant, unfamiliar sounds of the harbor reached her from the window she had opened. Now and then the whistling of a boat, or the sound of a buoy bell clanging—sounds she had not noted until now, when they seemed suddenly to fill the night with clamor.

She closed her eyes and thought of that strange little boy across the hall, and her throat tightened in pity. What a dreadful thing for a child to say—that his father did not like him, and that he did not like his father. Jemmy must have loved his mother very much, must miss her pitifully. She must try, somehow, to fill his loneliness a little, to help him against what must seem a hostile world.

She found herself wondering how Virginia had died. That was something Wade never talked about, would not discuss. Probably his wife's illness had been sudden and painful, leaving so deep and hurtful a shock that he could not bare it with words. She must think of these two, the boy and the man, and be nothing in herself. As her father had found contentment after her mother's death in service to others, so would she.

But Martin would not have slept in that room across the hall. And now she no longer felt old, but all too young and uncertain. She turned her cheek against the feather pillow and felt a wet streaking of tears. Tears were weak and she brushed them away impatiently. Doc had always said a fellow could do what he had to do if he had the gumption to try. And if she had no other possession in the world, she had gumption. He had seen to that.

If only this dull aching of loneliness would go away.

III

SOUNDS FROM THE harbor woke her early Saturday morning, and she lay for a little while listening to them, snug beneath warm covers. Her depression and concern of the night before had lifted and she felt eager to be up and ready

24

to meet the new day. If only her nose had not warned her that the room was icy cold.

While she lay gathering her courage to slip out into the chill air, Ellie's tap announced the advent of hot water. The little woman ducked into the room and set the steaming china pitcher in a white bowl on the washstand. Then she slammed down the window and inquired sibilantly if Miz Tyler wished a fire set going on the hearth. Lora hesitated, not knowing the custom of the house and wanting to ask for no uncommon luxuries. Quickly Ellie added that there were fires downstairs by now and breakfast would be dished up by eight o'clock.

Lora let the fire go and the moment the door closed she forced herself to get out of bed and hurry to the marble-topped washstand and the steaming warmth of hot water. She put on her old brown dress, then flung a fringed shawl about her shoulders and opened the glass doors. The first thing she wanted was a clear morning view of her new home. She would even brave the cold for that.

The shutters pushed open easily and she stepped out upon the gray-painted boards of an upper veranda. A cutting wind from the harbor made her draw the shawl more closely about her, but she would not be vanquished by its sharp touch. First she must see what she could of Dogwood Lane and Staten Island. This corner of the house was tucked into a curve of hillside and all about rose the sear, dry brown of woods which must be lovely when in leaf. The hill rose steep above the house, and trees cut off any possible glimpse of the Channing place which stood highest on the hill.

Lora walked to the front veranda for a better view. As it climbed toward the Tylers', Dogwood Lane made a sharp turn and then ran on a level along the hillside to the Lords' house. That must be the Lords' rooftop just visible through the woods along the road. Between the bare branches of a big horse chestnut tree which grew close to the veranda, Lora could see the wide brown hillside, dotted here and there with woods, sloping away toward flats along the water's edge. Here the peaked white tents of an army camp were visible and she could hear the silvery note of a bugle. Beyond lay the harbor, still and cold and gray in the haze of early morning.

Directly beneath the front veranda spread a wide patch of yellow-brown winter grass, with here and there a few traces of neglected garden. It would appear that the Tyler place had once boasted elaborate flower beds and shrubbery, but for some reason they had been allowed to go untidily to seed.

The cold was growing penetrating and as Lora turned to

hurry back to her room, she noted the long shuttered doors of a room at the front of the house. This closed room, according to Ellie, had been Virginia's. So she too had had a separate room in this strange house.

Lora sped back along the veranda, pausing in surprise just before she went through the doors of her own room. At this side of the house and around to the rear before what must be Mrs. Tyler's own windows downstairs, the garden had been kept neatly in order. Even though the bushes were bare and the flower beds only dead stalks at this time of year, there was evidence of loving care. In springtime this small area would be abloom.

How strange that Peter, or whoever tended the garden, had been permitted to let the rest of the grounds go neglected, while this one section was cared for so neatly. Wade had said that his mother got around downstairs quite well in her wheel chair, so she must know the condition of the rest of the yard.

The sound of a tapping on Lora's bedroom door drew her back to the room and she closed the glass doors behind her.

"Come in," she called, and Wade opened the door.

For just a moment she could only stare in astonishment. Always before she had seen him in his patched and shabby blue uniform. The fashionably clothed man who now stood in her doorway was a stranger to her eyes. He wore fawn trousers and a coat of broadcloth. There were pleats in his fine linen shirt and a cameo stickpin graced the carefully tied cravat beneath stiff white wings of collar. True, he exuded a pungent odor of mothballs, but that did not detract from the elegance with which he wore civilian dress. A tracing of shadow still showed beneath his eyes, and his cheeks were hollow, but he looked rested and was plainly enjoying her surprise at his appearance.

"You're very handsome this morning," she told him. "I'm not up to you in this old dress."

He crossed the room on his crutch and put an arm about her. His cheek felt smooth and clean-shaven against her own. "We'll change all that in a few days, Lora. We'll get you new dresses and then you can be as free of your old things as I am free of that filthy uniform."

She knew how he had grown to hate his uniform and the war that it represented. More than once she had pondered the impulse which had made him volunteer, when he was

26

such unlikely material for army life. Probably it had been an effort to escape the grief of his loss.

"I'm glad you're an early riser," he went on. "Mother will approve. Suppose we go downstairs where it will be warm."

She threw off her shawl and moved toward the door, but before he opened it he drew her back for a moment.

"Lora, you'll bear with my mother? She may be difficult at times, you know."

"Of course," she assured him. "I want her to like me. I want to like her."

He seemed oddly relieved and she wondered if he had feared some rebellion from her. It was true that she had an independent streak that he seemed to shrink from whenever it appeared, but people usually liked and respected her. Granted time and patience, it surely would be no different with Wade's mother.

He went on gently, "If you can win her, then we can live in peace in this house, and more than anything else, Lora, I want peace."

She cupped his face between her two hands and kissed him lightly. She too wanted peace and she would do everything in her power to please the old lady downstairs and win her liking.

In the hall she paused outside Jemmy's room and heard sounds of someone moving about, so the boy must be up. She would have liked to stop, but Wade went on toward the stairs.

"I talked to Jemmy last night," she said as they started down. "I like him, Wade. He's forthright and direct, but he seems a lonely little boy."

Again he glanced at her oddly and she had a fleeting impression that he was disturbed about Jemmy—as well he might be. Then they were at the door of his mother's parlor and Mrs. Tyler was summoning them in.

The rush of warmth and the smell of wintergreen were already familiar, as was the sight of the straight-backed figure in black waiting for them in her chair by the fire. This morning she wore a white lace cap with lavender bows which seemed a little incongruous considering the severity of the rest of her dress. The sight of it made Lora warm to her a little. If Mrs. Tyler had a touch of feminine vanity, as seemed possible with that cap and her well-kept hands, she might have her softer side and be vulnerable to affection.

"I've been wondering when you were coming down," Mrs.

Tyler said, though the little clock on the mantel pointed only to ten to eight. "I trust you slept well, Lora?"

"I don't think I stirred all night," Lora said. "And you?"

Mrs. Tyler reached for the heavy wooden wheels of her chair. "I never expect to sleep more than a few hours."

Even at this time of the morning she wore her rings and while the stones flashed a milder fire by daylight, their gleam was apparent whenever she moved her hands.

"Let me help you, Mother," Wade said quickly and managed, despite his crutch, to rest a hand on the curve of the chair's padded leather back and push it toward the hall.

When they reached the dining room, Ellie opened the door and closed it quickly. This room had a sombre air of stern dignity about it. No frivolous nosegays here, but a dim red paper on the walls, and furniture of dark walnut. The massive sideboard held silver dishes, branched candelabra and an impressive silver tea service. Behind polished brass andirons a fire crackled, but the room was big and draughty, less cozy than the sitting room they had just left. Lora suspected that it would be difficult to be gay in the cold, heavy gloom of this room.

Mrs. Tyler's chair was wheeled to the table and Ellie slipped extra cushions under her. Wade pulled out Lora's chair and touched her shoulder lightly as she took it. The old lady's quick eyes did not miss the gesture and if anything they grew a degree colder. Lora looked quickly away at the still life painting which hung above the sideboard—a stiff and depressing representation of dead game and fish. A forbidding picture, she thought, and wondered if Wade could be persuaded to brighten the room with something gayer in spirit.

"Why isn't that boy down, Ellie?" Mrs. Tyler asked as soon as they were settled.

"Gracious, ma'am, I've called him three times at least," Ellie defended herself. "I don't know what he's dawdling about."

Wade mentioned soothingly that it was still only five to eight, but his mother merely nodded to him and bowed her head for grace. Wade murmured the words of a rather long grace, during which Jemmy sidled into his place.

"Good morning, Jemmy," his father said when they all looked up. "It's good to see you again. I'm sorry to hear that you were ill yesterday."

Jemmy only mumbled a reply, giving no sign that he had not seen his father for nearly a year. His grandmother told

28

him sharply to speak up and Lora longed to say something warm and friendly to the boy, but the room forbade it. The heavy wine-colored wallpaper seemed to suppress any effort at cheer, and the dead game bird looked at them glassily, with its neck drooping over a table edge. Lora managed a smile in Jemmy's direction, but he looked soberly away without returning it.

It was a relief when Ellie arrived with a heaping platter of wheat cakes and ham, hot biscuits and coffee. When their cups had been filled and Jemmy instructed to drink up his milk and no nonsense, Mrs. Tyler turned directly to her son.

"There is no necessity for rush, of course, but I've been wondering how soon you will be able to return to the bank."

Wade did not look at her. He cut a piece of ham carefully before he answered.

"Not for a while, Mother. The trip to New York is too difficult for me at present."

"You are of course planning to take your rightful place again in your grandfather's bank?" Mrs. Tyler pressed the matter further.

Lora, all her instincts as a nurse alert, saw the beading of sweat that started out upon Wade's forehead. This was a subject she knew nothing about, though obviously it caused anguish to Wade.

"Suppose we talk about it when I'm well again," he said.

"This is what I have planned for, counted on ever since Wade was born," Mrs. Tyler explained to Lora. "That he should follow in my father's footsteps, do the things I could not do as well because of the handicap of being a woman."

Wade toyed idly with the food on his plate and his eyes did not meet his mother's. "In the meantime, while my leg is mending, I thought I might try my hand at something I've always wanted to do."

"What is that?" Lora asked, trying to put encouragement into her voice.

He looked directly at his mother. "I have always wanted to write. I've long had the idea for a novel in my mind. I used to think about it sometimes when we were on the march, or spending dull days in camp. Now is my chance to write it."

"A novel! What rubbish!" The old lady's deep-set eyes could light remarkably in moments of anger. "Nothing in your training has pointed in that direction. You will only fail and become discouraged."

"If it's what you want to do, I don't see why you shouldn't try it, Wade," Lora said quickly.

29

Mrs. Tyler turned upon her with a look which shifted the attack, but before she could speak, Jemmy burst into the conversation.

"Papa, are you really going to write a novel? What sort of story will it be? Will there be knights in it like Lancelot and ladies like Guinevere?"

"You were told to drink your milk," Mrs. Tyler said, and Jemmy picked up his glass absently, his attention still on his father.

But Wade seemed not to hear his son's words. Lora sensed the stiffening of resistance that went through him. He changed the subject abruptly.

"I walked around the house early this morning," he said. "It's quite evident that Ambrose has been coming down here."

"Of course he has." Mrs. Tyler helped herself to another wheat cake, showing an unexpectedly good appetite. "Peter has no genius for making things grow, as you are well aware. Ambrose understands what it means to me to have a garden to look out upon when I am tied to this house. In the spring that spot will bloom beautifully, thanks to the care he has given it all year."

"I believe I made a request before I went away," said Wade stiffly. "A request that no one from the Channing household be made welcome here."

"Ambrose has scarcely been made welcome," Mrs. Tyler retorted. "He comes in his proper capacity of gardener as he always has. He has the good sense not to expect to be accepted socially. Nothing ever made any difference to him in that."

Mother and son exchanged a look across the table and the silence was weighty with some significance which Lora could not grasp. She glanced at Jemmy and saw that he listened with intense interest.

It was Wade who finally shrugged and smiled at his mother. "Of course you must have your garden. And I have nothing against John Ambrose himself. It is the present connection. But now, Mother, I wonder if you'll agree to discuss the details of Lora's wardrobe with her sometime today? I know she'll need quite a few new things."

His mother nodded vigorously and reached for another biscuit. "She does indeed. Naturally I will supervise the matter."

Watching the biscuit disappear, Ellie clucked in pleased fashion behind Mrs. Tyler's chair. "Like a bird your mother's been eating while you were away, Mr. Wade. Now we'll get those roses back in her cheeks."

"That will be enough, Ellie." Mrs. Tyler sent the little woman scurrying toward the kitchen with a glance. "As I was about to say, Lora, after breakfast you may bring your fancywork down to my sitting room so you can keep busy while we discuss your new wardrobe."

"Fancywork?" Lora echoed. What with teaching school, keeping house and helping her father, there had been little time for ladylike graces. "I'm afraid I have no fancywork," she admitted. "But there are a good many things I need and I would be grateful for your help in making up a list."

Mrs. Tyler nodded. "We had a key which fitted the lock of your trunk, so I had it unpacked downstairs where I could look over your things."

Lora suppressed the flash of resentment that went through her. It didn't matter, she told herself. There was no need to have a sense of false pride about her poor possessions. Mrs. Tyler's next words startled her further.

"Lay your hands on the table," the old lady said.

Lora placed her rather square, rough-skinned hands palms down on the white tablecloth where the broken nails and reddened knuckles looked more unladylike than ever.

Mrs. Tyler inspected them in silence until Wade came gently to his wife's defense.

"She can take better care of them now, Mother. After all, she has been working very hard looking after me."

Lora returned her disgraced hands to her lap mutely. Once more Jemmy caused a diversion, and if he had seemed more friendly, Lora might have suspected that he did it deliberately to draw attention away from her discomfort.

"Isn't that a fine chair Uncle Adam made for Grandmother?" he asked his father.

"I was wondering where it came from," Wade said. "Adam Hume is Serena Lord's brother," he explained to Lora. " 'Uncle' of course is a courtesy title."

"Adam seems to have picked up a number of things in Libby Prison," Mrs. Tyler said dryly. "Fevers, new skills and new notions. Of course we had this chair, but he made the big side wheels and the small ones on the rear legs and fixed it up for me."

"How is Adam?" Wade asked.

Again it was Jemmy who spoke up. "He gets sick sometimes. But when he feels well he takes me for long walks. He's told me all about the fights they used to have at Libby

31

and about how some of the men were digging a tunnel to escape. He's still only a sergeant, Papa, but that's because he likes being closer to the men than if he had a commission."

The boy seemed almost cheerful now and eager to talk about someone who he plainly admired and considered his friend. But Wade looked away as if he were bored and Mrs. Tyler stilled the outburst by ringing for Ellie.

Wade pushed his mother's chair across the hall and Ellie began to clear off the dishes. For a few moments Lora lingered in the dining room with Jemmy, her attention again upon the depressing still life of dead game over the sideboard.

"That one-eyed fellow worries me," she confided to Jemmy. "We don't dare to laugh in this room with him watching us. What do you say we plot his downfall?"

The boy gave her a shocked look and bolted out of the room so that she could not tell whether he understood her whimsy or not. She made a little face at the glassy-eyed bird and went to join Wade in the hall as he came out of his mother's room.

"I've a few things to set in order," she said, "and then I'll come down to see your mother."

"Good. She wants to help you, Lora. But sometimes her ways are more autocratic than she realizes."

"I don't mind," Lora said. "I'm glad you're going to start writing, Wade. If it's what you really want to do, I don't think you should let anything stop you."

There was a troubled look in his eyes, but he smiled at her. "I want to try, at least. There are some old copybooks in the library desk. I think I'll see how a pen feels in my hand again. You won't mind?"

"Of course not. I'm very good at amusing myself. Perhaps this afternoon I'll go for a walk through the woods. I'd like to climb the hill and——"

He spoke quickly. "Not up the hill, please. I'd rather you stayed out of the upper woods, Lora."

She could only stare in surprise. "But why, Wade? I've always walked a great deal at home. I could never stay cooped up in a house all day."

He looked so strangely unhappy that she put a hand on his arm, and he covered it with his own scarred palm. "Walk along the lane and in the downhill area as much as you like. But I'll be happier if you stay away from the uphill side. Someday I'll tell you why. But not now, Lora. I don't want to talk about it."

He took his hand from hers and his eyes were cool as if

he saw her as a stranger. Without further comment he swung himself on his crutch toward the door of the library, calling for Ellie to come build him a fire.

Lora went upstairs, more puzzled than hurt. The web of mystery that the members of this household seemed so busy weaving troubled her. She did not like mysteries or arbitrary rulings. If something was disturbing Wade, then the sooner he talked it out, the better.

She could remember the way Doc used to say, "It's a funny thing, Lorie, but sometimes the sick ones you can't do much for will get a whale of a lot better if you just let 'em bend your ear for a while. Seems a silly waste of time, but I'm getting so I can catch a whole sixty winks and look awful interested while I'm doing it."

In her chilly room she threw a shawl about her shoulders and went to work unpacking the rest of the things in the carpetbag, rearranging her few possessions in an order that better pleased her.

A light, scratchy tap called her to the door and she opened it to find Jemmy standing there holding a plump bottle of liquid. Grandmother had sent it, he said, for her to rub on her hands.

"Thank you, Jemmy." Lora took the bottle. "I'll start using it right away." She uncorked it while he watched and poured a few drops into her palm. The odor of rose water was pleasant, but the glycerine stung as she rubbed the sticky stuff into her chapped skin.

"Have you decided about what I should call you?" Jemmy asked.

She had forgotten, she thought guiltily, but now, with the night's weariness flung off, a happy inspiration came to mind and she suggested it at once.

"A long time ago I had a brother just a bit younger than you. He used to call me 'Lorie,' and that was a pet name my father used too. So why couldn't we be brother and sister, and then it would be all right for you to call me Lorie."

He considered the matter solemnly, but he did not say what he thought of the name. "Would you like to see my turtles?" he asked, and Lora expressed immediate enthusiasm.

"I used to have some turtles myself when I was a little girl. Run and get them while I move things around."

He was back almost at once with a pan which contained rocks and sand and a sunken saucer-pool. Jemmy set it on the floor and Lora let her unpacking go so she could be in-

33

troduced to the three little brown-shelled creatures who had been jarred into pulling in their heads and feet.

"That one's Sir Lancelot," Jemmy said, pointing, though the three looked exactly alike to Lora. "And that's Merlin over there on the rock."

"Don't you have a dog or a cat too?" Lora asked.

Jemmy looked surprised. "Oh, no. Grandmother doesn't like animals. My grandfather kept too many. But turtles are very quiet, so she doesn't mind them."

"And what about playmates? Have you friends living hereabout?"

"There's only Temple Lord and his brother." Jemmy poked at Merlin, who had put out a cautious nose. "Eddie's too old. He likes bigger boys. Temple's close to my age, but he's a noisy sort of fellow and he doesn't care for books the way I do."

"What about school? Don't you have friends there?"

"Some," Jemmy said. "Temple and Eddie and I go to Mr. Sear's Academy. But the boys don't want to come here much because Grandmother makes them be so quiet."

"I see." Lora moved to safer ground. "Now I've met Merlin and Sir Lancelot, but you haven't told me the name of your third turtle."

"That's Guinevere," said Jemmy, and prodded the queenly one into a scramble across the sand.

"What—no King Arthur?" Lora asked lightly and was surprised at the stricken look Jemmy gave her.

"King Arthur died," he told her. Then he picked up the pan abruptly and carried it away, and though she left the door ajar, he did not return.

Poor little boy, she thought. To be allowed so few pets that he could be cruelly hurt by a turtle's death. It was one more thing to consider. There were more matters she wanted to talk to Mrs. Tyler about than the one of turning herself into a fashionable lady. But she would have to feel her way carefully and save the most important things until she was on sure ground.

First of all she was eager to take on duties in her new home, find ways in which she could aid in the running of the household. Then there would be war work she might get into also. Her nursing ability should be put to use, since there were so few women with experience such as her own.

Removing the last few things from the carpetbag, her fingers touched something rounded and smooth and she drew it out, knowing at once what it was.

Years before, when Martin was no more than twelve, his parents had taken him on a trip to the coast. He had gone swimming in the ocean for the first time and had walked for miles along a sandy beach. This satiny, cream-colored shell with the brown speckles was one he had found on that beach and had brought home with others he had picked up for her. The rest had been lost or scattered, but this, the prettiest of the lot, she had treasured.

The sudden sharp memory of Martin's smile, the very look of him, swept back upon her as she balanced the little shell on her palm. What an anguishing thing it was that a mere shell could remain intact and tangible, when Martin himself was nothing. She longed to fling herself across the bed and cry out the hurt that was in her. But she knew she must not. She could afford no such weakening indulgence before she went down to see Mrs. Tyler.

She thrust the shell quickly out of sight beneath handkerchiefs in a top drawer, straightened her shoulders and went downstairs to Mrs. Tyler's sitting room.

The old lady was still in her wheel chair, but when Lora came in she nodded toward a more comfortable wing-backed chair beside the fireplace.

"Think you can help me into it?" she asked. "You're not very big, but you look strong enough."

"I am strong," Lora told her.

She plumped up cushions in the other chair and then helped Mrs. Tyler over to it. The old lady clung to her heavily, but she was apparently able to take a few steps and with the aid of Lora's support she was lowered into the other chair.

"That's better." The old lady sighed in relief and patted her full skirts about her. "Sitting in one chair so long tires me. And the wings of this one protect me from drafts, so I'm more comfortable here. Now then, sit down and we'll get to work."

A basket of knitting waited on a nearby table and Mrs. Tyler took up a set of bone needles, and the gray yarn that was being fashioned into a sock. There was a little stool near the hearth and Lora brought it for Mrs. Tyler's feet, admiring the beautiful needlepoint covering as she set it down.

"Virginia made that," Mrs. Tyler said. "I had hoped that you were equally skilled in such arts. A great many things about the house were made by Virginia's hands."

There was more than a hint of reproach in the words, but Lora overlooked it. Mention of Virginia's name gave her an

35

opportunity she had waited for. The sooner a few mysteries which concerned Wade were cleared up the better.

She seated herself in a small armless chair on the opposite side of the hearth and folded her idle hands in her lap.

"Was Virginia ill very long?" she asked casually.

The twinkling of the needles ceased and the jeweled hands were forbiddingly quiet. "She was not ill at all. Her death was caused by a sudden and tragic accident. Wade has never recovered from the shock of it. This is a subject we never discuss in this house."

"I'm sorry," Lora said gently, and the bone needles began to move again. In the face of the rebuff she could ask no further questions.

"Bring that pad and pencil from the table," Mrs. Tyler directed. "You will need to write down a list of the purchases you must make in town. Right after New Year's when dressmakers aren't so busy we will get one in and have her go to work on your wardrobe."

Lora looked up from her poised pencil. "I'm not very good at fine embroidery, but I can make my own clothes. I've done it all my life."

"So I have observed," said Mrs. Tyler pointedly. "I think it would be wise to consult an experienced seamstress in this case. Someone who is up to date on styles. I would suggest an afternoon gown of silk foulard, perhaps. And of course several wool frocks for everyday. In gray and dark blue, I would say. Not that sallow brown you're wearing. Then you must have an evening gown or two for such affairs as you may attend. Wade used to go to a great many balls and parties when his wife was alive—that is, Virginia. But I doubt that he will care for such gaiety now. However, something in a green moiré might be suitable."

"I've never worn green," Lora explained. "With my coloring—"

Mrs. Tyler nodded. "Yes—I can see that you have not protected your skin from the sun. But a little lemon bleach will help that. And when spring comes you can carry a parasol."

"I've been wondering . . ." Lora set down the pencil, feeling that it would be better to change the subject quickly before her growing sense of dismay betrayed her. "I've been wondering what duties I might be able to help with about the house. I do like to be busy and I'm sure with this big house . . ."

"Ellie and Peter take care of everything," Mrs. Tyler said

curtly. "I hardly think they would welcome supervision other than my own. I still manage that very well myself."

"But if you aren't able to get upstairs, there may be some small ways in which I might help."

Mrs. Tyler put an end to the topic. "That will not be necessary. Perhaps this would be a good time to tell you something of our family background. Possibly Wade has not told you very much about these things."

This was apparently a favorite subject with Mrs. Tyler and the old lady went into zestful detail. Not about Wade's father or his side of the family, but wholly about her own. Jason Cowles's interests had been vast and assorted and it appeared that his daughter Amanda, who should have been a son, had been raised with a knowledge of business matters unusual for a woman. She knew about shipping, about imports from China and exports to England. And she knew banks and banking from the ground up. Her interest in these matters was lively and astonishingly keen, considering that she was an invalid who never left the house. The ship holdings were few now, but Mrs. Tyler had remained in control of the bank on lower Broadway and it was in this bank that she expected Wade to take his proper place and follow in his grandfather's footsteps. Mr. Niles, who was vice-president of the bank and her own personal adviser, was counting on this.

"There is a picture of my father, Jason Cowles, on the wall behind you," Mrs. Tyler pointed out.

Lora turned in her chair and saw the gilt-framed oval portrait which hung on the opposite wall. His daughter looked very like him. There were the same deep-set eyes, the same strong nose. Even the mouth wore something of the same grim line, though Amanda's lips were not so thin.

"He would never have approved of this nonsensical idea of novel writing Wade seems to have in his head," Mrs. Tyler said. "But I suppose I must let him amuse himself for a few weeks until he becomes bored or discouraged with it. Then I shall expect you to help me get him back into work that is more fitting for Jason Cowles's grandson."

Lora said nothing. She had already allied herself on Wade's side in this matter and she meant to make no promises to his mother. Now she managed to turn the talk to the next topic which she had in mind.

"Perhaps it's just as well that there are few duties for me to take up here at home," she said. "Since the need of

37

hospitals is so great I feel I must offer my services as a nurse as soon as possible."

"A nurse!" Mrs. Tyler echoed the phrase in the shocked tones she might have used had young Mrs. Wade Tyler suggested going into service as a scullery maid.

Lora went on quietly, but she was aware of a trembling that had begun inside her. "With the terrible flood of wounded coming into our hospitals and—"

"You are much too young for such work," said Mrs. Tyler flatly. "It would be entirely unseemly for a gentlewoman. You would meet coarse men, be subjected to intolerable insults. It is naturally unthinkable."

"Many of these men are too busy dying of dreadful wounds to have much time for insults," Lora said. "Perhaps you have not heard that gentlewomen of the South are serving in the most humble and ignoble capacities. Yet they are not degraded by doing so."

"The South!" There was venom in Mrs. Tyler's tone. "Don't talk to me about the South! In any event, we shall not discuss so ridiculous a matter further. Perhaps you may on occasion accompany Serena Lord when she takes fruits and sweets to wounded soldiers. It may even be possible to help some poor fellow write a letter home. I know the Sanitary Commission has asked for volunteers for such missions." The knitting needles flashed purposefully and the subject was closed.

Lora looked into the fire and wondered what Wade Tyler would have done if she had been so ladylike as to shrink from the sight of blood, or from the misery and helplessness which could engulf a human body. But she was beginning to realize that Mrs. Tyler never lost an argument and that she seldom saw any viewpoint other than her own.

Having dismissed the matter, the old lady returned calmly to the subject of Lora's list and made suggestions about yardage, buttons, trim, patterns and so on. The morning wore on until Ellie came to see if Mrs. Tyler would continue to have luncheon served in her parlor as she had been doing when there was only herself and Jemmy.

"That sounds very cozy," Lora put in. "That is, if you don't mind having it here, Mrs. Tyler."

"It's time you began called me Mother," the old lady reproved. "Very well, Ellie. You may set out the tea tables and call Mr. Wade."

While Ellie busied herself about the room, Lora got up to stretch her cramped legs. She was accustomed to active work and the sudden freeing of her time dismayed her no little. From the side window of the sitting room she could look out upon withered brown shrubs, leafless trees, and the orderly outline of the little garden that would bloom with the coming of spring.

As she watched two or three sparrows picking about energetically, a man came around the side of the house. He wore rough work clothes and a cap pulled down over grizzled hair. His face had the leathery, weather-beaten look of one who was much outdoors, and in spite of the cold he wore no gloves on his hands. He looked about for a moment and then reached into the lower part of a tree and pulled down a broken branch. He did not glance toward the window at all as he moved through the garden, seemingly on a tour of inspection.

"There's Ambrose, Miz Tyler," Ellie said, noting the man outside.

Mrs. Tyler turned in her chair so that she could look through the window. "I thought he would be down today. There was a storm yesterday morning and he never fails to check up on any possible damage."

As Lora watched, Jemmy scurried out the back door, without hat or coat, and flung himself into the old man's arms. John Ambrose looked up toward the house over Jemmy's shoulder and, seeing Lora in the window, touched his forefinger to his cap and gave her a friendly smile. She smiled back, liking him instantly. Then Wade came into the room behind her.

At a glance he saw what was happening in the garden and he reached the window quickly. With a sharp gesture he flung it open and told Jemmy to come into the house for lunch.

Jemmy would have continued to cling to his friend had Ambrose not released the grip of his small fingers and pushed the boy gently toward the house. When the old man looked up at Wade in the window, his smile was no less friendly than it had been for Lora.

"Good morning, sir," he said. "I came down to see if I'd need to do some trimming after yesterday's storm. But things seem right enough. Welcome home, Mr. Wade." Once more he made the gesture of forefinger to cap and turned away from the house without waiting for the man in the window to answer.

"Now that you've frozen out the room, suppose you close the window and come to lunch," said Wade's mother testily.

Once more Lora sensed undercurrents of emotion between these two which she did not understand.

Jemmy joined them, unsmiling and silent, and they sat down to the individual tea tables which Ellie had brought in. Lunch was a light meal with a fluffy omelet and popovers and hot tea. But it was anything but light in tone. Even the absence of the one-eyed bird did not lighten the atmosphere. Lora longed to find some way to inject a note of gaiety into the hour, but the energy and courage with which she had faced the morning were ebbing and she felt too limp to make any further effort at the moment.

Mrs. Tyler spoke with satisfaction of the list with which she was helping Lora. In a few days Lora must go over to New York and make these purchases. Of course she could not make such a trip unescorted, and Wade's leg would not permit him to take her over himself for a while. Mrs. Lord might have been called upon if her husband had not been home on leave. Though, on second thought, it was better to keep the scanty state of Lora's wardrobe strictly within the family. Ellie had a good head on her shoulders and she could accompany Lora on this trip to town.

Again there was a long silence, broken this time by an announcement from Jemmy.

"I showed Lorie my turtles this morning," he said, buttering a popover and not looking at his grandmother.

Mrs. Tyler put down her fork. "You must not call Lora by her first name, Jemmy. She is your mama now and that is the way you must address her."

Long lashes flew up as Jemmy widened his eyes defiantly. "I will not—" he began, but Lora spoke quickly before he could bring down lightning upon his head.

"Please don't mind, Mother Tyler," she pleaded. "You see, I once had a little brother and Jemmy reminds me of him. So we have decided that to start with we are going to be brother and sister. That way it will be all right for him to call me Lorie. I'm glad you've begun, Jemmy."

She smiled at him, but he returned her look solemnly and she had a feeling that he had used the name mainly to defy his grandmother.

For once Wade came to his son's support. "I see no reason why the boy should not call her Lorie if that pleases them both."

"We will discuss the matter another time," Mrs. Tyler said, and again silence lay upon the room.

Lora wished she could ask Wade what preparation the

40

writing of his book required, and whether he had actually started it this morning, but that, like so many other subjects, seemed to be a forbidden one, and she found herself growing more and more tongue-tied.

After lunch Wade, who still tired easily, went up to his room to lie down for a while, and Jemmy took the opportunity to disappear into the library. Mrs. Tyler, it seemed, also took a nap right after lunch every afternoon, so Lora was left to her own devices. The moment she found that she would have a space of time in which she could do as she pleased, she ran up to her room and dressed in outdoor things.

More than anything else, she thought as she tied her bonnet strings, she wanted to escape from the gloom of this house. She longed to gulp deep breaths of fresh air, stretch her legs in the stride of a good fast walk, and turn up the corners of her mouth in a smile.

On the way downstairs she met Ellie and told her she was going for a walk. Ellie had picked up something of her mistress's air of doubt over any purpose which did not originate with Mrs. Tyler. Her grunt suggested disapproval, but she offered no open objection. Lora closed the front door with a sense of escape and ran down the steps as if a reaching hand might snatch her back if she did not give wings to her feet.

IV

A HAZY SUN shone in the sky and here and there patches of the frozen road were thawing into mud. Lora leaped nimbly from one dry place to the next, or skirted the bad spots by following the dry brown grass along the road's edge. Her black gaiter boots were sturdy and meant for walking.

She chose the level stretch of lane that ran straight on toward the Lords' house. Above on her right woods crowded the hillside—birch, maple, oak, all wearing the dull brown of winter, with only the evergreens standing out in bold relief. Because of the trees she could not see the crest of the hill and the forbidden Channing house whose lights she had seen from a distance last night.

On her left the woods were more sparse. There were glimpses of the lower shore of the island with its mushroom tents and military activity, and the gray water of the harbor shining beyond. Across the water and down the bay she could see the buildings of New York, with the tall point of Trinity's spire towering above all else.

Here and there nearby in the shelter of rocks and shaded spots white streakings bore evidence of earlier snow, but it had long melted from all exposed surfaces. Perhaps it would snow again before Christmas, Lora thought. She looked forward to her first snowstorm with almost childish eagerness. Perhaps she and Jemmy could go outdoors and roll snowballs, even make a snowman. As a child she had loved to read about snowmen, but she had never seen one.

A chill wind whipped at her skirts and she quickened her step, thrust her hands with their thin gloves into her sleeves for more warmth. But she did not really mind the cold. After that stuffy house the bracing sting of a fresh wind was exhilarating. It made her want to skip and sing a little song to herself. She managed, however, to remember that she was Mrs. Wade Tyler and that she must behave with a proper dignity, though she grimaced to herself at the thought.

A short distance along the road, the sight of a lone chimney rising broken and black from a tangle of undergrowth brought her to a halt. Encroaching shrubbery and trees almost hid it from view of the road, but on peering closer she discovered evidence of what had once been a carriage drive, with the remains of a leaning iron fence beyond. Following the drive a few steps, she saw the crumbling walls of a house that had long ago been gutted by fire. There was something both sad and provocative about such ruins. She would have liked to pierce the protecting shield of vines and bushes and explore the old stones. But she remembered in time that this was the forbidden uphill side of the road and went regretfully on past the ruins.

A little further on a path opened up the hill, winding its way through the woods, and again she felt the tug of interest, the invitation to adventure. But again she set the impulse aside and went on. When she came upon a downhill path, however, she no longer resisted the invitation, but turned eagerly off the rutted road and followed a way which cut down through a clump of bare oak trees on a curving course.

Now the wide view of the harbor was clear and she could see the masts of many vessels, white sails and black smokestacks, and a dotting of tugs and small craft clear across to the Brooklyn shore. Far on the right the harbor narrowed and then opened into the sea. Lora stood for a long moment breathing deeply the pungent, not altogether pleasant odor of salt water carried shoreward by the wind. It was bracing, yes, but she would have to get used to it. She was more accustomed to the spicy scent of pines and the warm odors of sun-baked earth.

She paused near the edge of the woods, where a sloping brown meadow opened beyond and dipped downhill to disappear into more woods below. A dog barked, the sound of nearby voices came to her, and then the sharp, clear crack of a shot. Her stomach muscles tightened in immediate resistance to the sound and she stood utterly still, holding her breath. Then there was a second shot and she stepped cautiously into the open where she could have a full view of the bare expanse of hillside.

Across the meadow a target had been set up, its staring bull's-eye shining with fresh black paint. As a safety measure it had been placed against an earth embankment that would prevent all but the wildest shots from going astray. Some paces back from the target stood two boys—one a red-haired boy about Jemmy's age, the other a taller boy of perhaps thirteen years. The older boy held a rifle to his shoulder, and aimed carefully at the target. Once more the crash of a shot ripped the quiet and went echoing along the ridge of hills.

The boy who had fired waved his gun triumphantly aloft. "There!" he shouted. "I just got me another Johnny Reb!"

The smaller boy capered. "You sure did! You killed that no-good old Secesh deader than dead!"

Indignation swept through Lora and she hesitated no longer. She ran lightly across the meadow toward the boys, not sure of what she meant to do or say, but impelled into action because of the child's words. The two boys heard her coming and turned to stare in surprise.

"You shouldn't pretend you're killing *men!*" she cried breathlessly as she reached them.

The red-haired younger boy seemed less taken aback at her sudden appearance than did the older one.

"Who else would we pretend we're killing, ma'am? Who else but those old rebs?"

Lora managed to recover her breath and speak more quietly. "Have you ever known a Southern boy? They're just like you, really. And you shouldn't even pretend to kill."

Teaching school had given her an air of authority when she chose to use it, and the two boys looked not only astonished, but somewhat abashed. The older one glanced

43

sheepishly over his shoulder at a figure whom Lora had not noted until now. Near the edge of the woods a man sat cross-legged on the ground where he had apparently been watching the efforts of the two young sharpshooters. His hand was on the collar of a small, excited Airedale.

When he saw her eyes upon him he let go of the dog and got to his feet without undue haste. He wore a heavy blue jacket, but no cap, and his thick mane of hair was a darker rust color than the boy's. The little dog, released, raced toward Lora in friendly fashion and she bent to pat his head as he stood on his hind legs and pawed her skirt.

The man followed the course of the dog in a more leisurely manner, and as he approached she found herself contrasting his appearance and manner with Wade's. This man was somewhat stocky, rather than slender and tall. His features were rugged and he lacked any touch of elegance.

"Good morning," Lora said with dignity. "I couldn't help reproving these two boys for this game of killing Confederate soldiers."

His eyes were gray beneath rusty eyebrows and they gave no quarter but met her own without blinking.

"Maybe you can tell me just what you think this fight is all about?" he countered. "Maybe you've got a notion that nobody is killing real men in this war?"

"I know very well that men are being killed," she said quickly, "but that doesn't make me ready to forgive it, or to sanction it when I see such imitation on the part of little boys."

The younger boy capered again to get attention and the dog barked shrilly. "I know who she is, Uncle Adam. She's Jemmy's new mother. The one he doesn't want."

So this man was Serena Lord's brother who had been in Libby Prison. Never, she thought, could one have found a brother who less resembled a charming sister.

Adam Hume put out a hand and touched the younger boy's shoulder to silence him. "I don't like killing any better than you do, Mrs. Tyler. But we're in a war and if the North doesn't settle the matter soon, maybe young Eddie here and even Temple will be fighting the same war in a few years. And it's hard to win if you get to thinking about how the other fellow is no worse than yourself. Could be it's better to go in there hating him a whole heap—the way the rebs hate us. That's the only way to be a fighter."

Lora shook her head vehemently. "Fighting's no way to

44

settle anything. I think the South has some right on her side too."

"You sound like a rebel yourself. Are you?"

"I'm not on any side," she said. "I'm against war with every bit of me. My father came from the North, but he taught me to love life, not to waste it."

"You're spunky anyway," he said, appraising her with a look that made her tingle with annoyance.

She turned from him quickly and spoke to the two boys. "I know you're Mrs. Lord's boys."

They nodded, not quite sure how to take this softening in her tone. The younger boy bent to pat the Airedale's head, addressing him as "Whiskers."

"Why don't you both come over to our house to see Jemmy tomorrow?" she invited. "I'm sure he'd love to have you."

Temple spoke his surprise instantly. "But tomorrow's Sunday."

"Don't Staten Island folks go visiting on Sunday?" Lora asked. "We always did at home."

Both boys shook their heads and looked at Adam Hume, who answered for them shortly. "Not at the Tylers'."

"Then you must come another time," Lora said. She murmured a quick good-by which included Serena's brother, and started back up the path by which she had come. Her encounter with the Lord boys and their uncle had somehow upset her and taken the edge off her sense of adventure.

She reached the Tyler house and let herself in through the front door. The dim, chill hallway was silent and she found herself instinctively tiptoeing toward the stairs. Then, moved by a whim, she paused with one hand on the newel post. So far she had been faced by so many closed doors that she had seen little of this house. The front room opposite the library must be the parlor, and there was no reason why she should not look in and see what the room was like.

She opened the door softly and blinked at the thick gloom. Not only were the shutters closed, but heavy draperies had been pulled across the windows, shutting out any seepage of daylight and turning the room to shadowy night. Lora remembered the candle she had seen on the hall table with a packet of friction matches beside it and she got it quickly. The striking of a match sounded all too loud in the quiet hall, but she lit the candle and went into the dark parlor.

The draperies were of wine-colored velvet and most of the furniture was dark, well-polished walnut. A huge Bible lay upon a table in the center of the room and all about were

45

stiff, dignified-looking chairs. Lora held the candle high and moved toward a marble mantel above the cold hearth. From the wall above the mantel a portrait looked down at her.

Thinly her candle lighted the face of the man in the picture and for a moment she thought it was a portrait of Wade. But the full-lipped mouth was more sensual, perhaps a little cruel, and there was none of Wade's likable appeal in the portrayed gaze. One sensed something robust and hearty, but no great sensitivity.

This then must be Wade's father. It was difficult to imagine the grim old lady who held court in the rear parlor as the wife of this florid-faced man with the stamp of easy living upon him.

Lora moved on about the room, noting the stiff black haircloth sofa with its walnut frame, the whatnot in a corner, carrying a load of bric-a-brac.

Someone whispered from the doorway and she looked about to see Jemmy beckoning to her insistently.

"What is it?" she asked.

He put a finger to his lips and tiptoed into the room. "Ssh! Grandmother will hear you. You'd better come out quickly."

Lora lowered her voice, but she made no move to leave the room. "I'm just getting acquainted with your house," she told him. "After all, I'm going to live here and I want to see it."

"You're not supposed to come in the parlor," Jemmy whispered. "Grandmother only opens it for company, and on Sundays. We'll be here tomorrow. But if Grandmother catches you now she'll be angry."

"I don't see why she should be," Lora said gently, remaining where she was. Then she went on, not waiting for further objection. "That portrait over the mantel must be of your grandfather. Do you remember him, Jemmy?"

Jemmy stared at the picture and shook his head. "He died when Papa was only ten. And you know what—he was thrown from a runaway horse he was riding when he'd had too much to drink."

There was a certain relish for the lurid in Jemmy's tone and Lora dropped the subject hastily. Nevertheless, a sense of astonishment remained with her. It was doubly difficult to imagine Mrs. Tyler married to this handsome, reckless husband. But then, it was difficult to imagine Mrs. Tyler in the role of a young woman at all.

"Aren't you afraid of *her?*" he asked.

46

"Your grandmother? Why should I be?"

"My mother was afraid of her. Sometimes I had to protect Mama from Grandmother."

"There's no reason to be afraid," Lora told him. "We have to remember that your grandmother has had considerable trouble in her life." She glanced briefly at the portrait. "And that she can't move around like other people. Perhaps we'd be irritable sometimes too if we had to sit in a chair all day long and couldn't leave the house."

"I think she could leave it if she wanted to," Jemmy whispered, glancing cautiously behind him. "I heard the doctor tell her one time that there wasn't anything wrong with her that her own will couldn't cure. But she got so angry she sent him away and she won't have a doctor in the house any more."

Again this was not a subject to be discussed with Jemmy, but as they left the room and mounted the stairs together she thought about his words. The stifling, dominating spirit of Amanda Tyler was almost a tangible thing permeating the house. Could it be that a woman in a wheel chair was in some ways stronger than a woman who could walk?

I'll ask Doc about it, she thought before the pang of realization once more engulfed her, the knowledge that she could never ask him anything again.

Sunday came all too quickly, and with it a sense of restraint that made past solemnity seem almost frivolous. Sunday, as at once became evident, was a time for prayers and Bible reading and nothing else. The whole house was kept dark and voices low.

As Jemmy had prophesied, they spent the entire morning in the parlor. Shutters and draperies were not opened, but at least a lamp and candles pierced the gloom and a fire in the grate pushed back the chill air for a small radius. Mrs. Tyler's chair was placed at the center table on which rested the huge Bible and she read with keen eyes that needed no glasses the words of her vengeful God.

Lora sat on the slippery hair sofa beside Wade, her hands folded tightly in her lap, trying not to fidget. Mrs. Tyler's God was one whom she had not met before, and she wasn't in the least sure she believed in Him. To her father, God had been a close friend and confidant. One revered and respected Him, but with a feeling of love, not fear. He was a God who came into one's conversations frequently and in friendly terms. When Doc's hands and brain had done what they could for a patient, the whole thing was put up to Doc's good Friend. All higher decisions were accepted as just and proper, despite the pain they might bring to those who had not the wisdom to understand the mysterious purpose behind them. But this purpose was never regarded as vengeful punishment for past sins.

Mrs. Tyler's God came with fiery sword and merciless judgment. He had no sympathy or forgiveness for human frailty. The old lady bowed her head and prayed to him in a ringing voice.

"Thank you, Lord, for smiting down the enemies of our beloved Union. Deal just death and destruction on the wicked Confederacy. Bring victory soon to our forces and let the evil ones go down in helpless defeat!"

Her voice was grim as the voice of doom in the quiet room and Wade bowed his head with her. But Lora would not pray for the angel of death to destroy the South. She was not at all sure that the North was entirely right, any more than she was sure the South was right. These were brothers fighting one another and the death of one must eventually bring anguish to the heart of the other. Both were wrong, both were foolish.

She stole a look at Jemmy and saw that instead of praying he was watching her curiously. When she smiled at him he looked shocked and bowed his head, squeezing his eyes tightly shut.

The prayer was very long and once or twice Lora could not help the squeaking of the sofa beneath her. When it finally ended she released a sigh of relief without realizing it, and Mrs. Tyler looked at her sharply.

"Lora, I do not sense in you a proper reverence on the Lord's day."

Lora kept her voice low and steady, but she could not help speaking her thoughts. "The thing I don't understand is why your God is also smiting down the soldiers of the North."

Wade looked at her in distress and Jemmy wriggled on his hard chair.

There was a blazing light in Mrs. Tyler's eyes. "There is only one God and I will suffer no disrespect to Him in this house. Mortals like ourselves do not question any action of His. It is right that the wicked be punished."

"But I know many Southern people who believe in God too," Lora went on gently. "They are praying to Him just as we are. They think He will help their cause because *they* are right."

Mrs. Tyler turned to her son. "Wade, we have finished our prayers. Will you help me back to my sitting room, please? Then I trust you will take your wife aside and explain to her the customs of this house. I do not feel strong enough at the moment."

To Lora, she had never seemed less weak, but Wade pulled his crutch into place and stood up. He did not glance Lora's way again as he helped his mother wheel her chair into the hall. Lora stayed where she was, struggling against indignation which rose frighteningly within her.

The moment his father and grandmother were out of sight, Jemmy came to stand before her. "You're in disgrace," he said. "If you don't watch out she'll send you to bed without any supper."

Lora caught his two thin hands in her own, surprised at the fragility of his small bones.

"Jemmy," she pleaded, "God isn't like that. He is good and kind and forgiving. I don't think He goes around with a flaming sword killing people because He thinks they're wicked."

"You," said Jemmy, "will go to hell." And he twisted away from her and ran out of the room.

Noonday dinner was served in the dining room and it was heavy with solid food. There was fried chicken and thick cream gravy, hot biscuits, baked beans, mashed potatoes, and shortening-rich apple pie. The grace before the meal was extra long and given by Mrs. Tyler, who seemed to be hinting that while Lora did not deserve to partake of this repast, God was going to let her eat—this time.

Wade avoided Lora's eyes, though he made a special effort to engage his mother in conversation. Jemmy was not expected to talk, and Lora kept her silent attention on her food, fighting down a sense of nausea at the mere sight of gravy swimming on her plate. As Jemmy had said, she was certainly in disgrace, even with Wade. She nibbled at a wishbone and when she had picked it dry she slipped it unnoticed into her pocket to save it for a wish with Jemmy. But the rest of her food she could hardly touch—and thus brought a lecture on waste from Mrs. Tyler.

When the uncomfortable meal was over she attempted to draw Wade away by himself. She needed to talk to him, to make him understand that she meant no disrespect either to his mother or to God, but there were some things which she could not accept meekly. She had no opportunity, however, for Wade drove away from the house immediately after dinner.

When Lora realized he had gone, she went into Mrs. Tyler's sitting room, feeling that the quicker certain matters were cleared up the better. But Ellie was helping to make Mrs. Tyler comfortable for her nap and it was plain that the old lady meant to talk to no one. At least Lora managed a question about Wade.

"I saw him drive away," she said. "I wish he had taken me with him. I'd have loved a drive, and I imagine Jemmy would too. Do you know where he has gone?"

Mrs. Tyler looked up from slipping her arms into the sleeves of a lavender wrapper. "You would not have been welcome. My son has gone to visit his first wife's grave. It would hardly be appropriate for you to accompany him."

"Why would it not?" Lora asked. "I have only the kindest feeling toward Virginia." Ellie was helping Mrs. Tyler to the bed in the small adjoining room and Lora followed them to the doorway. But Mrs. Tyler did not answer until Ellie had gone scuttling off with a frightened backward glance for Lora. Then the old lady lay back upon her pillows and fixed Lora with a gaze in which there was nothing but open dislike.

"I should think," she said, "that it would be very plain to you that Wade is still in love with Virginia."

Lora swallowed against a dry throat before she spoke again. "I understood that when I married him. I have not fooled myself or Wade. But I will not believe that I mean nothing to him. I'm sure that he needs me now."

Mrs. Tyler merely closed her eyes and there was nothing for Lora to do but go softly from the room. She had never felt so futilely helpless in her life. She longed to do something decisive, release herself in action.

As she went down the hall she saw the library door closing just ahead of her and she pulled it open and walked in. Here too the shutters had been drawn and portiers swung across the windows to shut out any semblance of daylight. But at least a fire had been lighted and a lamp burned in the center of a table.

Jemmy might well have been eavesdropping, for he looked guilty when he saw her face. He picked up a book and scurried to the red damask sofa before the hearth, where he curled up, pretending to bury himself in the story.

Lora went straight to the portiers and flung them aside. Then she opened a window, thrust back the shutters and fastened them before closing it again. The outside world was bright with sunlight. Jemmy ceased his pretense of reading and came softly to stand beside her and look into the bril-

50

liant outdoors. A few sparrows hopped about the neglected garden and as he and Lora watched, a small rabbit scuttled across the drive and disappeared in a clump of bushes. Jemmy's voice was no more than a whisper.

"Don't you suppose God is out there too, even on Sundays?" he asked.

Lora looked down at him for a moment. Then she put her two hands on his shoulders, and this time he did not wriggle away.

"Let's go out there and see," she said. "Let's go right away and find out."

He looked at her with a mingling of fear and hope in his eyes. Then he nodded solemnly.

V

THEY PUT ON their coats and went outside without a word to anyone. Jemmy wore a striped stocking cap, a red muffler and red mittens which brightened him up considerably. He had turned into a surprising dynamo of excitement and Lora tried to quiet him by making the adventure seem as natural as possible. She wanted him to have no sense of wrong-doing about this. They belonged outside on the bright day of grace that had been given them before full winter set in. She did not hold with any notion that respect to the Lord could only be shown through moping indoors.

"Where shall we go?" Jemmy asked when they had left the driveway behind them.

"You choose," Lora said. "Isn't there some special place you know that you'd like to show me?"

He skipped along beside her, a bundle of nervous energy, and there was a look about him both speculative and purposeful. Already he had turned along Dogwood Lane in the direction she had taken yesterday.

"I know a place," he said. "A place up there in the woods."

When they had passed the ruins of the burned-down house and reached the narrow path cutting uphill, he turned onto it and Lora offered no objection. Since she was in full rebellion from unreasonable authority, she might as well add this to her score of disobedience. Wade's request had seemed unreasonable at the time he had made it and she meant to talk the matter over with him sooner or later; make it clear to him that it was not fair to ask her to bow blindly to rulings she did not understand. In spite of her desire and first willingness to please Amanda Tyler, there were certain things at which her nature must surely balk. It would be as well to make this clear to Wade in the beginning, rather than to pretend to be what she was not.

Here in the woods leaf mold lay thick upon the ground, making a soft carpet on the little-used path. Lora held her skirts away from snatching twigs as they climbed upward. Now there was an odd urgency about Jemmy, a kindling of some strange excitement that pulled him quickly on, despite the steepening grade of the hill.

Remembering small boys she had known back home in Pineville, Lora suspected what he was up to, though why he should seem so tense and excited about it, she could not tell.

"Is this a special place you're going to show me?" she asked. "A secret place?"

He glanced back at her over his shoulder in surprise at her understanding. "It used to be secret—sort of. But it's not —any more."

Halfway up the hill and around a turn in the path they came unexpectedly upon a clearing. Here sloping banks of brown grass led down to a small lake. On the far side birches graced the edge of the still water, their reflection white and pencil-slim. Beyond was another opening where the path picked up again and wound uphill.

With blue sky above and the sun high and golden, the surface of the little pool had a yellow shimmer which contrasted with drab surroundings like an amethyst set down upon a brown carpet.

Jemmy ran to the edge of the water, studying its quiet surface with a gaze so intent that he seemed to forget her presence. The pond was an irregular oval in shape, curving to fit the sloping banks, and not far from where Jemmy stood natural stepping stones led to a larger mound of rock that rose dry and brown well out in the water.

Lora went to stand beside him. "What a heavenly quiet spot. It must be beautiful in spring when the woods are in leaf and the grass is green. It's so still and lonely and secret. A lovely place to dream."

For some reason Jemmy shivered. "It's awfully deep," he said. "Higher even than my father's head. But when there's a breeze the water's not like glass the way it is now. You should see it when there are little moving crinkles all across it. Mama said it looked like quicksilver then."

"Did you come here often with your mama?" she asked gently.

He did not look at her. "We came here most every day when the weather was fine. We used to sit out on that big rock and sometimes she'd read to me and sometimes I'd read to her. About King Arthur and Ivanhoe and Rip Van Winkle and others."

"Perhaps we can do that again when good weather comes," Lora said.

Jemmy shook his head despairingly and she knew she had said the wrong thing. "No, never!" he cried. "Not ever at all!"

Of course, she thought, this place belonged to his memories of his mother. She should not have tried to usurp them. Perhaps she and Jemmy could find another outdoor reading place when warm weather came.

Moving quietly, with the strange tenseness upon him, he edged along the left bank of the pool to where the stepping stones began, his attention fixed upon the big rock.

"Sometimes turtles come out on the rocks in the sun and you can catch them. All my turtles came from here."

There was so strained a note in his voice that Lora glanced at him anxiously. Perhaps he should not come here where he had been happy with his mother. She wished she could find some way to comfort him, and knew helplessly that there was no way. Like herself, Jemmy could only wait for the healing of time.

He turned suddenly toward her and she saw how pale he was and how the blue of his eyes had darkened. His lips trembled and he had to tighten them fiercely before he could speak.

"Do you think I killed my mother?" he demanded.

Lora gasped and stared at him, shocked into silence.

"She couldn't swim," he said, looking back at the water. "She fell into this pool and was drowned. And maybe it was my fault. Maybe I killed her."

Lora found her voice with an effort. "Of course you didn't, Jemmy! Why should you ever think such a foolish thing?"

"I got my feet wet when I shouldn't have," he went on, his tone dull. "I catch cold real easy, so Mama put me to bed and she stayed with me reading most all day. But in the afternoon she wanted to go for a walk so she said she would come up here and see if she could find me a new turtle. Be-

53

cause King Arthur had died and I thought Guinevere was lonely. But when the wind blows and those rocks get wet and mucky from the pond, they can be awfully slippery. So that's what must have happened. She was trying to reach for a turtle when she fell off the big rock into the deep part. She never came home. And after a while Papa went to look for her."

He stopped desolately and Lora dropped to her knees and caught him to her, muffling his words against her breast. "Don't," she whispered. "Jemmy dear, you mustn't ever, ever think such a terrible thing again. If she slipped, then it was the slippery rock that was to blame—not anything way back like your cold, or even your wanting a turtle."

He pushed away from her, but not fiercely as he had once before. Now he wanted only to search her face, perhaps to find in it something that would free him from secret torture, make him believe. But even as she looked at him she thought in pity of Wade coming up through these woods to find Virginia . . . No wonder he had not wanted Lora to come here.

On the far side of the pond a twig broke sharply beneath a foot and Lora looked up, startled. At the place where the path opened again on the uphill side stood a figure that seemed outlandishly strange in a Staten Island setting. Half shielded by the trunk of a tree, a young colored girl of no more than eighteen years stood peering out at them with wide, liquid dark eyes. She might have seemed a wild thing herself in that verdant background, had it not been for her flamboyant costume.

She wore a full, bright-flowered cotton skirt with blossoms of crimson and green strewn against a yellow ground. A fringed red wool shawl was flung about her shoulders and a red bandanna had been tied in a jaunty bow atop her head. From her ears had swung huge gold loops, shining now in the sunlight. She was strikingly lovely with her warm brown coloring and great watchful eyes. She did not smile or speak, but simply stared for a long moment. Then, before Lora could recover from her surprise, she turned and fled back up the path in the direction from which she must have come, disappearing among the trees.

"Who on earth was that?" Lora asked.

Jemmy seemed relieved to escape his moment of dark emotion. He was markedly casual as he turned away from the pool.

"That's only Rebecca. If she's back, then that means Morgan Le Fay is home. Of course Morgan's not really Le Fay—

she's Morgan Channing. But she's sort of like Le Fay in the King Arthur stories so I call her that."

Of his own accord he turned toward home and she followed him willingly. There had been enough of the tragic and she sought for some subject which might distract and cheer him as they went downhill. An appropriate one offered itself easily.

"What are you planning for Christmas, Jemmy? Are you making presents for everyone? And when do we open them—Christmas Eve or Christmas morning?"

Looking back at her, a faint stirring of interest came alive in his eyes, but almost at once he shook his head.

"Grandmother says Christmas is a time for praying."

"Of course it is," Lora agreed. "But it's also a time to be happy and to make others happy. After all, it's the celebration of a very special Birthday. Don't you do anything about it at all?"

"We used to when—when Mama was here," he said. "But last year Papa was away and Grandmother was too sad. But I went to the Lords' for a party anyway. Mrs. Lord's mother was German and she always used to have a Christmas tree, the way German people do. So Aunt Serena likes to have one for Temple and Eddie. There were presents on it for me, too, and Grandfather came to the party."

Grandfather, Lora thought in surprise, remembering the handsome, florid face of the portrait in the Tyler parlor. But of course he must mean Virginia's father. She had not realized that he had any other grandparent living.

"I tell you what," she hurried on, striving to hold that look of interest in his eyes. "We'll have a wonderful Christmas this year. Perhaps if we can get one we'll even have a Christmas tree. Would you like that?"

He was an excited small boy now. Would he like it? Oh, and how much he would like it!

"I have some ideas for making presents too," she told him cheerfully. "We'll get to work on them right away and we'll have the nicest Christmas ever."

They reached the lane and, spurred on by urgent purpose, walked quickly toward home. Just before they reached the steps Jemmy slipped his red-mittened hand shyly into hers.

"I'm glad you've come, Lorie," he said, and then pulled away and ran ahead of her, engulfed by embarrassment.

A tingling of happiness went through her as she watched him run up the steps. Even if the skies fell she must try to help Jemmy. Then she saw Ellie in the doorway. Reading her expression, she knew that the skies were likely to start falling this very moment. But at least she no longer felt futile and helpless. Because of Jemmy and his need of her, courage swept back.

"Miz Tyler is up from her nap," Ellie told them, looking slyly pleased. "An' she wants to see you both right away. I don't mind telling you she's hopping mad. Such doings on a Sunday!"

"That will be enough," said Lora, surprising herself by becoming suddenly the mistress.

Ellie's toothy grin vanished and her eyes widened. She bobbed a curtsy she had not intended and murmured, "Yes'm, Miz Lora."

Lora held out her hand to Jemmy and they went down the hall together and into Mrs. Tyler's presence.

The old lady sat in the wing-backed chair before the fire and Lora saw that she had been reading from a small Bible in her lap. The look she turned upon them was dark and bitter.

"May I ask where you have been?"

"It was such a lovely day that we went for a walk in the woods," Lora said simply.

Mrs. Tyler's lips tightened to a thin line that resembled Jason Cowles's mouth in the portrait behind her. But before she could speak Jemmy put himself between Lora and his grandmother.

"It's not Lorie's fault, Grandmother," he said. "She didn't know about not going outside on Sunday. And I didn't tell her. So I'm the one to be punished."

Lora rested her hands on his shoulders and felt their slightness beneath her fingers. She knew he was trying to "protect" her from his grandmother, as he had once protected his own mother. But though she was touched by his gesture, Doc Blair's daughter needed no protection.

"I knew that you might be displeased, Mother," she said. "But Jemmy and I feel that God is out there in the woods just as much as He is in this house. We don't feel that *He* is displeased with us."

There was a flare of color to Mrs. Tyler's cheekbones, but she turned her attention upon Jemmy. "You at least knew you were doing wrong. You may go to your room for the rest of the afternoon."

The boy threw Lora a worried look as he left, but she smiled reassuringly.

"Do you mind if I sit down?" she asked when the door had

closed behind him. She would not stand there like a prisoner at the dock, but moved calmly to a small chair opposite Mrs. Tyler and held her hands to the fire. She felt surprisingly calm and unruffled.

"So you went into the woods?" the old lady demanded.

"Yes, we did. The woods on the uphill side." Lora looked up from the fire and met the other woman's gaze steadily. "Jemmy showed me the pool where his mother drowned. Did you know that he has some twisted idea that he is to blame for her death? Why hasn't someone helped him to get over that?"

The heavy lids came briefly down over Mrs. Tyler's eyes, but she was not one to reveal surprise easily. Nevertheless, Lora had the feeling that his grandmother had not realized this queer idea of Jemmy's.

"No one knows exactly what happened," Mrs. Tyler said. "The child was in bed at the time. Why should he blame himself?"

"Because he thinks his mother was trying to get him a turtle to replace one that died."

The rings on the old lady's hands flashed color as she moved them in dismissal of the notion. "What if she was? The boy reads too many books. But it is your conduct I wish to discuss, not his. I find it necessary, Lora, to point out the fact that you have not shown yourself properly willing to fit into the life of this household. You have flown in the face of my wishes as well as Wade's. I cannot regard your behavior as the dutiful conduct of a good wife."

"I want to be a good wife," Lora said. "But I don't think this can be accomplished by obeying edicts which seem unreasonable to me."

Mrs. Tyler sighed. "I suppose allowances must be made for the fact that you are hardly more than a child. It is to be regretted that you have been allowed to grow up in so willful and headstrong a manner. These qualities are not ones which will help you now. I cannot tolerate or permit them. Do you, or do you not want to make my son happy?"

"Of course I want to make him happy," Lora said earnestly. "But it seems to me—"

The old lady did not permit her to continue. "Today you have done nothing but upset him and increase his unhappiness. When he hears of your trip into the woods he will feel even more disturbed. Perhaps you had better go to your room now and pray for forgiveness and guidance."

Her earlier calm was treacherously forsaking her and Lora

longed to make the hot retort which rose to her lips. But she suppressed it and forced herself to rise without hurry from her chair.

"I'm sorry to have displeased you," she said, and went quietly from the room. But when she reached the staircase she picked up her skirts and ran all the way up in order to release herself in physical action.

Once in her own room, she went to work building a furious blaze in the fireplace, feeding on the small logs until the fire purred and crackled.

Because she had promised Jemmy a lovely Christmas she must refrain from open warfare with that autocratic woman downstairs. For Jemmy's sake and for Wade's she must find some way to possess her own soul and still give a pretense of submission to Amanda Tyler. But, oh, it was always so much harder when the time came than she ever anticipated.

The sudden clamor of the doorbell sounded through the house and she rose from her knees and went to her own door, opened it softly. Since there were not likely to be Sunday visitors, this must be Wade coming home. Would she be able to see him alone now and smooth things out between them?

She heard Ellie's shuffling steps and then the sound of her greeting.

A voice which was not Wade's said, "Mrs. Lord's compliments to Mrs. Tyler, and a welcome home to Mr. Wade and his wife. My sister has sent over some preserves and fruit cake."

It was Adam Hume, and Lora continued to listen at the crack of the door. Ellie led him back to Mrs. Tyler's parlor and the door below opened and closed upon him. Lora shut her own door thoughtfully. Serena's brother had been unpleasantly forthright in her single encounter with him, yet she sensed honesty in his directness. What was more, he had proved himself a friend to Jemmy Tyler. Because of that there was something she wanted very much to ask him. Something he might answer far better than Jemmy's father, or anyone else in this house.

She flung her shawl about her shoulders in order to be ready and when she heard again the sound of opening doors, she went out upon the upper veranda toward the front of the house.

When Ellie had closed the front door after Adam, she called to him softly. He turned on the drive, looking up through the branches of the big chestnut tree. Today he wore sober black broadcloth which seemed to pinch at his breadth of shoulder, giving him none of Wade's elegance. He had not yet put on his hat and his rusty hair shone in the sunlight.

"This is a pleasant surprise," he said. "I was told that you had retired with a severe headache."

She grimaced involuntarily and used Jemmy's term. "I'm in disgrace. I have no headache."

For the first time he smiled and resembled his sister Serena to a greater degree.

"I wanted to ask you something," she whispered. "Jemmy says you're his friend and I thought you might know what he would best like for Christmas."

He looked up at her with a certain speculation. "If you could manage it—a dog," he said. "I've never seen a boy who needed a dog more than Jemmy does. He's crazy about our Whiskers."

Lora put her hands on the veranda rail and felt the gray paint scaling beneath her fingers. "I'll manage it," she promised. "Somehow I'll manage it."

He turned his hat thoughtfully in his hands. "I'm not sure that you can. I doubt that his grandmother would readily permit him to keep a dog and I'm thinking it would take somebody a lot bigger than you to stand up to her. This could mean a major engagement—and, as I recall, you don't think much of fighting."

She turned away without replying, but he spoke again softly, his words faintly mocking. A tree branch had cut him from her view now, but she waited to hear and he knew she was still there.

"My sister Serena has an enormous curiosity, Mrs. Tyler. She has bidden me extract from you certain information if the opportunity arose. Of course she has also bidden me to be delicate about the extraction. But as you may have gathered, delicacy is not a matter in which I have any skill. She wants to know whether or not you have met Mrs. Channing."

He was of course being insupportably offensive, but somehow his honesty was a relief after the hidden currents and the evasiveness in the Tyler house. Besides, she herself was growing curious about this Mrs. Channing.

"No," she said, "I have not met Mrs. Channing. But since I have heard her name mentioned a number of times, I would like very much to know who she is." She stepped back to the edge of the railing where she could see him again.

He gestured in the direction of the hilltop. "So they haven't told you? She is the widow of a wealthy Southern planter,

59

Nicholas Channing. If you want to know more, you had better ask Wade or his mother. Here comes your husband now."

She saw the carriage on the lane in front of the house. It turned into the drive and Peter helped Wade out. Adam extended his hand in greeting, and Wade took it in a somewhat restrained fashion. At any moment, Lora thought, Wade would look up at her. He must surely have seen her on the veranda as he drove up. But he did not speak to her, even when Adam Hume took his departure after a too elaborate bow in her direction.

She saw Wade come slowly up the steps and disappear into the house, looking pale and very tired. She flew back along the veranda to her own room and through to the hall, where she could wait for him to mount the stairs. But he did not so much as glance her way when he came up. Instead he went straight to the door of the shuttered front room which had been Virginia's and went in, closing the door behind him.

Dismayed, Lora returned to the warmth of her own fire and curled herself on the hearthrug to think. The problems of this household seemed to loom larger by the moment. If only it were possible to get Wade and Jemmy away from this house, away from the domination of Amanda Tyler. What chance would there ever be for Wade to forget his lost love under this roof? There must be reminders of Virginia at every turn, and remembering could be a sickness. Worst of all, there was that closed room at the front of the house—always an invitation and a torment. Had it been kept as it had been when Virginia was alive? she wondered.

She sat very still before the hearth, listening with all her senses. But the only sound which came to her was the whinnying and stamping of horses in the stables and the faint, silvery tinkle of Mrs. Tyler's bell, with its everlasting summons of Ellie.

The feeling grew in her that Wade ought not to stay in there alone. That was why she was here—so that he might have someone to turn to in his need.

She got to her feet and went softly into the hall.

VI

AT THE DOOR of the room which had been Virginia's, Lora listened, holding her breath. She still heard nothing, and after a moment she tapped lightly on the wood panel. There was no answer, no whisper of sound. When she tried the knob it turned easily under her hand. At least he had not locked himself in.

She opened the door quietly and looked into the dim room. Faint light seeped through closed shutters, but here there were no portieres to reduce the room to night. A heavy scent of long-dried rose leaves enveloped her too sweetly in the unaired room.

She could see the bed with Wade lying face down across it and as she moved toward him the room emerged and made itself known to her. It was a pretty room, with frilly, feminine touches that bore no trace of Amanda Tyler's severity. Virginia too had had her haven of escape. But the scent of rose leaves and the stirring of long-quiet dust as Lora's skirts rustled about her made the air stuffy, and she wanted to get away quickly.

She put her hand upon Wade's shoulder. "Come, my dear. Come with me. You mustn't stay here."

He turned over and looked at her dazedly, as if grief had somehow confused him and he no longer knew who she was.

"Please come," she repeated in the firm tone she might have used to a child. "I want to talk to you, Wade. I *must* talk to you. But let's talk in my room, not here."

A little to her surprise, he sat up and she reached quickly for the crutch beside the bed and gave it to him. Moving at his own awkward gait, he followed her down the hall to her room. Here she made him comfortable on her wide bed, plumping pillows behind him, pulling off his shoes. When she had covered him with a quilt she went to poke up the fire and add more wood. Then she sat beside him on the bed, holding his scarred left hand as she had done so often in those long days when he had hovered between life and death.

He lay back with his eyes closed and she saw the shadows beneath them, and the grooved lines beside his mouth. If only she could get him to talk about those things which he

61

had always held from her. Putting his grief into words might be good for him.

"Tell me what she was like," Lora said softly.

He did not open his eyes, but his fingers tightened about her own and then relaxed. His words came slowly, faltering at first, then more quickly as memories crowded upon him. It was not of Virginia he spoke, however, but of his own childhood in this house.

"I can remember how different it was. When I was a little boy and my father was alive, that is. The house was always filled with his friends. There were always loud voices and people laughing, sometimes until late at night. Mother never cared for his friends any more than they cared for her, and she withdrew from them. On Sundays she made me keep the Sabbath with her in the same way Grandfather Jason used to keep it—with prayers and quiet and all the shutters closed. But we had to keep it by ourselves in the sitting room downstairs because my father would have nothing to do with gloom and solemn voices. He was a very hearty and popular man and I wanted with all my heart to be like him. But he was always so confident, so sure of himself, and that was a quality I lacked."

"And your mother?" Lora prompted.

Wade did not open his eyes. "She was determined that I should not be like him at all. I already looked like him and I suppose that frightened her into thinking that I might grow up a wastrel too. I suppose that's what he was, really, for all his charming ways. It's a mystery why she married him. But she was bound and determined that I must grow up in the solid mold of her own father, whom she'd loved and admired more than any other human being."

"Can you remember your grandfather?"

"He died before I was born," Wade said. "But I feel as if I'd grown up in the same house with him. Mother must be greatly like him. She wanted me to care about the shipping business and take an active interest in the bank as I grew up. When I was little she used to send me on trips to the docks sometimes with Mr. Niles. She would have taken me herself if that section had not been too rough for the presence of a lady. I loved the docks and all that busy life down there— but not in the way she intended that I should."

"Didn't your father mind what she did with you?"

Lora saw the twitch of a nerve near the corner of Wade's mouth. "I was ill a great deal as a child. I wasn't my father's sort, much as I'd have liked to be. He should have had a

62

boisterous, active child, and since I was neither he lost interest in me. I lived inside my own head too much to suit him."

He was quiet for a little while and the only sound was the chinking fall of embers in the grate, the only movement the rosy play of firelight on walls and ceiling. Lora sat very still, not wanting to break the spell of these memories.

As he took up the thread again, she could see the slender, handsome boy he must have been, eagerly absorbing the colorful life of the docks. But when he came home to his mother, it was not the business end he wanted to talk about. He had no interest in the size of a cargo, or the details of a bill of lading. His head was awhirl with visions of China and the Indies, his nose atingle with the scents of spices and tea. The dock workers were to him not merely employees of his mother's concern; the function of sailors was not solely to bring her ships safely to port. He saw each in an aura of his own and in terms of glamour and adventure. Words swirled excitingly through his mind and he tried vainly to capture all this magic on paper. He was forever "wasting" his time scribbling down impressions of the things he saw. All of which must have angered and disturbed his mother.

Lora could see her—that younger version of Amanda Tyler, straight-backed and strong of will, turning from the husband she should never have married to spend all her emotional strength on the son she loved so fiercely and possessively. As she listened, Lora began to understand something else that twisted her heart a little.

Though his mother had loved him, she had, as Wade grew older and continued to disappoint her, lost all belief in him. She never gave up trying to make him what she wanted him to be, but she could not suppress a contempt for what she regarded as weakness and failure.

"Virginia gave me back my belief in myself," Wade said.

He fell silent and Lora reached out with cool fingers to stroke the place between his eyes that sometimes throbbed with pain.

"I see her everywhere," he murmured. "But she always eludes me, slips away from me."

"This isn't a good place for you to live," Lora said, suddenly urgent. "Let's take Jemmy and go away from her. Let's be free of shadows."

He moved his head from side to side. "Such a move would kill my mother."

"It would not," said Lora firmly. "She is not made of stuff that dies easily. You and Jemmy are more important."

But he would not listen. "There's no place where I can escape. I will always see Virginia's eyes, reproaching me."

"Reproaching you for what? I've heard enough about her to know how good she must have been. She wanted your happiness. So why should that be changed now?"

Again he would not be persuaded. "You don't understand," he said, and turned his face away from her.

She knew there was no use now in urging him further. She continued to stroke his forehead and after a moment he caught her hand drowsily and kissed the back of it.

"Be like this always," he murmured. "Be the way she was."

For just an instant she wanted to snatch her hand away, but she controlled the impulse. She sat quietly beside him until he fell asleep. Then she tucked the covers about him and returned to her own long thoughts as she sat beside the dying fire. There she fell into a doze herself, with her head back against the cushion of a chair, and woke with a crick in her neck when Ellie came to call them for supper.

Wade awoke rested and more cheerful than she had seen him since they had left Pineville. A release into words had apparently helped.

It was a relief to find that Sunday supper was not a repetition of the gloomy midday meal. Apparently the stern Sabbath rules were somewhat relaxed with the coming of evening and even Mrs. Tyler seemed in a less bitter mood. It was likely, Lora suspected, that she considered everything to be settled to her own satisfaction, with the rebels in her house properly subdued.

No reference was made to the way in which Lora and Jemmy had slipped from grace, and Lora strove for an outward show of meekness that she knew was hypocritical, but which she was willing to don to gain what was now her first purpose.

Wade had risen from his nap in a gay and charming mood that made him very attractive. He had been like this sometimes during his convalescence and she had been drawn by his courage, his effort to make nothing of physical pain.

As the meal progressed, he entertained them with an amusing story of the company cook and of the ingenious way in which that inventive Irishman could eke out rations when the larder was low. And he told a story of a young drummer boy and how he had saved them all from danger early one morning when the enemy had tried a surprise attack.

The latter story appealed to Jemmy and he watched his father wide-eyed and without the look of veiled resentment which he usually turned upon him. There was even a grudging admiration in the boy's eyes and, observing him, Lora knew the truth with a sudden stab.

Jemmy's attitude toward his father was a shell of self-protection and nothing else. At the moment his small person betrayed his secret for anyone to read. But only Lora's attention was upon him; only Lora recognized that here was a small boy who longed to love and admire his father and to be loved and admired by him in return.

When there was a pause in the talk and they were still smiling over Wade's antic account, Lora drew a breath and plunged into the matter nearest her heart.

"What are we going to do about Christmas?" she asked. "It's only two weeks off and Jemmy and I have some plans."

Jemmy's eyes sparkled. "Papa, do you suppose we could have a Christmas tree the way Aunt Serena always does?"

"What nonsense," said Mrs. Tyler before Wade could speak. "I see no point in going to such fuss and bother. That is too worldly a way to celebrate Christ's birthday."

Wade put out his hand and covered his mother's. "I can remember how much fun we used to have at Mama Hume's Christmas parties before the old house burned down. When I was Jemmy's age I thought a Christmas tree was the most wonderful thing in the world."

"Oh, please, let's have one!" Lora cried.

Mrs. Tyler shrugged, but her sense of well-being held and she seemed not to regard this as a major rebellion. "I can see you're all against me. Very well, if Peter can find a tree, I will offer no objection. But understand—there is to be no mess about the house either before or afterwards."

"I'll clean up everything," Jemmy promised.

Lora winked at him secretly. "I have some ideas about presents. Let's go in the library after dinner and shut everyone out, Jemmy."

When supper was over they did just that, and the boy seemed more like the happy, energetic children Lora remembered from home. He helped her find paper and ink, and then rummaged in the cellar for the broken comb and old toothbrush she requested. A quick trip outside with a lantern enabled them to pick up several dry leaves, unbroken and clear of pattern.

Then, first spreading old papers carefully around on the library table, they sat down to the making of spatterwork bookmarks. Jemmy showed a surprising ingenuity and natural sense of artistry in creating designs. Lora made a special effort to praise the results he achieved and he wriggled all over in delight at her approval. He was a fine little boy, she thought. Somehow, somehow she must get him that puppy for Christmas. She would ask Wade about it very soon.

They worked in the library until Jemmy's bedtime, and then Lora went upstairs with him. She could hear Wade and his mother talking in the rear sitting room, but she had no desire to join them.

At Jemmy's door she paused, holding her candle high. "Call me when you're ready and I'll come tuck you in," she said matter-of-factly.

The solemn look came into his eyes, turning them midnight blue in the dim light. For just an instant she thought he was going to move away from her as he had the night she had come to this house. But she was his friend now and all day long he had been accepting her in small ways. If it was the memory of his mother kissing him good night, tucking him beneath the covers, that made his eyes darken, he did not at least hold this against Lora now.

"All right," he said briefly, and vanished into his room.

She went into her own room across the hall and released her breath in a long sigh. What a strange day this had been, with its moments of rebellion and of happiness too. She had a feeling that Jemmy already considered her an ally and was beginning to like her.

His voice reached her thinly through the door she had left ajar and she hurried across the hall to find him snug in his narrow bed. With little patting gestures she made a great thing of pulling up the quilt and tucking it securely in about the sides so that no chill draft could reach him.

"Toes warm?" she asked.

Just his nose stuck out over the edge of the quilt. "Warm as toast. Lorie, do you think we can really get a tree?"

"We're certainly going to try," she assured him. "And I'll have a surprise for you Christmas morning too. A special surprise from me." That was true enough. She'd get him something nice even if the dog proved to be impossible.

He wriggled happily. "Will it be something red?"

She shook her head.

"Blue?"

"Time to go to sleep now," she said, smiling.

"Brown?"

"Maybe. I'm not sure yet. Close your eyes and get sleepy."

She wished she dared to lean over and kiss him. But she knew better than to rush things. So she said good night and took her candle away, leaving him to dreams she hoped would be happy ones.

She undressed quickly and got into her warm flannel nightgown with the round collar she had edged with lace in one of the few small gestures she had been able to make toward a trousseau. She had not minded that she could not have pretty things. It had never been as if she were marrying Martin. She unpinned her hair and brushed it with long vigorous strokes before plaiting it into a heavy single braid.

When she had turned out her lamp and was about to crawl into bed, she heard Wade's light tap on her door, and his voice: "May I come in?"

A momentary stiffening ran through her. For just an instant her throat was choked and she could not answer. Then she went to the door and pulled it open. In the light of his candle she could see that he wore a handsome claret-colored dressing gown of patterned silk, looking elegant even now. She stepped back from the doorway and he blew out the candle and closed the door.

She went into his arms and lifted her lips to his, let him hold her close in the darkness. But the old wince of pain went through her because he was not Martin. She was gentle with him, and very tender, but even as his mouth found hers she knew the truth—about him as well as about herself.

She could only be lonely and longing in his arms. She could never for a moment forget that he was not Martin. Nor did she want to. The thought of such pretense would have revolted her. Yet as surely as she knew her own heart and mind, she knew his too, knew that by some dark magic he turned her again into Virginia, and that it was Virginia he held and caressed and loved. She could only pity him and give herself to his need.

Long, long after he had fallen asleep beside her, she lay thinking again about the long day. Pictures flashed through her mind without connection, springing into life of their own accord.

She remembered Adam Hume looking up at her from the drive in front of the house, telling her that it would need someone stronger than she, someone willing to do battle, to face up to Amanda Tyler. Then Jemmy's hurtful words when he had asked her if she thought he had killed his mother. And in a sudden flash of memory, the strange figure of that colored girl, Rebecca, looking out at them from the woods beyond the pool. Her face had been like a golden-brown mask, the eyes dark and staring without expression.

The vision, however, which pressed beneath her eyelids at the moment of falling asleep was simply the memory of that clear, still pool, shining beneath the golden sun. Virginia had said it was like quicksilver, but there had been no quicksilver movement to it today. It had been calm and quiet and innocent of guilt. Yet in those still depths a woman had struggled and died, and the painful mystery of her death still lay heavily upon this house.

VII

CHRISTMAS was only a few days off and today there was no bright sun shining upon the woodsy hillside. A gray sky blended into the waters of the harbor and a sharp wind rustled through dry leaves, whispered in the pines. Wade had said that morning that it looked like snow, but so far no drifting white flakes flecked the sky, though Lora watched for them eagerly. Somehow there had to be snow for Christmas Eve and Christmas Day.

She had not returned to these forbidden woods since her first climb into them with Jemmy that Sunday afternoon. Wade still did not know of their escapade, and Lora had wondered a little that his mother had not told him. Perhaps Mrs. Tyler was pleased with the new meekness and obedience Lora had managed to exhibit. Or perhaps the old lady was saving the knowledge as a weapon; something to use against her daughter-in-law if the need arose.

In any event, Lora felt that she had behaved so well for so long a time that she could not endure another moment of being a meek wife and daughter in that stifling house. Again Wade was working on his book in the library and Mrs. Tyler was napping. Jemmy was in school, so no one need know where she had gone this afternoon. Perhaps, walking in these woods, she could somehow retrieve something of her own will and spirit and soul.

Last week she had gone to New York with Ellie and shopped right down Mrs. Tyler's list. After New Year a seamstress would come in and Lora would then be clothed in a more seemly and fashionable wardrobe. Some of the material they had purchased was so beautiful that she'd longed to cut into it at once and make up at least one gown herself. But Mother Tyler would not hear of such a thing. She made it quite plain that she had no confidence in Lora's way with a needle, or in her knowledge of how a lady should be gowned. Since there was no place to wear lovely frocks anyway, Lora suppressed her eagerness, a little surprised that she was interested at all in such frivolous matters.

They had shopped for Christmas gifts that day too. Games and books for Jemmy, gifts for Mother Tyler and Wade. It had been fun to have ready money in her reticule for the first time she could remember. Now, even if there were no puppy, Jemmy would still be happy with what he received, not dreaming of what she had planned. Among other things she had bought him a little glass paperweight with a tiny snow scene depicted inside. When you turned it over the snowflakes flew for quite a long time, feathering down upon miniature houses and children and snowmen. She had found a leather writing case for Wade and a handsome morning cap for his mother, as well as two beautiful cashmere shawls, expressly ordered by Wade.

The stores had been an exciting experience for Lora— Arnold Constable's and Lord and Taylor's, gleaming and expensive-looking, with an astonishing wealth of goods on display. If her shopping companion had been someone less dour than Ellie, the day would have been even more of an adventure.

It was when she returned from her shopping trip that she had asked Wade about the puppy. The shocked look he had given her was far from reassuring.

"Mother detests dogs," he said. "My father filled the house with them when I was small and she had her fill of their racket and dirt. Later, after my father died, and she was rid of the lot, I wanted just one pet for my own. But she wouldn't hear of it. No, Lora, I'm sorry, but you must forget this idea of a puppy entirely."

She had not forgotten it, however. She had not given up. In her imagination a wonderful picture glowed and would not give way to such ugly reality, no matter how much anyone tried to discourage her. She could see Jemmy's rapt face, his delight when he found the puppy on Christmas morning. The picture was so real and clear that she could even see his grandmother's expression as she watched the little boy, see the softness come in to her eyes. With the fact an accomplished matter, not even Mrs. Tyler could be so cruel as to take the dog away from Jemmy.

However, when Lora had broached the subject with Wade again this morning, she had still been unable to gain his agreement and the interchange had left her feeling rebellious. That was why she had run away again to the peace of these woods and the usual release she felt when she indulged in vigorous action. She was a "doer," as Doc had always said.

When she reached the clearing where the pool hid among the trees, gray today, sightless beneath the gray sky, she was breathing quickly from the energetic climb. It was too cold to linger near the water, though she promised herself that she would come again to visit this beauty in the spring. Except for a sense of mystery, the place was not haunted for her. If Virginia's spirit hovered here, she felt sure it was a friendly, unvindictive spirit. Virginia had meant harm to no one and she would surely have been glad for the effort Lora was making with Jemmy.

On the other side of the pond the uphill path beckoned, and this time Lora did not hesitate. There was no reason why she should not climb through the woods and have a look at the Channing house that crowned the crest. She had no feud with Mrs. Channing or her household and she saw no reason why she should carry on some quarrel that had its roots in the past and did not concern her in any way. Besides, she was still curious, and as her father had always said, she could never stand wanting to know and not knowing.

The upper path meandered seemingly without purpose, as if it had once been traced by feet that wandered idly. But it opened at length upon the place where Dogwood Lane curved back on its course along the upper hillside and approached the great white house above.

At her first glimpse of the Channing mansion, Lora caught her breath in surprise. This expanse of graceful, gleaming white, with its columns marching across the front, was now a common sight in the South where the Greek revival was in full sway. But she had not expected to find it here. On this crest of Northern hill it became all the more impressive and commanding for the fact that it was unusual. Adam had said that Nicholas Channing had been a Southern planter. Apparently he had wanted to place a bit of his own South here in Staten Island.

As she stood on the rutted road below the house, recovering her breath and studying the windows without care whether or not the occupants saw her, the barking of a dog brought her attention to the open gateway through which the drive entered. Dogwood Lane went no farther along the hill, but ended before the Channing house.

Lora crossed the road and walked purposefully toward the drive. There was a gatekeeper's cottage set beside the stone wall. Beyond, a brown and white shepherd and her litter of puppies gamboled on the dry grass. A man stood watching them and at the sound of Lora's step on the gravel he turned and smiled. It was the man they called Ambrose, who tended Mrs. Tyler's garden in spite of Wade's disapproval.

She went to the gate, bidding him good afternoon. He touched his finger to his cap in recognition, noting her interest in the puppies.

"Funny little beggars, aren't they?" he said. "Come in if you'd like to look closer, Mrs. Tyler."

Lora went through the gate toward the place where the puppies rolled about on the grass. One fat little fellow with a white patch in his forehead nipped playfully at his tolerant mother and then rolled over and over in delight as she pushed at him with her nose. He had a roguish look about him, and he was obviously vain. While his brothers and sisters paid no attention to Lora, his alert gaze spotted her and he pranced over to present himself for her admiration. What a companion he would make for Jemmy! A demanding little dog who would insist on being loved.

Lora knelt and let him chew on her knuckles with his sharp little teeth. He never closed his jaws tightly, but he liked tugging at her hand and patting it with his paws.

"Do you suppose I could purchase one of these puppies?" Lora asked John Ambrose. "Are they for sale by any chance?"

The old man looked at her quizzically. "Just what would you be doing with a puppy down there, ma'am?"

"I want it for a Christmas present for Jemmy," she told him. "I've seen you at the Tylers'. I know you're his friend."

He rubbed a rough, brown hand over his grizzled chin. "You've got Mrs. Tyler's permission, ma'am?"

"No, I haven't," Lora admitted frankly. "She doesn't know anything about it. But I think Jemmy ought to have a dog and I'm going to get him one."

He shook his head, repeating the warning Lora had heard on all sides. "She'd never let the boy keep it."

"But why not? Every child needs a pet. And Jemmy's more lonely than most boys."

71

Ambrose reached for the puppy who played at her feet and picked him up by the scruff of the neck.

"That one," Lora pleaded. "That's the one he'd like best."

He rolled the puppy on its back and tickled the fat little stomach, to its intense delight. But he did not answer her directly. "I can remember one time I tried to get a dog for Jemmy's father in the days when I used to work down there. But she wouldn't have it then, and I don't think she's changed any now."

"You used to work for the Tylers?" Lora asked.

"I grew up down there." He regarded her frankly with keen eyes. "Spent my growing-up years working for the Cowles. And I stayed right on after Miss Amanda married."

What had happened, Lora wondered, to make him give up working for Mrs. Tyler after all those years and come up here to be Mrs. Channing's gardener? But this was no time to be curious about side issues. All she wanted was the possession of this engaging little puppy.

"If I give him the puppy on Christmas morning without Mrs. Tyler knowing about it ahead of time, she'd never have the heart to take it away from him. Will you sell it to me?"

"Maybe you're the one to manage it, at that," the old man said, and his look approved of her. "But anyway it's not up to me to dispose of the pups. If you want you can go up and ask Mrs. Channing yourself."

"I'll do that," Lora decided. She gave the puppy a last pat and started resolutely up the left wing of the drive.

The great white house awaited her coming, serene and proud, but it gave no sign by the least flicker of a blind that it noted her pigmy figure. Gazing out over the hillside toward the busy scene of the harbor, its air of superior indifference began to awe her a little as she followed the course of the drive. She had never set foot in a house as grand as this, and in spite of her strength of purpose she felt a little uneasy. Now she was truly on forbidden ground.

She crossed the brick veranda behind the pillars and went up the few steps to the center door. She hesitated only a second before she reached for the bell. She could hear the sound echo musically within the house. While she waited she turned to look at John Ambrose where he stood watching her near the gate. He made a slight signal of encouragement. Then she heard steps coming toward the door and braced herself for whatever welcome she might receive.

VIII

THE YOUNG COLORED girl, Rebecca, opened the door
and her dark eyes regarded Lora unflickeringly for an instant
before she veiled them with long lashes.

"Please come in, Mrs. Tyler," she said.

Her accent was softly Southern, yet without a slurring together of the words. The girl spoke like any well-educated
Southern lady. Lora was more ill at ease than she.

"I haven't come to call on Mrs. Channing," she said
quickly. "This is an informal visit. I wonder if I could speak
to her for just a moment?"

Rebecca's voluminous skirt was flowered green today and
matched the perkily knotted bandanna about her head. She
gestured toward a room on her left and went to open a door
for Lora, her gold hoop earrings swaying as she walked. She
moved with grace, her shoulders well back and her head high,
her feet treading softly on the dark mirror of the floor.

"Please sit down," Rebecca said, flinging open the drawing
room door. "I will tell Mrs. Channing you are here."

She closed the door and went soundlessly away. Lora, still
ill at ease, looked about the room. Pale roses bloomed against
the light green of the carpets. The room was so long that
two fireplaces were necessary, each with its marble mantel
and gift-framed circle of mirror above. Fires burned behind
elaborate andirons. Fires in a room like this when there was
no company!

Lora went to a nearby chair of gilt and rose damask and
sat down in it stiffly. Mrs. Channing must indeed be a lady
of wealth. Such chandeliers of crystal Lora had never seen
before, or such ornate plaster carvings at every corner of the
ceiling, such elegant green velvet draperies. Glass doors
opened toward the white pillars that ran along the front of
the house and Lora could imagine the view of harbor and
hillside which could be had beyond.

Every wall was graced with paintings, but they were of
foreign buildings, or woodland scenes, instead of the usual
family portraits which most people hung in parlor and drawing room. Turning about in her chair, curious and interested,
Lora saw that the only portrait in the room was a large one

73

which hung behind her on the wall at the far end of the room. This picture was oddly framed by dark-green velvet curtains which cut down past the single standing figure of a woman, setting it off effectively, though hiding whatever else the artist might have painted in his picture.

The figure in the portrait stood beside long French doors and there was a glimpse of white columns beyond, so the picture must have been painted in this very room. The woman was strikingly beautiful, with great dark eyes that seemed to challenge the observer. She had been painted in a yellow gown that set off her dark beauty but did not detract from the center of interest—her arresting face. Studying the picture, Lora did not doubt that if this was Mrs. Nicholas Channing, she was a woman to be reckoned with. If Wade had quarreled with her, it must have been a resoundingly good quarrel, to say the least.

She heard the turning of a knob just then and swiveled about in her chair to stare with innocent attention at the fire in the nearby grate. She did not glance up until the original of the portrait stood beside her.

"Mrs. Tyler?" said a cool voice which carried no hint of welcome in it, and Lora looked into a face that was far less beautiful than that of the woman in the portrait. Indeed, the artist had flattered her outrageously in his painting. This woman's mouth was too big, albeit the lips were as red as the painted ones of the picture, and she had a faint hump to her large, strong nose. Only her eyes were the eyes of the portrait, dark and arresting, but far more vital in life.

Lora gave her hand into the long-fingered one that was held out to her. Mrs. Channing barely touched her fingers and then withdrew her own hand quickly. She went to sit in a damask chair opposite Lora and regarded her guest with a look that was appraising and far from friendly. Unlike the vivid figure in the portait, she wore black with a great hoop skirt; black relieved only by the jade of her long earrings, and the jade and gold brooch at the V of her gown.

"It is very kind of you to see me," Lora faltered, sensing for the first time that there might be effrontery in her appearance here. If Wade brooked no friendship with the Channing household, it was equally possible that Mrs. Channing bore him a similar ill will.

"This is a surprise," her hostess admitted frankly, and her level look seemed to pry past any guard Lora might wear. "May I ask if your husband knows you are here?"

"No, he doesn't," Lora said hurriedly. "I'm here for my

own purpose. I happened to be passing on the road and I saw your shepherd dog playing with her puppies."

Winged brows raised questioningly. "Happened to be passing?"

Lora flushed, but she did not allow her own gaze to drop. If this woman meant to be direct, she would meet her on the same ground.

"No, that isn't true. The road ends here. I came because I wanted to see your house. I was curious."

Mrs. Channing said nothing. She waited, long hands, graced by rings of jade and pearl, quiet in her lap.

"I will tell you at once why I'm here," Lora said. "I would like very much to purchase one of your puppies. I want it for Jemmy Tyler."

A hint of surprise flickered across Mrs. Channing's face and there was a barely perceptible softening to amusement of her full red mouth.

"I will gladly give you your choice of a puppy if you can make Amanda Tyler accept it in her household," said Mrs. Channing directly.

Lora raised her chin ever so slightly. "I see no reason why she should not accept it."

The woman in the chair opposite relaxed against its back and her laughter was sudden and rich and unrestrained. Morgan Channing did not laugh like a well-bred lady and Lora was relieved at the sound.

"I'll confess that I didn't expect to like you," Mrs. Channing said. "But I think I'm going to."

There was a small bell of Chinese brass on a nearby table and she rang it with quick, vigorous flicks of her wrist. When Rebecca came into the room moving erectly but with always veiled eyes, Mrs. Channing spoke to her.

"Mrs. Tyler is staying to tea. Please serve it to us here by the fire, Rebecca."

The girl curtsied and went off without speaking. Lora found herself looking after her curiously and Morgan Channing noted her interest.

"Nick bought her for me one time when we were in the South. Some bad fortune had overtaken friends of his and they were forced to sell their slaves. Rebecca was brought up with the daughter of the house and taught lessons with her little mistress. She is something of a treasure."

Lora's look must have been one of inquiry because Mrs. Channing smiled wryly and went on.

"Of course she is not a slave now. I pay her a ridiculous

75

wage, considering that she needs no money and has no opportunity to spend it. She was given her freedom when the war started. Nick saw to that before he went on the trip on which he was lost at sea. Even though he was a Southerner he did not believe in slavery. Not that he could escape it in the South without impoverishing himself. Lately I've had a little trouble because Clothilde, the French housekeeper I recently brought home from Paris, does not like the girl. However, Rebecca is well trained and she amuses my guests."

Lora winced at the woman's careless tone, but she made no comment.

Mrs. Channing went on pointedly. "I'd like to know more about you. Tell me where you come from, Mrs. Tyler? Where did you meet Wade?"

Lora explained briefly that she had nursed him back to health after he had been wounded. She mentioned the border town where she had lived with her father, and Mrs. Channing seemed particularly interested.

"Having lived so close to the South, how do you feel about the war?" she asked.

That was a safer subject than to talk about Wade, and Lora expressed her own feelings frankly. Mrs. Channing listened, and although she made no comment, Lora sensed her agreement. This woman, too, hated the war. Whether or not Mrs. Channing's reasons were like Lora's own, there was at least this bond between them.

Rebecca brought lacquered Chinese tea tables of black and gold, set out sprigged plates and a silver cake basket. She moved unobtrusively and with grace. One sensed the training of a Southern mistress behind her, but Lora found herself wondering what might be hidden beyond the girl's exotic façade.

"How does Wade feel about this fighting, now that he's had a taste of it himself?" Mrs. Channing asked when Rebecca had left the room.

"He hates it too," Lora said. Mrs. Channing, as a near neighbor, if not a friend, probably knew well enough that Wade had gone to war driven by the pain of his wife's death. He had not wanted to fight, but only to escape—perhaps even in death.

Mrs. Channing nodded sympathetically. "There are many of us here in the North who are bitterly opposed to the war. We feel it should never have been fought and that the sooner it is stopped the better for our country as a whole."

"But how can it be stopped?" Lora asked. "It's too late now."

The other woman was silent for a long moment. Then she shrugged. "Let's not talk about gloomy things. Tell me, how do you like Staten Island? Has Wade taken you to any parties yet? There's quite a social life here, you know."

Lora sipped her tea and spoke readily of the inconsequential. After the stiff meals at the Tyler house it was a relief not to guard her tongue. She had, of course, seen little of the island, she explained, but the prospect of a social life sounded like fun. She hoped Wade would be willing to enter into it.

"He was gay enough in the old days," Mrs. Channing said thoughtfully.

"Then you've known him for a long while?"

Again there was a flicker of surprise across the moody face. "All my life. And I can assure you that once he is out from under his mother's wing he is popular enough. Especially with the ladies."

Was there a faint scratch behind her words? Lora was not sure. At any rate, time was flying and she did not dare stay away too long. As soon as she could manage it courteously she said she must go, and Mrs. Channing rose to accompany her to the door.

"Then I may really have one of the puppies?" Lora asked. "Of course I wouldn't want to take it now. But perhaps you could instruct your gardener to bring it down to our house Christmas morning?"

Mrs. Channing's hand paused within reach of the crystal doorknob. "My gardener?"

Lora was puzzled. "The man they call Ambrose is your gardener, isn't he? I spoke to him down by the gate as I came in."

"Gardener? I—suppose he is." Mrs. Channing let her hand drop to her side, and now there was wry amusement in her eyes. "How like the Tylers not to inform you about such things! He is also my father."

Lora could only stare. "But he—he called you Mrs. Channing most respectfully. . . ."

"He likes his little joke," the other woman told her dryly. "In return I call him Ambrose, and our masquerade serves me nicely at times. It saves me embarrassment with guests, since he prefers to remain what he has always been—a gardener."

Lora felt like a child who must blurt out puzzling questions, however rude. "Then you—grew up right on Tyler premises?"

"I did indeed," said Mrs. Channing. "In the servants' quarters with the smell of the stable below permeating everything." Her dark gaze swept the length of the rich drawing room, and again there was wry amusement in her eyes. "I said I would change all that when I grew up. And as you can see, I have."

Lora could find no words. She made an effort to recover from her surprise and moved again toward the door. But Mrs. Channing turned back.

"Wait a moment!" she cried and went swiftly toward the end wall of the drawing room where the portrait hung, her black skirts rustling over her wide hoop.

Watching in bewilderment, Lora wondered how she had ever thought this woman less striking than her portrait. No artist could ever catch such swift-moving vitality, or the ferment of nervous energy which seemed to drive her. Mrs. Channing might sit still and dark and silent as a night sky without stars. But she could also be the lightning which flashed across that sky with dramatic suddenness.

A long green cord with a tassel on the end hung down along one side of the picture. Mrs. Channing reached for it and as she pulled, the velvet draperies parted to reveal the entire portrait. The artist had painted a second woman who sat in a low chair, looking up at the figure in yellow. The second girl wore pale green and she was young and pretty, but with none of the arresting quality of Morgan Channing.

"My sister," Mrs. Channing said. "Virginia."

Lora was too startled to speak. This was Wade's wife; the woman who had come first in his life, the woman he wanted her to resemble. She stared in fascination at the sweet young face of the girl in pale green. Virginia had light hair with a golden touch to the ringlets about her face. She held an embroidery hoop in her small hands with a needle poised above it, as if she had just paused to look up at her sister.

"I was very fond of her," Mrs. Channing said carelessly. "She was a silly, rather insipid little thing. I never understood what Wade saw in her." The challenging gaze shifted suddenly from the portrait and fixed Lora candidly. "You are nothing at all like Virginia. How did Wade come to get over his great love?"

The suddenness of the question shocked an equally candid answer from Lora. "He wants to think I am like her," she admitted.

Mrs. Channing's unrestrained laugh rang out again. "This may be amusing to watch! Considering your behavior over this puppy, Wade could be in for a jolt one of these days."

"Not if I can help it," said Lora stiffly. Suddenly she wanted to get away from this woman and this room. But Mrs. Channing would not release her so easily. She walked to the door with Lora and opened it.

"We are going to be friends," she said confidently. "I have offended you now. But you'll forgive me in time. You will forgive because you are as direct as I am. Come see me again when that mausoleum becomes too much for you."

At the front door Lora managed to murmur a thank you for the tea and escape as quickly as she could. As she went down the same wing of the drive up which she had come, she saw an open carriage turning into the opposite wing. In it sat a handsome, youngish man with blond sideburns and rather intense blue eyes. He saw her and raised his gray top hat gallantly. She bowed in return and hurried on down the drive. Perhaps there had been reason for those two fires in the grate after all. Mrs. Channing must have expected company.

Ambrose was tending the gate after the passage of the carriage, and his ready smile lighted his face when he saw her.

"You're to have the puppy, are you?" he asked.

As she nodded a sudden realization struck her. There had been so many ramifications to the information she had just gained that she had not thought of this one till now.

"I'm sorry," she said. "I didn't realize before. You're Jemmy's grandfather, aren't you?"

"I thought Mrs. Tyler hadn't told you," he said, seeming more amused than hurt. "It's quite a blot on the Tyler escutcheon, you know."

She held out both hands to him on sudden impulse. "Jemmy loves you. I could see that. Come down to visit him soon."

He hesitated just a moment, then wiped his own hands apologetically on the seat of his work trousers before he took hers somewhat awkwardly. "Jemmy and me—we find ways to see each other. But not down there. It's better not, Miss Lora."

"You're to call me Lora," she said. "No Miss or Mrs. about it. You'll help me with the puppy, won't you? Because it's for Jemmy, you'll bring it down to me on Christmas morning?"

"And because it's for you," said John Ambrose gently.

She hurried across the lane to where the path led downhill. Then she turned and waved to him and he waved back. But as she hurried through the woods it was Morgan Channing who occupied her thoughts. The woman both attracted and repelled her, but more than anything else she made her feel uneasy, though Lora was not at all certain why.

IX

FOR ONCE ELLIE was not waiting with a summons to Mrs. Tyler's sitting room as Lora went up the front steps. The library door was ajar and Wade called to her as she went past. His voice sounded cheerful, unperturbed, so her absence must have caused no undue alarm.

"Come in," Wade invited. "Did you have a good walk?"

She nodded, and as she removed her bonnet she wondered what would happen if she told him the truth about her afternoon walk—that she had visited Morgan Channing and learned considerably more family history than either he or his mother had thus far given her. But of course she couldn't do that. Not yet, at least. She disliked the restraint such play-acting put upon her, but until Jemmy had his Christmas and was safely in possession of the puppy, she must be the very picture of decorum.

So she merely said, "A lovely walk," and went into the library. As she looked about, she was struck by the contrast between the heavy, dark furniture of the Tyler house and the gilt and damask elegance she had seen so recently at Morgan Channing's.

A large mahogany table strewn with books and newspapers stood in the middle of the room, its bulging claw feet resting on a carpet of Mrs. Tyler's favorite gloomy wine color. Wade motioned her toward the dark-red sofa drawn before the fire.

"Do sit down, Lora. You've come at just the right moment. I want to read you the first chapter or so of my book. Here, let me help you with your mantle."

When she was out of her wraps and comfortably seated on the red sofa, a pillow plumped behind her back and her feet on a small stool, Wade picked up a sheaf of manuscript from the desk where he had been working, and seated himself beside her. He had brought an inkwell which he set on a nearby

80

table, while he held a long feather pen in his fingers as if it helped his thinking to have it there.

But before he could begin reading, Lora put a hand on his arm. "Could Jemmy listen to this too? I know he'd be excited to hear the beginning of your book."

"It is not a story for children," Wade said a little coolly, and she did not press the request. But again she was troubled by the sense of some disturbing thing that lay deep in Wade and kept him from his son.

He read extremely well. The timbre of his voice lent itself to dramatic narrative and she was aware of its exciting quality. By his very tone and expression he made the characters and scene of his story come to life. She could not help but wonder if the narrative would have read half so well had she been reading it to herself.

The novel, Wade explained, was to be a romantic tale of Italy—a country which he had always longed to visit and had read much about. The hero was a handsome, adventurous young American who had fallen in love with a countess married to a husband too old for her. None of it seemed very real to Lora and she found herself listening more to the sound of Wade's voice than to the meaning of the story. Now and then she stole a look at his rapt face as he read. He seemed lost in the spell of the narrative and happier than she had ever seen him.

Occasionally he paused to make a quick correction in ink, then went on. It was obvious that the exercise of putting his story on paper was doing him good. When he finished the first chapter and laid down the closely written script, his eyes met hers asking for approval.

For just an instant she had to fight the impulse to tell him frankly that the story was not to her taste, that she thought these people both unreal and uninteresting. But she could not hurt him so, could not blight the healing that was apparently going on within him.

"It is surely as good as some of the romances I have read in *Leslie's Weekly*," she told him.

This at least was true. She did not see why an author should not tell about life as he found it among ordinary people. Why was all this tinsel melodrama necessary? But since it was what Wade was bent on writing, she must not speak her thoughts. Perhaps the writing of this manuscript would do him more good, perform a greater healing than any amount of nursing could achieve. And in that interest it was better to encourage him. If only he did not set so much stock in publication that later refusal of his book might cast him down to greater depths than before he had attempted the writing.

He shrugged aside her comparison with the novels in current magazines. It was quite clear that he thought his own writing superior to any of these.

"Of course I shall be grateful for criticism," he said stiffly, but she suspected that he would not be. It would hurt him so much that she dared not give it.

"I'm not qualified to criticize," she told him gently. "The story is most interesting. I'm anxious to learn how Hamlin gets into Maria's house."

"We'll postpone that for another reading," Wade said more cheerfully, stretching to get the cramp from his leg.

Lora was grateful for an interruption when Ellie tapped on the door and brought in a note addressed to Mrs. Wade Tyler.

"Mrs. Lord sent it over," Ellie said. "The man's to wait for an answer. I'll be back in a few minutes—there's something boiling on the stove." She went off in her usual scuttling manner.

The square of pale-mauve paper gave out a scent of lavender as Lora slit the flap and took a single sheet from the envelope. She read it quickly and her eyes lighted.

"Wade—Serena Lord is giving a party on Christmas Eve and we are invited. It's to be a dance and late supper." She held the note out to him.

He shook his head. "Naturally we cannot go."

"But why not?" she asked in surprise. A party and dance at Serena's sounded exciting and lively. A sudden desire for gaiety surged up in her.

"After all," Wade said, "there is a period of mourning to be observed for your father. And I have not felt like indulging in frivolity myself for a long while."

"Papa didn't believe in mourning," Lora told him quickly. "He never wanted me to wear black or go around with a long face."

She went to him, put light hands on his arm, gently pleading. His eyes softened and he bent to press his cheek against hers.

"You are a wheedling one," he said. "But have you forgotten that I cannot dance, thanks to my leg?"

"I won't dance either," she promised. "I'll sit beside you and we'll watch all the bright things that are happening, together. It will be wonderful just to dress up and—"

"Dress up?" he repeated. "But, my dear, you have no gown

82

that would be suitable to wear. Christmas Eve is almost upon us and I understand a seamstress cannot be had at this time."

For just a moment her hopes fell. Then she lifted her chin in a gesture of determination.

"I have the material now—that lovely garnet satin which is intended for a party gown. I can make the dress myself. I know just the style I would like. Please let me, Wade."

"Mother won't approve," he said, but he went to the fall-front desk and reached into it for notepaper. He brought a sheet to her and dipped the feather pen in ink before giving it to her. There was affection in his smile—as if she were a child he must indulge. "You may write our acceptance, Lora."

She rested the paper on the table and wrote eagerly, unable to suppress the feeling of pleasure that crept into her words and prevented them from being entirely formal. She knew Serena would understand and not condemn. Then Ellie was called back and dispatched with the note.

Lora could not wait to be off to her own room where she could spread out the rich material on her bed, loving the shine, the feel, the very smell of it. There was something heady about the scent of new material. She would make herself the most beautiful gown she had ever possessed. She would be a credit to Wade at the party, and that would please him, be good for them both.

Shears in hand, she hesitated only a moment when she was ready to cut. A certain courage was needed to cut blithely into the rich and lovely stuff. What if she should spoil it? But uncertainty did not hold her for long and the bright shears flashed confidently through the goods. She would need lace for trimming, perhaps, and velvet for bows. Tomorrow morning she would go down to the variety store on Bay Street and get whatever else she needed.

From the rear parlor downstairs she could hear the silver notes of Mother Tyler's bell calling Ellie, perhaps demanding details concerning the message from Mrs. Lord. But Lora worked on without heeding. Not even Amanda Tyler could stop her now.

At dinner Wade mentioned the party casually and Mrs. Tyler expressed some disapproval, but not opposition. Plainly she did not like the idea that Lora meant to make the gown herself, but she was surprisingly moderate in her remarks. Nor did she object Saturday morning when Lora announced that she must make a trip to the store. In face she offered the use of the carriage, though Lora refused it gently. She loved to walk and the distance to the store was not great.

After breakfast Lora donned mantle and bonnet and went out to the front drive. The day was bracingly cold and the usual fresh wind blew from the harbor. But there was a hint of sun breaking through the haze and brisk walking would quickly warm her.

She got no farther than the lane, however, before young voices hailed her, and she looked around to see a wagon drawn by a dray horse lumbering toward her. Temple and Eddie Lord were waving to her from the body of the wagon, while Adam Hume sat on the driver's seat flapping the reins. The dog, Whiskers, barked his own greeting.

"May Jemmy come with us, Mrs. Tyler?" Temple called, pushing back the green knitted cap on his red hair.

Lora looked inquiringly at Adam and he bowed from the seat of the wagon.

"Good morning," he said, elaborately formal, so that she knew he was mocking her again. "As you can see, we are off to purchase a Christmas tree. I understand a store on Bay Street has stocked a few. The boys would like Jemmy to come along, if you will so permit."

So far Mrs. Tyler had not sent Peter to procure a tree, either from the somewhat scrawny ones which grew in the woods, or by looking for one at a store.

"I'm sure Jemmy will want to come with you," Lora said. "I'll go call him. But I wonder—do you suppose you could get a tree for us at the same time?"

Adam's eyes seemed to measure her. "Why not come with us and pick it out yourself?" he asked.

She glanced uncertainly at the wagon. "You mean ride with you now?"

"Why not? There's room here on the seat beside me. And then you can be assured of getting the tree you want. I'll be happy to haul it home for you."

At home she would never have hesitated. She had ridden in farm wagons most of her life and thought nothing of it. But here, where she was hemmed round by so many restrictions . . .

"Are you afraid to be yourself?" Adam challenged.

Once more the irritation he always managed to rouse swept through her. She knew she sometimes gave in too quickly to impulsive action—Doc had often warned her about being headlong. But she did not want to live a life where she could never be free to do as she liked. Behind Adam's mockery lay a certain truth. She must not grow afraid to be herself.

"If you will wait," she said, "I'll go get Jemmy. We'll both come with you."

The boy was in his room reading and his eyes widened with interest when she told him they were going with Adam Hume and the Lord boys to get Christmas trees. While he was putting on warm things, she hurried to her own room and released the band that hooked about her waist supporting a tier of hoops. She could not clamber to the seat of a wagon in hoop skirts. And she did not mean to let that vinegar-tongued brother of Serena's imply that she was timid. There was no sensible reason why she should not go along and help Jemmy pick out a tree. She was not a child who must ask permission at every turn for the things she chose to do.

Part of a frayed string tore loose as she pulled her bonnet on too hastily and she had to resort to pinning. On the trip to town with Ellie she had made the purchase of two handsome new bonnets, but they were scarcely appropriate for wearing on such an errand. Jemmy was waiting impatiently at her door by the time she was ready and they ran downstairs together.

Ellie came into the hallway and Lora told her briefly that she and Jemmy were going to look at Christmas trees with the Lord boys. Ellie had been more respectful since the day when Lora had curtly reproved her, and she offered no objection. Wade, of course, was working in the library and there was no reason to disturb him.

Lora hurried down the front steps with Jemmy, feeling an odd exhilaration. This was escape and adventure and the fun of Christmas all rolled in one package. She had begun to think she would never be excited about Christmas again, but now there was a tingling in her at the prospect.

Adam sprang down to assist her to the driver's seat. She put her hand in his and went up the step lightly, glad to be free of cumbersome hoops.

"I was going down to Bay Street to make some purchases," she told him as he took his place beside her. "Do you think we might stop at my store on our way back?"

Adam nodded. "Yes, of course." He flapped the reins and the horse started ploddingly down the lane.

Lora glanced back toward the house and saw that Wade stood in the library window, watching them leave. She smiled and waved to him, but he did not return her gesture, and she found herself sighing.

"I suppose I shouldn't have come. I'm probably doing the wrong thing again."

"You're going to have trouble if you try to be what you want to be and what *they* want you to be at the same time," Adam said. "Sooner or later you'll have to go in one direction or the other. You can't walk east and west at the same time."

There was some truth in this. It was what she herself was beginning to feel, but she did not want to give him the satisfaction of agreeing with him. She pulled the knitted scarf she had thrown about her neck more closely under her chin to cut out the sharp wind and glanced at the boys in the bed of the wagon. They were already playing some game and absorbed in their own affairs, paying no attention to the two adults on the wagon seat. Jemmy had one arm around Whiskers.

Here was her chance to ask Adam a few questions. Since he was so direct himself he would scarcely object if she was equally so.

"Did you know Virginia Tyler?" she asked softly, looking straight ahead down the steepening hill.

He answered without hesitation. "All her life. Serena and I knew her when she was Virginia Ambrose and lived over the stable behind the Tyler house. The burned-out place you may have noticed along the road was ours. We lived there through our childhood right next door to the Tylers."

"Am I anything like Virginia?" she went on, still not looking at him.

She could sense his quick glance of surprise. "Of course you aren't. Neither in appearance nor in manner. What makes you ask?"

"I've wondered. Mrs. Channing too says I am not at all like her."

"Mrs. Channing?" he echoed. "So you've met Morgan at last? How did that come about?"

"I went up there," she said. "I heard barking and when I saw her shepherd dog and the puppies I went up to the house and asked for one. So I have my Christmas present for Jemmy."

Adam whistled a single long note. "Serena will love this. What do you think of Morgan?"

"I'm not sure," Lora said. It was a relief to be talking about her adventure, if only to Adam Hume. "She is very —dramatic. She seems to have a great deal of nervous drive. But she was nice to me when I asked for the puppy."

Adam reined the horse to one side of the road to make way for a buggy that wanted to pass, and he did not speak until they were plodding along again.

"It might be a good idea to remember that Morgan has never been known to serve any ends but her own. If she wants to make friends with you, then it is for some personal reason. It's just as well not to trust her."

She was inclined to agree with him, but because she so frequently prickled with resentment at his words, she could not wholly accept them now.

"You distrust nearly everyone, don't you?" she said.

He grinned at her, leaning to peer into her face around the rim of her bonnet. "That is indeed the case, my dear Mrs. Tyler. What else did you and Morgan talk about when you'd disposed of the puppy?"

It was none of his business, but there were more questions she wanted to ask. "We spoke of the war. Of whether there was any way to stop it before more lives are wasted. Do you think there is any way?"

"Of course there's a way. By winning it as quickly as possible. But since Fredericksburg victory hardly seems imminent."

"No," she said, shaking her head. "I didn't mean by more fighting. I mean by some peaceful way."

One wheel sank into a deep rut and she was flung momentarily against him. He put out an arm to steady her, but there was no gentleness in his touch.

"Just what peaceful way would you suggest?"

"I don't know. Aren't there those here in the North who are against the war and want to see it stopped? Those, perhaps, with power, with political influence?"

"Is this some notion Morgan Channing has put into your head?"

Morgan's words had seemed innocent enough at the time. Lora had no wish to involve her.

"It's something my father and I talked about often," she told him truthfully. "He believed the war could have been avoided. He still felt it ought to be stopped."

"Perhaps it could have been avoided if there had not been so many fools in high places. Fools and weaklings. I don't mean Lincoln, though I think he waited too long to act. But hindsight is always easier than foresight. It might have been avoided, but it cannot be stopped. Not without victory—and that means for the Union."

"The South is very brave," Lora said. "Her men are great fighters and—"

"The South is like a small boy grown too big for his breeches." Adam surprised the horse with a stinging flap of the reins. "Do you think I didn't hear the bragging during the time I was in Libby? The South has neither the men nor the strength nor the wealth to beat us in the long run. But I'll tell you what the South does have that the North lacks frighteningly. She has the will to win. And that's enough to make any intelligent Union man stay awake at night."

"Here's Bay Street!" cried Temple from the bed of the wagon, and all three boys stood up to look at the cluster of buildings, the banks and stores along the busy thoroughfare.

"I don't understand what you mean," Lora said.

"For a handful of months the North was fighting mad," Adam said. "Then she cooled off and lost interest. Her heart isn't in this fight. She hasn't anything concrete to fight for the way the South has. Your Southern soldier is in there to save home, mother and sweetheart—he thinks—to say nothing of preserving his sentimental ideals about the section he regards as his country. But war has scarcely touched the people up here."

"It has touched Wade," Lora said.

"Yes, the fighting men. But the rest have never been roused. The North mouths platitudes about saving the Union, but there's no real heart in it right now. What's more, knowing Wade, I doubt that even a spell of fighting turned him into a supporter of this war."

"I'm glad it didn't!" Lora said hotly. "I wouldn't want him to be like—like—"

"Like me?" Adam laughed out loud so that Eddie and Temple leaned against the front seat and demanded to know what was funny.

He did not answer them, but pointed ahead. "There are your Christmas trees. The custom is catching on so that we need not go out and pick them in the woods as we did when I was a boy."

There was traffic along Bay Street, drays and carriages, an occasional officer on horseback, privates on foot. Beyond lay the bay, a murky steel color this morning and choppy with whitecaps. Adam drew up to a hitching post and jumped down from the seat. The boys clambered out at once, Jemmy as eager and excited as the Lord boys, the Airedale leaping after them. Lora gathered up her skirts and reached one foot toward the step. But Adam came around and put his hands at her waist, swung her boldly down. She walked quickly away from him, following Jemmy toward stacked trees which stood outside the store.

Eddie and Temple were interested mainly in size. They

wanted the biggest tree on Staten Island. But Jemmy was more particular. He must study each one from every angle, examining it for symmetry and beauty of structure. He was difficult to please and took quite a while. Lora tried to help sympathetically and was grateful for Adam's patience and the fact that he did not tease Jemmy because of his search for perfection, as he did Temple and Eddie about their desire for size. The sense of Christmas excitement increased and even Adam lost his cynical air and became companionable and almost boyish.

When both trees had been selected and stacked in the back of the wagon, with their tops hanging out over the road, the boys wedged themselves, squealing, among prickly branches. Adam pointed out the variety store across the road and, somewhat to Lora's embarrassment, accompanied her, watching with frank interest as she made her purchases of velvet and lace.

"I'm making a dress for Mrs. Lord's party," Lora explained as the salesgirl wrapped up her packages.

"Then I'll see you there," said Adam. "I wasn't sure whether or not I'd attend. But now I may—that is, if you will promise me a dance."

"I shan't be dancing with anyone," she told him. "Wade won't be able to dance because of his leg and I shall stay beside him."

"You mean he'll keep you from dancing just because—"

"It is a suggestion I made myself," Lora said.

"And he accepted such a sacrifice? Well, it's a pity. I learned to waltz most gracefully in Libby." He was silent while she purchased candles for the tree.

When they left the store and crossed the road to the wagon, Lora pulled herself up quickly without touching his hand.

After they were settled for the ride home, he went on talking about the party.

"There'll be too many people there, of course. My sister's friends are legion. What's worse, she has no discrimination, but likes everyone. And Edgar encourages her."

A mingling of anticipation and uneasiness went through Lora. She had been to no parties such as this was likely to be, and the prospect was beginning to dismay her a little.

"I'm not sure I will fit in," she said half to herself, expecting no sympathy from Adam Hume.

But he looked at her more kindly. "Why not? You've only to be yourself. And of course curb your tongue a bit. You can't go asking startling questions or speaking out your mind the way you've been doing this morning."

"That is only with you," she told him. "Because you say what you think more than other people do."

His laughter had a pleased note in it, as if she had complimented him. For the most part they were silent on the way home and Lora began to regret the end of the trip. It had been more fun than she'd expected, considering that Adam had been her companion. Even while he irritated her, his directness was a relief after the devious ways of Mother Tyler and Wade's evasiveness. Now she remembered with increasing uncertainty that Wade had watched from the library window and had not returned her wave. At the time she had been intent on proving that she could be herself, but now the tree had been purchased and she was probably going to be treated like a child again—a child who must be scolded and sent to bed. This routine couldn't go on forever. Complete docility was not for her and never would be.

As they reached the gate to the Tyler drive, she looked back to see Jemmy squirm out of his nesting place among pine boughs and scramble to the ground.

"I'll get Peter," he called to her, and vanished toward the rear of the house.

This time Lora slipped quickly down from the wagon seat without waiting for Adam's assistance and was aware of his amused look. The library window was empty now, but she meant to give Wade no additional reason to object to her conduct.

Peter came out to carry Jemmy's tree around to the back of the house. Unlike Ellie, he seemed to be enjoying the prospect of Christmas.

"Thank you, Mr. Hume," said Lora formally, and Adam saluted her with the whip.

"You are welcome, Mrs. Tyler," he said with equal formality and urged the horse into a trot for home.

She gave the wagon no second glance, but followed the course of the tree around the house. Jemmy was chattering excitedly to Peter, pointing out the singular excellences of his choice. When Lora glanced up at the windows of Mrs. Tyler's sitting room, she saw the old lady there in her wheel chair, disapproval set in every line of her person. When she caught Lora's eye, she tapped on the window and beckoned to her to come inside at once.

Jemmy saw his grandmother and turned away from the tree, concerned for Lora. "Are you afraid?" he asked.

She touched his shoulder lightly. "Of course not. Your grandmother's not a dragon, you know. Someday I may need a knight in armor. But not right now. I'll run inside and see what she wants."

Jemmy returned her smile doubtfully and threw an anxious look in the direction of his grandmother. "Anyway, she can't say no about the tree now."

"She won't even try," Lora assured him, and went into the house.

She wished she might feel as brave inside as her words to Jemmy pretended. But she couldn't help the way her spirits dropped at the prospect of being summoned once again as a culprit before the judge's bench. There was no wrong-doing behind her, but her very youth seemed a handicap in the face of Mrs. Tyler's age and assurance. She might be as determined as the old lady, Lora thought, but it was hard to be as sure that she was right.

X

AMANDA TYLER sat alone in her parlor and Lora was relieved to find Wade absent. It would be easier to face his mother and speak for herself if he were not there to be considered.

"Adam Hume helped us to get Jemmy's Christmas tree," she said cheerfully as she closed the door behind her.

"So I understand. Will you assist me into my chair by the fire, please?"

Lora supported her in the few steps to the chair. When the old lady was settled, Lora took the small chair opposite and began to poke up the fire. The gesture was more to give her something to do than because the fire needed attention.

"Listen to me," said the old woman, and there was so stern a note in her voice that Lora looked up, the poker still in her hand. "Mrs. Wade Tyler does not demean herself by riding on the seat of a farm wagon. Nor does she arouse gossip by indulging in such indignities in the company of a man who is not her husband."

Lora set the poker down carefully so that it would make no clatter upon the hearth. "I have ridden in farm wagons all my life and I see no harm in it. As for being in Mr.

Hume's company—is he not an old friend of the family? And we were hardly alone with the three boys along."

In spite of herself, a note of appeasement had come into her voice. If she could just make Wade's mother understand her innocence of intention.

"There will be no argument," said Mrs. Tyler. "You have behaved disgracefully and there is no possible excuse. We expect you to learn the proper conduct for a lady in your position as my son's wife, no matter how difficult that may be."

Lora sat back in her chair, her hands clasped tightly in her lap so they would not tremble. Once more Mrs. Tyler was making her feel utterly young and futile and helpless.

"I want very much to please you and Wade," she said, hating the faint quaver that entered her voice. "But I cannot feel shame and guilt when I've done nothing shameful, nothing to feel guilty about."

Mrs. Tyler's gaze brightened with anger and she made no attempt to conceal her own feelings. "It does you no credit that you do not feel shame."

She might as well have everything out at once, Lora thought. "There is something else you ought to know. Yesterday afternoon I had tea with Mrs. Channing."

For once the old lady seemed momentarily at a loss for words. Then she rallied to the attack. "Does Wade know this?"

"No, Mother Tyler," Lora said. "I have not told him because I felt it might upset him. Of course he must know eventually. I have no desire to deceive him. But I don't feel that I must carry on a feud with which I've had nothing to do."

"Are you aware," Mrs. Tyler asked, "that this woman upon whom you have so foolishily called is the daughter of former servants of mine? Her high and mighty ways are scarcely due to birth. And of course she has no breeding."

"She was very pleasant. I don't see that her station at birth is of any consequence. After all, she is the sister of Wade's first wife—though this is something I would not have known if she hadn't told me."

The old woman sat very still and grim, her beringed hands gripping the arms of her chair. She looked into the fire, studying the flames as if she saw some vision there. For so long a while was she still that Lora began to feel uneasy.

"I'm sorry to have upset you," she said gently.

It was as though Mrs. Tyler did not hear her words. Her

whole attention remained fixed upon the flickering orange tongues in the fireplace and she did not glance at Lora as she began to speak.

"Perhaps it will be better if you learn a little family history," Mrs. Tyler said. "These are not things one discusses by choice with an—outsider." She paused again, lost in thought.

"I am Wade's wife," Lora said in a low tone.

"You are still an outsider in this house," Mrs. Tyler went on. "A stranger. You have not even begun to integrate yourself with our manner of life. It even seems to me that you are a stranger to my son. I do not know what reason drove you into marriage with him, but I think it was not love."

Lora sat very still. She had not expected this perceptive turn of mind in Wade's mother. But she had no secret to conceal. Wade knew about Martin. In the moments when he was completely honest he knew this had been a marriage of two lonely people who needed something to cling to. But it was impossible to explain this to Wade's mother.

Mrs. Tyler continued, her tone steady and cold, "I will now tell you a certain truth you should know before you make friends with the woman who lives in that monstrous house up the hill. From the time Morgan Ambrose grew into adolescence everyone knew that she had set her cap shamelessly for Wade. It was quite plain that she meant to have him at all costs. If I had not . . . prevented it . . . he might well have married her."

Somehow this "truth" which Mrs. Tyler seemed to think so important did not particularly shock or disturb Lora. After all, with Wade's charm, why shouldn't a girl like Morgan have been attracted to him? But that was all so long ago. Why should it matter now, or be considered a reason for carrying on a feud? She went on to a point which interested her more.

"Did you object to his marrying Virginia?"

There was a suddenly bleak note in Mrs. Tyler's voice, but a little to Lora's surprise she answered the question quickly and with a ring of honesty.

"I did not see that coming," she confessed. "The danger from Morgan seemed so much more imminent that I did not expect such a rebound."

"But since Virginia was the sort to make Wade a good wife, why should you have minded?"

Mrs. Tyler sat a notch more proudly in her chair. "It was hardly fitting for Jason Cowles's grandson to marry a servant girl. The shock for me was very great."

93

Lora felt a flash of pity for the girl Virginia. She was beginning to feel that she knew Virginia rather well.

"At least her marriage could not have been as bad for you as if he had brought Morgan here," Lora said dryly.

The old lady made a gesture of repudiation and the gems in her rings sparkled fiercely in the firelight. "I saw to it that he would not bring her here. But I realize that you have not the gentle upbringing to understand such matters. It is, I suppose, not your fault."

"That may be quite true," Lora admitted, though she felt that there had been nothing wrong with her upbringing. "But this is all so much water under a long-ago bridge. None of it matters now."

"You think it does not matter that Morgan has never in her life given up the pursuit of something she wanted?"

"I don't believe she wants Wade," Lora said stoutly. "It seemed to me that she does not even like him very well. What happened to make him give an order forbidding all of you to have anything to do with Mrs. Channing's household?"

"My son does not give orders in this house," Mrs. Tyler said tartly. "He merely made a request. Since he did not choose to explain his reasons, I did not question him. But tell me—if you do not think these past events important, what *do* you consider important?"

Lora had no need to hesitate. "Wade's happiness is important. I want to see him well and strong again, in spirit as well as in body. And I want very much to see Jemmy as happy as any other small boy. I want to see him free of the bad dreams that seem to haunt him. I want these things so much that I will even go now and tell Wade that I am sorry about riding in the wagon with the boys. I will say I am sorry, even though I have no feeling of wrong-doing. I *am* truly sorry if I have displeased him."

"But you are not sorry that you have displeased me?"

Lora rose from her chair. "I have already said that I'm sorry if I have upset you. But I am beginning to think that it is not possible to please you."

She waited for no answer but went to the door and into the chill of the hallway. She should not have said that. It had been childish slapping out at her adversary. But now Jemmy was waiting for her eagerly and she put aside the uncomfortable interchange with his grandmother.

"Was she very cross?" Jemmy demanded. "Did she say anything about the tree?"

"Everything's all right," Lora assured him. "She didn't even mention the tree."

"Then where shall we set it up? Peter says he can't bring it into the house till someone tells him."

"We'll get your father to help," she said, and held out a hand to him.

They went to the library and knocked on the door. There was a moment of silence before Wade called, "Come in."

"Wait here a moment," Lora whispered to Jemmy, and went into the room.

Wade was not at his desk writing, but stretched out on the red sofa before the fire, and he did not look around as she entered. Lora smiled at Jemmy and closed the door softly. For a fleeting moment she wondered how Wade's mother had prevented him from marrying Morgan. There had been something enigmatic in the old woman's words. Then he looked up at her and she went quickly to kneel on the hearthrug beside him.

"Your mother says that it was unseemly for me to go in the wagon with Adam Hume and the boys to help Jemmy pick his Christmas tree. I truly did not mean to do anything wrong. I went because—because I wanted to be myself. As I've told your mother, I have so often ridden in wagons at home that I saw no harm."

He sat up to search her face with eyes that were darkly blue like his son's.

"If it was wrong, why should Mr. Hume invite me?" she persisted.

Wade untied the strings of her bonnet and shook his head when he saw the pinned strip of ribbon. "All put together with pins and paste! Lora dear, Adam's pattern is hardly one for a young woman like you to follow."

He laid the bonnet on the sofa beside him and then fell to studying the palm of his left hand where the welts of the old scar showed in white ridges. Lora took his hand quickly and laid it against her cheek.

"You've never told me how you got that scar. The wound must have gone right through your hand. What a dreadful hurt!"

He pulled his hand away from her cheek and folded the fingers over the scar almost angrily. "That was a result of following Adam's lead," he said.

She knew better than to ask further questions. "Then I won't ever follow him again," she promised. "I don't really like him. He's an uncouth sort of person. But, Wade, Jemmy and I are waiting to ask you where we may set up the Christmas tree. Jemmy has picked out such a fine one and we're anxious to put it up."

He kissed her cheek lightly and she knew she had been forgiven. Wade, at least, would never hold bitterness in his heart as did his mother. Relief roused something of affection for him in her and she leaned against him for a moment before she stood up and pulled him to his feet.

"Do you suppose we could use the parlor? Would it upset your mother too much?"

He went into the hall with her where Jemmy waited anxiously.

"The parlor is of course the right place," Wade said. "Run tell Peter to bring your tree in, Jemmy. And Ellie might as well lay a fire in there so we can be comfortable."

Jemmy rushed off, while Wade led the way into the front parlor, threw back the heavy draperies and opened shutters to let in gray daylight.

They were all kept busy for the rest of the day. Lora set out the candles she had purchased that morning. Corn must be popped for the popcorn chains and cranberries threaded to wreathe the pine boughs with garlands of red. Mrs. Lord, who had heard from her boys about Jemmy's tree, sent over a box of "silver rain," slender, fragile strips which she had made up every year by a tinsmith.

That evening Lora brought the garnet dress goods down to the parlor and sewed careful seams while Jemmy and his father decorated the tree. For the first time in this house she felt warm and happy, watching them work together. For the moment something of the antagonism seemed to have died away and they were more like father and son than ever before. The only blight on the evening came when Mrs. Tyler sent Ellie to inquire how long Wade meant to leave her alone and helpless in the rear parlor.

Wade tossed a last wreath of cranberries over a branch and wiped his hands on his handkerchief.

"But, Wade," Lora protested, "we wanted her to come in here with us. She needn't have stayed alone."

"It doesn't matter. The tree is nearly done. Jemmy can finish the rest. I'll go read to her for a while."

So Lora and Jemmy were left alone to admire the tree. It was truly beautiful, with silver light dripping from every branch and the white garlands of popcorn, the red ones of cranberries, adding their own festive touch.

"It is the most beautiful Christmas tree in the whole world," Jemmy said solemnly.

"Wait till we light the candles," Lora said. And she thought, *Wait until we set a small fat puppy under these branches!*

He was reluctant to go to bed when the time came, so she walked upstairs with him. She would work on her dress in her own room just across the hall, she told him. But first she would tuck him in.

The ritual was an accepted one now, though she still did no more than tuck in the covers and pat his head where it lay on the quilt. Always at bedtime he seemed to hold himself stiff and still in a small knot of resistance. As if he feared she might bend over and kiss him, and as if there might be some disloyalty to his mother in the acceptance of her kiss. She was sure that was it because he accepted her completely now in every other way. When he came into the house after school he looked for her at once to see what she was doing, and now that vacation had begun he sought her out several times a day to consult her about one thing or another. But still he held her away at bedtime, and she did not urge or hurry him. There was time enough ahead.

She turned out his lamp and went to start a fire against the chill of her room. Then she settled near the yellow-sprigged lamp and her needle moved rhythmically in and out through bright cloth. As she sewed, she thought of Serena's party and how she would be as beautifully gowned as any lady there, and of how it was fun to have this gay occasion to look forward to.

XI

IT WAS Christmas Eve. Great white flakes had begun falling from a gray sky early that morning, and Lora and Jemmy had already made several excursions into the yard. Lora had not felt so young and free from weight and trouble for a long time. She pelted Jemmy enthusiastically with powdery balls and laughed when his return shots got into her mouth and eyes.

There had been nothing like this back home in Pineville. On the rare occasions when it had snowed, the stuff had melted as it touched the ground and was no more than a phenomenon to marvel at. But this was something you could press between your hands. You could feel the chill as it melted on your cheek, taste its cleanness on your tongue.

Dogwood Lane wore a new dress that transformed familiar contours and turned the stretch of road into a magic aisle, no longer rimmed by brown boughs, but all ashimmer in clean white.

As she dressed for Serena's party that evening, Lora was glad that the snow carried no reminder of Christmases at home. Tonight—just for tonight—she did not want to remember. Only once during the day had she taken out Martin's small shell and held it briefly in her hand. Then she had put it resolutely away and shut her heart and mind against memory of mistletoe and holly and the singing of carols. There might be these things too in Staten Island, but with white flakes whispering against the windows, and ridges of white rising along every sill, this was a different world and any resemblance to Christmases of the past could be forgotten.

"Are you ready yet?" whispered Jemmy urgently at her door.

"Not yet," Lora cried, laughing because he was as excited as she. "It takes a lady a very long while to dress for a party, you know. But I've promised—you shall be the very first to see me when I'm ready."

At Mrs. Tyler's instruction she had purchased a larger hoop on her trip to town, and now she dropped her new crinolines over it and reached for the garnet dress where it burned in bright warmth across her bed. A little breathlessly, holding the neck with care to avoid disturbing brown ringlets just released from curlwrappers, she slipped the dress over her head.

It billowed down about her in rich color and she buried her hands for an instant in its folds, reveling in the scent and feel of the stuff. It was hard to hook up the bodice because her fingers were shaky, and she considered running across to Wade's room to ask for help. But she still felt a little shy with him on such matters and, besides, she did not want him to see her until she was dressed to the last touch. Somehow tonight she wanted to see his eyes light with admiration that would be for her alone, unbeclouded by memories of Virginia. Pure female conceit, as she well knew, and laughed softly at herself because of it.

There was a small mirror over her dresser which she carefully avoided, not wanting to look until she was entirely ready. From a small bag of dark-red velvet she drew a string of garnets set in old gold. These were her only jewels and had belonged to her mother. Doc had given them to her on her sixteenth birthday, and now she clasped them about her throat with a feeling of love and pride. Their hue matched the color of the gown exactly and they glowed warmly against her sun-tinted skin.

She whirled about the room, pretending that a partner's hand was at her waist—then remembered with a faint twinge of regret that she would not be dancing tonight. But it didn't matter. Just to appear at Serena's on Wade's arm and sense that he was proud of her would be satisfying. With his wife in so beautiful a gown, he could not help but be proud, even though she had no real beauty, as she knew very well. She would smile at his friends and say little—that would be safest. And oh, she would be the very pattern of a lady!

Still holding off the climax of the moment when she would look in the mirror, she pulled up her skirts an inch or so to reveal the thin white lisle stockings that Mrs. Tyler had instructed her to buy. Never had she owned such stockings before. How thin they were beside the cotton or thick wool to which she was accustomed. True, there had been stockings of silk on sale at the same counter, but she had not even looked at them, knowing they must be extravagantly fragile.

Her new slippers were of soft black kid and they laced fashionably about the ankles. Now she turned one sole up for the dozenth time to admire the tiny heel which graced it. She would certainly be a very lady of fashion tonight.

At last had come the moment for the mirror and she knew she'd better hurry before Jemmy clamored at her door again. It was not a very large mirror and though she brought the lamp and set it near, she could not see much of herself at one time. But the round neckline of the dress, the puffed sleeves, her mother's garnets gleaming about her throat, looked very nice indeed. Her face did not please her, but then, it never had. At least the brown ringlets helped, trembling softly about her cheeks and giving her a less severe look than her usual drawn-back coiffure. Her longer back hair she had pinned into a high knot, held in place with a circlet of dark-red satin roses. Her eyes were bright and her cheeks glowed warm as the garnets about her throat.

She would do, she thought. Oh, she hoped she would do!

She went to open the door and Jemmy, who had been leaning against it, almost tumbled into the room. She whirled about for him, laughing at his surprise, waiting for his approval.

But he was not one to approve with easy carelessness. First he must walk all about her judiciously, looking her up and down. He even leaned over to fluff out the hem of her gown where the material had caught against itself. He took so long that she suddenly began to worry. If Jemmy didn't like her—

Then he stood back and his smile was one of approbation. "You're as beautiful as the Christmas tree," he said.

She swept him into her arms for a hug regardless of possible harm to her dress. He wriggled uncomfortably out of the squeeze and pulled her to the door.

"Let's go show Papa. Now that I've seen you first."

In full confidence she rustled down the hall and waited while Jemmy tapped upon Wade's door. He came to open it in his ruffled evening shirt, already looking the elegant gentleman, even in shirt sleeves and with his crutch beneath one armpit.

"I can't see you out there in the dark," he said. "Come in here where there's light."

There were two lamps burning in his room and the firelight added its own rosy glow. She stepped into the illumined area and waited again. Oh dear, she thought—these men! Now she would be subjected to another slow scrutiny that would keep her in a state of anxiety before approval could be given. How foolish to have hoped that his eyes would light immediately, that he would show astonished admiration. He was, of course, fully accustomed to ladies in ball gowns, while she had never owned so fine a dress before.

He wasted no time on the slow study Jemmy had given her. He took one close look and then swung himself toward the door.

"Suppose we go downstairs and show Mother, Lora. She will know whether it's right or not."

Right? A sudden uneasiness touched her. Why shouldn't it be right?

She picked up the skirts carefully lest they brush against the stairs and went down ahead of Wade. Jemmy came behind, a scowl between his dark, young brows.

As she went into Mrs. Tyler's sitting room, Lora tried to curve her lips in a smile. A look of gloom would never make her seem a lady dressed for a party.

"Stand there," said Mrs. Tyler, pointing. "Put your

100

shoulders back—don't slump. Turn around . . . no, not so fast. Turn slowly."

With her heart beating in her throat Lora turned in an agonizingly slow circle beneath Mrs. Tyler's critical gaze. When she had come full circle the old lady spoke one sharp word.

"Dowdy!" she said.

Lora turned to Wade, her eyes wide with shock, but he shook his head at her unhappily.

"I'm afraid she's right, Lora. I'm terribly afraid—"

"Of course I'm right," Mrs. Tyler said. "You can't take her to Mrs. Lord's looking like a frump. I knew she should never touch the material herself."

Lora could feel the flood of crimson sweep upward into her face. She felt utterly humiliated, ashamed. In her ignorance she had thought this dress finer than any she had ever seen. She had added her own little dressmaking touches of velvet and lace, believing that she created beauty.

It was Jemmy who broke the unhappy silence. "I think she looks fine," he said stoutly. "I think she'll be the prettiest one at the whole party."

No one paid him any attention and not even Lora could glance at him in gratitude, for fear her control would vanish and she would burst into childish tears of mortification.

Wade made a slight movement on his crutch and then reached toward the buttons of his shirt. "Well, I'll get out of these togs. It's too bad, Lora, but I'm afraid we can't go to Serena's party."

Mrs. Tyler reached for her bell. "I'll call Peter. He can deliver a note of regret. Mrs. Wade Tyler is ill tonight."

It would be true, Lora thought. She was ill. Ill with foolish disappointment, ill because she had been shamed in Wade's eyes. She blinked and turned away, the tears already starting. Before she could escape, Wade saw them.

"Good heavens, Lora," he said, "did this party mean so much to you?"

Lora rushed blindly toward the door, her full skirts rustling silkenly about her, but Wade was there to stop her with his free arm.

"Wait, Lora. Hold the bell, Mother. I've an idea. If this party means so much, there is still something which can be done. Sit down, my dear, and wipe those tears."

He handed her a big linen handkerchief and there was no course but to obey. Though all she wanted was to escape to the shelter of her room where no eye could see her misery.

"You'd think the skies had fallen," Mrs. Tyler said testily when Wade had gone out. "The young have no sense of proportion."

Lora dried her eyes while Jemmy watched unhappily, wanting to comfort, yet not knowing how.

"I still think you look fine," he said.

"And I suppose *you* are an authority on ladies' fashions?" said his grandmother.

"I only know how nice she looks," said Jemmy simply.

They could hear Wade's halting progress down the stairs as he returned, and Jemmy ran to open the door. Lora did not look up as he came into the room. She pressed his handkerchief against her eyes and fought to control her tears.

"Look at this," Wade said gently. "If you can wear it—"

She looked up then and saw that he was holding over his free arm a magnificent gown of pale-green brocaded taffeta. Even flung in a heap on his arm it breathed perfection in every careful seam, in the draping and heavy scallops of pale lace. Obviously this gown was a masterpiece of its kind.

"That's my mother's dress!" cried Jemmy.

Wade ignored him. "It came from Paris, Lora. Why not try it on?"

She looked away from the gown quickly. "I—I never could wear green. It makes me look sallow."

"At least it will not make you look a frump," said Mrs. Tyler. "You're too thin for it, of course, but go put it on and let's have no more nonsense. You wanted to go to this party, didn't you?"

Lora knew she could not say that she didn't want to go now, not if she had to wear Virginia's dress. She could not say that everything had been spoiled, that she had wanted to go as herself, in a gown that she felt became her and that was her own. Such contradictory notions could not be explained away with words. She rose limply to her feet.

Jemmy blocked the door. "You can't wear my mother's dress! You're not my mother. I won't let you wear it!"

His grandmother pointed a silencing finger at him. "That will be enough from you, young man. Go to your room at once."

Lora could not even rouse herself to come to Jemmy's defense. She went to her husband and took the green dress from his arm. The moment she touched it Jemmy stormed out of the room and ran clattering up the stairs. They heard the distant slam of his door and Mrs. Tyler shook her head.

"The boy is becoming incorrigible. You have been spoiling him, Lora."

Lora made no answer. She carried the dress into the hall and up the stairs. In her own room her fingers ripped at the hooks she had sewed so lovingly to the garnet-red bodice. She pulled the dress off feverishly, let it fall in a bright heap on the floor. It was only something for the rag bag now. She would never put it on again.

The green gown pulled at her ringlets as it went over her head, but she hardly noticed. Nothing seemed important or even very real. She moved like a puppet, indifferently. The dress had tiny cap sleeves and a bodice far more immodest than she had ever worn. Her shoulders and bosom were white above the green, unlike the fading tan of her face and hands. Before she went downstairs her fingers sought the garnets at her throat. They felt hard beneath her fingers, and at their touch her will to act returned.

She would not remove the garnets. They were something of herself and she would wear them tonight.

In the hallway she considered looking into Jemmy's room, but in this gown she did not dare. There would be time enough tomorrow to talk to him, try to make him understand that there was no usurping of his mother's place because she had donned this dress tonight. Besides, tomorrow was Christmas, and there would be the puppy for Jemmy. In the face of that, all else would fade in significance.

She looked at Wade as she entered the room and saw the quick veiling of his eyes. What had he expected? Had he thought that because she wore this dress she would become Virginia? All desire to weep was gone and two spots of color burned high in her cheeks. Not the bright hue of excitement now. Her blood coursed dark and angry in her veins.

"It's not perfect," Mrs. Tyler said. "You don't fill it out enough, but the length is right. And at least you will look as Mrs. Wade Tyler should look. But take off those garnets. I have my jewel case here and we can find something more suitable."

The old lady opened a case of black leather and selected a strand of pearls from a tray lined with green velvet.

Lora shook her head, strong in her silent anger. "I will wear my garnets," she said quietly. "They are mine."

She met Mrs. Tyler's gaze without faltering and it was the old woman's eyes which dropped first.

"No matter," Mrs. Tyler said. "Though pearls would go

better with the green. At any rate see if you can find rings that will fit your fingers."

Lora's hands were sturdy and not slim of knuckle like Mrs. Tyler's, and she found only one ring of sapphires and diamonds that would go over the fourth finger of her right hand. As she slipped it on she glanced again at Wade.

"Won't someone recognize this dress?" she asked.

He shook his head. "I think not. It was worn only once or twice. No one but Serena is likely to recall it. Well, now that you are a lady of fashion and are to have your party after all, we must hurry and get ready." He seemed to rouse himself, make a visible effort at cheeriness.

She went with him out of the room and he brought her another garment of Virginia's—an embroidered cape of purple velvet with a heavy, quilted lining and a bit of fur at the collar. She tied a finely crocheted white scarf over her hair and met Wade at the doorway downstairs.

They went back together to bid his mother good night and then hurried down the path Peter had shoveled to the road. The cutter waited for them, and Wade tucked her warmly beneath the buffalo robe and got in to take the reins himself. He no longer accepted help from Peter because of his crutch as he had done that first night.

The snow had stopped falling and the night was sparkling clear beneath the stars. Every branch glittered with snow crystals and only the road had been marred by the passing of sleigh runners. The drive was a very short one and during it Lora's spirits began to rise a little.

She would rather have been herself, wearing her own gown, but her tears of confusion and disappointment seemed to have washed her free of emotion. As they drove between crowding woods with the world white and glistening in the starlight, a sudden thought came to her of that quiet pool sleeping beneath a covering of ice up there on the hillside, and she shivered. But she shook the vision off swiftly and looked toward the lighted windows of the house ahead.

She had not seen Serena Lord's house closely until now. Though she had walked this way often, some shyness had always made her turn back before she could come upon it beyond its hedge and clump of trees. She had not wanted the occupants of the house to think she was spying.

But now it rose generously expansive beneath the stars. It was not beautiful, perhaps, as Morgan's house was beautiful, but it was warm, inviting, friendly, with no meanness about it. Tonight brilliance glowed at every window and in the great bay of the drawing room downstairs a Christmas tree stood alight with candles, gay in holiday splendor. An unexpected tingle ran through Lora and her fingers tightened involuntarily on Wade's arm.

He patted her hand kindly. "What a child you are. All those stormy tears over a mere party."

She managed a smile, but she did not explain what she could not entirely understand herself. There had been more behind her tears than disappointment over a gown and a party. There had been a reaching for some intangible thing which had only escaped her.

One of Serena's servants came to take the horse and cutter, and Lora and Wade went up the cleanly swept steps and into the bright hallway. One could sense that fires burned in every grate. Warmth swept to meet them, mingling richly with the scent of pine needles and ladies' perfume. Here was none of the repelling chill of Tyler hallways.

Serena herself came to greet them as they hurried in out of the cold. She wore a great hooped gown of golden yellow and her red hair fell in fashion-approved ringlets about her face.

"Lora Tyler!" she cried in a welcome that was warmly real. "I'd hoped to see you again long before this, but what with having Edgar home . . . And Wade—how fine you look tonight. You'll have to keep an eye on him, Lora. There are hearts ready to flutter at sight of him, as they always have."

Wade made some easy, laughing answer, then other guests came in behind them and Serena motioned Lora up the stairs to the room at the top where the ladies were laying aside their wraps. Wade stepped back beneath the bannister as Lora went up the stairs, and she glanced down at him. For the first time since she had known him there was a hint of excitement rising in his eyes. Now that he was here, Wade too was responding to the contagion of a party.

"Hurry," he said to her. "No other girl will do."

She knew it was play-acting. He was only trying to be kind because of her disappointment. So she play-acted too, smiling down at him before she ran up the steps.

The bedroom at the head of the stairs was alive with feminine chatter and Lora entered hesitantly. A half-dozen girls and women were taking off their wraps, or waiting their turns before the room's several mirrors. They all seemed to know one another and for a moment no one paid any attention to her.

Lora tightened with uneasiness as she slipped the velvet

cape from her shoulders to reveal her green brocade frock. What if Wade had been wrong? What if these women had known Virginia and remembered the dress? If she saw recognition or pity in their eyes, she would want to run away.

But she stiffened herself firmly and called her own notions nonsense. There was no reason for anyone to pity her. Boldly she flung aside the cape and laid it with the heap on the bed. A momentary hush fell upon the room, and she was sure without looking that eyes were upon her. She steeled herself to raise her own and meet their curious gaze.

One girl smiled and came toward her with outstretched hand. "You're Wade's wife, aren't you? I'm Hester Wylie. It's wonderful to have you come to our island."

There was no resisting Hester's friendly ways, and in a moment the other women had gathered about to meet her. Lora found herself taking their hands shyly, returning their smiles, no longer fearing their eyes.

She went downstairs with Hester and heard the sound of a gay polka from the drawing room. Wade stood at the door, watching the dancers, and Lora saw with a pang that he still looked white from his illness. Nevertheless, there was a keyed up, handsome maleness about him which as a nurse she had always been too close to see. He leaned on his crutch, watching the dancers flash by the door, and he seemed for an instant a stranger to her, so that she approached him shyly.

Hester saw him and ran ahead of her to kiss him frankly on the cheek. "Wade, it's wonderful to see you! There now— I hope Herbert is watching. The only time he stops taking me for granted is when Wade Tyler is around."

Lora was relieved to see Wade rise to this banter and manage a gallant reply. She glanced past him into the long room where candles were multiplied to a myriad number by the reflection from many windows. Breathless couples swept by in the polka and there was laughter and the sliding sound of feet on the waxed floor. The Christmas tree loomed brilliant in the bay window, crowning the bright scene.

Across the room near one fireplace she saw an arresting couple who were not ruffling themselves in the quick dance. The woman was Morgan Channing and she wore a gown of creamy-white satin trimmed in velvet bands of turquoise blue. Her smoothly combed hair had been caught in a white, besequined snood which tied on top of her head with a narrow white velvet ribbon. Her lips were bright with rouge and there was a burning intensity in her dark eyes. It would seem that all her attention was for the handsome young man with blonde sideburns who stood before her—the man Lora had seen in the carriage that day on the hill. But just for a flickering instant Morgan's eyes shifted from his face and swept toward the door, then back again. She had seen Wade, of course. But she had not tried to catch his eyes, and she did not move to greet him.

Edgar Lord found Wade and Lora cushioned seats near a window at the far end of the room, and from that moment on they were not left alone. Wade was as charming and gay as though no dark shadows had ever fallen on his life. Everyone seemed to like him, and Lora began to realize how popular he and Virginia must have been in the happy days before the war. Moreover, he began to expand and grow more confident under this feminine attention and admiration. He had a need for this sort of thing, Lora thought guiltily, that she could not fill.

She knew his friends were curious about her, though they hid their interest in a well-mannered way. There were some who gushed a little and told Wade that she was "sweet" and "shy." Listening and watching, smiling, saying little, she felt increasingly ill at ease. She did not think that she was either sweet or shy and she wished Wade would not be so pleased with these labels.

Pineville, she thought restlessly, was far removed from this glittering party world, but Pineville had more reality. True, the blue of uniforms was in evidence tonight on every hand, but that was the only reminder of the war. What did these pretty, richly gowned women know of dirt and blood and death? Or even of the deprivation of war? War had not yet truly touched them—not in the sense that it had put its harsh stamp upon women of the border towns and women of the South. The gay party Lora had looked forward to with such eagerness seemed suddenly tinsel, and those who danced were paper puppets.

She had been reaching for a rainbow, she thought, pretending to herself that rainbows were tangible. Now she knew that what she had reached for was only forgetfulness, just as Wade too reached for some anesthetic that would deaden the sense of pain, permit an escape into a carefree, happy world. But there was no such escape for her.

Across the room Morgan Channing moved into the arms of her tall blond escort and joined the dancers for the first time. Lora followed them with her eyes. Of all the women in this room Morgan alone seemed flesh and blood reality. One could sense the force that drove her, the intentness of purpose that made other women seem limp as paper dolls. What was that purpose? Lora wondered.

Hester Wylie, seated nearby with her pleasant Herbert, whispered behind a gauzy fan.

"Morgan's gown is from Paris, of course. An Empress Eugenie style. Who is the handsome one she is dancing with?"

A man near Wade answered her. "That's Murray Norwood. A so-called Peace Democrat, like our fine Seymour whose inauguration New Year's Day as governor of New York will set us well on the road to treason. Somehow I do not like the smell of Copperheads any more than I like the stink of secession."

Tinsel fell away for a moment, uncovering the gray look of war beneath the glitter. But after a tiny, shocked silence, the tinsel covering was tugged back into place with quick words and laughter, and the moment might have been forgotten had Wade not, to Lora's surprise, challenged the speaker.

"As I understand it," said Wade courteously, "there is no taint of treason on Seymour. He is against the war—and so has been elected. But he is not against the Union."

The man who had spoken said, "Pah!" rudely and would have argued further had not his feminine companion pulled him a little frantically out upon the floor among the dancers.

"Plainly not a gentleman," someone said lightly as they whirled away, but Lora saw Wade's gaze move speculatively toward the man with Morgan Channing.

Now and then some gentleman bowed before Lora and asked her to dance, but each time she shook her head, smiling, and Wade was pleased. Once or twice she wondered about Adam Hume. Strange that he should not be in evidence at his sister's party. Perhaps he simply did not care for the folderol of a ball. Lora suspected that no one could make him do what he did not wish to do.

During the next break in the music Edgar Lord came toward her across the room, broad of shoulder and handsome in a new blue uniform with brass buttons shining. He smiled down at her, bowing.

"You've not been dancing, Mrs. Tyler. But tonight we permit no lovely ladies to sit and watch. May I have the honor?"

Again she shook her head. "Thank you, but since Wade is unable to dance as yet—"

"I've never known Wade to be so unkind a taskmaster,"

Edgar said, and turned his friendly smile on Wade. "You'll surrender the lady, sir?"

"To a superior officer, yes," said Wade, laughing. "Of course you must dance with Edgar, Lora."

She rose reluctantly. Now that she recognized tinsel for tinsel, she did not want to be betrayed again into grasping at make-believe. And yet—the music, starting up again, was heady and her rebel body longed to fling itself into the giddy steps of a polka. Edgar danced beautifully and was easy to follow. He took care of their sketchy conversation himself and did not expect too much from her. They whirled breathlessly in among the dancing couples and once they came very close to Mrs. Channing and the handsome Murray Norwood. Morgan saw her and flashed a smile of recognition, her gaze dropping briefly, meaningfully, to Lora's green gown.

For a little while Lora had forgotten her dress. Morgan's frank look made her suddenly self-conscious. Here was one who would remember this gown—Virginia's sister. No matter which way she turned, Lora could not escape Virginia. Even now there might be whispers going on behind her back because Wade Tyler's new wife had no party gown of her own, but must wear Virginia's.

"I'm making you dizzy," Edgar said, looking down at her in quick concern.

She tried to smile. "It has been such a long time since I've danced."

He whirled her through the door and into the hall. "Wait, I'll get you a glass of water. You look a little faint."

She did not feel faint, but she let him go for the water. It was just that the house seemed suddenly hot and the lights seemed to swing in dizzy arcs before her eyes. She sipped the cool water slowly when he brought it and wondered how she could escape.

He was perceptive, this kindly husband of Serena's. "You needn't go back right away," he said. "I won't tell if you want to run off from the partying for a little while. Wade is in good hands."

"Thank you," she said gratefully, and when he had carried her glass away, she turned toward the stairs. But she did not go up them after all. There might be ladies in the upstairs room rearranging their ringlets and indulging in feminine chatter. She did not want to face their curious gaze, but only to escape for a few moments by herself.

At the far end of the hall was a pair of French doors, probably opening upon a rear veranda. Nearby upon a hall tree hung a woman's black wool shawl. Lora acted swiftly. She caught up the shawl and flung it about her shoulders. Then she went to the doors and opened them, let herself through into the quiet and chill of a glass-enclosed veranda. Softly she pulled the doors shut behind her and knew she was alone.

XII

THE SUDDEN SHOCK of cold cleared her head and stopped the reeling. She breathed the cold cleanly into her lungs, freeing them of warm air, stuffy with the scent of perfume and heated bodies.

How silly to be so shaken because of a look from Morgan Channing's observant eyes.

"I don't *want* to be Virginia," she told the darkness softly, and went across to the far windows, pulling the shawl more snugly over her bare arms and throat. The only light on the veranda streaked across from a window in the drawing room. Beyond that patch of light she could see the dancers.

She turned away, seeking the view that dropped steeply down the white-blanketed hillside. From here the harbor lights were visible, with black stretches of water between. Out toward the Narrows a ship, all agleam, was coming in on Christmas Eve.

Behind Lora the veranda doors opened, startling her. She glanced about and saw a man coming toward her in the darkness.

"So you ran away?" Adam Hume said.

She hid her feeling of distress because her retreat had been discovered. "How did you know?" she countered.

"I was in the dining room stealing tidbits from the hors-d'oeuvres trays. I saw you. Here—have a bite of caviar."

He held out a tiny round of bread without apology for his fingers. She had never tasted caviar and she bit into it daintily.

"Look," she said. "Down there on the water. A ship is coming in."

He reached past her and unhooked a latch, pushed the window ajar. An icy thrust of wind cut through Lora's shawl and she drew back hastily, but Adam made no move to close the window.

110

"Listen—sometimes you can hear them. Be very still."

At first nothing came to her but the rattle of icy boughs on the hill below, where snow had blown away and left dry winter bones to clatter. Then, faint from the water, came a faraway singing, now full, now dim with the breathing of the wind. It was no Christmas carol they sang on the homeward-bound ship, but another tune—"Home Sweet Home."

Adam closed the window and the sound was shut away. Now the music inside drowned out all other music and dancers went whirling about the floor again.

"A waltz!" Adam cried. "As I've told you, I learned to waltz most beautifully in Libby. Will you honor me with this dance, Mrs. Tyler?"

Plainly he meant here and now, on this dark veranda. She drew away from him quickly.

"Oh no—please! I must go back inside."

"How fearful you are," he said, and put his hand firmly at her waist. "See—you're cold. This will warm you quickly. And we have the floor to ourselves."

She was light on her feet and once she had loved to dance. With a last worried look toward the lighted window, she gave herself up to the lilt of the music. This was a reckless thing to do. Suppose someone should find them here? Suppose Wade should turn about and peer through the window behind him into the darkness, or wonder where she was and come to find her. But the music sang and the chilled blood tingled to warmth in her veins.

"How could you learn to waltz in Libby?" she whispered.

He did not trouble to lower his tone, and it was probably true that the music hid their voices safely.

"There are times when it's better to invent things to do than to sit around and go mad with idleness. So we held balls on occasion. Those of us who weren't too weak or listless participated. Some of the men wore blanket shirts and shaving curls over their ears, and we pretended we were in a house like this, forgetting about the war as those people in there have forgotten."

His hand was hard at her waist and his fingers hurt her side. She drew stiffly away from him in the dance.

"They haven't forgotten," she told him. "I thought that too, but they're only pretending. The war is there, near the surface."

He made a sound of derision. "The men perhaps, yes—those who wear uniform. The others, and some of those ninnies of women—it has never touched them at all."

111

"Let's hope it never does," said Lora gently. "Why should you want it to?"

He looked at her in the dim light. "I suppose I do want it to reach them and hurt them."

"But why? Why should you be angry because they haven't been touched?"

The music ended and he let her go abruptly. She was warm enough now, not minding the chill of the veranda.

"I suppose when you've been in the thick of it," he mused as if he were anxious to find a valid answer to her challenge, "and have known how little your own people care at home, how ready they are to talk treason, even in their letters to camp—well, maybe that's why I want to wake them up. Until they do wake up we'll never win this war."

She could not answer him. She knew too little about the North, and she did not believe in this fighting anyway. As a new waltz started she moved toward the door, but his hand touched her arm.

"You're not running away?"

"I must go back now," she said.

"What are you afraid of? Why do women always scuttle like scared rabbits when they step out of the accepted pattern?"

His scorn pricked her again, but she would not let it anger her this time. "I'm not afraid. It's simply that this is not what I want to do. I think you rather enjoy danger, Mr. Hume, even to the point of drawing others into danger with you. Does it give you some sort of satisfaction, perhaps?"

He let her arm go and opened the doors to the hall, looking first to see if anyone was there.

"Go back then, little rabbit," he said, and she saw that he was laughing at her. "You're dangerous yourself. You see through a man as no lady ever should."

She hurried back inside and flung off the shawl before anyone should guess where she had been. When she turned back to him his laughter had stilled and she saw that he was staring at her dress.

"You should never wear green," he said shortly.

So he too remembered. She almost ran back to the lighted room, slipping between the dancers to find her way to the safety of Wade's side. She wanted nothing to do with danger. She wanted only peace and safety and a healing of old wounds.

A short time later Serena Lord, buxom and shining with happiness on the arm of her husband, came to invite their guests to refreshments. Ladies and gentlemen began to file into the dining room where a lavish repast was spread upon table and sideboard. A maid in white uniform and a house-man in white coat stood ready to serve, but Serena hovered about to see that everything went smoothly, and Edgar took up his post near the bottles of wine and champagne.

Lora waited while Wade, never liking to be thought help-less because of his crutch, filled her plate. She drew back into a corner of the dining room where she could watch the bright crowd and wonder about these people. How happy Serena Lord looked tonight, for all that she wore the normal concern of a hostess. Envying her a little, Lora saw Serena glance the length of the room to meet her husband's eyes. A look of such affection and respect flashed between them that there was about it an almost physical touching. It was the way a husband and wife should be able to look at each other across a room, with secret recognition and deep love.

Lora dropped her gaze hastily because she had no right to spy, but her interception of that look made loneliness rush through her. In spite of herself, her eyes sought Wade's at the far end of the table. Not with hope, or for reassurance, but only because there was no one else she could look to. He saw her glance and raised the plate, smiling, as if food were her only interest. To him she was hardly more than a casual dinner companion, and there was an aching in her throat for something she would never know.

Wade came toward her on his crutch, her plate held in his other hand. She turned half away, knowing he would not want her to watch his awkward approach, and her eye was caught by the handsomely arranged tray on a stand nearby. Along the studiously scalloped edge of the pattern two small rounds were missing. Rounds of caviar, undoubtedly. She smiled in amusement and managed to recover herself before Wade reached her.

Adam was nowhere in sight, so probably he had made some further raid on the dining room and was off eating alone. Once during the evening Lora had heard Serena ex-plaining that her brother was not very well—the fever, you know. But Lora thought him surly and inconsiderate. Re-gardless of his own dislike for society, he might have sought to please his sister.

"Here you are, my dear," Wade said, handing her the plate. "Let me settle you somewhere while I take care of my own."

"I don't mind waiting for you here," Lora assured him. "Don't hurry."

Morgan Channing and her blond companion came into the room just then and Lora's interest quickened as if she were attending a play. Wade could not escape these two now, and she wondered what the unpredictable Morgan would do if she came face to face with him.

The encounter followed almost at once. Wade had not seen the two step into line behind him. Reaching toward a bowl of potato salad, he jostled Murray Norwood's arm, and turned at once in apology. The flare of color to his face when he saw Morgan so near at hand was more than Lora had expected. She watched him, startled now, for the first time putting some belief in the things his mother had said.

Morgan spoke before Wade had completed his apology to Mr. Norwood. Her manner was as easy as that of a lady who meets an old friend whom she has seen no longer ago than yesterday, but Lora found the look she turned upon Wade less casual.

"Good evening, Wade. May I present Mr. Norwood? I think you and he may have a number of interests in common."

Wade set down his plate and took the other man's hand. He looked as if he wanted to ignore Morgan but could not do so without being conspicuous. He spoke to her restrainedly, managing an exchange of pleasantries with Norwood before they started on about the table. Morgan had veiled the quick intensity of her first look and now seemed a little contemptuous and amused. This belied Mother Tyler's belief that she still wanted Wade, Lora thought. Surely a woman could not love a man and look at him so scornfully. At least she—Lora—could not.

That was one reason, she thought as she went back to the drawing room with Wade, that she was glad to see him tonight in this gathering of clever, well-to-do people. She liked the affection with which they seemed to regard him. Even if she could not love, she wanted their respect and admiration for Wade to grow.

They found their former places in the drawing room empty and took them again. Soon the room buzzed with the voices of returning couples and there was the clink of silverware against china, the high laughter of women, the deeper voices of men.

Strangely, Lora found herself trying to pretend that her own position was similar to Serena's, to imagine that she and Wade, just for these hours, were drawn together in the closeness of a true marriage relationship. It was as if by playing

114

this role she could shut away all doubt, forget the mockery that had looked out at her from Adam Hume's eyes.

But the fragile web of pretense collapsed when Wade reached out with his napkin to wipe at a spot on her billowing green skirt.

"I'm afraid you've dropped a bit of mayonnaise on your gown," he said regretfully.

She wiped at the spot with her own napkin and his hand fell back to finger the green brocade almost caressingly. After that Lora could no longer pretend. As the evening wore on and Wade's still-lagging strength began to fade, she sensed his own withdrawal from the gaiety about him. For him too the tinsel had fallen away.

In the dark early hours of the morning, when they drove home through falling snow, they had little to say. Obviously Wade was lost in memories of his own and wanted no breaking through on her part.

Lora went up to her room and lighted a candle. There, where she had left it in the middle of the floor, the garnethued gown burned like a dark flame. She picked it up and hung it away in the wardrobe sadly. The green dress she carried back to Virginia's room to replace in the wardrobe there.

In the light from the candle she carried she saw with a start that Wade lay across the bed. When he heard her he sat up.

"I must ask you not to come in here again," he said, and his tone was colder than she had ever heard it.

She did not speak to him at all. She drew her robe close about her and hung the green gown away as quickly as she could. She did not look at him again as she turned and went out of the room, her shadow swaying up the wall as she moved. There was nothing in her now of pity or gentleness. She felt only a despairing impatience for the man on the bed, and she did not in the least care whether or not he knew it.

XIII

IN SPITE of her few hours of sleep, Lora awoke while it was still dark on Christmas morning. For a few moments she lay quiet and warm beneath her quilts, feeling the weight of unhappiness pressing her down. She could not recall in the fog of sleep why she must feel unhappy, but knew only that despair lay waiting to engulf her as soon as she could remember.

Then recollection of the party and the ending last night swept back. But now she put the memory aside. Today was Jemmy's day and neither she nor Wade mattered. That was why she had set herself to waken early.

She knew very well what little boys were like. This was Christmas and surprises had been prepared. No weight could hold a small boy down on such a morning, and she must be ready for him. Jemmy might have no belief in Santa Claus, but he believed in the coming of presents, since she had prepared him, and he would not be disappointed. She had not seen Ambrose again since the day she had arranged for the puppy to be brought here Christmas morning, but she felt sure she could count on Jemmy's grandfather.

Yesterday she had found time to wrap the presents she had bought for him in town, including those which should come from Wade. There were other packages to go under the tree as well; the writing case for Wade, the cap and shawls for his mother. And of course Jemmy had been busy making and wrapping things he meant to give.

Lora gathered up her packages and stole softly downstairs through the still, cold house. It wouldn't hurt to start a fire even though it was early. She set her parcels down and knelt before the hearth in the parlor. The kindling responded with a lively snapping and when she was sure the blaze had caught she returned to distributing packages beneath the tree.

Before long she heard a creaking on the stairs and a moment later the door opened a crack and Jemmy looked in uncertainly.

"Come in by the fire and get warm," said Lora cheerfully, as though he had never stormed at her last night because of the green dress.

Relieved, he sidled into the room in his nightshirt, his own arms filled with tissue-wrapped packages. Over one arm hung a long red and white striped stocking. He distributed the parcels beneath the tree and then turned to her doubtfully.

"I didn't know if I was supposed to hang up a stocking. Of course I don't believe in all that chimney stuff, but I thought—"

"Of course you're supposed to," Lora said. "But it should have been hung up on Christmas Eve. Don't make such a mistake next year. Now you'll have to scoot back to bed while somebody fills it. It's much too early to be up for good anyway. Your papa will be tired after the party last night. We must let him sleep."

"Tell me about the party," he said shyly. "Tell me what you did and how everybody looked. Was Uncle Adam there? Did you dance with him?"

She shook her head. "You're not going to wheedle me like that. I'll tell you later, not now. If you really want that stocking filled, you'll have to go back to bed right away."

"You are a tyrant," he said. "You are a queen tyrant."

"And you," she told him, "are my faithful slave. Depart, slave."

The slave actually giggled, sounding younger than she had ever hear him sound. He made her a low salaam at the door and "departed."

When she heard the stairs creak again she busied herself stuffing his brightly colored stocking with the small gifts she had prepared for just this purpose. The little paperweight with its snow scene went into the toe and on top of it went an orange with a green ribbon tied about its plump sides. Next a loose handful of nuts to fill up the cracks, another orange and a small packet of sweets, a little calendar with a bright angel pictured on it, and right at the top, hooked over the stocking edge, the wishbone she had saved, graced with a big red bow.

By the time she had done the unhappy weight with which she had awakened had lifted a little and she hummed to herself as she stood back to examine the effect of her work. The packages looked gay and inviting, and by spreading them out to the best effect she had accomplished an illusion of plenty. There should have been more, if only others beside herself and Jemmy had taken an interest. But with the arrival of the puppy everything else would dwindle to unimportance, so quantity would not matter.

As she thought of the puppy her heart began to thump, both in anticipation of Jemmy's joy, and in uneasiness over what his grandmother might do. But this morning she felt strong, even ruthless. She would face up to this whole household if necessary. Jemmy should have his puppy and he should keep his puppy, if Lora Tyler had anything to say about it.

A tormenting voice in her mind inquired whether she *would* have anything to say about it, but she thrust it away quickly. This morning she had all the natural optimism and courage of her youth. She would even fight Wade for Jemmy's sake today. She no longer felt angry with Wade, but she did not feel particularly pitying either. She was beginning to think that perhaps pity was not good for him. Perhaps Virginia herself had not been altogether good for him—not when she had made him so dependent that he thought he was nothing without her.

She went back up the stairs with her long braid swinging against her back, her spine stiff with determination. One thing at a time. This morning—Jemmy.

She knew she could not go back to sleep, so she lighted a fire in her room and dressed in her old brown wool. She wished she might have had something new and festive to wear on Christmas Day. She had a bit of holly, however, to pin at the white collar of her dress, and that gave her a more festive air.

Jemmy had not gone back to sleep either, and when he had dressed, he came tapping at her door for company. She let him in gladly and they sat before the fire while she told him about the party—weaving the details out in storybook fashion. But she did not tell him about the reckless moment when she had danced with Adam Hume on the dark veranda. That was something she wanted to forget. Nor did either of them mention Virginia's green gown.

At breakfast Mrs. Tyler too wanted to hear about the party. Who had attended? What had been served? Wade did not come to the table until rather late and he looked so white and drawn that his presence dampened the Christmas enthusiasm which Lora and Jemmy had been building between them. Again, in her account to Mrs. Tyler, Lora made certain omissions. She did not, for instance, indicate that Morgan Channing had been at the party. A little to her surprise, Wade was less careful.

When Lora ran out of things to tell, he said flatly that Morgan had been present in the company of a certain Murray Norwood. Had his mother ever heard of him?

Mrs. Tyler had not, but she would inquire of Mr. Niles when he came to see her next week. Mr. Niles reported to Mrs. Tyler frequently.

"The name sounds familiar," Wade mused. "It seems to me that I've heard it in some political connection. Last night someone sneered that he was a Copperhead."

"Fit company for Morgan," said Mrs. Tyler. "With all that love she developed for the South after she inherited her husband's property, I'd not put treason past her."

"Nevertheless," Wade said, "I can't agree with the Unionists. The Lincoln program has embroiled us in this futile war and it will never get us out without countless wasted lives."

Mrs. Tyler bristled, as she always did at any reflection cast upon the Union or President Lincoln. Lora was sure that the President himself was far less vindictive and bloodthirsty than some of his firmest supporters.

"Wait until he releases his Proclamation freeing the slaves," Mrs. Tyler went on. "Mr. Niles says it is probable that he will do so early in January."

"And what can such a proclamation do?" Wade asked wearily. "I read the proposed draft of it in the papers and it sounds hopeless. It would free the slaves in every state that is fighting the Union—where they cannot be freed anyway. But it would not free them in our own states. What logic is this?"

"Very shrewd logic on Mr. Lincoln's part," his mother said. "The freeing of any slaves may have an emotional impact on the North which it sorely needs. Yet the President cannot risk turning the border states against us. Full freedom must come later."

Lora found herself listening to the old lady in surprise. It was remarkable, really, how close she kept in touch with what was going on, how eagerly, and sometimes indignantly, she followed the news in several papers and looked forward to the visits of Mr. Niles. Lora had heard rumors last night of such a proclamation, but she was much more ignorant of the country's doings than was Mrs. Tyler.

There was a knocking on the back door just then and Lora started nervously. That would probably be Ambrose with the puppy and it was all she could do to refrain from running to the door. She had worried ever since rising over this matter of getting the puppy into her own hands before anyone else realized its existence. If Mrs. Tyler were to see it first—

But John Ambrose had thought the problem out himself. In a moment Ellie came to the dining-room door, looking mildly suspicious. It was for Mrs. Wade Tyler, she said, and mentioned no names.

"Well, tell whoever it is to come in. Don't stand there," Mrs. Tyler ordered.

Before Ellie could comply, Lora slipped from her chair and hurried to the door. Ambrose was waiting in the kitchen with a small covered basket in his hands.

"Good morning, Mrs. Tyler," he said pleasantly. "It's that matter we spoke about," and behind Ellie's back he gave her a hasty wink.

"Yes, of course," Lora said. "Please come in, Mr. Ambrose. If you'll bring the basket right in where the Christmas tree is . . ."

They left Ellie in the kitchen, clearly popping with curiosity, and hurried to the parlor. Not until the door was closed behind them did Ambrose reach gently for the thin covering that lay over the basket. He drew it part way back to reveal the snug little ball of warmth that lay sleeping within.

"I've been teaching him to lap his milk and he's a fine scholar. His belly's full now and he'll sleep a while, but don't leave him alone too long. He's a mischievous one."

The puppy whimpered faintly in its sleep and put out a pink tongue to lick off any remaining drops. Ambrose drew the covering back and Lora took the basket.

She knelt beneath the Christmas tree and put the basket around toward the back behind the other presents, half hidden by the tree trunk. This, of course, was the climax to be opened last—if the puppy himself would permit. She rose and held out her hand to Jemmy's grandfather.

"I can never thank you enough."

She could feel the rough hardness of his hand as he pressed hers. "We'll all thank *you*, ma'am, if you can fix it so he gets to keep this little feller."

"I shall fix it," Lora said firmly. "But now I'd better go back before Mother Tyler sends someone to investigate."

She would not let him out the back way, but took him to the front door, and opened it for him.

"Merry Christmas, Mr. Ambrose," she said.

"Just make it John," he told her. "I'd feel more comfortable. And Merry Christmas to all of you, Mrs. Tyler."

"Lora," she reminded him. "After all, John, we are friends."

He reached into his pocket just before he went down the steps and drew out a small tissue-wrapped package of his own.

"Will you do me the favor of putting this under the tree for the boy? He doesn't have a good knife of his own as every boy should, and this is a fine one."

"I know he'll be proud of it, John," Lora said, and took the package from him.

When she had put it with the others beneath the tree and assured herself that the puppy still slept, she went back to the dining room. Mrs. Tyler looked up from her wheat cakes, instantly suspicious.

"Who was that? Why was he not brought into this room as I directed?"

120

Lora put a light hand on her arm. "Mother, this is Christmas. We're all permitted our secrets at Christmas time. And this is a secret no one can know about till later."

Mrs. Tyler snorted indignantly, but Lora saw only the shine in Jemmy's eyes. No matter what happened, that shine must remain.

It had been unthinkable, of course—from Mrs. Tyler's viewpoint—that they open Christmas presents before breakfast. But once the meal was over, Jemmy, who had eaten practically nothing, could be held back no longer. Even Wade thawed a little and smiled at the boy's excitement. But he did not look at Lora. He had avoided her eyes ever since he had come downstairs and he had not spoken to her directly.

Now he pushed his mother's chair down the hall and Jemmy ran ahead to open the door. Ellie was kneeling before the hearth turning embers into a roaring blaze. As she rose and started from the room, she gave Lora a quick, frightened look. So Ellie had not been able to contain her curiosity, Lora thought. She must have investigated the contents of the basket Ambrose had brought, and her look of shock was not reassuring.

When they had all settled around the tree, the picking of packages to be opened began. They must each choose in turn, Lora said, and each package must be opened before they went on to the next. But first of all Jemmy's stocking.

"Excitement's not good for the boy," Mrs. Tyler muttered as he took down the striped stocking and pulled out the contents eagerly. But no one paid any attention to her.

The wishbone he hung over one ear, to save for an important wish. Then each orange and practically every nut must be exclaimed over as valuable treasure. The paperweight in the toe threw him into a state of delight and he turned it again and again in his hands to watch the snow fly. Lora had to assure him that the fun was only beginning before he would pay attention to anything else.

"Now he'll throw up all day," said his grandmother gloomily. But she had spotted the large oblong package that was marked with her name and now she demanded that it be brought out.

So Grandmother Tyler opened the next package and examined her shawls. Lora had chosen them doubtfully, feeling that it would not do to give her something too drab and elderly, yet not sure how far she could go in brightness of hue. It was the memory of the beribboned morning caps which the old lady wore that had decided her choice. So one shawl was a soft, powdery blue, and the other glowed with a deep rose color.

There was a certain response to this luxury evident in the way Mrs. Tyler held them in her hands, spread their loose folds on her lap so that color spilled over her black dress. But her lips pursed in habitual protest and Lora spoke quickly to allay criticism.

"You're too young a grandmother to wear nothing but black," she said lightly. "Fine cashmere goes with nice hands. The blue is for your eyes, and the pink for your cheeks."

"Flattery will get you nowhere," said the old lady tartly. "Well, let's get on with this nonsense." But she continued to warm her hands with the brightness of the shawls.

Wade opened a bookmark made for him by Jemmy and tried to be appreciative. But his heart was obviously not in his thanks and Lora reached quickly for John Ambrose's gift to his grandson. Jemmy unwrapped the knife proudly and did not hear when his grandmother said he would now have a fine chance to cut off a finger.

Then it was Jemmy's turn again to choose a package. He crawled to the foot of the tree on his hands and knees and looked over the spread of gifts thoughtfully.

"Do hurry," said his grandmother. "This is growing tiresome."

Once more Lora dared to speak up. "Part of the fun of Christmas is to make everything last as long as possible."

Jemmy threw her a quick, pleased look and crawled closer until pine needles hooked themselves into his dark hair. At that moment a certain rustling and creaking of wicker arose from behind the tree, to be followed by an odd whimper. Lora's heart thudded, but now there was nothing she could do. The moment had come.

"What's back there?" Mrs. Tyler asked sharply. "Something made a noise. Jemmy, pull it out at once."

Jemmy needed no direction. He had heard the small, endearing sound too, and swept other parcels recklessly out of his way as he crawled beneath the tree. The basket tore the tissue paper laid about the tree as he pulled it out, but Jemmy did not care.

For out of the basket had emerged two light-brown ears, a pair of bright, mischievous eyes and a wet, black nose. Next a brown paw and a white paw appeared on the basket's edge as the puppy investigated this strange new world.

Jemmy stared as if he could not believe what he saw. The puppy yapped in baby fashion and showed sharp little teeth and a pink tongue. Jemmy looked at the three grownups almost in agony. Wade had risen to his feet, his shock and distress plain. His mother stared, completely at a loss for words.

"Is it—is it for me?" Jemmy asked faintly.

Lora dropped to her knees beside him and put an arm about his shoulders. "Of course it's for you, darling. It's your very own puppy—from all of us."

Mrs. Tyler made a choked sound, but Lora did not look at her, or at Wade. She pulled back the cloth covering and Jemmy lifted the fat little animal tenderly from the basket. A miracle had happened in this house on Christmas morning. With a soft cry he buried his nose in warm fur. The puppy, however, was far from docile and he wriggled and nipped at Jemmy's ear until the boy laughed and held him away.

Behind them the old woman found her voice. "Take that creature out of here at once! Wade, you know that I can't abide dogs. I suppose this is your foolish doing, Lora?"

Jemmy held the dog so tightly that it yelped and Lora turned to face Mrs. Tyler. She was still on her knees, but she raised herself straight as her spine could hold her.

"I had hoped you would want to be one of the givers," she said. "But if you don't wish it, then Wade and I—"

"Lora, please," Wade said. He looked almost ill.

"Very well," said Lora, and she let scorn bite into her voice. "If neither of you wants to come in with me on this gift, then it shall be from me. From me to Jemmy—a puppy for his very own."

"It is I who make the rules in this house." Mrs. Tyler's eyes were alive with anger. "Put that creature down instantly, Jemmy. Wade, if you will not take it away yourself, go and call Peter."

"It's mine," Jemmy said. "Peter shan't take it."

Wade went out of the room as if he were glad to escape and he did not return. The old woman and the little boy faced each other in the light of Christmas morning, but of the two the woman was older and still the stronger.

"Put it down," she said levelly.

With a little sob Jemmy gave up. He dropped the puppy down upon the tissue and ribbons beneath the tree and fled from the room, his arm tight across his mouth. Lora made no move to stop him. All this was so much worse than she had imagined. Somehow she had hoped that the spirit of giftgiving might soften this impossible old woman to being humanly kind. But that had not happened and Wade had not stayed to help his son. So now the battle was posed—as she had seen it must be all along—between herself and Mrs. Tyler.

"Come in!" said the the old woman sharply to Peter's knock. Lora scooped the puppy into her arms and got to her feet. She rubbed her cheek against its hard little head where the white patch showed, and stroked its fur.

Peter came unhappily into the room. It was clear that he knew from Ellie what might happen and that Wade's summons had confirmed his fear. Mrs. Tyler pointed a straight forefinger at the puppy in Lora's arms.

"Take that creature out of this house at once!"

Peter played warily for time. "Where would you like me to take it, ma'am?"

"What difference does it make? Drown it if you like. Leave it in the woods, give it away. But get it off my property!"

Peter took a tentative step toward Lora and held out his hands silently.

Lora smiled at him. "No, Peter, it's not going to be that easy. *I* say that the puppy belongs to Jemmy and that he shall stay. If you mean to take it from me you will have to use force."

The man's hands dropped to his sides and his lean face looked utterly lugubrious. "If you please, ma'am, what do I do now?"

"Take it from her," Mrs. Tyler commanded.

Lora's laugh was light. "Remember, Mother—I am not a lady. And I am strong and young. If Peter touches me—" She did not finish, but walked boldly toward the door, carrying the puppy in her arms.

Behind her Mrs. Tyler made a choking sound of rage, but Peter lifted not a finger as she walked past him and out of the room. In the hallway she paused for an undecided moment. Then she went into the library where Wade sat on the sofa before a cold fireplace, his elbows on his knees, his head in his hands. In spite of her anger a faint stab of pity went through her. He was still ill with his wounds and the experience he had been through. Nevertheless, she spoke to him coolly.

"Jemmy is going to keep his puppy, Wade. His need is more important than the whims of your mother."

He did not even look up at her. "I thought you were gentle. I thought you would bring peace and happiness to this household—"

"Perhaps you should stop thinking about *you* and think about Jemmy. What sort of father are you?"

He looked up quickly, but she waited for no answer. She turned about and went quickly through the door. Up the stairs to her room she carried the puppy. For a moment she thought of taking it into Jemmy's room, but since the battle had not been fully won, she could not risk that.

In her own room she turned the key in the lock and set the puppy on the floor. Then she pulled up the rag rugs and flung them over the back of a chair, removed her slippers from beneath the bed. A bare floor would be safest until this fat little thing had learned manners. Jemmy must give him a name soon. They would need something to call him by.

Feeling too restless to sit in the rocker before the fire, she strode up and down the small room, rubbing cold hands together, while the puppy made small attacks on her skirt hem as she went by and yapped his excitement. She began to talk to him softly as she paced and at the sound of her voice he perked up his ears and sat back on his small haunches to listen with puzzled interest.

"We've only won the first skirmish, you know. I expect Mother Tyler has a great deal of ammunition left. But I don't really know what she can do unless she puts me out of the house along with you."

The puppy sneezed and rubbed at his nose with one paw.

"If only you were bigger, so you could be my bodyguard. As it is—"

For the first time something unfamiliar in the room caught her attention and she stopped in her pacing. Someone had placed an oblong pan upon her dresser—a pan containing rocks and sand and a half-buried saucer-pool. Three small turtles snoozed in the cool sand.

Why had Jemmy brought his turtles in here? Had he feared that they too might be taken from him? Or—was there some other meaning?

She ran suddenly to the door and unlocked it. Then she slipped out before the puppy could bounce after her. Across the hall Jemmy's door stood closed, but she turned the knob and flung it open. The room was empty and Jemmy's coat and cap were gone from the clothes tree that stood near the head of his bed.

She knew now why he had left the turtles in her room. He had entrusted them to her in his absence. Jemmy Tyler had wasted no time at all. He had run away.

After the late party last night the whole h
asleep. No, Jemmy Tyler was not here, the maid

XIV

LORA STOOD quietly in Jemmy's small room, trying to think. He could have gone only a few moments before, so he was not far away. She had no concern that physical harm might come to him before he would be found. But the danger of spiritual harm was great and she wanted to think carefully about what was best to do.

Someone should go up the woods path, since it was quite possible that he had gone up the hill to his grandfather. Perhaps she had better set Peter on that course at once. Then she herself would go over to the Lords' and see if he had gone there. She ran back to her room for her mantle and bonnet, and as she went out she remembered to lock the door and take the key with her. There would be no stealing away of the puppy behind her back.

Then she went downstairs to the library, where Wade still sat with his head in his hands.

"Your son has run away," she said. "I think you'd best send Peter up to Mrs. Channing's to see if he has gone there. I am going to the Lords to look for him."

There was dismay in Wade's eyes now and he got up at once. From within the parlor where she kept lonely vigil with the Christmas tree, Mrs. Tyler was ringing her silver bell furiously, and Ellie came padding in from the back of the house.

"You may tell Mrs. Tyler that Jemmy has run away and that I'm going down to the Lords' to see if he is there," Lora directed, and went out hurriedly.

The snow was not deep and the wheels of vehicles coming to last night's party had packed it firm in places so that walking was not difficult. Nevertheless, unused to snow and icy ruts, Lora slipped once or twice and caught her balance with difficulty.

As she passed the opening to the uphill path she tried to tell whether Jemmy had gone that way, but Ambrose's feet had left marks both ways and Jemmy might well have stepped into his tracks. At Serena's she rang the bell and waited impatiently for a sleepy maid to come to the door.

No one but the boys were up as yet, the maid told Lora.

126

After the late party last night the whole household was asleep. No, Jemmy Tyler was not here that she knew of.

As Lora hesitated, wondering where to turn next, Adam Hume came down the stairs.

"Merry Christmas," he said, and then noted her expression. "Is anything wrong?"

She went to the foot of the stairs. "It's Jemmy. He has disappeared. His grandmother tried to take the puppy away from him. He didn't realize that I wouldn't have let her take him. I'm afraid he has run away."

"To his grandfather's?" Adam asked.

"I thought of that. Peter has been sent to look. I'd hoped he might have come here. Do you know any place else?"

Adam leaned against the newel post, thinking, while the maid went away to her duties.

"I know one possibility. It's not very sensible, but I've heard him mention it—and he might try."

Lora would have questioned him, but he ran back up the stairs. "I'll get into my coat and take the cutter. He might have gone downhill. Suppose you go home and I'll drop in later, whether I find him or not."

There was something comforting about Adam's way of quick decision, quick action. She hurried back to the house and just as she reached the gate he drove by, saluting her with his whip. He was apparently never one to waste time or words.

Wade was waiting in the hall as she entered the house. He leaned upon his crutch, contrasted in his helplessness with her recent glimpse of Adam.

"If I could just get out and look myself—" he began.

She thrust the unfair comparison from her mind. "Adam has gone," she told him. "Don't worry. Jemmy can't have gone far. The important thing is what we are going to do when he comes back."

He returned her look coolly. "You realize that you have brought this whole thing upon us with your foolish act. Why didn't you tell me what you were planning to do?"

"Because I wanted Jemmy to have a dog," she said, and went past him up the stairs. She could hear the silver bell chiming its summons from the parlor again as she went into her room.

The puppy had left a puddle in the middle of the floor and he had managed to get a corner of the bed quilt between his sharp little teeth and make a nice pulpy mess. Lora sighed and went about cleaning up.

"It's a good thing I'm convinced that you're worth all this trouble you're causing," she said.

When she had taken off her things, she locked the puppy in the room again and went down to the parlor. Wade and his mother were in conference there and the old lady looked up angrily when Lora came in. Surprisingly, Wade smiled at his wife.

"I'm trying to persuade Mother that if we keep this little dog out of her sight and train it well from the beginning it will really not be much bother and will not intrude upon her at all. Apparently it means a great deal to Jemmy."

"He should not be rewarded for running away," said Mrs. Tyler. "In any event no further argument or discussion is possible. I will not have a dog in this house and that is final."

Lora went closer to the hearth and sat down on a low footstool, but her gaze did not leave the old woman's face.

"Did you never have a pet of your own as a child?" she asked gently.

"My father did not believe it healthy to keep animals in the house. I agree with him thoroughly. When my husband was alive beasts overran the place and I wanted only to be rid of them."

"Then I'm very sorry for you," Lora said. "You've missed so much. Doc—my father, that is—always said a boy couldn't grow up healthy unless he had a dog to love him."

"Then your father was not a doctor I would care to consult," Mrs. Tyler snapped.

That was probably true, Lora thought, though she said nothing. Doc's notions would likely have shocked such a patient.

Before Mrs. Tyler could find further words the doorbell rang again and Lora sprang to her feet.

"That must be Adam. Perhaps—"

But Mother Tyler's words stopped her before she reached the door. "Remember—the dog goes."

"No," said Wade, "he stays."

Lora forgot the door and turned quickly, her eyes on Wade's flushed face. "Do you mean that?"

"The dog stays," he said again, looking at his mother. "He stays or Lora and Jemmy and I leave this house."

They could hear Ellie in the hall, then Adam's voice. Lora pulled open the parlor door and saw Adam stamping the snow from his feet on the mat, with Jemmy, little and cold, beside him.

"Jemmy!" she cried. "Come quickly where it's warm. You've frightened us all. Come in, Adam." She did not realize until she had spoken that she had dropped the "Mr.," but formality did not seem to matter now.

Adam drew Jemmy into the warm room with him and said good morning to Wade and his mother.

"I found this young man on his way to Camp Herndon down on the flats. He was going to enlist in the Union Army as a drummer boy. It took a bit of persuading to get him to believe that they aren't taking drummers quite so young as yet."

"I'll make them take me!" Jemmy looked about him with stormy eyes.

"The puppy will miss you, darling," Lora said. "He's upstairs in my room waiting for you now."

Jemmy's eyes widened in disbelief. "But Grandmother—"

"Your father says you are to keep him, Jemmy. Wade, tell him so!"

He turned a look of disbelief upon his father and Wade smiled a bit wanly. "That's right, boy. No one is going to take the little dog away from you."

Lora stole a hasty look at Mrs. Tyler. The old lady was watching Wade in outrage. Her face was crimson and she looked as if she might be holding her breath. There would still be trouble here.

But Jemmy waited for no other corroboration. He tore out of the room and Lora went after him, close to tears. She saw Adam's look as she brushed past him, and for once there was no mockery in it, but only admiration. She did not care what Adam thought. She ran after Jemmy and found him tugging at her door.

When she had unlocked it, they went inside together. The puppy had taken to chewing on the rungs of a chair, but he turned from this interesting occupation to welcome them with joy. Down on his knees went Jemmy and already the little dog seemed to know the smell of his master for he paid no attention to Lora, but fairly leaped into Jemmy's hands.

"He's mine," said Jemmy in wonder. "He's really mine. That's right, isn't it, Lorie? Papa said so."

Lora blinked the moisture from her eyes and sat down on the bed to watch this loving reunion. "That's right, Jemmy. Now you'll have to name him. We can't go on calling him Puppy and 'it.'"

Jemmy took his nose out of the puppy's neck and held the

small, wriggling body at arm's length. But no name seemed to come to him.

"What do you think, Lorie?"

"Well—he has a white star in the middle of his forehead. You could call him Star. Or you could call him Spot, or—"

But Jemmy dismissed her list with a disapproving head-shake. "I don't like dog names. I want a special name. If he was a little girl dog I might call him after you, Lorie. Because you gave him to me. Papa said I could keep him, but maybe it would mix things up if I gave him Papa's first name."

"I think it very well might," said Lora solemnly.

A light came into Jemmy's eyes and he gave the puppy a little shake. "I know! I'll call you Hamlin. Hamlin's the hero in Papa's book and that will do perfectly."

Lora looked at him quickly. "You mean your papa has read you his story?"

"Well, no, not exactly," said Jemmy, setting Hamlin down on the floor. "But it's always in the library desk and so one afternoon I just read it."

"Your Papa might not approve of that, you know. Not without his permission."

"Mm," said Jemmy doubtfully, and then poked the puppy with his toe. "But I *want* to call him for my father in some way."

"You could keep his whole name secret for now," Lora suggested, "and just shorten it to Ham."

"Ham," said Jemmy, trying it out thoughtfully. "Ham, come here, sir. Come here, Ham."

The puppy cavorted over to him at once and put on a wriggling performance that nearly shook him in two.

"He knows that's his name," Jemmy said in delight. Then a sudden thought seemed to strike him and he looked at Lora. "When's your birthday, Lorie?"

"Goodness! It's not till July. Whatever made you ask?"

"We'll have a party for you," Jemmy cried. "And I'll start making you a present today."

"But this is Christmas," Lora said. "And I have presents from you."

"I know. But I want to do something special for you, Lorie. Like you've done something special for me."

Her eyes misted again and she did not attempt to blink the tears away.

XV

NOT UNTIL LATER did Lora know what had happened in the parlor that day after she and Jemmy had run upstairs. Mrs. Tyler had risen from her wheel chair before Wade could stop her, to take several steps across the room and collapse at his feet. She had been in bed ever since.

She had refused to see the doctor Wade had sent for, nor would she allow Lora to come near her. She simply lay on her pillow with her eyes closed most of the time, eating little, withdrawing from life. Lora suspected that the cure would be simple. They had only to get rid of Jemmy's dog and his grandmother would recover promptly. But so far, to her surprise, Wade had refused to make this concession.

Not even President Lincoln's January first Proclamation of Emancipation, of which Mrs. Tyler had approved so intensely, served to rouse her interest.

"She is trying to die," Wade said dully. "I've seen her do this before. That time when she fell downstairs. Sometimes I think she would rather die than not get her own way."

He sat on the sofa before the library fire, while Lora stood at a window looking out at the thawing landscape. It was mid-January and after a stretch of extremely cold weather the sun had come out bright and warm. Snow ran in dirty rivulets down the hill and the road had turned to a sea of slush.

"She's behaving like a spoiled child," Lora said. "What happened when she fell downstairs? How long ago was that?"

"Immediately after my first marriage." Wade leaned over absently to add more wood to the fire. "It was a shock to her when I married Virginia and after the fall she went very close to death."

"How did she come out of it that time?"

Wade did not answer for a moment, remembering painfully. "Virginia managed it. She was so sweet and loving that no one could resist her. Not even Mother. Even she came to accept Virginia, though she could never forgive what she regarded as a lowly background."

He sighed and Lora, hearing, went to him quickly and dropped on her knees beside him.

"You haven't let me talk about it, my dear. But now I must. I think you were splendid on Christmas Day when you

131

told Jemmy he could keep his dog. It has meant everything to him. I'm sure you must have noticed the change. He even whistles sometimes now, as a boy should, and he looks at you with his heart in his eyes. But you still hold him off, Wade. Why?"

He moved restlessly. "I'm not holding him off. It's just that I—know nothing about small boys. I don't know how to talk to him, or what to say."

"Anyway you stood up for him. That's what matters."

He looked at her in the cool way that was growing familiar. "I didn't do it for Jemmy alone. I'm trying to hold to something of myself this time. Always before, my mother has forced me to her pattern. And for me, that is a pattern of failure."

She leaned against his knee, eager now, and earnest. "You must be what is right for you to be. Just as I must be what is right for me. Believe in yourself, Wade."

The chill which put distance between them went out of his eyes. He rested a finger beneath her chin, tilting her head toward the lamplight. "You're always so *alive*, Lora. I've felt that in you from the beginning. Perhaps that was the thing which drew me toward you when I was near death. Perhaps I thought you might help me to be alive again. When Virginia—"

"No," she said, drawing away from the touch of his finger. "Not Virginia. Not me. You must do it yourself, Wade. That's the only way there is."

His smile was not altogether happy. "You're still young enough to believe that a mountain can be moved if only you push at it hard enough."

"Perhaps I do," she said. "Perhaps it's even true."

He bent to kiss her cheek lightly and stood up. "I must go and read to Mother now. She pretends not to listen, but I think it pleases her nevertheless. Though in the end she'll win, I'm afraid. She always does."

"Not this time!" Lora cried valiantly. "Wade, what of your book? Don't you work on it any more?"

"Sometimes," he said. "But perhaps that's only a dream—something make-believe. A waste of time." He picked up a volume from the table and went out of the room.

Lora sat where she was on the hearthrug beside the sofa. The feeling of his kiss was still light on her cheek and she reached up to touch the place with her fingers. Strange that when he kissed her she could always feel more lonely than before. But her loneliness wasn't important. If only there were some way in which she could really help him.

Just then there was a yelping and scampering up the front steps and she heard Jemmy coming home from school. She roused herself and went to the door of the library. It was wiser for both boy and dog to keep as quiet as possible when they came inside, but these days in his new confidence that his father would stand by him, Jemmy did not always remember.

Lora smiled and put a finger to her lips. But this time Jemmy did not need the warning. He bent to pat the little dog and soothe him so that he uttered only an excited yap or two. Then Jemmy peered down the hall and up the stairs with an exaggerated air of secrecy, before he beckoned Lora into the library. Once inside, he closed the door and held out an envelope to her.

"Rebecca brought it," he said. "It's a note from Morgan Le Fay. Rebecca saw me on the road when she came out of the woods and she said to give it to you when no one else was around. She's waiting on the woods path for an answer."

Lora slit the envelope with a brass paper knife from Wade's desk. The note was brief. Could Lora visit Morgan Channing any time this afternoon? Something important had come up and Lora's help was urgently needed.

Why should she go? Lora wondered. She neither liked nor trusted this woman. And yet at the same time she was intrigued by her. The note was both puzzling and provoking, and it certainly aroused her curiosity. There could be no harm in at least finding out the reason behind this invitation.

"What is it?" Jemmy asked. "What does she want?"

Lora tore the note into small bits and dropped them into the fire. "Mrs. Channing wants me to come up to see her for a little while this afternoon. If Rebecca is waiting in the woods I'll go back up the path with her now."

Jemmy's eyes took on a shine of conspiracy. "I won't tell, Lora. If anybody asks I'll say you're having a nap in your room."

"Thank you, Jemmy," she said quickly, "but of course you musn't do that. I'd be very unhappy if you told fibs to keep me out of trouble. There's nothing wrong about going up to see Mrs. Channing if I choose to do so."

"Just the same, I won't tell," he promised her.

There was no convincing him that intrigue was not necessary in this house of intrigue and though she could not admit it to him, she would be glad of his silence until she had time to discover what Morgan Channing wanted.

For the last two weeks a seamstress had come daily to the house. In spite of Mother Tyler's indifference to what went on, Wade had seen to the matter. As a consequence, Lora's new wardrobe had begun to blossom and she could now put on a soft wool dress of turtle-dove gray, most stylishly made and trimmed with velvet of a darker shade. She felt quite another person in it, though she smiled at herself for gaining confidence from the mere donning of a new frock. At least she need not mount the hill today with the knowledge that she would seem dowdy and countrified beside the impressive Mrs. Channing. Her new bonnet was gray too, with a touch of warm pink color under the brim, and her gray mantle was far warmer than her old one.

Jemmy, playing with Hamlin on the drive before the house, looked up as she came down the steps.

"You look nice," he said. "We'll take you to Rebecca, Hamlin and I."

Their course down the muddy road was somewhat less than elegant, but Jemmy was a help in guiding her along the least soggy patches of grass beside the road. Hamlin wallowed happily to his ears in mud and then had to be restrained from leaping upon Lora in the ecstasy of farewells.

"I'll take him right home and give him a bath," Jemmy promised. "Here's Lora, Rebecca."

Rebecca said good afternoon in her usual soft-voiced manner and turned at once to lead the way uphill. Lora waved to Jemmy and followed her. The springy path of dried leaves made more comfortable walking than the road, but Lora had to give considerable care to her swishing skirts.

As the young colored girl went ahead, straight-backed as Amanda Tyler, with her head held proudly high, Lora felt her old curiosity sweep back. More than once she had wondered about her life up there in the Channing mansion, wondered about her as a person.

"How do you like it here in the North, Rebecca?" she asked of the straight back ahead of her.

Rebecca did not so much as glance over her shoulder. "It's fine up here, ma'am," she said.

"Do you have friends here on Staten Island?" Lora went on, probing a bit more personally.

There was the briefest of pauses before the girl answered. "I wouldn't rightly say I've got much time for friends, ma'am."

134

"But you must have time off and friends to visit?"

"Watch the mud there, ma'am." Rebecca turned to hold back a flapping branch.

Lora sensed that she had been mildly rebuked. By no least word did Rebecca mean to betray her real self to a strange white woman. This was no new thing to Lora. There had been many Negroes in the town she had come from, and they had always been friendly, courteous, helpful—but you never knew what they were thinking. You never penetrated past the special face they turned toward white folks. Only Doc had been able to get past that guard and get them to talk to him, forget their caution, be themselves.

When they reached the turn on the path where it wound about the woodland pond, Rebecca moved more quickly and kept her gaze from the shimmering pool, as if she shrank from looking at it.

"I suppose you knew Miss Virginia, didn't you?" Lora asked, still seeking a way past the guard that held her off.

Rebecca moved more quickly than before. "Yes'm," she said. "A real nice lady she was. That was a sorry thing that happened, ma'am."

For an instant she glanced around at Lora, but her eyes were blank, unrevealing. They saw, but they did not betray.

"Wait!" Lora cried. "I'm out of breath. Let's stop a minute and rest, here by the pool. How beautiful this place must be in the springtime. I can hardly wait for warm weather. I'm afraid I'm not used to real winter. Did you have trouble getting used to the cold, Rebecca?"

The girl shivered, but Lora could not be sure if it was because she had mentioned winter, or because of the nearness of this pond where Virginia Tyler had died.

"Yes'm," the girl said dutifully. "It was real hard to get used to." She stood with her back to the pond, resembling some wild, richly plumaged bird about to take flight.

Lora walked down the bank to the edge of the water. "Jemmy says it's very deep out there."

"I reckon that's right." The girl turned suddenly, showing her first sign of emotion. "Mrs. Tyler, this is a bad place. If you want to rest, we can go a mite higher up the hill."

But Lora took quick advantage of this slipping mask. "Miss Virginia's death must have been a tragic thing for everyone, Rebecca. But it was an accident. That doesn't make this a bad place. We musn't blame the water, or the trees, or that rock out there, you know. The *place* is still beautiful and good."

135

The girl watched her, wide-eyed for a moment. Then heavy-lashed lids drooped once more over dark eyes and she started quickly up the hill as if she did not care whether or not Lora followed. She almost ran now, as if some demon from the pool pursued her, and Lora followed after, knowing there was no use in trying to dispel whatever haunting lay upon the pool for Rebecca.

They reached the big house without further conversation and Lora was ushered in at once into the drawing room, where only one fire burned today. Somehow the room looked austere and cold and less richly glamorous than it had to Lora's eyes the first time.

Rebecca took her wraps silently with only a murmured acknowledgment when Lora thanked her, and went off to summon her mistress. This time Lora did not seat herself timidly before the fire, but walked boldly across to the French doors to look upon the brilliantly sunlit view. How wonderful it must be to occupy the very crest of the hill, instead of being tucked away in a hollow below. From the upstairs windows of this house, both sunrise and sunset vistas must be magnificent.

When she had her fill of the view, Lora turned back to the room. Her eyes searched out the great portrait at the far end, but today the painting of Morgan and Virginia had been hidden by the green velvet draperies pulled completely across the picture.

Mrs. Channing came in so softly behind her that Lora was unaware of her presence until she spoke. "How nice of you to come, Lora. I may call you Lora, may I not? I dislike formality between friends."

She wore black again today, with only a pearl brooch and earrings to relieve its somber hue. Yet she was not in mourning for her husband, since she had been gay in white and turquoise the night of Serena's party. Black suited her, Lora decided. It heightened her dramatic quality, whitened her skin and made her dark eyes all the more brilliant.

Morgan had not missed the look of interest Lora had been giving the hidden picture. She nodded carelessly toward the pulled draperies.

"Sometimes I weary of looking myself in the eye. Particularly when I am my own sole company."

Lora smiled uncertainly and took the chair which a gesture from Morgan indicated. This woman always made her faintly uncomfortable and a little unsure of herself.

"I've been away, you know," Morgan said. "To Albany."

Lora had not known. In the tight little world of the Tyler household, concerned more than ever with its own problems, little news of the outside world had penetrated for the last two weeks.

"I attended Governor Seymour's inauguration on New Year's Day," Morgan went on. "Mr. Norwood is very close to the governor, as well as being an old friend of my husband. Nicholas was always interested in the political scene and he could never keep me from becoming interested too. I like to be near the seats of the mighty."

She laughed at Lora's puzzled expression, and rang the little bell at her side as a signal for Rebecca to serve tea.

"I can see that you don't approve of a woman who interests herself in politics," she went on. "But I cannot see myself sitting idle and alone in this great house. I want activity and life about me. Important activity."

"It isn't that," Lora confessed. "It's just that—well, the other day you seemed to speak very sincerely about wishing there was some way to stop the war. And now—"

"I am sincere," Morgan broke in. "That is why I've asked you to come here to see me today."

Rebecca moved unobtrusively and hardly lifted her gaze from the tea tray and the passing of small cakes. Her gold earrings tapped her cheeks gently as she bent to serve, but what she was thinking, what private longings or antagonisms she might feel behind her golden brown mask, there was no telling.

When she had gone from the room, Lora stirred sugar into her tea and spoke thoughtfully. "Did you know that Rebecca is afraid to go past that pool in the woods?"

Morgan shrugged. "That's natural enough with these people. I presume they are all ignorantly superstitious."

Lora let her words pass, though Morgan's tone caused a prickling of sensitivity along her nerves. She had spent too many years in the company of her father to accept so careless a dismissal. There was more behind the masked exterior of this colored girl than Morgan knew.

"What sort of life does she have up here?" Lora went on.

Morgan looked as surprised as if she had inquired whether the mantelpiece spoke French. "Life? How should I know? She serves me well and I pay her well. I'm not concerned about her personal problems. I doubt if she has any." The subject was evidently unwelcome and she changed it quickly. "How charming you look today, Lora. Gray becomes you far better than green."

137

Lora set her teacup down and met the other woman's eyes. "I did not wear your sister's gown by choice the other night. I'm sorry if it disturbed you."

"Why should it disturb me? I've told you there was little affection lost between my sister and me. From the time when we were small children, we had no common meeting ground. It's a fable that blood relatives should necessarily like each other. But I haven't asked you here to talk about Virginia or Rebecca. From something you said the other day I gathered that you would lend your help if you could, toward any movement which might lead in the direction of halting this dreadful bloodshed."

"That's quite true," Lora said.

"Good. First, I'd like you to know that we have Governor Seymour on our side. Of course, he cannot come out openly and officially oppose the Administration. Not with any show of force, at least. But he will sanction what we do and will lend us behind-the-scenes support. Have you heard of the Knights of the Golden Circle?"

"Vaguely," Lora said. "I've heard them labeled Copperheads."

"Many people don't understand their work and purpose," Morgan said blandly. "The Circle is opposed to the continuation of the war. Its members want a peaceful settlement with the South and they are by now many thousand strong in the Middle West. Murray Norwood is one of those chosen to start new castles in the east."

"Castles?" Lora asked.

Morgan smiled. "Between you and me, Lora, I will acknowledge that there's a good deal of the small boy in many men. They like to dress up, use passwords and exchange secret handshakes. They love the mystery of the secret society and all the trappings that go with it. 'If I go to the East . . .' and 'What of the night?' 'Morning cometh,' and all the rest. But let them have their ritual if it appeals to them. Let them have it if it will stop the war."

She had set her tea and cakes upon the table beside her and was leaning earnestly toward Lora. There was no doubting her sincerity now, or her driving intensity.

"But what can they do?" Lora asked.

"You've heard of the coming draft, have you not?"

"I don't know much about it, I'm afraid."

"What an ignorant little thing you are! Don't you realize that the Union cannot possibly win this war unless it has more men? But men of the North are no longer flocking like sheep to throw their lives away. If President Lincoln cannot raise his quota the war will stop because it will be impossible to fight on. Stop the draft in New York State, as they are going to stop it in other states, and we stop the war bloodlessly."

"But *how* can the draft be stopped? If the government—"

"Ah, but you don't know the power we have on our side. We have a magnificent leader out in Ohio—Clement Vallandigham. And Governor Seymour himself is opposed to the draft. We have only to organize and stand fast."

Lora sighed. "I'm afraid I am ignorant of all this. In any case—what do you want me to do?"

Morgan glanced toward the closed velvet draperies and grimaced. Then she rose and strode the length of the room to fling them open so that her counterpart, more beautiful, but less vital, looked down upon the room. Morgan turned and came toward Lora, her smile flashing.

"Now there are two of us on my side," she said. "You can never hold out against us both. And the thing we ask of you is so simple, so easy. We need someone of influence here on the island. Someone who is strongly against the war and who is liked and trusted by other islanders. A man, of course." She paused, watching Lora.

"You mean—Wade?" Lora asked, more puzzled than ever.

Morgan returned to her chair and took up her teacup again with a gesture elaborately casual. "Of course. And you are the one who can draw him into this."

"I!" Lora cried. "I'm afraid I have little influence with him. Besides, what could Wade do? His mother is very ill just now and he is not well himself. He has taken no part in island life since his return."

"But he did at one time," Morgan said. "And he will again if it is urged upon him. He had a taste of it the other night at Serena's party. Perhaps you haven't seen enough of that side of your husband to judge. He has always been extremely well liked and influential too, thanks to his name and position. We need to draw men of his sort in with us. Will you help us, Lora?"

Lora moved her hands in a gesture of helplessness. "You must know how he feels about—well, about this house. He would never, I am sure, agree to come here."

"I appreciate your delicacy, but we need not mince words." Morgan's smile was wry. "It is I whom he wishes to avoid, not the house. However, as you must know by now, it is child's play to wrap Wade around your finger. You can get

139

him here if you try. Not for my sake. I am nothing in this. But to meet Murray Norwood. Once Murray talks to him I feel certain that Wade will be with us. Then he can use his influence to draw others to help us."

Lora shook her head, quietly stubborn in the face of Morgan's assurance. "I don't want to wrap Wade around my fingers, or to see anyone else do it. I want him to think for himself and do what he believes is right."

Morgan nodded tolerantly. "You are honest, my dear, but you are also very young. There are certain facts you must face sooner or later. Believe me—I have known Wade all my life and I know he will always need a stronger hand to mold him, guide him."

Lora moved restlessly in her chair. There had been times lately when she had almost thought the same thing. But on Christmas morning Wade had stood up to his mother in the matter of the puppy. No one had made him do that. No one had forced his hand. In fact, the greatest pressure had been in the other direction, yet he had not so far given in to it. So there must be some core of strength in him that was his own. He had even confessed that he was struggling to hold something of himself away from his mother.

"I think it quite possible that you underestimate my husband," she told Morgan firmly.

For just an instant Morgan's eyes flashed anger, and though she suppressed it swiftly, there was a tinge of irritation in her laughter.

"You are a young wife in love," she said. "I apologize. You must learn to know Wade for yourself, of course. I had no right to say such a thing. Suppose we start over. Two tremendously important factors remain. I believe you are sincere in wanting to aid in the cause of bringing this war to an end. I also believe you are sincere in wanting to help your husband recover from the shock from which he still suffers. To speak frankly—the shock of my sister's death. Am I not right?"

"Of course," Lora said.

"Very well. Help him find something he can throw himself into—something he can do that counts. There lies the way to recovery. You have only to persuade him to see Murray Norwood."

Rebecca returned softly to the room bringing fresh hot water for the tea, replenishing the cake basket. Morgan waved her aside somewhat impatiently and waited for her guest to speak.

There was a reasonableness about Morgan's words, Lora had to admit. She had touched on the truth concerning Wade and her counsel was good. Yet Lora felt helpless to judge the worth of the cause she proposed to work for. The word "Copperhead" had a smell of treason, as that man at Serena's party had said, and she knew nothing of this so-called Circle.

"I just don't know," she said at length. "Perhaps if it were only a matter of meeting Mr. Norwood, talking to him—"

"But that is all we ask," Morgan said quickly.

"Meeting him elsewhere. Not here," Lora added.

Morgan shook her head. "I am part and parcel of all this. Murray needs me, needs my house and whatever else I can contribute. The men who work with him must accept my presence and my help. I am accustomed to entertaining constantly. No one thinks anything of the flow of guests to my house. This is an ideal location for a castle. But this is not something I expect you to run about and announce to the four winds. I weighed you carefully before I decided to make this gamble in talking to you."

"I understand," Lora said. "But as for getting Wade to come to this house, I know it's impossible."

Morgan went on as if she had not spoken. "First you will tell him that Murray Norwood is interested in a plan which will oppose the draft and become a force in halting the war. Say nothing of the Circle. Let us tell him about that. He may set the time for meeting Murray himself and the meeting will be in this house."

Lora shook her head. "The whole thing is hopeless. I don't know anything about the quarrel between you and Wade, but I know he becomes very angry when your name is so much as mentioned."

"I realize that," Morgan said, her tone studiously light. "A childish notion on Wade's part. We had no quarrel. Nevertheless, there is one weapon you can use to bring him here. An infallible weapon."

Lora waited, instinctively ready to resist this woman's persuasiveness.

Morgan leaned forward in her chair and Lora noted that there were amber flecks of light in her eyes; an amber that seemed to glow when she was moved to intensity.

"Make him angry," Morgan said. "Tell him that he is afraid of me, tell him that is why he avoids me. Tell him you think the war a more important cause than his own feeble fears. If you make him feel he must prove his courage, he will come. I know him, Lora. I know him clear through."

Lora regarded the woman before her with increasing distaste, but she managed to answer quietly. "The method you suggest would not be mine. I have too much respect for my husband."

She rose with a dignity which put her on the same footing with Morgan in spite of her lack of years.

"I really must be getting back home now. It was kind of you to invite me here today, but I'm afraid there is no way in which I can help you."

She was aware of Morgan's anger, though the other woman's manner remained carefully unperturbed.

"What a contrast with Virginia you must make for Wade. How much suffering you must inevitably cause him!" There was malice in Morgan's laughter as she walked with Lora toward the door.

Lora found herself surging with resentment against this woman. But she would not give Morgan the satisfaction of suspecting how indignant she was. At the door her hostess held out her hand and Lora put her own into it briefly.

"I will expect to hear from you," Morgan said. "Not for my sake, or for yours. But because I believe you truly want to help Wade. And this is an opportunity for doing so."

Lora made no answer. She said a polite good day, and went down the driveway, sensing that Morgan stood in the doorway staring after her.

All the way home she pondered Morgan's words and motives. Was this a simple matter of politics as she professed, or was there in this woman a purpose which concerned Wade far more personally than she claimed?

XVI

BY THE END OF January Lora had still said nothing to Wade of the request Morgan had made of her. She did not mention her recent visit, though she had told him of her first trip up the hill and that she had obtained the puppy from Morgan. He'd been distressed at first, but had eventually forgiven her.

She had not, however, been able to dismiss her talk with Morgan from her mind. It was just possible that Morgan was right and Wade ought to have something like this to fling himself into. If Morgan's cause was honest and just, the chance at least should be given Wade. But how could she be sure? And how was she to broach the subject to him without incurring his displeasure and gaining only an angry refusal?

Matters in the Tyler household were no worse, though little better than they had been. Mother Tyler had decided not to die after all, but merely to remain in bed as an invalid. However, she consented now to sit up, demanded constant waiting on from Ellie, and wanted Wade at her side too much of the time.

True, she was not as yet winning the fight in which Jemmy's puppy was a mere symbol, but she was winning in other ways and Lora could only watch in distress. Wade had done little more on his book because he could never be permitted uninterrupted time to himself. No sooner would he shut himself in the library to work, than the silver bell would ring demandingly and Ellie would come tapping at the library door with some request from his mother. Once Lora had quietly given orders that Ellie was not to disturb her master on any account, let the bell ring as it might. Whereupon Mrs. Tyler had had a relapse and been ill for several days.

More than anyone else these days Lora missed her father. He would have had the wisdom and experience to deal with these problems. And he would have had the patience. Lora found her own patience wearing thinner by the day, until she was afraid that she might throw caution to the winds and stride into the sickroom to take matters impulsively into her own hands. This, she well knew, might be disastrous because the battle was one she was helpless to win. She could only stand beside Wade and offer what comfort she could.

These days Jemmy was the one happy member of the household. He and Hamlin—whose full name had not been disclosed to Wade—even stole away from the house sometimes on Sundays because Adam was full of dog knowledge and was aiding Jemmy in the development of Hamlin's personality and everyday good manners. Sunday rules had relaxed a bit for them all, now that Mrs. Tyler was bedridden. At Lora's suggestion they had taken to going out to church, instead of conducting gloomy prayers in the parlor. This, for the moment, was their only contact with social life.

Whether Jemmy sensed the tension among his elders, and the cause of his grandmother's self-imposed illness, there was no telling. It was enough for him that he had been able to keep the puppy. When, on the rare occasions of a visit to his grandmother, she would emphasize to the boy that the pain of her headaches was brought on by the noise of the dog scampering through the halls, or barking at night, Jemmy would turn a bright, blank look upon her and announce that Ham was sorry and didn't mean to hurt her, and was really trying very hard to learn.

Lora had an account of these sessions from Ellie and knew that neither old woman nor small boy ever won or was defeated. But the tension in the household increased and Lora dreaded the possibility of a real explosion.

Mother Tyler's constitution was probably ironclad. She could make herself ill if she tried, but she would probably never will herself to go down in complete defeat. It was Wade who would be more likely to give in under the strain. Lora felt increasingly that she ought to find someone from whom she might gain advice. Her thoughts turned often to Serena Lord.

One bleak morning when it was snowing again, she bundled herself up and walked along Dogwood Lane toward the Lord house. Edgar's leave had ended and he had rejoined his company, so she would not be intruding on Serena's brief hours with her husband. The maid showed her into the dining room, where a fire blazed and where Serena, her red hair hidden beneath a house cap, her plump person encased in a voluminous apron, sorted piles of linen heaped on table and sideboard. Adam was helping her, having been pressed into such female service somewhat against his will.

Lora almost bumped into him as he came through the dining-room door bearing a pile of sheets as high as his head. He grinned at her around the mound in his arms.

"Good morning, Lora Tyler. You're a welcome sight. Do intercede for me and obtain my release from bondage."

"Nonsense!" cried his sister briskly. "You've nothing else to do and you can run up and down stairs better than I. How nice to see you, Lora. Do come in."

Lora glanced doubtfully at the heaps of linen, but Serena forestalled any apology or effort to withdraw. She gave Lora's wraps and bonnet to the maid and waved her to a chair before the fire.

"There! You shall sit and talk to me. A linen inventory is a tiresome task and Adam doesn't feel talkative this morning. I've been pining for company."

The room was doubly cheerful and warm in contrast to the snow blowing against the windows and the piling of white drifts in the garden. The air was fragrant with a scent of lavender and orris root sachet.

"I would not have waited much longer for you to visit

me," Serena told her cheerfully. "You've had more than enough time to settle into your new life. Now you must get out and make friends, my dear, have some outside contacts. We see you only at church. How is the elder Mrs. Tyler?"

Through Jemmy's visits to Adam, Serena must know something of the situation at the Tylers', but Lora could not tell how much Serena read between the lines. She explained briefly that Wade's mother was somewhat better and then sat silent for a little while, watching the fire, wondering how best to broach the subject of the unhappy struggle for power in which Wade's mother was engaged. She looked up to see Serena's understanding gaze upon her.

"Mrs. Tyler is doing the same thing she tried to do when Wade married Virginia, isn't she?" Serena said.

Lora nodded, reassured by the fact that she need make no explanation to Serena Lord. "One thing that puzzles me is the fact that she seems not to have attempted this when her husband was alive. From the little I've heard now and then, Jack Tyler must have flouted her wishes and done exactly as he pleased. But she didn't take to her bed then."

Serena counted swiftly down a stack of pillowcases and made a mark on a sheet of paper. "For Amanda to take to her bed would never have worked with Jack Tyler. He'd have been happy to have her out of his way. She knew that, so it was the last thing she'd do. But she can hurt Wade and make him feel guilty. I'm surprised that he hasn't given in long ago on the matter of the dog. Just for the sake of peace, if nothing else."

"I'm afraid he still may," Lora said. "That's one reason I wanted to talk to you today. I'd like to help him, and I don't know how. I'm afraid I don't even understand him very well."

Adam came in empty-handed just then and overheard her last words. "If anybody who knows him can explain Wade to me, I'd like to hear about it. I'd never have expected him to stick up for Jemmy's dog in the first place."

Lora winced at the implied criticism. "I don't see why everyone underestimates him!" she cried.

"You like to play the mother, don't you?" Adam scoffed.

He might have said more, but his sister made a shooing gesture with her hands. "That will be enough. Off with you to that freedom you've been begging for. Lora and I want to talk woman-talk. No—let the towels be. We can't have you constantly popping in here disturbing us."

Adam sighed exaggeratedly. "You can see what a henpecked brother I am, Lora. But since freedom has been offered me, I'll escape before my sister changes her mind."

Serena shook her head as he went out, and a lock of bright hair slipped from beneath her cap and curled against her cheek. "Don't mind Adam. I'm worried about him. He needs to be engaged in some furious activity. With these bouts of fever still laying him low, he can't return to action, or even work for long at any job. But now we'll be able to talk without being picked on."

Lora sensed again the warm sympathy she had felt in this woman that first night when Serena had spoken to her on the ferry.

"If I knew more about the past perhaps I could understand better how to help Wade," she mused. "He must have had some quarrel with Mrs. Channing, though she denied it, and no one will tell me what it was about."

Serena sorted towels into piles thoughtfully. "If there was a specific quarrel I haven't heard the details. But there was a time when we all thought Wade would marry Morgan. Did you know that?"

"Mother Tyler told me," Lora said.

"She would! There was always a spark between Morgan and Wade when they were young. Morgan went after him in her headlong way, but it always seemed to me a stormy affair with more quarreling and passion in it than any real liking. Fortunately he came to his senses and turned in what must have been relief to Virginia."

"How did he come to his senses?" Lora asked. "What happened to make him turn to Virginia?"

Serena shrugged. "Again I can't give you the details—we only heard rumors afterwards. But I believe it was Morgan herself—some frightful thing she did that shocked Wade into seeing what she was."

"Mother Tyler hinted that she stopped the affair and broke it up."

"I don't know," Serena said, "but I do believe he's still a little afraid of Morgan."

"I don't see why he should be."

Serena paused in her sorting. "Even my Edgar admits that she has a decided attraction. More than one man whom she hasn't particularly wanted has played moth to her candle. The funny thing is I've felt a bit sorry for Morgan at times."

"Why ever should you?" Lora asked in surprise.

"Because as a child it couldn't have been easy to be the homely, unloved one of the family, with Virginia so pretty

146

and sweet and lovable. And able to take so easily what Morgan wanted most."

This was a new and startling conception of Morgan which Lora found hard to accept. "Mrs. Channing homely?"

"Oh, not now. Not since she has learned poise and has gained a position in the world with Nicholas' wealth behind her. As a woman she has come into her own. But as a strong-willed, disliked little girl, she had a hard time. Virginia and I were the only ones who really stood up for her and we were the wrong sex. She didn't care whether or not we liked her. Wade was the one she wanted and she was ready to fight for his admiration, even while she antagonized him. But she was such a wild, lonely little thing I had to feel sorry for her."

Lora could only listen in silence, finding it difficult to reconcile her recent glimpses of Morgan with the picture Serena remembered.

"I'll never forget something that happened on my fifteenth birthday," Serena went on. "Let me see—Morgan would have been thirteen at the time. Wade and Adam are the same age—a year younger than Morgan, and Virginia would have been eight or nine."

Serena left her sorting and came to pull another chair close to the fire.

"This is as good a time as any to tell you about it," she said, thrusting the bright lock of hair back under her cap and smoothing out her big white apron. "I need a rest and we can have this time to ourselves. Would you like a cup of coffee, Lora?"

Lora shook her head. "No, thank you. Please tell me the story. I'm anxious to know something that will give me a better understanding of all these things."

"My birthday falls in August, when it can be very hot here on the island. So mother gave me an outdoor party that year. Some of my older friends were there, of course, but by the time this incident occurred they'd gone home, and only the neighbors were left, and a few grownups. Mama always invited the Ambrose children to our parties, even though Mrs. Tyler didn't approve of such social recognition. At any rate, the five of us were out in the side garden, quite replete from being stuffed with ice cream and cake and candy. Virginia was building a little house of twigs and stones and leaves, while Wade and I were helping her. She was such a good, amiable child that we all loved to please her. Adam was prowling around shooting Indians or something—he always had to be active—and Morgan was swinging in the hammock, looking cross because no one was paying much attention to her. Of course we lived in my father's house then—the Hume place near you. The house that burned down."

She sighed, remembering sadly.

Lora watched the fire as she listened and as Serena's quiet voice went on building pictures in her mind, she could almost see the children as they had been on that long-ago day in August. Virginia, small and fair-haired, with a dimple that was forever showing with her ready smile. Serena, older, tolerant and kind. Adam forever restless, ready for any scapegrace adventure. Wade pale because he didn't eat well and was often kept indoors, but always eager to be liked. And, finally, Morgan, with ragged, dark hair that would never stay within the confines of a braid or ribbon, her nose that was too big, and her stormy, dark eyes and sulky mouth.

As she listened, Lora could almost hear the words of the careless women on the porch—adults, sure that the children were intent on their own affairs, not listening to grown-up talk.

It had been one of Mrs. Hume's guests who had started the whole thing. She had looked at Morgan swinging sullenly in the hammock and had shaken her head at her friends.

"What a pity the Ambrose girls are so different. The little one is quite charming and appealing. Even without a good family background she will probably do well in her own circles. But the older child is a fright. So bad-tempered. So plain."

"Hush," said Mrs. Hume uneasily. "She may hear you."

The other woman shrugged. "Someone should take her in hand. She has been trying to spoil the party for the others all afternoon."

Mrs. Hume threw a quick look at the seemingly indifferent Morgan and took her friends into the house. Morgan waited exactly two minutes and then swung herself out of the hammock. She came over and stood glowering at the small house of twigs that Virginia was building.

The other children had heard and they looked at her uncomfortably.

"Don't pay any attention," Serena told her. "Mrs. Dickson is just an old busybody."

Adam scalped his last Indian and joined the group, his eyes alight at the prospect of trouble. "Just the same, what she said was true. You *have* been trying to spoil things for us all afternoon, Morgan."

Wade was about to place a V-shaped twig upon the roof of

the house when Morgan swung her foot and kicked the whole thing from beneath his hand. The bits flew in all directions and Virginia cried out in dismay. It was possible that Adam who was no respecter of the feminine person, might have tackled Morgan then and there and given her a good pummeling, but the girl was too quick for him. She sprang away with a derisive laugh and climbed the iron fence that ran along the front of the house.

"Get down, Morgan!" Serena ordered in her role of the eldest. "If you fall on those spikes you'll kill yourself."

But Morgan only balanced on the narrow ledge that ran on either side of the spikes, pulling her skirts high and laughing at them all.

"Maybe I'm a fright, but I'm braver than any of you!" she cried. "I can walk this fence all the way to the gate, and I'll bet the rest of you are scared to try."

"No one wants to try," said Serena reasonably. "And we don't want to see you hurt."

Virginia hid her face in her hands. "Make Morgan come down," she quavered.

"Fraidy-cats! Fraidy-cats!" cried Morgan, and started her reckless traversing of the fence, putting one foot almost carelessly before the other, down beside the spikes of the palings.

Adam said, "Who's afraid? Anybody can walk that old fence." He was after Morgan in a second and up behind her, moving with an easy, sure balance, completely confident and unafraid.

Morgan reached the gatepost and jumped down, her dark face glowing with triumph. But she was not yet done with her taunting.

"Wade's-a-coward, Wade's-a-coward!" she chanted.

Wade stood up, staring at Morgan angrily. Virginia caught his hand and clung to it, but he shook her off and went toward the fence. Adam had jumped down by now and even he didn't want to see Wade attempt the feat.

"Hey!" he called. "Don't climb up there. You get dizzy too easy."

Serena knew she should run into the house for her mother, should scream, should do something, but she was suddenly helpless, frozen in dreadful fascination, as they all were, watching Wade climb the fence and stand white and shaky on its top, looking down at the spikes beneath him.

One step after another he took, obviously frightened and fighting his own fear. Serena had begun to think he would make it after all when, three steps from the end, his vertigo

149

won out. He swayed, tried to recover his balance, and put out a hand to save himself as he fell. He screamed just once as the iron spike went through his palm, and then he was on the ground, his hand impaled on the fence.

Serena recovered her power of voice and screamed wildly for her mother. Little Virginia went into sick hysterics at the sight of blood and Wade's agonizing pain. It was Adam who tore down the lane shouting for Ambrose at the top of his lungs. Morgan, who had caused the whole thing, only stared in horror.

There were no men at the party, only frightened women, and it was Ambrose who came running back with Adam to take charge of the crisis. It was he who removed Wade's hand from the spike and caught the boy when he fainted. It was he who stanched the blood and carried his limp body back to his mother's house.

The birthday party broke up in confusion. No one spoke to Morgan. No one told the grownups just what had happened. It was Morgan herself who told her father. She went back to the Tylers' and sat on the back steps until Ambrose came out, looking grave and a little sick himself. Virginia had been put to bed by her mother by that time in the servants' quarters. But Morgan could not rest till she had told her father what had happened, had castigated and humbled herself.

"Years afterwards Ambrose told me about it," Serena said to Lora. "Morgan always had to do things in extremes. She asked him for a whipping, even pleaded for one. I suppose the poor thing felt she could expiate her guilt if she hurt herself enough. But Ambrose wasn't the beating sort of father." •

"She should have been whipped," Lora cried indignantly. "What a wicked thing to do!"

"Children often do wicked things." Serena's tone was gentle. "But that doesn't mean they are wicked. The punishment Ambrose gave her without intention was worse than any whipping. I believe her father has always been the one person whose love and admiration she really wanted as a child. She and her mother were never close, and Mrs. Ambrose died shortly after Virginia was married. She always wanted her father's respect. And she tried to gain it in the wrong ways, as children do so perversely sometimes. But Ambrose is simple and good and there's no cruelty in him. He could never understand Morgan and her behavior must always have bewildered him, even while he wanted to help her."

"Did Wade's mother know what really happened?" Lora asked.

"Gracious no! I can't think what she'd have done to Morgan. Wade never told her, and no one else dared. But I heard Mother Tyler use the accident against him one time when he was older. She said, 'Remember—if you put yourself on an iron fence, you've got to be man enough not to fall off.' "

Lora shivered. "What a dreadful thing to say." In her imagination she could see Wade, hurt in spirit as well as in his physical body. He must have felt that he had proved himself a coward, though in fact he'd showed more courage than either Morgan or Adam, who lacked the imagination to be afraid in the first place, and so were in much less danger.

"Afterwards," Serena said, getting up to return to her sorting of towels, "Morgan couldn't do enough for Wade, and of course everything she did was wrong. She had a genius as a child for alienating those she wanted to have like her. I really believe she was more sensitive than Virginia and I'm sure she suffered deeply in the knowledge that her younger sister could always gain easily what she could never have. Only her suffering was all within herself and for herself. She never stepped into anyone else's shoes to understand his feelings. So there it is, Lora. Not a very pretty story."

"It helps me to understand why Wade must dislike her," Lora said.

Serena shook her head. "That's the strange part. He never seemed to hold what happened against her. He distrusted her, but she had some sort of fascination for him too. He blamed no one except himself for the accident. I don't think he regretted getting up on that fence so foolishly. He only regretted falling, and he never blamed Morgan for that. No, this late avoidance of her has its roots in the more recent past. But I don't really know what might have caused it."

Tenderness for Wade welled in Lora's heart. She could see the picture more clearly now. Even though there were still gaps she could understand far better.

She fell to watching the fire again. "He needed Virginia a great deal, didn't he?"

"Yes," Serena said, slapping her hand at a frayed towel as if it offended her. "He needed her, of course. But I'm not at all sure her way was good for him."

Lora looked up quickly. "Sometimes I've thought that myself. And yet his mother's way hasn't been good for him either. And there isn't any other way. Either you love a person as he is and forgive him his faults, or you can't forgive those faults and you try to make him into something else. At least I can understand why he's having such a hard time recovering from the accident of Virginia's death."

Serena glanced at her uncertainly and then came to a decision. "There are some who say her death was not an accident. Perhaps that is something you ought to know."

Lora blinked in bewilderment.

"You might as well know what has been rumored, though you needn't believe it. I'm not sure that I do myself. But there have been whispers of suicide."

"Suicide? But why? Surely Virginia wouldn't . . ."

"Wade admitted to some quarrel with her a week or so before her death— something he blamed himself for. That was strange because Virginia was never the sort to quarrel. However, there is Mrs. Tyler to consider. I suspect that she did her best to make Virginia unhappy. Perhaps she succeeded beyond her hopes."

"But Mother Tyler has only praise for Virginia now," Lora protested. "She keeps holding her up to me as a model wife."

Serena lost her tolerant attitude for the first time. "Of course! She has to find some way make *you* unhappy. Oh, but she makes me furious, that old woman! I can be generous to Wade and even to Morgan—but I can only see blame as far as Mrs. Tyler is concerned. She would go to any lengths to gain her own ends. Why do you suppose Wade and Virginia had separate rooms in that house? His mother took care of that. Anything to keep them apart. She told Virginia that Wade didn't sleep well at night, that he had never been strong. Separate bedrooms were a necessity. Since Virginia was never one to stand up to her, any more than Wade could stand up to her, that was the way it was. Virginia had been brought up with her parents servants on the premises and she lacked Morgan's strongheaded ways. But we've talked of unhappy things long enough, Lora. I've just tried to give you the glimpse of the past that you asked for. The present is something else. The present is you, my dear . . . and, frankly, I think you're the very best thing that has ever happened to Wade. Much better for him than Virginia."

Lora could only shake her head despairingly. She was not in the least sure of this herself.

The doorbell startled them with its ring and Serena's brow puckered. "Oh, dear, someone to spoil our visit, I'm afraid."

A moment later Adam came knocking on the door to ask if their woman-talk was over, as a matter of great importance had arisen. He ushered in Hester Wylie, the young woman whom Lora had met the night of Serena's party. She greeted them both gaily and plunged at once into the purpose of her errand.

She was planning a February sleighing party in a week or two and wanted Serena's help. Adam had already promised to escort his sister, and of course Wade and Lora Tyler must come too.

"We must get Wade back into the middle of things," Hester said to Lora. "I'm sure neither of you is having fun stuck in that dark old house."

"And, after all," said Adam, "we must have our fun."

Hester made a face at him, undaunted. "We're not forgetting the war, you know. We're planning this especially for some officers who are home on leave, and for a certain ex-prisoner of war named Adam. I wish Edgar could be here, too, Serena, dear."

"So do I," said Serena, and Lora thought guiltily that she had been so concerned with her own affairs that she had not even asked about Edgar. How much Serena would miss him, and how courageously she concealed it.

Before Lora went home that morning, the plans for the sleighing party had been endorsed and abetted by Serena, and Lora had been drawn into an agreement to persuade Wade to come.

When she broached the matter to him that evening in the library, she found that such persuasion was not too difficult. The Christmas party had given him a taste of the social life he had once indulged in so heartily and this affair promised a few hours' release from the gloomy atmosphere of the house.

He had led a difficult day at the beck and call of his mother, and Lora could read the discouragement in his eyes. Her mood of tenderness, aroused by Serena's story, held and she reached for his left hand where it lay idly on the sofa between them. She took it into her own, tracing the white welts of the old scar on its back.

"Serena told me how this happened," she said softly. "She gave me the whole story of that day."

"Serena is a gossip." Wade would have drawn his hand away, but she laced her fingers between his.

"This was not gossip. I want to know all about you. I want to know things that happened when you were young. You were a brave little boy to walk that fence that day."

"I wasn't in the least brave. Morgan was right—I was a coward about that fence."

153

"But you climbed it," Lora persisted. "You went ahead in spite of being afraid—that's what really makes bravery."

"A man is judged by his successes, not his failures," Wade said. "But this is something I no longer want to think about or discuss."

She could sense his withdrawal, but she had so few opportunities to talk to him alone that she held to her purpose.

"Everyone likes you, Wade. Jemmy wants so much to love you. He needs to love you. But you hold everyone off while you convince yourself that you are—well, somehow unworthy. Do you do this because you could never fit the pattern your mother chose for you?"

"I have always disappointed her, if that's what you mean."

There was a warning in his voice which would have discouraged her if she had been less intent on her own designs. But this was her chance to launch into the subject which Morgan had brought up to her.

"Your mother isn't the world. There are others who believe in your talents, others who need your help."

He watched her, his guard still up. "What lies behind all this maneuvering, Lora?"

"I'm not being very clever about it, am I?" she admitted. "Very well—I'll tell you straight out. Two weeks ago Mrs. Channing invited me up to her house for tea."

She could sense his stiffening. "You declined, I trust?"

"No—I accepted. I saw no reason for declining. I don't want to carry on old feuds. The matter Mrs. Channing wanted to talk to me about is bigger and more important than any small feud."

He rose impatiently to replenish the fire. "Have I not enough worries at this time, Lora? Must you add to them by striking up a ridiculous friendship with this woman who has done nothing but injure me?"

"This is scarcely a friendship," Lora said. "I believe you are as interested as I am in any plan which might lead to a halting of this dreadful war."

"And what has Morgan Channing to do with such plans?" he asked over his shoulder, prodding the fire with impatient thrusts of the poker. "Why should she even care?"

"I'm not sure why." At least, Lora thought, she had caught his interest, and she went on quickly. "Perhaps she likes the sense of power she gains from mixing into politics. Perhaps she's in love with this Murray Norwood and is interested for his sake. I don't know. It might even be that she has holdings in the South that will eventually become worthless or lost to her altogether if the war goes on. Is that possible?"

Wade set the fire screen in place and wiped his hands on a linen handkerchief. "It seems quite likely. Nicholas left her considerable property in the South and if I know Morgan she would dare anything to cling to her wealth. But is so selfish a motive any reason why we should trust her?"

"Don't you see, Wade?" Lora leaned toward him earnestly. "It doesn't matter if her motives are selfish, providing they are sincere. There are very definite plans afoot which this Mr. Norwood is mixed into. Mrs. Channing says even Governor Seymour approves of them and will be behind them unofficially."

"And where do I fit into this little fantasy?"

"Mr. Norwood needs you. He needs men here on the island who are liked and have some influence. There are ways in which you could help."

"Influence—I?" His laughter was unbelieving.

"You have only to talk to him. Nothing more if you decide against it. Let Morgan know when you would be available for a meeting with him at her house."

In the silence of the room the distant, insistent ringing of a small silver bell reached them.

"I'll have to see what she wants," Wade said wearily. "Ellie has probably gone to bed by now."

Lora put a quick hand on his arm. "First, tell me, Wade—you will see Mr. Norwood? Perhaps there's nothing to all this, but if you'll just talk to him—"

"With Morgan behind him, and in her house?" Wade asked. "Indeed I will not. I'll have nothing to do with the matter, or with either of them."

And he went off to answer the summons of his mother's bell. Lora leaned her head against the sofa and toasted her feet before the fire. At least she had made a first attempt. Since her talk with Serena she was sure that something must be done to draw Wade from his retreat into himself and into the past. He needed to be coaxed out of this house, given a chance to put his hands to some work that he could feel was important and worth while. Something that would make him look outside himself.

It occurred to her that there was another step which might be managed in connection with the sleighing party. She would ask Serena about it tomorrow.

Her thoughts turned again to her visit with Serena that

morning and the rumor that Virginia had taken her own life. Was there something more here which Wade and his mother had not published to the world? Did Wade himself believe this? If he did, how much greater his suffering must be than she had suspected.

XVII

FEBRUARY turned obligingly snowy and by the time set for the sleighing party the roads were packed with frosting. All the island sparkled beneath the sun or shone in gleaming purity under the moon. Now the bare branches of the trees made a fragile tracery against the white, adding to this winter beauty.

The evening was frosty and clear, and cold stars hung like bits of ice in the dark sky. There was much champing of bits and the stamping of horses' hooves as the Lords' sleigh waited in the lane for its load. Bells arched above the harness and chimed musically at every move the horses made. Two other sleighs were to join them farther down the hill and by the time the party was on its way there would be some forty young people and married couples in the group.

Lora wore the plainest of her new dresses—a gown of dark-blue wool, but without hoops, of course—and she and Wade were well bundled into coats, with wool mufflers around their heads and ears, and warm mittens protecting their hands. All seats except the driver's had been removed from the big sleigh and the body filled with fresh, clean straw. As Lora and Wade reached the Lord house, they found Adam and some of the other men carrying out hot bricks, well wrapped in strips of old blanket. The ladies remained snugly indoors until all was ready, but Adam barred Lora's way, laughing down at her when she would have mounted the steps.

"Hello, Lora. Hello, Wade. No, you don't—no scooting inside! All you fragile little ladies can come out now and pile aboard. Somebody's got to keep these bricks warm."

Adam had a striped stocking cap, which probably belonged to Eddie, pulled well over his ears, and a red plaid muffler wound twice about his neck. His nose was pink with the cold and his eyes very bright. He looked, Lora reflected, like a boy who had been let suddenly out of school and was intent on action and mischief. There was about him somehow a quality both irritating and engaging.

The ladies came hurrying out the door, bundled to their ears, twittering and laughing, and even those men who were in uniform were released and gay for the evening. One after another the ladies were helped into the sleigh and settled themselves in the straw, like nesting birds.

Before Lora found a place she stood for a moment looking out upon the drive, watching the open door from which light spilled brightly as guests ran down the steps. She was searching for two faces in particular, and she did not see them. Serena, puffing a little as her brother helped her unceremoniously into the sleigh, caught her searching look.

"It's all right," she whispered. "We're picking them up at the ferry landing. Mr. Norwood had to make a trip over to town and Morgan went to meet his boat. I don't know why you're anxious to effect a reconciliation between Morgan and Wade, but I've done what you asked. She and Mr. Norwood are joining us."

Lora settled down in the straw, pulling a hot brick toward her feet, and a few moments later they had all piled in. She was not sure how it happened, but the married partners seemed to have separated for the trip out. Wade was near the back of the sleigh with Hester Wylie beside him, while Adam Hume managed to take the place next to Lora. She was not entirely pleased at his company, but managed a polite smile.

"Good," he whispered under the racket the others were making. "I'm glad to see the corners of your mouth turn up for a change. You've been worrying too much lately."

She had no answer to that. Her worries were none of Adam's affair and she doubted that he would understand them. From time to time she was aware of his eyes upon her, without mockery now, and she could not be sure what he was thinking.

The driver cracked his whip and the four horses put their weight into the pull. The idle jingle of sleigh bells took on a steady and musical rhythm to the trot of the horses. Beneath the runners snow squeaked and crunched and a cold wind whipped into their faces. Lora found herself snug and comfortable beneath the buffalo robe, with a brick hot at her feet, and she relaxed into an enjoyment of this new experience, paying little attention to the silent man beside her.

There were starts and stops as other sleighs joined the party, and from the shelter at the ferry landing Morgan and Murray came hurrying to take their places in the Lords' sleigh. In spite of herself, Lora found her attention fixed on Wade as Morgan approached. She had to lean forward just a little to see his face and she was aware that Adam drew back at her side to give her a better view. Once more she saw the darkening surge of color beneath Wade's fair skin, saw how quickly he turned to speak to Hester as if he had not seen Morgan at all.

Unbidden, Serena's words came to mind. Serena had said Wade was afraid of Morgan. Why? For what reason, unless perhaps that he distrusted himself where she was concerned? But that was something Lora did not want to believe. Wade had truly loved Virginia. There was never any doubt about that.

Morgan, as might have been expected, had not dressed as plainly as the other women. She wore a long fur cape and carried a muff with a bunch of artificial violets pinned to it. A crocheted scarf wound her head more decoratively than the clumsy caps and mufflers of the other women and her eyes were ashine with some inner excitement. As she got into the sleigh she threw Wade no more than a careless glance and greeted him as casually as the others. Settling into the straw beside Adam, she turned a single questioning look upon Lora.

Murray Norwood had been on business in the city and had made no concessions in the way of dress. He was obliging but not exactly bubbling with gaiety as he folded his long legs beneath him next to Serena. By way of complete incongruity he wore a top hat, and Hester began to tease him about it.

"What a target for snowballs!" she cried. "You'll bring an attack upon us sure as anything!"

He gave her a slightly chill smile and pulled the buffalo robe to his chin. But he did not remove the hat. Murray Norwood fitted a drawing room far better than he did a straw-filled sleigh. It was probably a tribute to the spell Morgan had cast upon him that he was here at all.

Now the line of sleighs was mounting Richmond Turnpike, climbing the long hill toward Silver Lake. A fine misting of snow had begun again and the stars were veiled. Someone started a rollicking tune, and soon they were all singing. "Jingle Bells," of course, and other sleighing songs. Then the beautiful, but always mournful "Lorena," which had become popular with the soldiers of North and South alike. There were the inevitable war tunes, too: "Tenting Tonight" and the stirring words which Julia Ward Howe had set to the tune of the John Brown song, "The Battle Hymn of the Republic."

158

Perhaps it was the latter which started the war talk. Lora had wanted for a little while to be like the other women and forget everything but this beautiful night, and the lovely hills and valleys of Staten Island as they unfolded about the sleigh. There were woods on every hand now, with only an occasional sign of habitation. A string of small lakes shone in the starlight, with the dark form of a mill at the far end. But the talk drew her back to unhappy reality.

It was gloomy, discouraged talk. Grant had been repulsed at Vicksburg and the pattern of defeat and inaction went on.

"The draft must come soon," one captain in blue was saying. "We need men desperately. After our losses at Fredericksburg, we must draft or enlist. And enlistments have fallen off alarmingly."

Where other ladies might feel it wise to keep silent when their men talked of such matters, Morgan never hesitated to speak her mind.

"What if there is no draft?" she asked. "I've heard that Governor Seymour doesn't approve of such coercive measures."

"If there's no draft the South will beat us," said Adam.

"Perhaps not," Murray Norwood put in blandly. "Perhaps if we offer to cease hostilities, we can make terms with the South even now. I doubt that the Southern states can be eager to continue the fighting."

"Then you don't know the South," Adam said. "Why should she stop when she's got us practically on the run?"

There was a murmur of indignation and denial, and several men began to talk at once. Lora found herself watching Morgan as she listened. The sleigh had turned down the Clove Road and was nearing a section where gaslight illuminated the streets again. In the cool, greenish glare Morgan's eyes were alert and watchful, her wide mouth curved in a faint smile. Lora could not forget the picture Serena had painted in her mind of a young girl with wild hair, a nose too big for her face, and angry eyes that defied a disapproving world. Was that girl still there, hidden beneath the polished exterior of this confident and handsome woman?

Tongues were turning sharp and feeling had begun to run high on the question of the draft by the time the sleighs reached the Shore Road and the lights of the Pavilion Hotel came into view ahead. The ladies sighed with relief, glad enough to have attention come back to them, eager to put all thought of war aside for one gay night at least.

Wade had taken no active part in the debate over the

159

draft, but Lora had noted that he listened to every word and seemed to be turning the matter over in his mind. She wondered if Mr. Norwood might not succeed if he approached Wade while he was in this thoughtful mood.

She stood up with the others, brushing herself free of snow, glad to leave her slightly cramped position and return to warmth and light. In her preoccupation she might have forgotten Adam had he not been there, ready to lift her down from the sleigh. Wade had gone ahead with Hester, escorting her into the hotel—which was proper enough, since each man must look after his partner. But Lora wished she need not be left to Adam's tender mercies.

As they went toward the lighted doorway, he spoke softly in her ear. "If you keep trying to run away from me, I shall get the idea that you're afraid of me. Are you?"

She glanced up at him in annoyance. "Why should I be? As a matter of fact, I wasn't even thinking about you."

He laughed and bent toward her. "Sometimes you tempt me just a little. What if I should try to make you think of me?"

She did not trouble to answer that as they went up the steps together. This was merely Adam's reckless way of playing with danger, and she meant to give it no thought. There were more important matters demanding her attention tonight.

When the ladies had put aside their bulky wraps and emerged in hoopless gowns to rejoin the men, she was glad to see that partners were again coupled with original partners. Other sleighing parties around the island had come for the dancing tonight and the big ballroom was alive with music and whirling figures.

Morgan, Lora noted, wore no warm wool dress of modest colors like the others, but was brilliant tonight in emerald green, her shoulders bare and lovely. It did not seem to matter to her that her costume did not suit the occasion. She seemed to scorn convention and do as she pleased.

Wade, still hampered by his crutch, and in some discomfort after the cramping restrictions of the sleigh, seemed nevertheless in vastly good humor. It must have been a relief to escape from his mother's tempers for an evening. He would not hear of it that Lora should sit beside him this time throughout the dancing, and when Adam came to seek her as a partner, Wade insisted that she dance.

At least she was grateful for the fact that a figure dance was forming. Adam would have to keep his wits about him and watch his steps. The audacity of his remark about making her think of him stung more in retrospect than at the time he had said it, and she was quite ready to reprove any further boldness. She drew herself as tall as her slight height permitted and looked coolly away from the laughter in his eyes.

Tonight, though some of the same people were present, the atmosphere was very different from that of Serena's party. The crowd was more boisterous, thanks perhaps to the rougher clothes and the more informal atmosphere lent by the sleigh ride. Adam swung Lora breathlessly through the figures of the dance and when the music changed to a waltz after the more active number, he drew her into his arms without asking for the privilege.

She looked up at him, ready to utter some sharp reproof, but he returned her look with such unexpected and penetrating kindness that she faltered and held back the words.

"Just this one waltz and then I'll let you go," he said. "Smile, Lora. Turn up the corners of your mouth. Forget the things that trouble you."

She did not feel like smiling, but she let him whirl her into the graceful steps of the dance and lost herself almost sadly to the music. He did not speak until the dance was over and he was taking her back across the room toward Wade.

"I see your husband is having an interesting conversation," he said.

She saw what he meant. Wade was not alone in the line of small gilt chairs. Murray Norwood sat next to him and the two were absorbed in conversation. The two men rose as she approached and made a place for her between them. Adam bowed his thanks formally for the dance, looked straight into her eyes for an instant, and then disappeared into the crowd.

Mr. Norwood seemed not to mind her listening presence, and went on with what he had been saying. He was talking about the draft and about the one thing which might halt hostilities—a stopping of the draft before it got under way.

Wade asked the same question Lora had. "But how can any group set itself against the government to prevent the draft? That in itself would be treason."

"A strong word," Mr. Norwood said smoothly, "and not at all what is intended."

Wade was doubtful. "The government would back its order with force, naturally. Police, even the army."

"The government is not going to shoot down loyal citizens. And we would still be that."

Norwood went on quickly when Wade made a little gesture of rejection. "This is not the place or time to give you the details, Mr. Tyler. There is strong organization behind this move. If sufficient opposition is raised to the draft throughout the North the government will be helpless to enforce it. The voter's voice still counts. I ask only that you attend one of our meetings. We cannot of course admit you to the inner circle unless you decide to join us, but through the kindness of Mrs. Channing it is possible that an arrangement be made so that you can learn something of our cause."

Wade's interest was evident, and this time he did not flush angrily at the mention of Morgan's name. As she listened, Lora glanced about the room, looking for Morgan, and saw her dancing with Herbert Wylie—perhaps purposely giving Murray Norwood his opportunity with Wade.

"I still don't see what use I might be in this cause," Wade said doubtfully.

Mr. Norwood reached into his pocket and drew out a small brown object which he tossed idly in his hand. "Every man we can raise is needed. But in particular we need men of intelligence and influence."

"Influence?" Wade's laugh had a wry sound.

"Influence indeed. Mrs. Channing has told me of the time when the young bloods of the island followed your lead with some enthusiasm."

"In matters of getting up parties, perhaps. The war has sobered young blood."

Mr. Norwood opened his hand, revealing the object which lay upon the palm. "Do you know what this is?"

"A nut or acorn of some sort, I presume."

"It's a cross section of a butternut," Mr. Norwood said. He held it toward Lora. "What does the pattern resemble, Mrs. Tyler?"

She looked at it for a moment. "Why, it's a little like two hearts intertwined."

"Exactly. That is why the butternut is worn as a badge of honor out in Ohio where the movement is many thousands strong. Those intertwined hearts stand for the common people of the North and South, together as brothers. Not separated by a rich man's war, or by emotional nonsense concerning the slaves."

Lora glanced at Wade, not altogether trusting Murray Norwood's smooth manner and persuasive words. Yet—any movement to stop the war, even if one were not altogether in agreement with the ideas of the leaders, seemed worth considering. Wade, too, seemed to be weighing the matter, still not convinced. Mr. Norwood returned the butternut to his pocket. "Now is our time. The movement is already strong in the West, but only beginning here in the East. Our people at home are sick of war. The fight has gone out of our men. They are deserting in huge numbers every day. Confidence in our leadership is shaken. The papers scream alarming details of what the North has not accomplished. People are ready to accept peace on any terms. This is the time to act. If we can prevent or stop the draft, the war will be over. It *must* be over."

There was an intensity about the man which was compelling. The bright room, the sound of music and laughter faded into mere background before the fire of his sincerity.

Wade nodded thoughtfully. "I will at least come to your meeting, sir. If you will permit me, I will come and listen, but I will promise nothing more."

As the last measure of the music died, Lora saw Herbert Wylie bringing Morgan toward them across the floor. The party was moving into an adjoining room for supper now, and Lora rose with the two men. Wade was not aware of Morgan's nearness until she spoke directly to him.

"I hope you are coming in with us, Wade," she said.

Wade bowed gravely but made no promise. Morgan took Mr. Norwood's arm and they moved in the direction of the adjacent dining room.

At the table Wade found places for himself and Lora which were nowhere near Murray and Morgan. But now Wade was less quiet than on the trip out in the sleigh. She could sense again his winning charm, see why there must have been a time when he could easily draw men and women about him. Perhaps this talent had been some compensation for his mother's lack of belief in him at home.

Waiters brought steaming-hot oyster stew and the sleighing party ate with appetite and relish. There was no war talk now, but only a somewhat feverish effort to snatch at this moment of being together in this bright room where the distant roll of drums could not reach them.

Lora, however, found herself growing more quiet as the gaiety about her increased, watching rather than partaking. Adam, too, was sober, eating stolidly as if his only interest were in the food set before him. Once his eyes met Lora's and she was aware that he had noted her area of quiet, and in a sense saluted it across the table. He was no longer asking her to laugh.

After the late and leisurely supper they all piled into

sleighs again and went jangling off along the Shore Road, following the water's edge toward home, instead of cutting back across the island. This time Lora stayed close to Wade. He seemed glad to have her there within the curve of his arm as they nestled into straw that was once more warmed with hot bricks supplied by the hotel.

She was comfortably weary now, dreamily-aware that the night had cleared and a big moon which had risen overhead was silvering the dark waters of the Kill Van Kull. A few lights sparkled on the Jersey shore, and there was the sequin brightness of vessels and small craft anchored out in the Kill. The movement of the sleigh was smooth, soft-flowing, and sleigh bells sounded elfin in the night.

"Comfortable, Lora?" Wade whispered, and she nodded her head against his shoulder. It was comforting to let all disturbing matters fade away and pretend again for a little while. Pretend that she was married to someone she loved and who loved her dearly. Not Martin. She quickly shut away the thought of the past and moved closer to Wade.

She was growing drowsy now. Wade's arm was around her and for a little while she could feel safe and protected. A make-believe safety, yet she held to the warm, comforting feeling of it as she dozed.

Once, when the sleigh jolted over a rutted place where the snow had been worn through at a crossing, her eyes flew open and in the brief interval of light from a lamp she saw that Adam, next to Serena on the other side of the sleigh, was watching her. She closed her eyes quickly, refusing to rise to any challenge in his. She could even be sorry for Adam tonight. Adam had nothing, no one. Only his own bitter self to live with.

She snuggled more closely into the curve of Wade's arm. When the road grew dark she felt the touch of her husband's cheek against her own and was comforted.

XVIII

MARCH BLEW IN tempestuously, melting the snow on tree branch and hillside, reducing Staten Island roads to a sea of mud. The *Richmond County Gazette* printed the usual indignant letters of protest from readers who felt that the paving of roads was a necessity which should be postponed no longer.

In a corner of the Tyler yard the willow tree leaned with the wind, its tracery of branches streaming outward like a woman's long hair. Wind moaned down chimneys and whistled at every crack of window or door to which it could put its blustery mouth. On such a day it was good to remain inside snug and warm by a fire.

As far as Mother Tyler was concerned, the status quo within the house had remained exactly that. The old lady still kept to her bed, refused to have anyone but Wade, Peter, or Ellie come near her, and had occasional relapses over the presence of the growing puppy. She read nothing but her Bible and she quoted her Lord's words often to Wade, giving them her own stern interpretation of criticism upon this household.

Lora had been only too glad to accept banishment, though at times it made matters difficult for the rest of the house. At least there had been some escape for Wade, since the night of the sleighing party.

He had attended a meeting of the Circle at Morgan Channing's house, and while he had been thoughtful and guarded about what had happened, Lora saw that his interest had been fired. Early in March, when a mass meeting was held in New York with Clement Vallandigham as the speaker, Wade went across with Murray Norwood and Morgan. Lora would have liked to go herself, if only for the sake of some activity and excitement, but Wade said firmly that these were a man's affairs, and he preferred her to take no part.

Like Virginia, she thought rebelliously. But she would in no way disturb this new interest which sparked his life. She suspected that he did not tell his mother what he did, or where he went, and this must have added one more burr of irritation to the old woman's bed of self-inflicted pain.

Wade had come home from the New York meeting talking familiarly of "Val," apparently caught by the electric quality of this erstwhile congressman from Ohio. Vallandigham had not won re-election last fall, but he was still a leader among the Peace Democrats and there were those who whispered that he was also a leader among the Knights of the Golden Circle—in fact, that the two bore a close relationship. It was enough for Lora that Wade had come to life and seized upon a mission which kept him at least occupied, if not entirely happy.

Lora had come into the dining room this afternoon to

complete some unfinished business. Wade was out on an errand of his own and Jemmy was not yet home from school. She would perform her nefarious deed and surprise the two of them tonight at dinner.

What she would like, she thought, was to pull every shred of dreary red wallpaper off the walls of this room and start afresh. But she knew she had better approach her reformations with a less revolutionary attitude. Even a small advance at a time would do.

From its position of honor above the sideboard, the game bird hung its limp neck over a painted table, glaring at her with one dead eye.

She nodded to it cheerfully. "You've made us uncomfortable long enough. Down you shall come. And I'll find something cheerful to put in your place if I have to paint it myself."

Ellie leaned a shoulder against the dining-room door to push it open and stuck in her head. "You call me, ma'am? I thought I heard somebody talking." Her hands were covered with flour and dough from bread-making and she held one under the other to keep from dribbling bits on the floor.

"That was I you heard, Ellie," Lora said. "I was talking to his nibs up there." She gestured toward the picture on the wall.

Ellie's eyes widened and Lora laughed softly. It was better never to laugh out loud in this house, since that would set the silver bell across the hall to ringing.

"Don't worry," she said. "It's all right as long as I talk to a picture on the wall. It's when I start talking to myself that you need to be concerned."

Ellie's sense of humor was not outstanding, but since she presumed this to be some sort of joke, she cracked her thin mouth into the semblance of a smile.

Just then Mrs. Tyler's bell rang piercingly. The long winter days had somehow made its silver note grow sharper, less musical with constant use.

"Oh, Lor', ma'am!" Ellie wailed. Lately even her own devotion to Mrs. Tyler had worn a little thin. "This dough's got to be babied along now, and there she goes wanting me."

"You go back to your bread," Lora said. "I'll see what she wants."

"Better not," said Ellie, making futile wiping motions with her sticky hands. "There's a divil in her these days—pardoning the word, ma'am. Goodness knows what she'll do if *you* go in there."

166

"Nevertheless, I am going," said Lora, suddenly determined. "You just finish your bread."

The bell rang again insistently and Lora crossed the hall and opened the door which had been forbidden to her ever since Christmas.

A fire burned low in the sitting-room grate, lending some slight warmth to the bedroom beyond, and the air was stuffy with sickroom odors. The sitting room looked unlived in without the familiar figure in black in the chair before the fire. Jason Cowles's visage brooded from the wall more grimly than ever.

"Why must you take so long when I call you, Ellie?" demanded Mrs. Tyler in pettish tones from the dim bedroom.

Lora went quietly to the door. "Ellie's hands are covered with dough, Mother, so I've come to see if I can help."

The old woman was a hulk beneath the mound of quilts and in the dim light from a shuttered window Lora could just see her eyes, dark and shadowed in a white face, staring at her balefully.

"I will not have you in this room," Mrs. Tyler quavered. "Where is my son? I have given orders—"

Lora went straight to the bed and stood beside it. "There's no one else home just now. Shall I get you some water? Or your medicine?"

Tears of weak rage blurred Mrs. Tyler's eyes. "I will not be mocked when I am ill. It is not good for me to be so upset. Go away and send Ellie to me at once. I—I'm so miserably uncomfortable."

Lora ignored the outrage in the eyes that watched her, and felt beneath the bedclothes with a practiced hand. "Of course you're uncomfortable with everything bunched into a wad of wrinkles. I'll have you easy again in a jiffy."

She returned to the sitting room with no heed for the sputter of protest which followed her and came back wheeling the big leather chair before her. Then she went to the bed, released the covers gently from the clutch of Mrs. Tyler's fingers, and flung them to the end of the bed. The old woman lay shivering in her flannel nightgown, gasping at the violation.

"Now then," Lora said, "let's move fast so that you won't get chilled."

She reached for the thin hands, ringless now, and pulled the old woman to a sitting position.

"I'm too weak for this!" Mrs. Tyler wailed. "Go away, you wicked girl!"

"Of course you're weak, lying in bed all this long time. But never mind that—I'm going to have you feeling better than you've felt in a long while. Come now—over to the chair."

"I'm going to faint!" cried Mrs. Tyler.

"That's all right," said Lora. "I know just what to do for a faint. Quickly now—I won't let you fall."

She gave all her support to Mrs. Tyler's dead weight, half carrying her the few steps to the chair. Then she lowered her into it, quickly wrapped a quilt about her, tucked it around her bare feet, and turned her attention to remaking the bed. The old lady did not faint, but she watched her tormentor with eyes bright with helpless rage.

When the sheets had been pulled taut and every wrinkle banished, Lora turned cheerfully back to her charge. "I know how much you'd like to punish me, but you can't punish anyone when you let yourself go to pieces like this. If you want things your way you have to get up and fight for them. Now then, back to bed, and I'm going to give you the best back rub you've ever had. Fainting won't do you a bit of good."

There was alcohol among bottles and jars on a shelf and Lora turned the old woman quickly over on her stomach, pulled the covers up to her waist and pushed up her nightgown so that her thin back lay bare. If there was one thing Doc had taught her how to do well, it was to give a back rub to a bedridden patient. She went vigorously to work, rubbing and kneading with palms and strong fingers, seeking out nerve centers, relaxing knotted muscles.

The stiffness went gradually out of her patient, gradually the old woman relaxed and resisted Lora's hands no longer.

"You're going to feel wonderful now," Lora said. "You're even going to stop being indignant with me for helping you."

When she had completed her ministrations and had her patient covered and warm again, she hurried to the kitchen for a basin of warm water, winked at the alarmed Ellie, and returned to wash Mrs. Tyler's face and hands and comb her thin, snarled hair. Through it all, the old woman lay with her eyes tightly closed, weak, helpless, with her impotent anger fading in spite of herself.

"Gracious," said Lora, drying Mrs. Tyler's fingers, "you don't even take care of your hands any more. Do you know your hands were the first thing I noticed about you? They made me so ashamed of mine. Where's that rose water and glycerine?"

She found the bottle and made a ceremony of rubbing the lotion into drying skin and roughened knuckles.

"Now for your rings. They're in this case on the table,

aren't they? We'll have you all dressed up by the time Wade comes home. What a lovely diamond this is. I used to watch it shine in the firelight when you moved your hands. But nothing shines in this dark room. And you can't get well with no fresh air to breathe."

"Fresh air is dangerous when one is in a weakened condition," Mrs. Tyler protested.

Lora went to the window. "My father didn't hold with that idea," she said as she opened the shutters.

The March wind seized the unexpected opportunity and whooshed into the room, setting window curtains flying and book pages fluttering. Lora permitted it to play havoc for no more than a minute, and then slammed down the window right in its face. But she left the shutters open and arrows of sunlight did swift battle with the room's dark corners, lancing cheerfully from polished wood, warming bright quilt squares to life.

Mrs. Tyler drew a deep lungful of cold fresh air and shuddered through her entire being.

"Now what do you plan, may I ask?" she demanded fiercely of her tormentor.

Lora laughed out loud. "There! I knew I'd have you feeling better. You sound practically like yourself. Would you like to sit up in bed for a while and read? Here's your Bible on the table and I'll fix the lamp for you. You may have your bell back now and I'll return to my own work."

"Work?" Mrs. Tyler echoed. "What work?"

Lora paused in the bedroom door. "Right now I'm taking that dreadful picture of a dead bird off the dining-room wall. I'm sure it is giving us all indigestion."

Mrs. Tyler pulled herself up in bed. "I will *not* have that picture touched! Do you hear me? That painting—"

Lora put her hands saucily on her hips. "How can you stop me if you stay tied to your bed?"

She whirled out of the room and returned to her task, tingling from the encounter. She set a newspaper on a chair and climbed up to take the picture from the wall. She was holding the thing in her hands when Jemmy came running in, just home from school. Usually he went straight through the house and around to the yard where Hamlin had a home in the stable. But when he saw the dining-room door ajar and Lora balancing on a chair with the picture in her hands, he came in to find out what she was doing.

"Hello, Jemmy." Lora held up the picture for him to see.

169

"This is not going to stare at us any more while we're eating," she told him.

His eyes widened. "What will Grandmother say?"

"She has already said it. Oh dear—there's a dark blotch on the wall where the picture has hung for so long. We'll have to find something right away to cover it. Have you any ideas, Jemmy?"

"We could take a picture from somewhere else," he suggested. "Maybe the one of the Parthenon from the library. But then I suppose that would leave a spot on the wall there. Or that Three Graces one from my room. I'm awfully tired of that. Or—Lora, I know! There's a lot of old stuff in the attic. Pictures, too, I think. We could go up there and find something."

Lora handed him the picture and got down from the chair. "Fine—if you'll help me. Do you want to go tell Hamlin you're home first?"

He ran out to the yard and was back again while Lora was getting a shawl from her room. Jemmy showed her a door in the upper hall that opened onto ladder steps and she brought a candle to light their way. He went first to push up the trap door and climbed ahead into darkness.

"Ooh, it's shivery up here!" he cried. "Hurry, Lora, bring up the candle."

She climbed to the top of the ladder, kicking back her skirts lest she trip, and set the candleholder on the door. Then she climbed the last steps into attic space. The roof pitched upward in dark beams above them, and Jemmy's shadow sprang up the wall, long-legged and grotesque. All around were gathered the collections of generations past. Trunks and boxes, pieces of broken furniture, piles of discarded books. It was an orderly array, however, as was to be expected in Amanda Tyler's house.

On a wall rack were set several guns and some pistols and Jemmy regarded them with interest.

"My grandfather—Papa's father—used to go hunting quite often. Those are his guns. They used to keep the ammunition up here too, but once I tried to load a pistol and after that Papa hid every bit of it. Of course I'm older now and I know I'm not supposed to touch guns, though Adam lets me sometimes."

He found the pictures stacked with their faces against the wall. While Lora brought her candle over and held it close, Jemmy acted as showman, turning frame after frame out from

170

the wall. There was a grim print of the stabbing scene from *Hamlet*, and a fiercesome one of Lady Macbeth sleep-walking.

The latter fascinated Jemmy, but he agreed that it would be no better than the bird for a dining-room decoration. There was a still life of fruit which might have been more suitable, except that the painted articles bore little resemblance to reality.

"Morgan Le Fay painted that," said Jemmy. "I guess she used to paint quite a lot when she was a young girl. I can remember a much better one than this."

He turned another half-dozen candidates around and then brought out a garden scene, with a stiff little girl in flounced skirts daintily sniffing a spray of lilac.

"There! This is the one Aunt Morgan did when she was older. That's my mother in the garden. Mama liked it. She used to have it hanging in the downstairs hall. Let's put this one up, Lorie."

Lora regarded the picture with some doubt. True, it was bright and gay, and if the hand which painted it had been less than expert, it was still preferable to the picture of dead game. But she did not want to hang a picture of Virginia, even when it so little resembled Virginia, where they must all look at it every day. Especially since that picture had been painted by her sister Morgan. But how was she to explain the matter diplomatically to Jemmy?

She held the candle high, playing for time, and its flame wavered and guttered as wind buffeted the house, wailing gustily through attic cracks.

"We don't have to decide now, anyway, Jemmy. I'm getting cold up here. If the space goes empty for a while it won't really matter. Perhaps you can go to New York with me soon and then we'll find something together that will be just right."

Jemmy shook his head. "I think this one's fine. Lorie, when it's warmer do you suppose we could come up here and look in some of the trunks? Just for fun."

"I don't see why not. We'll ask your father if we may. But, Jemmy—about that picture—"

He was already lugging it toward the stairs, however. "I like this one. Let's go down, Lorie. It's cold."

She started after him uncertainly, wishing now that she had never tampered with the picture until she had another ready to take its place.

"Of course your mother liked the picture, because Morgan was her sister. But we can't expect your father to like it as

171

much when it isn't a very good painting. You know how he—well, he doesn't exactly approve of your Aunt Morgan."

"Oh, yes he does," Jemmy said, resting the frame on the floor near the trap door. "He likes her a lot, really. Else why would he be kissing her the way he did that day in the woods? Bring your candle for the stairs, Lorie."

She followed him, stricken. This was just the talk of a small boy. Jemmy had a vivid imagination at times and didn't always distinguish between truth and fantasy. But she had to ask the question that came to her tongue.

"When did this happen, Jemmy? How long ago?"

He answered her guilelessly. "Oh, it was way last year—no, before that. Before my mother—" He broke off and started down the steep flight ahead of her, still carrying the picture.

She went after him, blowing out the candle as she reached the bottom step, and closed the door carefully behind her. She kept her voice steady, casual, as she asked the next question.

"Can you remember, Jemmy, whether you ever told anyone about this?"

"I told my mother," Jemmy said, his interest still on the painting. "Lorie, I *like* this picture. If you don't think it's right for the dining room, could I have it in my room, please? Could that old Three Graces one go down in the dining room for now?"

"A very good idea," Lora said, relieved to have the problem so easily settled.

They went into his room to remove the old picture and hang Morgan's water color in its place. All the while Lora kept a careful guard on her thoughts, her expression, her words. Not for a moment must Jemmy suspect the turmoil within her. When Jemmy sat down on his bed to admire the painting in its new place, Lora, carrying out the one he disliked, paused in the doorway.

"Did your mother say anything special when you told her?"

"Anything about what?" asked Jemmy blankly. "Oh—you mean about Papa and Morgan Le Fay in the woods? She just said she was glad Papa liked Aunt Morgan. The hollyhocks in the picture are especially nice, don't you think? Do you like hollyhocks, Lorie?"

"I love them," said Lora, and carried the Three Graces down to the dining room.

Jemmy did not come with her this time and she climbed upon the chair, held the picture experimentally over the darkened spot on the wall. It wasn't quite right, but it would do for now. She slid the wire over the hook until it was exactly balanced. Then she stepped down from the chair and stood off to study the three rather buxom Graces without really seeing them at all.

It was as if she feared that the moment she stopped working actively at something, stopped pretending to be busy, a whole dark field of thought might engulf her, and she was afraid of what it might bring.

If Jemmy had actually come upon his father in a love scene with Morgan Channing in the woods, if he had told his mother innocently enough—what had this knowledge meant to Virginia?

Lora crossed the room to French doors that opened upon a little side veranda, and stood looking out upon whipping branches and dry leaves tumbling across the yard. This house, tucked against the hillside, had some shelter, but how wild and windy it must be today up on Morgan's hilltop.

The thoughts swept back, engulfing her. Serena had said there had been some whisper of suicide. But she wouldn't, she mustn't think of that. How terrible would then be the blame heaped upon Wade. Had Jemmy told his father? she wondered. Did Wade dream of what Virginia knew? Lora was sure that whatever had happened had been Morgan's doing, yet Wade could not be completely exonerated. If this was the burden he carried in secret—the fear that his wife, because of his own action—!

No wonder he detested Morgan, did not trust her. But surely Virginia must have known what her sister was like. Surely she would have put no stock in Jemmy's words. Not when she was so confident and sure of Wade's devotion.

Or had she been? What depth of attraction existed between Wade and Morgan to have burned anew after the passing of so many years? Had it perhaps never died out entirely?

Carriage wheels crunched upon the drive. That would be Wade now, coming home. She ran upstairs to her own room. Not until she had sorted these troubling thoughts into some semblance of order could she face him again. He must not read this guilty knowledge in her eyes.

XIX

AFTER DINNER that night Mrs. Tyler summoned Ellie to her room to assist her into the wheel chair for the first time in weeks. She ordered a fire built in her sitting-room grate and had herself wheeled into the dining room where she could see exactly what vandal's act had taken place behind her back. Having looked at the substitute picture, she sent for Wade, lecturing him thoroughly and then asked for Lora.

Lora had been pretending to read in the library when Wade came to fetch her. The look on his face as he came in was reassuring.

"What on earth have you done to Mother?" he asked. "She ate a whopping good dinner in her room and now she's ready to lick her weight in wildcats. She seems to be spitting mad at you and enjoying life thoroughly."

Lora released her breath in a long sigh. "Thank goodness! All I did was give her a good back rub, bully her a little, and tell her if she wanted to run this house her own way she'd have to get up and do it."

"Well, she's up—and you're in for it," Wade said. "She wants to talk to you right now. And I'm coming along to watch. But don't count on any help from me. This is your party."

He squeezed her arm lightly as they went down the hall to Mother Tyler's sitting room and she knew he was not displeased.

The old lady was once more in her easy chair by the fire, its high wings hiding her face as Lora entered. Her hands lay folded in her lap, atwinkle with the rings Lora had set upon them that afternoon, and she held a lace handkerchief daintily between two fingers.

"Good evening, Mother," Lora said. "I'm glad to see you up and looking so well tonight."

"Thanks to you, it's a wonder I'm not in my grave," the old lady said tartly. "Sit down and stop staring at me." She looked at Wade. "Nearly froze me to death this afternoon, she did, and tried to break all my bones."

"Evidently it's done you good," Wade said.

Lora took the chair opposite her, smiling faintly. Amanda

174

Tyler could no longer frighten or intimidate her. Not since Lora had felt this day the dry, aging flesh beneath her fingers, turned the frail body in bed, treated her like any other bedridden patient. Now she knew the vulnerability of Amanda Tyler's flesh.

Wade drew up another chair and waited, like a spectator at a play. The performance, as he must have known, lay between these two women and needed no interference from him.

"I have been in the dining room," Mrs. Tyler went on, "and I have seen that ridiculous print you've put in place of the excellent game painting which hung there before. I will not have three such simpering ninnies looking down at me from my dining-room wall."

Lora said mildly, "It was the best Jemmy and I could find."

"Well, it won't do. On your next shopping trip to New York I shall expect you to get something more suitable in the way of flowers or fruit."

"Yes, Mother," Lora said, her lips twitching.

"Mind you, that game bird painting is a fine one. My husband paid a large sum for it. It was the sort of thing he liked. But by this time I believe it has earned its worth in service. As a matter of fact, I always detested the thing. But I do not like to see good money wasted."

The audience was plainly over, and Mother Tyler turned her attention to a heap of papers on the table beside her.

"Everything has been neglected, Wade. Everything. I want Mr. Niles here tomorrow without fail. There are a number of matters I wish to discuss with him."

She said nothing at all about Jemmy's dog. Indeed, there was no mention of it then, or at any time in the next few weeks. Mrs. Tyler's recent illness was ignored by herself and never mentioned by other members of the household. The only difference from the old life was that sometime during each day Lora went down to the old lady's room and gave her a vigorous alcohol rub. There was little conversation between them during these occasions. Weak flesh surrendered to ministering hands, and for that little while there was no question about who was in control. At all other times, however, Mrs. Tyler was again herself, despotic and demanding. But Lora no longer felt the sting. She had somehow placed herself beyond the reach of Mother Tyler's whiplash.

Wade too escaped to some extent these days, being caught up in an active part in Murray Norwood's plans. He had substituted a cane for a crutch by now and got around with much greater ease. Lora knew he still suffered from his wounds at times, as he probably would all his life. But at least he had an active interest now and there had been no recent retreat into the dark room at the front of the house.

One April morning Lora awoke to find that a thick bank of fog had moved in from the sea to envelop Staten Island. When she stepped outside after breakfast she found that the day was almost balmy and that a little breeze stirred the mist into drifting shapes along Dogwood Lane. It was so warm that she needed only a shawl for a walk today. She was eager to explore this secret mist-wreathed world and set out briskly.

There had been little rain and the road was dry and rutted. Lora walked aimlessly, ready to follow any whim. There was a lift to her steps in response to the feeling in the air that anything might happen—a feeling that was part of the coming of spring.

These days everything was so much better at the Tyler house than she had ever thought it could be. Lately Wade had even returned to his writing in the library, and it was good to see him busy and occupied. If her own place in his life was a quiet one which required little of her, she was all the more grateful to have it so. If they could be friends and comrades, that was enough and she served some purpose in life.

The troublesome thoughts that had haunted her for a while after Jemmy's revelation had faded to the background of her mind. Such matters which belonged to the past were better forgotten. Understanding them could not change what had gone before. Let old wounds heal and old griefs die. The important thing was not to prod the wounds anew.

A sea breeze parted drifting mist along the road and a tall black skeleton chimney emerged from the new-budding branches around it. The old Hume place. Lora had always wanted to explore it—and when could there be a more suitable time than now when it was touched by soft fog fingers of mystery? Always before the place had been too cold or too damp for such exploration. Today was perfect.

Lora had worn her old brown dress without the restraint of hoops, and now she gathered up her skirts and hopped across the ditch that separated road from ruin. Once there had been a carriage drive bridging the ditch, but water running down the hill had worn a channel through.

Traces of the old driveway were still to be seen beneath encroaching grass and the rank overgrowth of weeds. Lora

176

picked her way between a bush that would burst into white snowball blooms and a hydrangea, unbeautiful now with its lack of blossoms, and tripped over something hidden beneath the grass. As she bent to see what it was, a faint shiver ran through her. Once an iron fence had stood here. There were still rusting portions which had fallen flat and lost themselves in the undergrowth. Immediately beneath her foot lay a spike of iron. The picture Serena had drawn for her of the happenings at her fifteenth birthday party flashed back and Lora pulled her foot away and went on hastily.

A flight of five steps mounted upward, with a graceful arch of doorway above them. Steps which led nowhere, a doorway into emptiness. At either side stretched the remains of crumbling, blackened walls. Even nearby objects wavered in the mist, their colors deadened in the gray light, changing their outlines even as she looked. Beyond the empty doorway where mist rolled in billows there was nothing—as though you might step from doorway into empty space.

For just a moment Lora experienced a feeling she'd had sometimes as a child. One shivered at the unknown, yet enjoyed the shiver, aware that it was only imagination which formed strange shapes and figures, at the same time half believing they were real. Lora went up the steps and paused beneath the arch. There was a little platform of brick here, and then a dropping away into what was now a grass-grown interior. She felt for the ground with one foot and then slipped down into the cup of mist gathered among the ruins. Here the new grass, bright with the upsurge of spring, was like velvet beneath her feet as she began to trace her way through the outlines of what once had been rooms.

There were only heaps of rubble, a few charred timbers where interior walls had stood, but she could still make out the shape of rooms, the doorway openings. Where a blackened chimney rose, still firm and strong, a hearth lay open to mist and wind, with the broken marble of a mantle above it. The sight was somehow more lonely than all else.

Long ago a family had lived here. They had laughed and loved, quarreled, died. Wade as a little boy had spent hours between these walls. So must Morgan and Virginia. Serena and Adam had lived here. Perhaps if she listened intently she could hear the echo of old laughter, old tears. She might even hear Wade's cry as he fell from the fence that dreadful day. For this, surely, was a haunted place.

But only the distant sound of foghorns and whistles from

177

the harbor broke the listening silence and the ruin lay hushed and quiet about her.

On a warm and sunny day unhaunted by mist, this might be a place to come with Jemmy if she wanted to get him back into the pleasant habit of reading aloud outdoors. They could bring an old quilt and spread it in the shadow of the chimney, have this wild, lonely place to themselves, read to their heart's content. Reading aloud had been so much a pleasure of her own childhood that she wanted to share it again with another child. Perhaps such a sharing would bring about a closer understanding between herself and Jemmy.

The misty air was brighter now, and there was a luminous glow touching it from above. Soon the sun would dispel the mist and this would no longer be a place of memories and mystery.

Still exploring, she started through a broken doorway, her skirts brushing over bright new grass, catching on the reaching branch of a sassafras bush which had sprung up in this once forbidden area. She bent to release her skirt from the reaching twig and felt the hard little nubs of bursting life against the dry wood.

Her fingers moved along the nubby twig, her imagination already envisoning the full blooming of spring that lay only a little while ahead. She must watch for it this year. She must be conscious with all her senses of the tiny unfurling of leaves, of the delicate tracery of color that would burst into lush growth in so short a time. This was a magic not to be taken casually for granted as it had been in the past. Perhaps it was this sudden awareness of the awakening life about her that made her catch the tiny flash of gold beneath the bush which had snatched at her skirt.

She knelt and reached beneath the branches. Some small piece of metal it was. Perhaps a forgotten possession of those who had lived in this house before the fire. She held the circlet on her palm and turned toward a gleam of sunlight slanting through the fading mist. It was a hoop of gold hung from a small gold hub, with fine gold wires which had fastened into a pierced ear lobe. A gold hoop earring. She recognized it at once—she had seen a pair such as this and remembered them well. This was Rebecca's earring.

But how had it come to this place? At some time in the weeks since Lora had last seen Rebecca with this very ring swinging against her brown cheek, she must have come to this ruin. The ring must have slipped from her ear without her knowing it, so that she had come away without it. But why had she been here in the first place?

178

Lora moved out of the ruins and back to the road where mist still rolled before the breeze, thinning now, preparing to lift altogether. Still pondering the puzzle of the earring, she walked slowly up the road toward the woods path that led uphill to Morgan's house. Perhaps she would climb the hill and return this hoop to Rebecca. Providing, of course, that it could be managed without Morgan's knowledge. Somehow, Lora suspected that Morgan would not approve of the girl's mooning about in old ruins. Yet why should Rebecca not do just as Lora herself had done, if the spirit moved her —wander in the woods, explore? What else had she to do with her spare time?

There was a sound of footsteps on the road and Lora looked up from the bit of jewelry in her hand. Her fingers closed over the earring to hide it and she walked more briskly, as if there were real purpose behind her steps.

Out of the mist before her a man loomed suddenly, and of the two, he was the more startled. His skin, darker than Rebecca's, bespoke his blood, and he wore the rough clothes of a workman from the docks. There was anxiety in the look he turned upon Lora, though he dropped his gaze quickly and touched his finger to his cap in greeting.

"'Morning, ma'am," he said, and went quickly by while her answering good morning followed him. She glanced at the gold earring and then thoughtfully after the tall figure disappearing into the mist. Had Rebecca a friend after all? Had there perhaps been rendezvous held in the ruins of the old Hume house? But she must jump to no hasty conclusions. The man's presence on the road very likely meant no more than some mission to the Lords' or the Channings'. Nevertheless, the look in the man's eyes, so hastily hidden, remained to be considered. Lora turned onto the path, her decision made, and hurried uphill through the woods.

XX

LORA EMERGED UPON the high curve of the lane where sunshine glowed bright and golden on the sea of mist below. The tall columns of the Channing house made white exclamation points of grace in the shimmering light.

Hamlin's mother barked as Lora approached and John

Ambrose came out the door of the cottage by the gate. He smiled when he saw her.

"Good morning, Lora. A fine day it's going to be, now that the mist is burning off. If you've come to see Mrs. Channing, I'm afraid she's still abed. But I can send Rebecca—"

Lora shook her head. "It's not Mrs. Channing I've come to see, but you, John. I'm what my father used to call busting with curiosity. There are so many things I want to know about."

"Fine, then," he said. "Let's have a talk right now, if you don't mind coming into my small place."

He led the way up the steps of the stone cottage where he evidently had his living quarters separate from the big house. Lora stepped into a bright, cozy room where a fire burned in the big stone fireplace and light poured in at every window. The furnishings were plain, with no woman-touches to be seen. A long deal table without cloth, where breakfast dishes still waited, stood in the middle of the floor. There were several straight wooden chairs, and two somewhat battered rockers, one of which John Ambrose pulled toward the hearth for Lora. Under a window stood a wooden sink with a pump beside it. Simple enough quarters, but comfortable for a man who lived alone. Strange, nevertheless, when he was the father of the woman who lived so comfortably in the great empty house at the hilltop.

Perhaps he read her thoughts as he added a log to the fire. "I could have rooms up there if I liked," he said. "But for me this is more what I'm used to, more comfortable. I dress as I like, come and go as I please, and there's none to bother or fuss because I wear no long tails or high hat."

Lonely though, Lora could not help but think. And surely not what Virginia would have wanted for him. Where had he and his wife lived when Virginia was first married? she wondered.

She rocked comfortably for a few moments, the earring still hidden in her hand. Ambrose began clearing the table, carrying dishes to the sink. She was glad that he chose to keep busy while she sat there sorting her thoughts.

"You've done a lot for the Tyler household," he said, pumping water into a pan. "Jemmy tells me you've even got *her* sitting up again running things."

Lora nodded. "Was Mrs. Tyler always like this? I mean so domineering and—and sometimes unreasonable?"

"She has a lot of her pa in her," Ambrose said, rubbing a cloth over a big homemade cake of brown soap. "Old Jason

180

Cowles was all iron and nails and I guess she took after him pretty much. Too bad she couldn't have taken after him till more—they'd have both of 'em liked that. I mean if she'd been a boy."

"I know. I'm surprised sometimes at the way she thinks like a man about business and the war and outside affairs. It's a wonder she ever married. And yet she can also behave like a spoiled, petulant woman."

Ambrose paused with a big white coffee cup in his hands and looked out the window absently. "There was always plenty of woman in her, in spite of the way her pa tried to tamp it out and make her all man. Those rings she wears and the way she keeps her hands so nice. But mostly the woman part got buried where you couldn't see it so easy."

"Was she unattractive as a girl?"

"Well—maybe to some. She got the idea in her head that she was too plain for any man to like, and anyway her pa kept 'em all away from her. Maybe that's how she came to fall so hard for the first fellow who came along after he died."

"I saw her husband's picture in the parlor," Lora mused. "He looked like a handsome, reckless sort of person. I've wondered what he saw in her and she in him, when they were so different."

Ambrose snorted and began rescouring the cup. "What would he see—a fellow like that!—except all the money behind her? And she an innocent about men's ways, for all that she was in her thirties and knew shipping and banks inside out."

"I believe you like her," Lora said softly.

He looked around at her then, his eyes as sharply blue as Temmy's beneath grizzled brows. "I have liked her for a good many years, ma'am," he said simply, humbly.

Oddly shamed, Lora turned from his direct gaze and began studying a rough bookshelf set up beside the fireplace. There were several well-worn volumes on it and she read their titles curiously. Something by Benjamin Franklin, a collection of Emerson's essays, a volume by Matthew Arnold, and some titles by Sir Walter Scott. She knew now where Temmy must hold his visits with his grandfather—here in this very room with its books and serene atmosphere. She was beginning to understand the keynote of this man to which she had responded from the first. It was a quiet response that had nothing of despair or defeat in it, which refused to become overwrought by any contact with the tempests of the world. Undoubtedly John Ambrose had sailed

181

stormy seas before he had reached this haven of quiet where the hurricane could no longer rock him.

"I'm sorry," Lora said at last. "I've seen Mrs. Tyler only as someone who has hurt Wade and Jemmy—not as a woman who has been hurt herself."

Ambrose had gone back to his dishwashing. "I'm not standing up for the hurting things she does to people," he went on. "It's just that I can't forget the day when she came back from her honeymoon with Jack Tyler and began to live as a bride in that house where she'd grown up under her father's thumb. It didn't take long for Mr. Jack to show his colors. But how could she have known what to expect when she'd pretended all her life not to care for men, and when they cared so little for her? She was an easy mark for the first fortune hunter to spot her. And once they were married, he didn't keep up the pretty ways that had won her. He held the purse strings then, according to law, and he could do as he liked. So he filled the house with his dogs and his friends and his liquor. He even started bringing women in when he was drunk enough. But the second time that happened I knocked him down and he didn't try that again. Not in her house, anyway."

Lora looked at the old man in surprise. He smiled at her expression and dumped out his pan of water.

"You're wondering why he didn't fire me? Well, to tell the truth, he did. But me and my family just stayed on for a while and he let things drift. Besides, when it came to a real scrap, I think he was always just a mite scared of that wife of his. Mostly she shut herself in her own rooms and had nothing to do with him. But one time when he tried to interfere with something she wanted to do about Wade, she told him to keep hands off or she'd take one of his own guns and deal with him for certain. Scared him good, I guess. Even scared me, for fear she'd really do something crazy like that. Maybe that's why he didn't make firing me stick. She wouldn't have it and he'd learned to know a brick wall when he saw one."

"What a terrible childhood for Wade," Lora said sadly.

Ambrose wiped a cup and hung it neatly on a hook in the cupboard nearby. "Worse than you can guess, ma'am. Because, while he wasn't like either of his parents, he was more like his father than he was like her. But she was bound she could change nature and turn him into the spittin' image of old Jason, his grandfather. Everything he was good at she made nothing of, and she nagged and prodded and pushed all the time to turn him into what he wasn't. Even his papa

ot sorry for the boy sometimes, but he didn't dare interfere,
nd anyway he wasn't much for the father stuff—not him. I
ever saw a little tyke who needed to be loved more than
at Wade boy. He did fine, too, away from home. Girls al-
ays liked him and lots of the boys did too—except the real
oughnecks. He was plenty smart when he forgot that his
other thought he was stupid. Outside, people listened to
im and made a lot of him. And he warmed to that the way
emmy warms to you."

"Virginia listened to him, didn't she?" Lora asked gently.

His back was to her and he didn't speak for a minute. He
ung up his dish towel and came toward the fireplace.

"Virginia thought he was Apollo and Lancelot and Abe-
rd rolled into one. But I guess he didn't believe all that
imself. Maybe in a way he was leaning on her belief, in-
ead of his own. That's why you're good for him—he's be-
inning to find out he has some belief in himself after all."

"But am I good for him?" Lora murmured. "I hadn't
ought of it like that."

He reached toward the mantelpiece for a pipe in a cracked
owl, then remembered his company and drew back his hand.

"Please smoke," Lora said quickly. "My father always
moked a pipe. I like it."

He took the pipe down and packed it with tobacco, held
taper to the fire and lighted the fragrant weed. Then he
rew the other rocker up to the fire beside her.

"One thing I can't understand," Lora said, "is why Wade
hould include you in his feud with Morgan."

"That's simple enough," Ambrose rocked for a moment
nd drew on his pipe. "He offered me a home in his house
fter we lost Virginia. My wife had died a while back. But I
ecided to stay with Morgan. Funny thing, Lora—maybe it
nakes no sense, but no matter how much of everything Mor-
an's got these days, I still feel like I need to be around,
tanding by. Just in case what she's got doesn't turn out to
e enough after all."

"I'm sure she doesn't appreciate that."

"It makes no matter. Something inside me bids me do this.
But you can guess how much it peeved Wade. He wanted
othing to do with her, and when I chose to make my home
ere, he was mad enough to include me in the way he felt
bout her."

"Thank you for telling me these things," Lora said. "I'm
ot prying idly—I want so much to understand. Serena has
old me a few things too. So has Jemmy. And even Morgan.

I can fit all the bits and pieces together and begin to see the pattern. But, John, I'd hate to feel that human beings can only be what they are *made* to be. I don't want to believe that Wade, or Jemmy, or Mother Tyler, or I can only be part of a set pattern that was fixed in the beginning."

"I know what you mean, Lorie," he said.

Her eyes blurred at the sound of the name he must have picked up from Jemmy. Hearing him use it was like hearing it on Doc's lips.

Ambrose reached toward the bookcase beside him and pulled a volume from the shelf. "Just the same, Lorie, there's a weaving to start with we can't much help. There's a casting of the colors and a starting of the pattern that we've nothing to say about. Something's handed us and we have to go on with it. But the going on is up to us."

He paged through the book and she saw that it was by Matthew Arnold.

"Listen, Lorie," he said.

"The will is free:
Strong is the Soul and wise and beautiful:
The seeds of godlike power are in us still:
Gods are we, Bards, Saints, Heroes, if we will."

Lora sat very still and the words seemed to echo in the room long after Ambrose had closed the book. His voice had not been made for reading as was Wade's. His words lacked any cultured cadence, but she sensed wisdom in this man and a simple goodness.

A log fell with a small crash in the grate and Lora came back to the present with a start and felt the circle of gold still held within her palm. She uncurled her fingers and showed the earring to John Ambrose.

"I found this in the woods today. I think it belongs to Rebecca."

He nodded. "She'll be glad to have it back. Her mother gave her that pair long ago, she said. She felt bad about losing one of them."

"I found it in the ruins of the Hume house," Lora told him.

Ambrose puffed on his pipe, but did not look at her.

"I wonder what Rebecca is really like," Lora said. "I don't think Morgan regards her as a person at all."

"You'd like to return the earring to her yourself, wouldn't you?" Ambrose asked. "Suppose I go look for the girl and send her here. Won't take me a minute."

184

She waited while he went out of the room. Once she got up and looked through the windows on the downhill side. But the woods shut off the view and there was only the cool brown of clustered maple and oak across the road.

Rebecca's step in the doorway was so light she might not have heard her entry had not the door squeaked as the girl closed it. She stood there with her back against it, bright in her usual gay plumage, looking at Lora guardedly. Against her cheeks hung hoops of tortoise shell.

"Mr. Ambrose says you want to see me, ma'am," the girl murmured.

Lora tried to make her smile reassuring. "Good morning, Rebecca. Come in and sit down, won't you?"

The dark eyes gave her a quick, bright look of suspicion as Rebecca came into the room. Reluctantly she seated herself on the very edge of a chair and waited for whatever might come next.

"I found your gold earring this morning," Lora said. She leaned toward the girl, extending it on her palm. "It was under a bush in the old Hume place."

"Oh!" Rebecca gasped. "We looked all over for it." She took the earring while mingled relief and pleasure flashed briefly across her face. Then it was dark and shuttered again. "I reckon I'd better go back now. Mrs. Channing will be needing me real soon. Thank you for finding this, ma'am."

Lora watched her helplessly. She wanted to offer her help if Rebecca needed it. Yet there was no way to get past her suspicion, her distrust. At least she had betrayed something when she had used the word "we."

"I'm glad you've found a friend," Lora said gently.

Rebecca clasped her hands together, the earring pressed between her palms. "Mrs. Channing doesn't want me to—to have—friends. You don't know how Mrs. Channing gets when she's mad."

"Mrs. Channing can't keep you from having some sort of social life," Lora protested.

"She can if she wants."

"But you're not a slave. You can do as you like. It's not for me to interfere, but if you wanted to leave her employ tomorrow you could easily get work elsewhere."

Rebecca shook her head. "I can't leave. She'd make real bad trouble. Besides, she pays me more than I'd get most places."

"What can you do with money if you have no life of your own?"

"I can't—" Rebecca stopped, but this time her eyes met Lora's searchingly, not as a servant's but as the eyes of another woman looking for an assurance that she could trust.

"I'd like to help you, Rebecca," Lora told her. "If there's anything I can do—"

For the first time her sincerity seemed to penetrate the other girl's guard. Rebecca spoke softly, in a little rush of words.

"I'm saving to buy freedom for my mother and my little sister, ma'am. They're still back home and they belong to Mrs. Channing. But she said she'd sell them to me if I save my money. That is, if I'm a good girl and do just like she wants."

For a moment Lora was at a complete loss for words. What a brutal weapon to hold over the girl's head, to cow her with, and make her a chattel. Why should Morgan want to do so cruel a thing? Besides, she was a Northern woman—she had no right to talk of buying and selling human beings.

"You need pay no attention to that now," Lora assured her. "President Lincoln has freed all slaves in the states that are fighting against us. So your mother is free. She can come here any time."

Rebecca shook her head disbelievingly. "Mrs. Channing says the President's Proclamation don't rightly mean much. She says it won't mean much unless the North wins the war. And the way she thinks, the North isn't going to win."

Unexpectedly a flash of denial went through Lora. "Of course the North must win!"

The thought surprised her. Until now she had believed her whole being to be set against war itself, wanting neither side to win. This unexpected upsurge of loyalty for the cause of the North indicated a change of which she had been unaware. She recovered herself and went on.

"I'm going to see about this, Rebecca. I'm going to see if I can find some way to help."

The girl twisted her hands nervously. "Mrs. Channing says she'll sell them quick as a wink if she thinks I'd try anything. No'm, Mrs. Tyler—I guess my way's right for me. It'll take a long while, I reckon, but—" Her words were lost in the sudden opening of the door.

The hand which had pushed it open was plainly an angry one, and Lora turned in her rocker to see Mrs. Channing herself in the doorway. Morgan had flung a wool mantle over her wrapper and nightdress, her dark hair hung thick and heavy over her shoulders, and there was wrath in her eyes. She took in the tête-à-tête before Rebecca could rise from her chair, her indignation centering upon the colored girl, ignoring Lora.

"So I am to ring for a half hour in the morning without being answered?" she cried. "When I go in search of you, Clothilde tells me you are down here. What is the meaning of this? You are having your morning tea, perhaps? Or perhaps you are entertaining the neighbors in your own right?"

Rebecca said nothing. She stood submissively before her mistress with downcast eyes. Lora had been too shocked by the outburst to move, but now she too rose to her feet.

"Good morning," she said, trying with her calm greeting to draw Morgan back to quiet and reason. "You mustn't blame Rebecca for this. It is entirely my fault and—"

"It is no one's fault but Rebecca's," Morgan snapped, not troubling to glance in Lora's direction. "She knows where she is to be in the morning when I waken. She knows her duties exactly. But lately I've noted some uppitiness and I won't stand for it an instant. These people must be kept in their place. Well—what have you to say, Rebecca?"

The colored girl hesitated a moment, then held out her palm with the gold earring upon it. "Mrs. Tyler found this one—on the path and brought it to me. Mr. Ambrose told me to come down here and see her, ma'am."

"And are you in Mr. Ambrose's employ or mine? Mrs. Tyler's or mine?"

"Yours, ma'am," said Rebecca in a low voice.

"Give me the earring," Morgan commanded. "I've never liked that pair anyway."

Rebecca made no move to obey. She stood like a woman of bronze, scarcely breathing.

"Please listen, Morgan," Lora pleaded. "I understand that Rebecca's mother gave her that pair of earrings. It's natural that she should treasure them and be glad to have the missing one back. If I had known I was interfering with your rising time—"

"Give it to me!" Morgan repeated.

Rebecca took a step backward and put her hand behind her. For the first time she raised her eyes and looked at Morgan directly, not as servant at mistress, but gaze for gaze, as woman to woman.

"Such impudence!" cried Morgan. Her hand flew up and struck the colored girl a resounding smack across the cheek. Rebecca's golden skin turned ashy, except for the place

187

where dark blood surged up beneath the blow. But she stood proudly and her eyes did not falter.

Lora went to the girl's side and touched her arm gently. "Go now, please. Fix Mrs. Channing's tea, or whatever you must do." She squeezed her arm gently, secretly, impressing her friendship. At her touch Rebecca turned and went from the room, moving with her usual soft and graceful step.

Morgan stood where she was, angry, distraught, unbeautiful now with her skin rage-mottled, her nostrils distended. Without speaking, Lora reached for her shawl and flung it about her shoulders.

"Good day, Mrs. Channing," she said formally, and went toward the door.

Morgan seemed to see her for the first time, and for the first time to be uncertain. "Wait, Lora! It wasn't your fault, of course. Though I should think you would know better than to take the side of one of her kind."

Lora said nothing. She opened the door and went through it without a backward glance. John Ambrose came quickly to open the gate for her and she knew that he surmised what might have happened.

"Don't let her do anything to Rebecca," Lora whispered as she went through the gate.

The old man shook his head sadly, and it was not in promise. "I've never in my life been able to keep that one from her headlong ways. I'm sorry, Lora."

She went down the hill slowly. The sun was high and warm now—a true spring day bestowed as a gift before May was here to sanction spring's appearance. The breeze that had blown the mist away rippled the surface of the little pool in the woods. A soft, rippling motion sped across the surface. Like quicksilver, Lora thought, remembering Jemmy's words.

She stood beside the water, thinking unhappily of the scene which had just been enacted on the hilltop. The young Morgan of long ago who had turned in a rage to kick down a house of twigs and then teetered her way recklessly along an iron fence was still there, untamed, beneath the present Morgan's polish. Such rages were something Lora had never witnessed and even the memory made her a little sick. Perhaps there could be an illness of the spirit, just as there was physical illness.

The words John had read aloud returned to her mind: *The will is free . . . Gods we are . . . if we will.* But demons too, she thought, destroying ourselves and those about us . . . if we will.

188

She turned away from the pool, found the place where the path opened on the downhill side. For the first time she was shaken in her conviction that she had been right in helping to persuade Wade to work with Morgan Channing and the Knights of the Golden Circle.

XXI

IN THE WEEK or so that immediately followed, Lora saw nothing of those who lived on the hilltop. Apparently quiet reigned again and Rebecca had made peace with her mistress. Lora did not forget her promise to the girl, but she had as yet thought of no way in which she could help her.

Then one night in April Wade came home from a meeting at Morgan's bearing news.

Lora had gone to sleep, but his tap at her door woke her and she called to him to come in. Only embers burned on the hearth, but he knelt to renew the fire without lighting a candle. Lora lay beneath the covers and waited till the fire was going and he had pulled up a hassock where he could sit before the warmth and stretch out his lame leg.

Every now and then he came to her room like this to talk for a while and then went away again. Sometimes a sudden flare of love-making might follow, but more often not. It was as though Wade were gradually coming to accept her as a person in herself, instead of as a substitute or as an image he could put into Virginia's place. Now he made love to her only when caught up in the old, dangerous make-believe, and she was relieved to find these times coming less often.

She had an affection for him, yes. Perhaps even a growing affection, but it was not that of sweetheart for lover, or wife for husband. She still shrank within herself at his kisses and could only lie inert beneath his touch.

Often when he came home after one of these meetings he was keyed up, tense, eager to release himself in talk with her before returning to his own bed. And these times she was coming to value, as she might have valued the confidences of a brother of whom she was fond. In this role of listener she could give herself gladly and even find satisfaction of a sort.

Lora turned on her side, watching him from the warmth beneath the quilts.

"Is it going well?" she asked. From the first she had found Wade entering into the spirit of secrecy that bound the Circle and its doings. He seldom talked of what went on at Morgan's. Thus she took care never to ask a pointed question, but only those of a general sort which would reveal her interest without making her seem to pry.

"We've had wonderful news from the Middle West," he said. "Norwood has received a report of the draft being stopped in several sections, or at least so successfully resisted that it has been postponed."

"I hope this is managed without violence," Lora said anxiously.

"There's been none to speak of, I believe. Of course one can't make that absolutely sure. The human element is too uncertain. But Norwood assures us there will be no armed revolt, if that is what you mean. Often a quiet show of force is all that is necessary. And desertions are on the increase all the time."

Lora lay quiet, wishing she might ask more direct questions, obtain details which would quiet her doubts, and enable her to better understand what was happening.

Wade changed the subject carelessly, as if he might have said too much. "Adam is down with another bout of fever. I stopped in to talk to him tonight, but he was in bed with his shivers and sweats, and much too miserable to discuss politics."

"You aren't planning to draw Adam into this, are you?" Lora asked uneasily.

"Why not? He can't be any lover of war after what he's gone through in prison."

She turned beneath the covers. "I've heard him storm about the way men aren't enlisting. And I think he'd like to shoot every deserter. He seems bitterly intent on winning the war on the Union side. It might be just as well not to talk to him about these things. He could cause you trouble if he liked."

"Perhaps you're right." Wade stared into the fire again for a space of time, lost in his own thoughts.

"How is Morgan?" Lora asked cautiously.

"Raging mad tonight," said Wade. "Mad as any spoiled child who has lost a toy. That colored girl, Rebecca, has run away."

Lora sat up in bed. "Oh, Wade! The poor thing! Though you can't say she's *run away* when she's perfectly free to come and go as she pleases."

190

"But she hasn't done that. She hasn't given notice and left her job properly. She has simply disappeared. Into thin air. She must have sneaked away at night because her room hasn't even been slept in. Morgan didn't know she'd gone till she started to ring for her the next morning."

Lora sighed. "Morgan must have driven her into a corner to make her go. Did you know that the girl was working there because Morgan said she'd let her buy freedom for Rebecca's mother and little sister?"

"Sounds like Morgan," Wade said dryly. "No, I didn't know that. But the mother and sister are free now anyway, if they want to be free."

"I told Rebecca that. But she felt it didn't mean anything. And perhaps it doesn't unless there is still some way to get through Southern lines and escape to the North. I wonder where she's gone."

"If she has any money she could go anywhere, I suppose."

"I don't think she'll want to spend it on herself. She'll be trying to find some way to get her family up here. Now I wish I'd tried to take a real stand with Morgan."

Wade turned from the blaze so that he could look toward her shadowy corner. "*You?* Take a stand with Morgan? What do you mean?"

She told him then what she had held back till now—the story of what had happened in John's cottage on the hill, of Morgan's rage and of the way she herself had been helpless to do anything but walk out.

When she was through, Wade came over to sit on the edge of the bed, where he could see her better. "What a stormy petrel you are! Always out in the middle of the gale, stirring things up. I haven't held it against you that you wouldn't listen to me and must go to Morgan's anyway. But now you've raised the sort of rumpus that is sure to occur if anyone crosses her. Let her alone—stay away from her."

Lora pulled the covers up to her chin and looked at him rebelliously over the edge of the quilt. "You're blaming me for what happened. That isn't fair!"

"Nevertheless," he said, "if you hadn't climbed the hill to talk to Rebecca, none of this would have happened. You could simply have given the earring to Ambrose and he'd have returned it quietly. You'd not have stirred up this hornets' nest."

His words seemed to her the last straw. "I'm not afraid of Morgan," she said, "even if you are."

She could sense the stillness of him, the angry tightening.

191

She could have bitten her tongue for speaking so pettishly, but the way people catered to Morgan made her furious. Someone had to show the woman that she couldn't ride rough-shod over those who were weaker than she.

"Why should I be afraid of Morgan?" Wade asked coldly.

There was no turning back now. He was already angry, so perhaps this was the time to go ahead, to step boldly into the dark labyrinth.

"I'm not quite sure why you're afraid of her," she said. "Jemmy calls her Morgan Le Fay and says she's like that plotting queen. And of course there are those who say she has always wanted you and that she'd cheat and lie and steal to get you."

He put a hand upon her shoulder, pushing her back against the pillow. "What are you talking about? Say what you mean!"

"There was a time something happened," she said, not moving, though his fingers hurt her shoulder. "A time I don't understand—up there in the woods. Perhaps it isn't true at all. Perhaps it's just one of those stories that go around. About you and Morgan."

His fingers tightened. "Jemmy? Jemmy's been telling that beastly story again?"

"Then it's not true?"

He let her go and turned away. For a long moment the only movement in the room was firelight flickering on the ceiling. Then he got up and went toward the door without speaking.

Lora slipped out of bed, her long braid swinging against her back as she hurried across the room. She stepped between Wade and the door, her shoulders against it, pity and under-standing welling up in her. Now—now she was beginning to see all the sad, ugly pattern.

"So that's why you turn away from Jemmy? Because he told his mother and because you think Virginia . . . But it isn't true, Wade! I don't believe it! Virginia knew her sister. She'd have forgiven you for whatever happened. I think she'd have forgiven you for anything."

"It wasn't a matter of forgiving." His tone was so low that Lora could barely catch the words. "She wanted me to have whatever I wanted most in life. If she came to believe—it was just the sort of thing she would have done."

Lora put her hand across his mouth. "No! You mustn't say it. You mustn't think it. And you mustn't go on blaming Jemmy for something he did so innocently."

He drew away from her hand. "I blame only myself. But when I look at the boy I remember. Now, if you'll let me by—"

For the first time she understood fully his inner torment, which was so much worse than she had imagined. It was one thing to suffer the tragic loss of a dear one, but something far worse if you carried as well a sense of guilt about her death.

She wished she might fling her arms about his neck, cling to him, try to heal and comfort by the very nearness of her body. Perhaps even dispel the doubt and confusion that was part of her own being at times with the physical reality of caresses. But she would not play Morgan's role. She slipped away from the door and ran barefooted back to her bed.

Once again warm beneath the covers, she held her breath as he went out, heard him close her door, go softly down the hall. She listened intently as another door opened, closed again, and only then did she relax in relief. It was his own door, not Virginia's.

She overslept the next morning. When she opened her eyes bright April sunshine burnished the windowpanes, birds proclaimed the day, and the air was alive with the tingle of spring.

She yawned widely and stretched to her very fingertips. Last night's unhappy ending reached out to possess her mind, but she would have none of it. Today she would laugh at Wade if he gloomed, tease Jemmy lovingly, coax a smile from Mother Tyler. And right after breakfast she would go to see Serena, taking along a basket of fruit for poor Adam at the same time. Serena might help her in the matter of Rebecca.

Unfortunately her brave plans began to go awry almost at once. She came downstairs in her new gown of dove gray, to find Mrs. Tyler and Jemmy already at breakfast. The boy was not eating, and his grandmother was obviously in a towering dudgeon.

"I *am* sorry to be late," Lora apologized, slipping into her place. "Has Wade overslept too?"

Jemmy threw her a tragic look and began to fiddle with his porridge spoon.

"Eat!" said his grandmother, and Jemmy forced the spoon to quivering lips.

"Has something happened?" Lora asked. "Where is Wade?"

"That," said Mrs. Tyler coldly, "is what I should like to know. My son has never turned against me with thoughts he would not share until you came into this house, Lora. Perhaps you had better tell me where it is that he goes in the evening and why he is so often out of the house all day long."

"He doesn't tell me either," Lora said mildly. "I believe he is working on some effort that has to do with the war. Why don't you ask him yourself?"

"I have no wish to pry," said the old lady inconsistently. "At least he has come to his senses about one thing this morning."

Jemmy's mouth trembled uncontrollably. He set down his spoon and ran out of the room and up the stairs.

Mrs. Tyler began an indignant complaint, but Lora did not stay to listen. She set her napkin down with a hasty "Excuse me," and hurried after Jemmy.

Sure enough, he was being sick in his slop pail. She held his head gently, supported his small convulsed body until he was quiet again. Then she helped him to the bed, drew off his shoes, and pulled the quilt over him.

"No school today," she said cheerfully. "But it's too beautiful a day to stay inside. So get well fast. This afternoon I'll show you a wonderful reading place I've found outdoors. We'll take some books and blankets and go there. A secret place just for us."

"I don't want to," Jemmy said. "I don't want to go anywhere."

She sat on the bed beside him and patted his hand, noting that the bones no longer stood out so clearly beneath the fine-grained skin. Jemmy had been eating well in the past few months.

"You don't have to tell me," she said, "if you'd rather not talk about it. But it would make it easier for me to help if you could tell me what happened."

He blinked to hold back the tears, his forehead still moist with cold sweat. She reached out to wipe his face and then left the handkerchief in his hand.

"It's Hamlin," he said after a futile effort to stop his tears. "Papa says he has to go. This morning Ellie must have left Grandmother's sitting-room door open and Hamlin got in there before I was up. I guess it was a new place for him because he's never allowed there, and he must have thought it was fun. He didn't mean to do anything bad, Lorie."

Jemmy gulped and Lora patted his arm gently.

"One of those shawls you and Papa gave Grandmother for Christmas was on a chair and Hamlin dragged it down and played with it all over the room. He chewed a hole in it and tore it in some other places. Grandmother heard him and rang and rang her bell, but Ellie was busy in the kitchen and she didn't come right away. And then I heard the ringing and the barking and I came running down, right after Papa."

He choked back a sob and went on. "Grandmother was furious when she saw her blue shawl and she said Hamlin would have to go. I tried to explain that he didn't know any better because he is a very young dog. But—but Papa wouldn't listen. He looked so queer and angry. He said this was enough and Grandmother was right. He—he called Peter in and told him to take Ham out and get rid of him—to give him away at once."

Lora held the small hand tightly. "And then what happened?"

He sat up in bed to tell her despairingly. "I—fought Peter when he came in. And when Papa held me I—I kicked him, and I bit him on the hand. But he didn't do anything to me. He just looked at me in the most awful way and said I'd done more damage in my life than I'd ever realize. Then he told Grandmother he was going out and he didn't even stay for breakfast. Lorie—what did he mean? Did he mean my mother and—the turtles?"

"No darling," she said quickly. "Of course he didn't mean that."

"I'd rather have him thrash me than look at me the way he did."

She held him close, and for once he did not rebel at the embrace, but sobbed with his face against her neck, words still spilling out.

"Don't let them take Hamlin! He's my family, Lorie. He's all I've got. The Union doesn't sell families away, like the South does with slaves. Lorie, you *will* help me?"

"Of course I'll help you," she whispered, her lips close to his ear. "You've got me, you know. And you've got your papa. All mothers and fathers get cross with their children sometimes, and sometimes the children get cross at them too."

"It's not like that!" cried Jemmy knowingly. "He hates me. I know he does. And I hate him too!"

She could feel anger tightening in him, pulling him taut. Gently she pushed him back upon his pillow.

"You can't help me if you keep this up. And I'll need your help if we're to save Hamlin."

He quieted a little and stared at her darkly, not daring to hope.

"First I'll have to talk to Peter. But I can't do anything unless you stop crying and try to get a nap. Never mind school today. You just rest now. And this afternoon we'll go out to that place I mentioned. We'll talk about what can be done. Make plans. We'll work things out somehow, Jemmy. You know I'll stand by you."

Crooked over the top bar of his bed hung the wishbone Lora had put in Jemmy's stocking for Christmas, its red bow still gay. She reached for it on sudden impulse and held it out to him.

"Here! Now's the time for a wish."

He hesitated a moment and then took one end of the bone. They both wished silently and Lora gave the signal to pull. The larger half came away in her fingers and Jemmy's tears started again.

"You see—I won't get my wish! It's no use, Lorie."

She laughed out loud, surprising him. "What if I wished the same thing you did? So either way you couldn't lose?"

Such trickery caught his fancy and he managed a smile, relaxing a little. Now he made no protest when she tucked the covers around him, or when she opened the window wide to let in the warm smell of spring. She left his door ajar as she went out, so she might hear if he called. Then she went down to breakfast.

It was a relief to find that Mother Tyler had finished and had been wheeled back to her sitting room. When she had eaten, Lora went in briefly to let her know that Jemmy would stay in bed this morning, and that she was going to take some fruit to Adam Hume, who was down with fever again.

There was a gleam in the deep-set eyes as the old woman regarded her. "Have you seen what that dog has done?" She reached for the ragged shawl from the table next to her.

"Yes, I know," Lora said. "I'm very sorry. But I think Jemmy is being torn much more seriously than your shawl, and I think he is more important. Now I must get Ellie to help me with a basket for Adam, and—"

"Fortunately my son does not place my feelings so low on the scale of his consideration," Mrs. Tyler broke in. "He has ordered Peter to get rid of the dog. Something which should have been done long ago. What I can't understand is how he can be visiting Morgan's house these days, as Ellie tells me he is. He knows how dangerous and destructive she can be."

"It is a political matter," Lora said.

196

"Morgan's main interest is not in politics and never was. I had thought he would be on guard against her all the rest of his life after her wicked attack on me."

Lora had started toward the door, but now she turned back quickly and saw the gleam of triumph in the old woman's eyes.

"So you don't know what happened?" Mother Tyler snapped. "Well, I shall tell you now so that you will be more careful in your association with this dreadful woman. It happened years ago when Ambrose and his wife were working for me. They had gone away for the day and I went out to their quarters to speak to Morgan."

She paused dramatically, watching Lora, knowing well she had her full attention.

"I went to tell her that under no circumstances would I permit my son to marry her. And if he did I would disinherit him. Morgan was curling her hair at the time and she became livid with rage. She snatched up the curling iron from the spirit flame where it was heating and attacked me with it. She would have struck me in the face with the hot iron if I hadn't flung up my hand to save myself. I must have screamed when the iron burned me across the palm and Virginia, who was outside, ran to fetch Wade."

Lora listened in shocked silence. Mrs. Tyler turned her right-hand palm up and shuddered as she traced the place where the iron must have burned across the flesh. When she looked at Lora again the gleam was more intense than ever.

"You can understand that my son would not marry a girl capable of so vicious an act."

"Yes," Lora murmured. "I can understand."

Mrs. Tyler sighed and closed her hand. "What I did not see was that Wade, horrified by Morgan's behavior, would turn for comfort to Virginia, who was only waiting to enfold him in her gentleness and love. But at least I hope I have made it clear to you that my son will never turn against me, as you have tried to turn him."

Lora said nothing. She slipped out of the room and went into the kitchen, still shaken by the story she had heard. All this was in full character for Morgan. In these sudden violent rages to which she was prone, she was quite capable of doing physical harm. Rebecca was better off away.

While Ellie prepared some fruit and molasses cookies for her to take to Adam, Lora questioned her about Hamlin.

"Peter's already took the pup off," Ellie told her. "And a

good thing, I say. The critter has caused enough trouble around here."

"But where did he take it, Ellie?"

"He didn't say where he was going, ma'am." Ellie paused with an apple in her hands and there was spite in her look. "You ain't figgerin' to do anything 'bout it, are you, ma'am?"

"I'll do what I can," Lora said. "There, that's fine. Perhaps this will cheer Mr. Hume a little."

Ellie was not interested in Mr. Hume. "I guess you never seen Mr. Wade get real mad, have you, ma'am?"

Lora took the basket and went out of the kitchen quickly. Before she left she looked in on Jemmy, saw he was asleep, and hurried from the house.

At the Lords' Lora found Serena floured to the elbows and singing as she worked. Serena loved to make her own bread and rolls and would relinquish the task to no cook she had ever had.

"You're just what Adam needs!" she cried, when Lora explained her basket. "He's in a vile mood and I know you're the one to stand right up to him and put him in his place."

Lora shook her head, smiling. "What a reputation I'm getting. I don't want to put anyone in his place."

"He's sitting in the sun on the terrace right now. So do take the basket out to him yourself. And scold him a little for the good of his soul."

"But I've really come to see you," Lora protested.

"That's nice. But let me finish this chore first. I like to concentrate on talk for its own sake. We had towels and pillowcases interfering last time. Run along—right out the door there. Get a knife from the drawer first so you can coax him to eat some fruit."

There was nothing to do but obey and Lora went out to the rear terrace, where flagstones made a level space before the hill dropped steeply away. Adam sat glumly on an iron garden bench, with a blanket under him and a muffler of plaid wool around his neck.

"Good morning," Lora said cheerfully. "Serena has sent me out to scold you, but I'm not sure what for. I'm sorry you've been ill and I've brought you these. How are you today?"

He looked up, unsmiling, and she saw how sallow his color was, and that there were shadows beneath his eyes.

"I'm all right," he said. "This thing leaves as fast as it hits me."

She set the basket down beside him on the bench, but he made no move to touch it.

"I'll peel you an orange," she said.

She seated herself on the bench without invitation and chose a big golden sphere from the basket. But before she settled to the peeling she took a deep breath of warm, sunny air. The waters of the bay seemed a deeper blue than the sky today and the sails of the many vessels which dotted the water were dazzling white. Even the mushroom encampment at the foot of the hill gleamed in every detail and the bustle of soldiers on drill, artillery wagons, moving horses on parade, were plainly evident.

"There'll be action now with spring here," Adam said, regarding the encampment dourly. "Both armies will be on the march. The waiting is over."

She knew how he must long to be back where he could be part of this movement himself, and she tried to distract him by bringing up a problem nearer home.

"Did you know that Mrs. Channing's colored maid has disappeared?" she asked.

"Rebecca? I've always wondered how she endured serving her charming mistress this long."

Lora explained what Rebecca had told her about saving money and Adam made a grimace of distaste. "It seems to me the girl will be better off away from the place."

"I'm not sure," Lora said. "I believe there was a man coming up to see her secretly. But she's young and she can't have been around much by herself. She could easily fall into the wrong hands. And I know she'll be upset and worried because of what may happen now to her mother and sister. Do you suppose there's anything we could do?"

Wedges of orange peel were coming away from the fruit beneath her fingers as she worked the knife. When he did not speak she looked up to find him watching her in his quizzical way.

"What about you, Lora?" he asked.

She flashed a startled look at him. "I? What do you mean?"

"Don't you live any life of your own?"

"I'm doing very well, thank you," she said stiffly. She broke the orange into sections and held it out to him. He took a section, bit into it with strong, even teeth, his look still appraising her.

"I've really come to talk to Serena," she said, rising. "So I'll go back inside now."

Unceremoniously, he pulled her down beside him on the

bench. "Running away again? Serena is busy and happy. I am neither. Perhaps I can help you on the matter of Rebecca."

"Do you mean you know where she might be?"

"There are quite a few Negro families down on McKeon Street. It's probable that's where she is. If you like I'll go there tomorrow and see what I can find out. Though why you should bother—"

"Because she's alone. Because she's only a little younger than I am and friendless. And she's in trouble."

"And you care only about people in trouble," said Adam wryly. "One of these days perhaps you'll find out that Lora is important too, and that she has problems. Then what will you do?"

"I have a problem right now," she said quickly, ignoring the direction of his words. "Jemmy's dog has chewed up an expensive shawl that belonged to Mother Tyler and Wade has given in to her demands that the dog must go. This morning Peter took him off somewhere and I must find a way to get him back."

Adam did not tease her this time. "Poor Jemmy. You're right, of course. Take that dog away and he will be right back where he was before you came to the island. We'll keep Ham for you here, if you like, till you straighten things out."

"Thank you," she said. "I hope Peter has taken him up to John Ambrose. The dog will be all right there until I've had a chance to talk to Wade."

"Unless Morgan is mad enough to refuse to have him on the premises. She doesn't forgive easily, that one. And you must have riled her over Rebecca."

"What makes her that way?" Lora mused. "She has everything—position, money, beauty. She could be a wonderful person if she chose."

"She has everything but what she wants most," Adam said, "and that makes her dangerous. Probably she has no real resentment against Rebecca. The girl was the scapegoat of the moment. Though I'll admit that Morgan never gives up an inch of property she thinks she owns. Regardless of anything written on a paper, she probably looks upon Rebecca as her property."

Lora sat quietly, staring out toward the blue waters of the harbor. She was sure she would never understand Morgan Channing as long as she lived.

"When you married Wade you must have thrown a pretty crimp into any new hopes she may have raised after Virginia's death. She can't love you for that."

"That's nonsense," Lora said. "But tell me what happened after Virginia married Wade. How did she take that? And where did Morgan and her father and mother live then?"

"That was a funny thing. She didn't carry on the way we expected her to. She took the whole thing in a queer, tight-lipped sort of way, as if for the first time in her life she was beaten and knew it. Wade rented a small house for her mother and father, since obviously they couldn't remain on the premises as servants after he had married Virginia. Morgan went to live with them.

"Mrs. Tyler wouldn't receive Virginia's parents socially. Nevertheless, Virginia began to take Morgan around to parties, and buy her clothes. She tried her best to share her own good fortune with her sister. At first people stood off—but they liked Wade, and no one could resist Virginia. So in a year or two Morgan was going everywhere with her new gowns and the fancy airs she mimicked from ladies she met. She was always clever enough. And she knew she had a natural appeal for men which she didn't hesitate to use."

"I suppose she met Mr. Channing through Virginia?"

Adam nodded. "Before the war quite a few Southerners sent their families to Staten Island during the summer. The better hotels here catered to the resort trade from the South. Nick was a widower and he used to escort his sister and her children North every year before returning home to his own affairs. But the summer he met Morgan he stayed on for a time, and she had a good chance to set her little claws into him. He was handsome, though considerably older than she, and he had position and money. More money than Wade. Morgan married him before he had time to catch his breath, and then she got him to build her that big house on the hill so they could live up there part of the year. Of course she wanted to be where she could lord it over those who had snubbed her—and to be near Wade."

Lora listened in silence. More small pieces falling into place, forming the pattern.

"Have a piece of orange," Adam said. "You're not enjoying your own handiwork. Incidentally, have you any idea what Morgan is up to now with all this entertaining she's doing? A mixed lot she has coming up there now, with that Norwood fellow always in evidence."

"I don't keep track of my neighbor's business," Lora said primly.

He grinned at her. "Meaning that I do? Of course I do. What else have I to occupy me? Wade is moving with an odd lot, if you ask me, from the rumors I've heard. Norwood is running with the Circle."

"What circle?" Lora asked carelessly.

"The Golden Circle. The Vallandigham, Fernando Wood bunch. Peace Democrats! Maybe. But more likely rampant Copperheads favoring the South. And that, my innocent one, is treason."

"I don't know much about politics," Lora said. "Only what I pick up here and there. But isn't it possible that some of these people are just as sincere as you are? What if they truly want to stop the war?"

"I've no doubt at all that they want to stop it—by stabbing the Union in the back, by driving her down to defeat in her own territory."

Lora bit into a piece of orange, tasted the tangy juice on her tongue. His words were adding to the uneasiness that already stirred within her. But she knew Wade would never throw in his lot with those who planned treason. She was sure of that. Unless—since he was more idealist than realist—they tried to hoodwink him, use him. That was a new and disturbing thought.

She repeated the old argument she had heard from Morgan and from Mr. Norwood when he was talking to Wade. "Isn't it possible that if the draft was stopped in the North the Union might be forced to negotiate with the South so that a peaceful resolution could be brought about and all the fighting stopped?"

"The United States government would not look lightly upon such notions. Try to stop the draft and the army and militia will put the resistance down in short order. Even if it means bloodshed."

"But haven't there been some places in the Middle West—"

"It seems to me that you know a good deal about these matters," Adam broke in. "Who has been telling you these things?"

She could feel the flush rising in her cheeks, but evidently he did not expect an answer.

"Vallandigham and his crowd are going to have to step softly or find themselves in hot water. I suppose you know about General Burnside's recent order?"

She shook her head.

"That somewhat hotheaded gentleman has ordered the arrest of anyone guilty of seditious utterances likely to obstruct recruiting. This Val, who has made himself the hero of the Peace Democrats, has been doing just that. It remains to be

202

seen whether this order will muzzle him. If it does not and he is arrested there may be the devil to pay from his supporters. In any event, if Wade has got himself mixed up in any of this, my advice to you is to get him out of it as quickly as possible."

"I'm sure Wade is quite capable of running his own affairs," Lora said stiffly. "And I'm also sure he'd never have anything to do with treason."

"Let's hope so," Adam said, but his tone was dry.

Lora rose with what she hoped was an air of dignity and bade him good morning.

At least Adam had stopped sulking, for he grinned at her with his old mockery. "Thank you for your visit, Mrs. Tyler. You've done me no end of good."

She went into the house without answering him and stayed a while longer, visiting with Serena. She told her about Rebecca and that Adam had offered to look for the girl down on McKeon Street. Serena promised to see that he kept his word.

Soon after, Lora went home to find that Peter had returned, and that, as she had hoped, he had taken Hamlin up the hill and placed him temporarily in John Ambrose's friendly hands.

"I don't know if Mr. Wade will approve, ma'am, but it just seems like I couldn't take the boy's dog off and give him to strangers."

"The more fool you," said Ellie, listening to his words disapprovingly. "There'll be the old Ned to pay with both his nibs and her nobs when they find this out."

XXII

WADE STAYED AWAY from the house all day and all evening. His mother complained and fretted, but finally went to bed. Lora sat up in the library, comfortable in her old warm wrapper. The air had turned cool after the summery day and a fire felt good again. Tonight a high wind was blowing and rattling the windowpanes, setting dry vines scraping across library windows—the only sounds in a still house.

Lora had curled herself on the sofa before the fire with a copy of *Leslie's Weekly* in her lap, but as often as not the pages, with their vivid drawings of battle scenes, lay unheeded and her thoughts wandered uneasily.

If Wade had gone to New York for the day and evening, he had missed the last boat home by now and there was no point in sitting up waiting for him. On the other hand, if he were on the island he might come home at any moment and she had the feeling that she wanted to be up when he came in.

That morning, after she learned for sure that Peter had taken Hamlin up to John Ambrose, she had gone in to tell the secret to Jemmy. She found him awake and listless, but when she gave him her news about the dog he recovered quickly enough. Nevertheless, Lora kept him away from his grandmother and brought up a tempting lunch on a tray. When the old lady lay down for her afternoon nap, Lora took Jemmy out to a sunny nook in the Hume house, where dandelions already dotted the bright new grass and yellow forsythia hung above their heads over a crumbling wall. They read aloud to each other, talked lightheartedly, and nibbled the molasses cookies Lora had brought along for a special treat.

Reassured that Hamlin's absence was temporary, Jemmy was no longer despairing. Late in the afternoon she let him run up the hill by himself to visit the dog and his grandfather.

Now all that remained was for her to make good her promise that Hamlin would soon be returned to the arms of a welcoming family.

The vine, still dry with winter leaves, clattered against the window and at intervals wind whined down the chimney. She wished Wade would come. The later the hour, the more uneasy she grew. Sometime after midnight she went out to the kitchen and set the kettle on the stove.

Even if Wade did not come at all, a cup of tea would be comforting. But as she returned to the library, she heard the sound of a hackney out on the drive and a moment later Wade's key clicked in the lock.

She waited for him at the library door, and was aware of his lack of pleasure when he saw her. But she hurried to take his hat and help him off with his coat, pretending not to notice.

"You've had a long day," she said cheerfully. "Come in before the fire and rest a minute. The kettle's heating on the stove and we'll have a cup of tea in a little while."

Perhaps he had expected stormy words from her over the dog, and when she said nothing about what had happened that morning, he seemed to relax a little. He did not object when she plumped up pillows behind him on the sofa and covered his legs with a comforter as he stretched out. She sat down on a hassock close to the fire and began to talk of inconsequential things.

"One of these days would you mind if Jemmy and I rummaged in the attic trunks?" she asked. "Jemmy thinks it would be fun, and I'd like to give him the pleasure. If you don't mind, of course."

"Do as you like," Wade said listlessly.

He looked tired, as he did often these days, and she was afraid he was trying too much for his newly returning strength. A movement made him grimace and she knew his leg must be paining him again, as always happened when he asked too much of it. When he seemed at length to doze, she tiptoed out to the kitchen and prepared a big brown earthenware pot of tea. There were still a few cookies from Ellie's last baking, and she set up a tray attractively with a linen cloth and a sprig of the forsythia she and Jemmy had brought home that afternoon. From the dining room she brought one of the nested tea tables and set it at Wade's elbow to hold the tray.

He roused himself sufficiently to smile at her. "You're spoiling me," he said.

She smiled serenely as she poured the tea. With silver tongs she dropped two lumps of sugar in his cup, and added cream. Then she poured tea for herself and sat down once more on the hassock, watching the fire. After a while her silence, or perhaps the stimulating warmth of strong tea, seemed to urge him into words.

"Norwood offered to take me on his rounds in New York," he began, "so I went over with him this morning. I've been there most of the day. We came back here for dinner and another meeting on the island. The movement is growing, Lora, and there's power behind it."

Nevertheless, there was a puckering between his brows.

"Do you still feel that what these people are doing is right?" Lora asked quietly.

He stirred his tea, still thoughtful, as though torn by indecision.

"Not all of it. In theory, in principle, I can be with it. Even in much of the choice of action I can go along. But there are aspects I distrust. Mind you, this is to go no farther than these walls, Lora."

She nodded, waiting for him to go on. The tea was hot

205

and a little bitter. She had brewed it strong and heartening.

He went on, still puzzling aloud. "As long as we work with men of reason, men of integrity, I can feel satisfied that the movement is honorable and its purposes worthy. But there are those in the group who are not preaching the passive resistance I had been led to expect. Today we went into quarters of New York where the very word 'draft' is enough to stir up violence. I'm not sure how this unlettered and even criminal element is likely to behave when the time comes. I heard one man assure the audience that Lincoln's government was highhanded and oppressive. And he quoted Vallandigham in saying the draft was unconstitutional."

"But don't political parties always talk like that?"

"This seemed a deliberate effort to incite. I heard murmurings about how the Negro freedmen coming North would take away the jobs of New York citizens. There seems to be a mounting resentment against the Negro which is both regrettable and dangerous."

Lora listened, her dismay growing. None of this sounded auspicious.

"If you don't like the way things are going, isn't it possible to withdraw from the whole thing?" she asked.

"I'm not sure I want to do that," Wade confessed. "So far I'm not sure of what the actual plans are, or where this whole thing is going. I doubt that either Morgan or Norwood trusts me completely. So far I've been kept on the outskirts of the movement, not admitted to its inner circles. Perhaps I can do more good by going along than by stepping out. If the worst came to the worst, I might be able to swing my weight in opposition."

"Is there any danger to you in this?" she asked uneasily.

He hesitated just long enough so that his answer was not completely reassuring. "I'm scarcely involved. But I know they're raising money out west to arm deserters. Editors who are in the movement are publishing demoralizing pieces in the papers. Copies are then sent to soldiers to encourage desertion. I don't like it, Lora. This has its ugly aspects."

She reached for his hand and held it, that being the only comfort she could offer.

His smile was suddenly contrite. "And you, my dear? I know I left you a difficult situation to handle when I went out this morning. I was pretty angry and upset."

"I'm afraid you did," she admitted frankly. "Jemmy got sick again and had to be put to bed. Your mother was practically shooting out sparks of triumph and lording it over us. And Peter had already taken the dog away."

Wade set his cup and saucer down and leaned back against the pillows.

"Why did you treat Jemmy like that?" Lora asked directly.

He made no effort to defend himself, or to bring up the matter of the ruined shawl. He was plainly regretful now.

"The boy was there before me," he said miserably, "and suddenly all I could see was the harm he had done in telling Virginia about that day in the woods. Then he had told you the same story too, and I was cut to pieces all over again— remembering. When the matter of the shawl came up it gave me a chance to punish him—through the dog."

"And you've been sorry all day, haven't you?"

"Of course," he said simply. "It's not the boy's fault, but mine. Yet I can't help the way I feel about him. And now the thing is done."

Lora let his hand go and settled back on the hassock, clasping her fingers about her knees. "The dog has been taken only as far as Morgan's. John Ambrose has him. He can be brought back whenever you like."

"Then get him back tomorrow. Settle things with my mother, Lora. You can handle her better than anyone else."

Lora thought about that. She could do what he asked easily enough. And if she performed this service he would be relieved and grateful. He would need to take no further blame upon himself if his mother became ill again, or otherwise behaved badly.

"Lora," Wade said softly, "what are you thinking? Where have you gone?"

She looked at him then, seeing clearly what she must do. "I've been thinking of what you've asked of me, Wade—to get the dog back and deal with your mother. But the order was yours and the responsibility is yours too. I think you must stand by what you've done, or else undo it yourself."

There was disbelief and hurt in his look. Then he closed his eyes again. She rose and carried the tray out to the kitchen. She set the dishes in the sink and nibbled the last cookie. When she returned to the library she found that he had not moved. But he opened his eyes when she came in and looked at her.

"There's nothing I can do," he said coldly. "You must understand that. If you will not help, then the dog must stay where he is. I will not stir everything up all over again."

"If that's the way you wish it," Lora said. She picked up his cane which had fallen to the floor and put it in his hand. Then she said, "Good night," softly and went out of the room.

Later, while she was undressing, she heard him climbing the stairs in his slow, painful way. She blew out her candle and crawled between cold sheets, shivering at their touch.

She was not at all sure what she had done was wise, or kind, or sensible. Even now she longed to run to his room and tell him she would take the responsibility herself and do as he asked. Then he would be happy again and the forlorn look would go out of his eyes.

Unbidden, Adam's words returned to her: "You only care about those you can help." Was this her own weakness perhaps? Were she and Virginia sisters, all too prone to make others dependent upon them?

She slept fitfully that night and was early awake Saturday morning. Everything in her resisted the day ahead. It was a day which was likely to be fraught with hurt and resentment and argument. Or if not these things, then a cold, armed truce in which resentment seethed beneath the surface. That rain washed against the windowpanes was a matter which suited the mood of the day.

At breakfast Mother Tyler was cheerful and triumphant. How fine, she said, that they were having a little rain. Not only because the farms on the island needed it, but because the woods were too dry and that always made for fire hazard. Too often in both spring and fall, fire swept through the beautiful island woods, destroying them.

The old lady ate as she had not eaten in a long while, and she talked of news in the papers, of the last business word given her by Mr. Niles. She asked Wade no pointed questions about his absence the day before and did not mention the dog. But she wore her victory like a crown and because of it vitality seemed to surge through her.

Wade was remote, retreating into a shell of absent-mindedness that seemed to give him some protection. Behind it he need not recognize the cause of his mother's good humor. He need hardly see his son or Lora. Right after breakfast he said he was going to work on his book and shut himself away in the library. Jemmy was quiet as any mouse. He knew wherein lay the cause of his grandmother's cheerful mood, but Lora saw by the secret look he gave her that he was putting every confidence in her promise to get back his dog, and that he was willing to bide his time until she could manage the matter. She was distressed, however, to see the expression he turned upon his father, who seemed not to notice his dark look at all.

Mrs. Tyler did not wait for anyone to trundle her wheel chair back to the sitting room. When she had folded her napkin, she turned the wheels herself and sent the chair vigorously toward the door. As Ellie ran to open it, Mrs. Tyler spoke over her shoulder to Lora.

"I know just what I'd like this morning, if you're free, Lora—a good back rub. If the day clears later and the sun comes out, perhaps I'll sit on the front veranda for a while. When Ambrose comes to spade the garden I want to talk to him. I've got some notions of my own on the subject this year."

Lora followed her into the sitting room where she was out of Jemmy's earshot.

"I'm sorry, Mother," she said evenly, "but I've made plans for Jemmy this morning. After the loss which has been inflicted upon him he needs comforting. I won't have time for your back rub today."

Mrs. Tyler looked plainly shocked at this open defiance. "Don't be ridiculous! You can see that the boy is already over his upset about the dog. He never had one before, and he doesn't need to suffer over not having one now. Besides, it was not I, but his father, who gave the order. You needn't try to take it out on me."

"Would you like Ellie to rub your back?" Lora asked, moving toward the door.

"Come back here!" the old lady cried. "I'm not accustomed to having people leave while I'm speaking. As I said before, you've been badly brought up, Lora. You need to learn courtesy for your elders."

Lora returned calmly to stand beside Mrs. Tyler's chair.

"I am listening," she said.

"Then do as I ask," Mrs. Tyler snapped. "Jemmy and his imaginary sorrow can wait. Surely the comfort of an old woman must come before that of a small boy."

"Not for me," Lora told her quietly. "You are strong and healthy and ought to be up and around, instead of babying yourself in a wheel chair. Now, if you don't mind, I'll go tell Ellie you want her."

"I do *not* want Ellie!" Mrs. Tyler raged, and now there was a shrill note in her voice. She enjoyed a fight only so long as she was winning.

But this time Lora went out the door and down the hall, leaving the silver bell ringing indignantly behind her.

Jemmy had already climbed the stairs to his room. When she looked in on him he was playing with his turtles, though without any great enthusiasm. Turtles must seem insipid company after a boisterous, affectionate little dog.

"Do you think Hamlin misses me?" he asked as Lora looked in the door.

She nodded her conviction. "I'm sure of it. Just as you miss him. But you may go up and see him again when it stops raining, and in the meantime I hope you'll be patient. If Hamlin comes back this time, let's make sure he'll never be sent away again. Next time Peter might have to take him somewhere else. So let's wait awhile, Jemmy, until everything can turn out for the best."

He nodded and looked out the window. "It shouldn't ever rain on Saturday."

"Why not?" Lora asked. "A rainy Saturday is just right for doing things you don't do other times."

"What things?" he asked, a faint interest stirring.

"Well, we could explore the attic. You said you'd like to—remember? It would be warm enough up there today, since the sun beat on the roof all day yesterday. I'm going to put on an old dress and cover my hair with a sunbonnet to keep out cobwebs and dust. Then I'm going to dip into some of those old trunks and see what's there. Your papa said I might. Of course, I wish I had a helper—but if you're too busy with your turtles—"

He dropped Lancelot back on his sand pile with a plop and grinned at her.

"You make schemes, don't you, Lorie? I like surprise schemes."

"I'm a very scheming woman," she said. "I'll call you when I'm ready," and she went into her room to change her clothes.

Her blue sunbonnet was an old, faded one she had often worn in the yard back home, though somehow it had never prevented her skin from turning brown. Mostly because she could never resist the temptation to lift her face to the sun's warmth and soak it in through her skin. At least the bonnet would keep the cobwebs away.

"You look funny," Jemmy said as they climbed the attic stairs in single file. "Like a farm lady who's going to milk cows."

"You're wrong," she told him. "I'm an island lady who is going to open trunks."

They had brought a half-dozen candles today and Jemmy

set them around in places where they would do the most good and not catch anything on fire. Rain pattered cozily over their heads and gurgled in pipes and gutters. Shadows retreated to the corners, or swung themselves up the slanting beams of the roof, hovering there like giant birds. It was not exactly warm in the attic, but at least the cutting chill of winter was gone.

The nearest trunk offered itself and Jemmy raised the lid eagerly. There were the usual old clothes, hats, shoes, faded artificial flowers. Jemmy found a battered top hat and set it on his head, where it slid down to his ears and made them both laugh. There were dust and cobwebs aplenty and now and then the explorers sneezed, but this was undoubtedly a wonderful way to spend a rainy Saturday morning.

Now and then things which had belonged to Virginia turned up, but Lora noted that while Jemmy identified them and looked at them sadly, he did so without bursting into tears. The terrible urgency of sorrow had lessened in him with the passing months, just as it had in herself. The hurt was there, but the thrust was not as painful as it once had been. One could bear now to be reminded, and even begin to remember the comforting things that at first faded in the immediacy of loss.

The third trunk they opened contained something different and Jemmy pounced upon it in delight.

"There are Papa's old toys, and even toys that belonged to my grandmother when she was a little girl. Mama showed them to me once when I was little. Lorie, do you think Grandmother could ever have been a little girl?"

Lora laughed. "I'm sure she was. A little girl with griefs and disappointments and pleasures just like our own, Jemmy."

He pulled out a doll with a painted china head and kid body that must have been his grandmother's, and studied it thoughtfully, but she suspected that he did not believe her words.

She reached in next and pulled out a funny-looking clown that had obviously been homemade. Its suit was of black alpaca, with tufts of yellow yarn making pompons down the front. The cotton-stuffed head had been painted with goggle eyes and an enormous turned-up grin which had faded to a pale pink outline with the years. Orange-colored yarn had been sewed to make a shaggy, bright wig that topped the fellow off.

"That clown belonged to Papa," Jemmy said. "He gave it

211

to me to play with when I was little. I wondered what happened to it. Grandmother made it for him. I used to sleep with it at night and Papa did too, when he was a little boy."

Lora perched on the corner of a packing case and held the clown in her hands. There were other toys of Wade's coming to light now—a cart with one wheel, a garland of painted wooden spools, blocks with pictures of children rolling hoops pasted on them and curling off at the edges. But the clown intrigued her most, and she continued to hold him.

"Look," Jemmy cried, pulling out several copybooks, "these must have been Papa's composition books."

But he was more interested in toys than in schoolbooks, so he dumped them beside Lora and reached into the trunk again. She picked one of them up and leafed through it idly. He had written a neat and decorative hand, that small boy. She glanced at the slanting writing on one page and saw that his description was of a visit to the docks, and read a few lines, her interest caught. The writer's excitement and response to the color and life, to the odors of spices and tea, came through his words. What a shame that his mother had scorned these efforts and had discouraged them. It seemed that there was talent here—more than had been revealed in that stilted effort at a novel which he had read to her. She would take these books downstairs and read them more carefully.

From the distant reaches of the house the jingling sound of the doorbell reached them and Lora went to the head of the stairs to listen. In a few moments she heard Ellie padding upstairs in search of her, and she turned to Jemmy.

"It must be for me. Do you think you could put things back by yourself, Jemmy? We've really spent a long enough time up here for one morning. We want to leave something to look forward to on another rainy Saturday."

He was reluctant to stop, but agreed with a sigh as she hurried downstairs, still carrying the clown and the stack of copybooks.

"It's Mr. Adam," Ellie told her, puffing from her climb upstairs. "He wants to see you, ma'am. I've shown him into the parlor."

Adam. That must mean news of Rebecca. She thanked Ellie and hurried past her down the stairs, not even seeing her astonished look. She went into the parlor, where Ellie had lighted a lamp against the usual gloom, never thinking of her appearance until Adam stared at her.

212

"Good morning," he said. "Is this a new style? The wearing of sunbonnets on a rainy day?"

She remembered then and set the clown and copybooks down while she untied the strings and pulled the bonnet from her rumpled hair.

"I've been in the attic," she said, as if that explained everything, and then hurried on. "Do sit down, Adam. Have you found out about Rebecca?"

He took a chair, looking amused. "I've seen her," he said. "I've talked to her."

"That's fine!" Lora drew a breath of relief. Rebecca had been steadily on her conscience ever since she'd learned about the girl's action. "Then she's all right?"

"Yes—and in good hands. The young fellow she's been seeing has a very sensible and intelligent mother. Rebecca is staying with her. But the girl is upset and concerned over what she has done. She must have run away when her position became intolerable, and has been worrying about the consequences ever since."

"She doesn't want to return to Mrs. Channing, does she?"

Adam shrugged. "I know she fears that Morgan may take some action to punish her through her mother and sister. I tried to assure her that there was little possibility of that while the war is on."

"Morgan would find a way to pull strings if she wanted to," Lora said. "Do you think the girl would return to her employ?"

"From what she said, I gathered that she would. But she's afraid that Morgan would never take her back now. That's where you come in."

Before Adam could explain, the door of the library opened and Wade came across the hall to the parlor.

"Good morning, Adam," he said. "I heard voices and wondered if something was wrong."

Lora explained about Rebecca, and Wade, limping over to a chair, listened remotely.

"I'm sorry for the girl," he said, "but I heartily dislike having Lora meddle in Mrs. Channing's affairs. If you're interested in this matter, Adam, perhaps your sister, Serena—"

"Let's go back to the beginning," said Adam, still amused. "This visit of mine to McKeon Street was made at the request of your wife. So I presumed that anything further which might be done would have to come from her."

Wade threw Lora a look of disapproval. "Had you consulted me, I could have made this trip to McKeon Street myself to find the girl. I don't quite understand—"

"Then perhaps you'll go to see Morgan about her?" Lora asked hurriedly.

Adam did not wait for Wade's answer, but rose with an air of relief. "At least there's nothing more I can do about the matter 'and I promised my sister not to be late for luncheon today. So if you'll excuse me—"

He managed to bow himself out of what promised to develop into a family disagreement, and took his leave of them both with a flourish, in which there remained an irritating amusement.

When he had gone Wade turned to Lora in despair. "My dear, why must you be so headlong?"

She suppressed a twinge of indignation and turned to pick up copybooks and clown. The clown's goggle eyes seemed to regard her meaningfully and she had to return his wide smile with a faint one of her own.

"What did you call this fellow?" she asked. "I suppose he had a name?"

Wade looked at the doll in blank astonishment. "Where on earth did you find that?"

"Jemmy and I have been exploring the attic. He said you used to sleep with this when you were a little boy."

"I suppose all children sleep with their toys at some time or another. Why have you brought the thing downstairs?"

Why had she? In a way, she knew. "I thought he might tell me things about you," she said.

Color darkened Wade's face, but his look softened. "What a strange little person you are, Lora. I never know where to find you next. I thought we were discussing Rebecca and Adam—and here you've turned me to the subject of a toy I had when I was small."

"I want to hear his name," she repeated.

He hesitated a moment. "Well, if you must know— Jupiter. A most unsuitable name for a clown, but I thought it was just right at the time."

"Jupiter," said Lora softly. "Certainly a power to guard you through the night. And I've more treasure trove," she went on, holding the copybooks up for him to see.

This time he moved toward her as if he would take them out her hands, but she held them away, laughed in his face and ran into the hall and up the stairs. Near the top she turned to look down at him and saw that he was watching her with an odd, puzzled look.

"The trouble is," she said, "you try to make serious sense of me. How did your book go this morning?"

His lips tightened again. "It has gone where it belonged— into the kitchen stove. I read through what I'd written this morning and I recognized it for the trash it was."

He went into the library then and closed the door behind him. She stood for a moment staring at the door, then went more slowly up the last few steps.

Jemmy had come down from the attic, having put things back by himself. He had heaped a pile of loot on the floor of his room and through his open door Lora could see him kneeling beside it, examining his treasure.

She went to her own room and put the copybooks in a dresser drawer. Then she carried the little clown to the window, where daylight touched him through rain-streaked panes.

"So your name is Jupiter," she whispered. "Jupiter, the all-wise, the all-powerful. If you're all that, then perhaps you can help me. Perhaps you can teach me what he is really like."

XXIII

LORA WAITED until Monday before she made any move in Morgan's direction. For one thing, she preferred to act on a day when Jemmy would be in school and when Wade had planned to be in another part of the island on some business of the Circle.

Then, too, she wanted to be sure she did not act on impulse. Too often she seemed to leap into events without proper forethought. But the more she considered now, the more she felt that she must be the one to talk to Morgan and find out how she felt about having Rebecca back.

After breakfast, as soon as Jemmy and Wade were gone and Mother Tyler was settled before her sitting-room window where she could see Ambrose the moment he put in an appearance, Lora started up through the woods to Morgan's house.

Saturday's rain had lasted only through the morning and the thirsty earth had soaked it up. By afternoon everything was turning dusty again beneath the sun. Tree branches still withheld their full treasure in nubs of green, waiting for the right combination of sun and rain to release them into a largesse of bloom. Only the bold advance guard of forsythia and dandelion were really in blossom.

She had just reached the pool when she saw John Ambrose coming down the higher path and went to meet him on the bank.

"She's waiting for you by her window," Lora told him.

"Then her spirits are fine this morning?"

"They've been fine ever since she got rid of the dog. But I don't think she deserves to feel fine at everyone else's expense. Would she listen to advice from you, John?"

He shook his head wryly. "Never in all that lady's life has she listened to anyone but her father. But I'll bring the little dog down any time you say."

"We'd better wait," Lora told him. "I would like my husband to give the order."

Out in the pond something moved on the big sunny rock and fell into the water with a splash. Lora watched ripples widening across the still surface.

"Turtle," the old man said. "They like the sun."

"I wish spring would hurry," Lora said. "It will be so beautiful here."

"Aye," he said. "It will be."

She remembered then and turned to him contritely. "I'm sorry. About your daughter, I mean. You must hate this place—"

He shook his grizzled head. "There is no wickedness here to hate. It's not in me to hate a pool of water, any more than I do the poison ivy when it stings me."

This was almost what she had said to Rebecca. She was glad he felt that too. Now she took her courage in her hands and spoke her puzzled thoughts to him.

"Virginia would never have died by her own hand, would she, John? What is the truth of what happened?"

He stood for a long moment watching the now quiet water. "I've heard what they say," he told her at last. "I think she would not. But then—I would never have thought she would marry Mr. Wade either." He looked at Lora—a straight, sober look. "I'm not one to understand the strange things women do. But still, I feel she would not."

"I never knew her," Lora said softly, "but I feel that too. If only Wade could believe it. It would be better to have it only Jemmy's turtles than what Wade thinks happened."

He gave her a quick touch of the cap and turned away

down the hill, and she knew that sudden emotion had moved him. She went on uphill, lost in her own thoughts, and emerged at the top to find a faint haze in the air and a smell of smoke. Sometimes there were brush fires along these hills and the wind would carry the smoke for miles. But little breeze stirred today and she wondered where the haze was coming from.

Both Hamlin and his mother bounded to greet her as Lora let herself through the gate. At the sound of their barking a woman stepped to the railing of the upper gallery of the big house. It was Morgan Channing and Lora raised a hand in greeting, as though they had not last parted on anything but friendly terms.

Morgan bowed gravely, but made no returning wave. She remained at the rail waiting for Lora to come up the drive.

"Do you smell the smoke?" Lora asked as she approached the house. "There must be a brush fire burning."

"I came out to see if I could locate it," Morgan said. "But I can see nothing from here." She seemed to be waiting for Lora to state the purpose of her visit.

"May I speak to you for a few minutes?" Lora asked.

Morgan nodded somewhat distantly. "The door is open. Won't you come upstairs? Clothilde is busy at the moment and I'd like to search out this fire."

Lora ran up the few steps and beneath the graceful fanlight of the front door. She had never been upstairs in this house before and she looked about with interest as she mounted the curving staircase with its mossy-green flowered carpeting. Morgan waited for her in the wide upper hall and led the way at once to an unused bedroom at the rear. Here the furniture stood shrouded against dust and the room was dark. Morgan went to French doors and flung them open.

"There's a balcony here," she said, "where we'll have a good view."

Lora stepped out upon the small balcony with its wrought-iron rail, and found that she could see out over rolling hills and into the deep cut of a valley. Few signs of habitation were visible. Brush or thick woodlands climbed hill and dale and only the villas of the wealthy encroached upon this first rim of hills overlooking the bay. Here and there a strip of road could be seen, and sometimes a clearing that marked a farm.

Beyond the servants' quarters and stables the hill dropped steeply down from the crest. Morgan pointed to the opposite rise of hill.

"There's the fire. If the day remains still we're probably all right. But with the woods as dry as they are, I don't like it. Well, there's nothing we can do, so come in and tell me why you wanted to see me."

Her tone was hardly cordial, but she led the way to a small upstairs sitting room that was scarcely any more cozy than the vast drawing room below. The circular mirror over a marble mantel was heavy with gilt ornament. Stuffed birds and artificial flowers set in the middle of the mantel were covered by a dome of glass, and on either side stood a tall Italian vase. The carpet was thickly flowered in yellow, its color repeated in heavy draperies and the silk of quilted chairs.

One could easily get mental indigestion from such rich fare, Lora thought as she seated herself somewhat stiffly in a chair indicated by Morgan.

Her hostess wore her favorite black today, but without jewels to relieve the somber effect. Her face seemed paler than ever, her eyes intensely dark by contrast. Lora suspected that Mrs. Channing had not been sleeping well of late.

Morgan twined her fingers in her lap and stared at Lora without welcome. As usual, she was direct and made no gesture toward superficial courtesy.

"I should not have thought you would return to see me so soon after your last unfortunate visit. You have some special purpose here today?"

"I'm not here to plead for myself," Lora said quietly. "I've come about Rebecca."

"Yes?" said Morgan, waiting.

"I have wondered if you intended to take any steps about the girl? After all, she was useful to you and—"

"I shall take steps the moment I locate her," Morgan said. "She will return here to work or I will bring charges against her."

"Charges?" Lora echoed, taken aback. "What has she done?"

Morgan's wide mouth curved vindictively. "Theft, naturally. These people always steal."

"That isn't true!" Lora cried indignantly.

"I'm not accustomed to having my word doubted," said Morgan, and Lora glimpsed a wayward and hoity-toity little girl behind the words. "Any number of articles have been missing since Rebecca left. Of course it will be my word against hers, and who will believe anything she says?"

Lora could only stare at her in dismay. She longed to tell

218

this woman that she would take Rebecca's word against hers any day, but she knew open accusations would do no good at this point. In any event, since the girl wanted to return, perhaps this simplified matters.

"You will need to bring no charges." Lora managed by an effort to keep her voice steady. "We have been in touch with Rebecca and I believe she will return to you if you want her. But I think in the interest of decency you will need to promise her some better treatment."

Morgan sprang to her feet and paced to the window and back. "How dare you tell me what I must do! I will promise her nothing. She will come here on her knees. Perhaps you don't know how thoroughly I hold her in my hands."

"Because of her mother and sister? I do indeed know. But must you humble her further? Isn't it possible to be kind?"

Morgan turned from the window. "When did anyone ever trouble about kindness with me? Don't talk sentimental nonsense! I am beginning to think you as silly as Virginia."

"Very well, Mrs. Channing." Lora stood up with an air of finality. "I shall visit Rebecca myself and advise her not to return to your house. I believe there is no way in which you can harm her mother and sister at this time. When the war is over they will no longer belong to you. They do not now, in fact. As for your charges against Rebecca, I can only believe you are mistaken and they would come to nothing."

Morgan took a step toward her and Lora had an uneasy moment of wondering if the woman was capable of doing her physical harm. Then Morgan seemed to make a visible effort to control herself. Surprisingly, she flung out her hands in a gesture of capitulation.

"Very well! Bring her back and I'll promise what you ask."

This sudden giving in seemed strange coming from Morgan Channing and Lora was a little puzzled.

"Why do you want her back so much?" she asked curiously.

Something flickered in Morgan's eyes and was gone. "She is well trained, useful to me. There's no point in being difficult about the matter if she wants to return. She should be punished for her behavior, but since you ask it, I will waive that."

Lora rose. "Thank you," she said gravely. "I will let her know as soon as possible."

She put no trust in Morgan's words, but after all, if Rebecca were mistreated again it would be easier for the girl to leave the second time. And she herself would keep in touch with affairs through John Ambrose.

She went into the hall ahead of Morgan, into a thin haze that stung her eyes and made her cough. A window stood open at the rear of the house and a breeze was blowing white mist into the hall. Only it was not mist.

"The wind has come up and the smoke is blowing this way!" Morgan cried.

She ran toward the empty rear bedroom and Lora followed her onto the balcony and stood beside her looking out over tree-studded hills. As was its custom on Staten Island, the wind had come up suddenly and now the burning on the opposite hill was no longer a smudge of smoke, but had seared its way to the valley, leaving a black path behind it. A great flaming area was now visible.

Lora choked as a gust of wind blew the white smoke their way. Morgan twisted her hands together.

"If this wind holds, my house is in the fire path! And we've nothing but brush around us. I'll have to find my father. Something must be done!"

She was already running toward the stairs and Lora hurried after her. "Your father's gone down to our house. I met him in the woods when I was coming up. I'll hurry home and send him up here."

"Get Wade too," Morgan cried. "And Adam. Every man you can find. I'll have the stable boy give the alarm."

Morgan ran toward the rear of the house and Lora went out the front door and hurried down the drive. On the way she paused to look back at the house, her eyes searching the second-story level. Yes, there was a fire mark of copper nailed near an upper window—an oval plate with crossed torches and the insurance number. So the fire companies would not turn back from the house for lack of pay.

She plunged breathlessly down the hill, tripping now and then over a root across the path, sparing herself not at all. The smoke haze had not yet crept down the hill and John Ambrose was digging placidly in the patch of garden at the rear of the Tyler house. Mother Tyler sat watching him critically through the open window where her chair had been wheeled.

"There's a fire coming up through the woods toward Morgan's house!" Lora cried as she ran into the yard. "Morgan says you'd better come home at once, John. Peter can go up there too, and I'm going to fetch Adam."

"Lora!" Mrs. Tyler called from her window, and the girl turned impatiently in mid-flight.

"I can't stop now," she told the old lady. "If Wade comes

220

home you'd better send him right up there. They may need every man they can raise. I'll come back as soon as I can."

She had seen woodland fires at home and knew what this ruthless foe could do.

When she reached the Lords' she did not wait for the polite ringing of the bell to be heard, but pounded on the door and shouted for Adam. He came at once, with his sister behind him. He still looked sallow from his recent attack of fever, but at least he was well again.

"There's a fire coming up the hill toward Morgan's house," she told them. "If the wind stays as it is now there may be real danger."

Adam assured Serena that there was nothing she could do and came with Lora at once. Together they started toward the hill path and Lora had to trot to keep up with Adam's longer stride.

"You'd better go home," he advised. "And keep a watch-out. If this thing gets out of control it could burn its way down this side of the hill too. Though the Channing grounds and the upper curve of Dogwood Lane make a natural fire-break which may help."

"I'm going with you," Lora said. "There'll be things I can do at Morgan's and they'll need every hand."

He threw her a quick look, but offered no objection. They saved themselves for fast climbing and did no more talking until they reached the level of the pool and stopped a moment for breath. Adam did not look too fit, and Lora regarded him doubtfully.

"Perhaps you shouldn't be doing this. After all, you've been ill and—"

"Don't trouble being sorry for me. I'm all right," he said shortly. "Have you talked to Morgan yet about Rebecca?"

Lora nodded. "This morning. She's going to take her back. Though first she was full of threats about bringing charges against her, punishing her—I don't know why she gave in so quickly."

"Well, let's get on," Adam said and they hurried upward again.

Ambrose and Peter were already on hand. Clothilde, the French housekeeper, and the other women servants were drawing water from the well, while men stood on ladders throwing pails of it upon the roofs of stable and servants' quarters nearest to the danger. Over everything hung the ominous white haze and the air was uncomfortable to breathe.

The bells of rival fire companies could be heard clanging

221

up the hill and in a few moments the horses of the Zephyr Company appeared, pulling the heavy engine up the drive, while volunteer firemen overran the grounds. A few were equipped with red hats and shirts, but most of them had come dressed as they were when the alarm sounded. Hose was quickly lowered into the well and volunteers manned the hand pump.

Lora stood for a few moments watching the single, thin stream of water begin the doubtful task of watering down the space of brush back of the Channing grounds. The second fire company had arrived shortly behind the first, but its men stood idly by, watching the progress of the fire up the hill. It was likely that they would not lift a finger unless the first company agreed to "slice the melon" by sharing the insurance company's reward. The sight made Lora indignant, but she knew there was no way to oppose this ridiculous system. Not even if the house burned down.

She went to work in the kitchen, setting a huge coffee pot on the stove. The reviving powers of the brew would be needed in the hours ahead while all hands worked at the emergency.

Through the kitchen window she could hear the not too distant crackling of flames. The stifling smell of the fire now pervaded the entire house and her eyes smarted constantly.

Morgan came up from the cellar carrying a stack of gunny sacking to be taken outside and soaked with water, in the event of hand-to-hand fighting with encroaching flames. She glanced at Lora, apparently taking her efforts for granted, and ran outside at once with her burden.

Lora found big china cups kept for the use of the servants and filled them with the steaming liquid. These she set on a tray and carried outside to serve to whoever needed a respite. Again and again she made the trip, for the coffee was accepted gratefully wherever she went.

The scene was one of furious activity by now. More distant neighbors, attracted by the blaze, climbed the hill to help. All were pitching in with a will except for the idle volunteers, who stood about cracking jokes at the expense of the working company.

But still the flames ate their way upward and the sound of the roaring grew constantly louder. One could feel a pulsing of heat in the air, even at this distance. The wind blew in uncertain bursts and there were moments when it seemed that it might shift to another direction. But always it veered again to the uphill attack.

Now many of the men had stripped to the waist in the warming sun, facing the still fiercer heat of the fire as it blazed up the hill toward them. Lora could not refrain from keeping a nurse's eye out for Adam, who should certainly not be up here doing such work as this when he had been so recently ill. But she did not see him among the groups she visited.

After she had handed around her current serving of coffee she looked for him deliberately and saw that he was working alone at a distance from the others, chopping at scrubby dry brush, working toward the line of a firebreak that had been started immediately back of the servants' quarters. Lora set her tray of empty cups down and picked up the last cup of coffee she had been saving for him. Then she walked behind the buildings to the place where his ax lifted and fell against the brush. It looked as though there would be little time left before the whole fight would become a hand-to-hand matter, with only wet gunny sacking and that single weak stream of water to fight the devouring fury.

Adam saw her coming and threw down his ax for a moment as he wiped dripping sweat from his forehead. He grinned as if he were really enjoying himself. His shirt was streaked with soil and plastered against his body, and he took the time now to pull it off and toss it in a heap on the grass. His muscular shoulders and stocky torso shone wet in the sunlight.

"Hello, Nurse," he said. "You couldn't be more welcome."

He reached for the cup she held out to him and drank the coffee in a few deep draughts. As he drank he stood with his legs braced and his hand shook a little when he gave back the cup.

She began to feel sorry that she had summoned him to this task. "You shouldn't be doing this," she told him. "Couldn't you work at something less strenuous? You're quite likely to collapse and then the others will have to stop work to come and carry you into the house."

"I'm not the collapsing kind," he told her, and weaved a little on his legs.

She put out a hand to steady him and he startled her by catching it in his own. There was a daredevil light in his eyes. Before she could pull away, he drew her into the circle of his arms and put his mouth hard upon her own. She could feel the damp warmth of his body beneath her hands, taste the salt sweat of his kiss. For a queer, heady moment her pulses quickened in response and her lips were soft beneath

223

his own. Then she pushed away furiously, wiped her palm across her mouth.

As suddenly as he had drawn her to him, he held her at arm's length, laughing down at her, recognizing fully her instant of surrender.

"Your—fever has returned," she cried desperately, hating the tremor in her voice. "I'll send someone here at once."

He had picked up the ax to return to his work, but now he let his hand fall and leaned on the handle. "Wait! I'm suffering from no fever. I kissed you because that was what I've long had in mind. And if you were not a rabbit—but since you are, you'd better scurry for safety, lest I try again."

She could find no words stinging enough with which to demolish him. She picked up her skirts and fled toward the house with the hateful sound of his laughter ringing behind her.

He was a dreadful person—uncouth, unpredictable, dangerous. Her blood burned with hot anger and her hands trembled. She could only hope that no one had seen what had happened. But now the roar of the fire was frighteningly near and she put the thought of Adam out of her mind.

Tiny, fluttering tongues of the enemy advance reached to the very edge of the cleared space, like the flags of an invading army, and smoke rose blue above the spreading area of fire. Every gust of wind carried drifting smudges of ash. The defenders stood ready with wet sacking to flail at any lighting spark and the firemen rested a moment at their pumping and held the hose ready to quell such attack as might be made on the roof or wall. If only the wind would cease its irregular blasts, the stable might be saved. Long since, the horses had been removed and tethered in the lower woods at John Ambrose's direction and the carriages moved to safety. But the servants' quarters were over the stable and now Clothilde and others were pitching their belongings out the window, or carrying them away tied in bed sheets. Now and then Lora glimpsed John Ambrose moving capably and calmly among the excited throng.

There was no time now for coffee; the real battle was about to be posed. Lora carried her tray of empty cups to the kitchen and set them down with a rattle as the disturbing memory of Adam's kiss swept back. Even more disturbing was her realization of the momentary response she had given him. She dampened her handkerchief and scrubbed her mouth free of his kiss. But there was no time to waste on personal resentments. She must find something else useful to do. Perhaps she could help remove valuables from this house, in case the danger increased.

She went into the hall, meaning to look for Morgan, when she heard the sound of raised voices from the front of the house—as if some argument was going on. This was no moment for ordinary manners and she hurried to investigate.

The drawing-room door was ajar and she pushed it wide without ceremony. Morgan and Wade stood with their backs toward her. Morgan seemed to be resisting valiantly some request which Wade pressed upon her. Lora broke in on them at once.

"Morgan! The fire has reached the cleared places now. If it jumps to the stable anything can happen. Have you packed up what you want to save? You may have to abandon the house."

Morgan looked at her as blankly as though she had forgotten the fire. But Lora's words seemed to encourage Wade in his purpose.

"It has to come down," he insisted to Morgan. "You musn't risk having it burned to ashes."

Anger blazed in Morgan's eyes. "I am still mistress of this house. I'll be happy to see it burn with the house, if the house must burn!"

Wade turned away from her to stride the length of the room as swiftly as his limp allowed him. And now Lora saw his purpose. The draperies had been pulled back from the painting of Morgan and Virginia, and as Wade went toward it she saw the kitchen knife in his hand and realized that he meant to cut the canvas from its frame.

Morgan, however, flew down the room ahead of him, her state plainly one of near hysteria. "Let it burn, I tell you! I won't have Virginia staring at me any longer with those pale eyes. All along I've wanted to see that picture destroyed."

"Don't behave like the heroine of a bad play," Wade said coldly, and there was a lash to his tone. "I'm only trying to save a valuable work of art. There are other possessions about the house which you should be giving your attention to, as Lora has pointed out."

Morgan seemed to go suddenly limp, and he pushed her aside easily, reached toward the picture with his knife.

Lora ran to help him. "Here—I'll push this desk over. Then I can stand on it and reach the higher part of the picture. It should be saved for Jemmy's sake. Give me the knife."

There was surprise in the look Wade turned upon her, but

225

he handed her the knife and would have helped her clamber onto the desk.

But just then a shouting from outside reached them. Morgan started as if she had wakened from some spell and ran out of the room. Something had certainly occurred outside. Lora tossed the knife onto the desk.

"Let's see what's happened," she said to Wade, and he limped beside her as she went toward the rear of the house.

They stood at the back door together, watching the frantic scene in the yard. Flames were running up the ridgepole of the stable roof, hissing as the single stream from the firemen's hose harried them futilely. They darted along the shingles, zigzagging downward, and the crowd in the yard watched the doomed building helplessly. In a few moments a fierce burst of light behind the panes revealed that the interior too was blazing.

But now at last the wind, having satisfied its capricious will, seemed to be dying out altogether and no more sparks and burning embers were being carried across the bare expanse of yard toward the main house. At only one point did the fire seem to have leaped across the firebreaks. Along the rest of the line it seemed to be satiating its appetite among the stubble, burning itself out in black patches.

Adam came toward them across the yard, streakings of soot smearing his upper body, his hair and eyebrows singed. Lora looked away from him quickly, standing very close to Wade.

"You should have arrived sooner," Adam said dryly to Wade. "We could have used an extra hand."

"I'm afraid I'd have done you little good as a helper," Wade admitted.

Lora could only turn a furious look upon Adam, hating the flush that rose in her cheeks. Even as she turned purposefully away from him, she knew that he had noted it and was amused.

Now the stable and the quarters above were burning fiercely and even the firemen had given up wasting further water on the conflagration. Off to the left and right down the hillside the fire seemed to be dying out—balked on one hand by a stony meadow which had long been cleared of trees, and on the other by a road which cut through the woodland, edged for a distance by a low stone wall.

Adam stretched himself upon the ground, looking really ill now and no longer able to stand. He fumbled with his shirt, buttoning it on, then folded his arms across drawn-up

226

knees and leaned his head upon them. If he were ill, let other hands succor him, Lora thought, still angry and shaken.

Wade touched her arm gently. "I think there's no further use in staying here. We ought to get back to Mother. She'll be worried. But first let's ask Morgan if there's anything else we can do."

There was a crash and a shower of sparks as the stable roof fell in, but now more smoke than flame shot up and the blaze was quite evidently eating itself out.

Morgan was nowhere in sight and they went through the back door into the house. Clothilde met them in the hallway, plainly distraught. She was a thin, nervous woman, dressed in black with a white apron tied about her waist.

"Please!" she cried to Lora and Wade. "Madame Channing does the so terrible thing. Please, you will go to stop her."

She waved them toward the drawing room. Lora and Wade went quickly to the door.

Morgan had climbed upon the desk Lora had pulled before the picture and she stood upon it with her legs braced and the kitchen knife upheld in her right hand. She was hacking roughly at a space near the center of the picture, and the white gash above the knife showed what damage had already been done.

"Morgan! Stop!" Wade cried. He went across the room as quickly as he could manage with his cane. When Morgan turned he reached up and twisted the knife from her hand.

"Give it back to me!" she cried, stamping her foot on the inlaid desk top. "You wanted the picture of Virginia, didn't you? Well, I was going to give it to you. I don't want it—so the thing might as well be cut in two. Then I can be free of the way she watches me."

Wade stepped out of her reach with the knife. "I can't stop you if you choose to do something hysterical. But it isn't necessary to ruin the picture. I'd thought to save the whole thing, not deface it that way."

She stared at him for a long moment and then crumpled suddenly on the desk, her black skirts billowing about her. She put her head in her hands and began to sob uncontrollably. Clothilde, who had hovered in the background, ran toward her and began to wave a bottle of smelling salts near her nose. Morgan flung up her head and slapped the green bottle from Clothilde's hand. It struck a chair and shattered, staining the carpet. For a moment the pungent odor was choking.

"Get that away from me!" Morgan cried. "And go! Go

away, all of you! As if I hadn't had enough to bear today." She stared angrily at Wade. "What do you know of how it is —having her up there on the wall staring at me, blaming me? I've tried to hide her face behind those draperies, but she looks at me right through the cloth. Day and night. What am I to do? What am I to do?" She rocked her body back and forth in torment, her head in her hands again.

Lora turned to Wade. "I've seen this sort of thing before. Clothilde and I will manage. Please go home. We musn't keep your mother waiting any longer. I'll follow as soon as I can."

Morgan's state was quite evidently something Wade was glad to escape. "Don't stay too long," he said, and went out of the room.

Lora took Morgan's arm firmly. "We're going to get you to bed now. A good sleep will make you feel better. Come along with us."

The quiet, authoritative tones of adult to child seemed to have some effect. Morgan sobbed convulsively, but she slipped obediently from the desk. Lora silenced Clothilde's clucking with a glance and put her arm about Morgan's waist, led her quietly from the room. Adam stood in the hallway, leaning against the newel post as if he needed to cling to something to stay erect. But Lora had no interest in a second patient. When he would have spoken she shook her head at him sternly and it was likely that Morgan, her handkerchief to her eyes, did not even notice him as Lora led her up the stairs.

When Morgan had been undressed and given hot milk to drink, she lay back upon her pillows and closed her eyes. The hysteria had gone out of her and she was drowsy and spent. Lora sent Clothilde away to help settle the servants into temporary quarters in the big house and to summon Morgan's father here. Then only the two of them were together in the darkened room.

Discovering that it was afternoon and she was growing hungry, Lora had accepted the glass of milk and thick slices of homemade bread and jam Clothilde took time to bring her. She ate now and watched Morgan drowsing in the big bed.

But Morgan was not asleep. Once her heavy lids fluttered open and she stared at Lora. "Why are you being kind to me?" she demanded.

"You need me," Lora said simply. She smiled, attempting

228

to keep her tone light. "Adam says I can never keep away from anyone who needs me."

A faint light of interest sparked into the dark gaze. "I saw you kissing him this morning—down there at the far corner of the yard."

Lora said nothing. There were no words which would place the blame on Adam and exonerate her. She could only wish that of all people Morgan had not seen what happened.

"I don't blame you for turning elsewhere. Not with Wade for a husband. Why do I still want him, Lora? Why should I fight anyone to get him when I know he's not worth it?"

"Be quiet," Lora said. "Don't say things you'll be sorry for. Things that aren't true. You don't want Wade, and I'm not turning to Adam. Go to sleep."

Morgan's eyes closed and she lay very still. When Ambrose came quietly into the room she did not stir or open her eyes. Lora put her finger to her lips.

"I'll stay a while," he whispered. "But I think she'll be right enough now."

Lora thanked him with a smile and made her escape.

Downstairs she paused at the drawing-room door and looked in. The desk had been returned to its accustomed place and the green velvet curtain hid Virginia, hid the slashed place between the two figures where Morgan's knife had cut through the canvas.

Lora sighed and hurried to the front door, inexpressibly glad to be free of the emotional tumult of this house. On the front steps Wade sat, his cane beside him, one leg outstretched. He looked up as she came down the steps.

"I've been waiting for you," he said.

XXIV

WADE GOT TO HIS feet unsteadily and smiled down at her.

"You didn't climb that long hill again just for me?" Lora protested.

"Why not? You've been helping up here, and I came too late to be of any use. The least I could do was return after I'd set Mother's mind at ease. I thought I might see you home and keep the dragons in the woods away from you."

229

Remembering the betrayal of her own lips in the moment when Adam had kissed her, she winced. She could not accept Wade's consideration as sweetly as it was given. If he knew, he would not be here.

But when he offered her his arm as formally as if they'd been going for a Sunday stroll, she took it and went down the steps with him. Her knees felt shaky and more than anything else she wanted to reach the haven of her own room, fling herself across her bed and forget everything in the oblivion of sleep.

Wade spoke only once on the way down. "So Morgan is haunted too," he mused. "I hadn't suspected that."

"You mean you think she blames herself in some way for—"

He nodded unhappily, and Lora wished she had the strength and wisdom to argue with him. She doubted that Morgan felt the slightest self-reproach, even though she suffered some aberration about the picture.

No dragons appeared in the woods and they made the rest of the trip downhill in silence. He seemed to understand her weariness, and though he could not know the mingled emotions which had swept through her that day, he sensed her need for withdrawal and made no effort to intrude small talk upon her.

Back at home he left her at the foot of the stairs and returned to his mother's sitting room. Lora went up to find Jemmy waiting for her at the head of the stairs.

"I wanted to go up to Morgan Le Fay's!" he cried. "I wanted to see the fire, but Grandmother wouldn't let me. She said I'd be in the way. Is Hamlin all right, Lorie?"

"Quite all right, Jemmy, and you'd better not go there today. It's all over anyway and everyone is tired and busy. You can go up tomorrow and see what has happened."

He leaned toward her, sniffing as she reached the top step. "You smell real strong of smoke. Was it scary, Lorie? Tell me about it. Papa shut me out when he came back to tell Grandmother. She said it was too exciting for me. But I *like* excitement."

"Of course," said Lora. "All boys do, even when it isn't good for them. But now I need to get a warm bath and lie down for a while, Jemmy. I'm so tired and my head hurts. Tomorrow I'll tell you all about everything, and that's a promise."

Any appeal to his sympathy always reached him, and Jemmy pleaded no further. Lora undresssed and bathed herself from head to toe in the zinc-lined tub in the bathroom. She brushed her long hair to bright luster and rubbed her head roughly with a towel, striving to be rid of the sickening odor of smoke. Then she closed the shutters in her room and got limply into bed.

There could hardly be a more grateful moment in life, she thought languidly, than the first instant of consigning a weary body to the softness of a feather mattress, the moment of relaxing mind and body, of surrendering as quickly as possible to sleep.

For a little while the events of the day flashed in muddled sequence through her mind. Then slumber came and washed away the senseless pattern. For a long while her sleep was so deep that it did not seem that she dreamed at all. But when her consciousness hovered near waking she had an awareness of the passage of time. When she lifted her heavy lids she found the room dark except for a faint glow of moonlight edging the shutter slats. She had slept into the night.

She blinked the heaviness from her eyes and they became gradually accustomed to the gloom. Something in the room was changed, was not as usual. She turned on her side, the better to see the shadowy bulk not far from her bed. A rocker creaked and she came widely awake. There was someone in the nearby chair, watching, waiting for her to waken.

"Jemmy?" she inquired softly.

The figure in the chair moved and threw aside a quilt which had wrapped it.

"Not Jemmy," Wade said.

He went to her dresser for a candle, and she closed her eyes for a moment against the sharp arrowhead of light. When she opened them Wade had returned to his chair and was rocking gently back and forth.

The candle flame made only a small aura of illumination behind him. It left his figure in shadow, faintly outlined, his face invisible. The senseless flashing in her mind had ceased. She was quiet now and there was peace.

He is my husband, she thought. *I do not want to be angry with him, or to pity him, or to condemn him. I want only to learn to love him.*

This was a thought so strange that she could only wonder at it. Oddly, it carried no sense of disloyalty to an old love. The girl she had been in the past would always belong to Martin. But that girl was a cocoon from which someone new had grown and the new entity was lonely and longed for love. Nevertheless, a desire for love was not love itself, she thought

231

warily, but at least it gave her an increased tenderness toward Wade.

"Why did you stay with me?" she asked. "Why did you watch while I slept?"

"I was lonely," he said simply. "I wanted to be near you."

He too, she thought, and was touched. She wished she might go to him easily and naturally, as a wife should; put her arms about him and her lips upon his in this new tenderness. But there was a shyness in her, a lack of certainty that held her back. She must not be betrayed into the pretense of giving when there was so little in her to be honestly given.

She raised herself on one elbow. "What time is it?"

"Near midnight," he said. "Lora—" There was a warmth, a softness in his voice, almost an affection. She swerved away from it quickly. She was not ready, nor was he. Tenderness was not enough.

"I'm ravenously hungry," she said. "I've had only a bite to eat this afternoon, and no dinner at all. Do you suppose we could raid the kitchen for a midnight meal?"

He withdrew almost perceptibly, so that the thing which had been there a moment before was gone. But he was not resentful, despite his withdrawal. There was still kindness in his tone.

"Of course we can. I'm hungry too. Here—let me get your wrapper."

He brought it for her from the wardrobe. Not her old, worn one, but the feminine gown of pale blue which had been his gift, opened days after the unhappy fiasco of Christmas and never worn. Now she slipped it on and let him bring her the blue slippers he had given her to match.

"There!" he said. "You look frivolous now, and small and helpless."

"And you'd like me that way?" Lora could not resist the challenge.

He had moved toward the door, the candle in his hand. Its yellow flame gave his face a golden warmth, as if the gray cold behind it had begun to thaw a little. He shook his head at her, smiling.

"Only if frivolous and helpless is what you are," he said. "I'd like to know you as you are, Lora."

She followed him into the hall without answering, while he lighted her way. There was danger in this new softening toward her. Because she felt suddenly guilty, she tried to make their midnight meal a gay adventure. They closed the kitchen door with secret laughter, lest they awaken his mother, and behind the shutters they lighted only candles, lest one of the servants see brighter lamplight and come to investigate.

There was cold chicken left from dinner in the icebox, and a bowl of potato salad. She poured glasses of rich milk, dipped that very morning from the huge cans brought around by the milk cart. Lora ate hungrily, while Wade nibbled a bite here and there without the appetite he had claimed.

"Did you get Morgan quieted after I left?" he asked, when they came to a halt in their self-conscious effort to be gay.

"We had no trouble," Lora told him. "I put on my schoolmarm manner and she turned right into a weepy child and did what I told her to do. She went to sleep almost at once."

"No more accusations or dramatics?"

Lora considered the question and decided on frankness. There had been too much of secrecy and subterfuge in this house.

"She blurted out that she still wanted you and would fight anyone for you."

Wade flung down his napkin. "Why must she always want whatever is denied her? Even as a child, the thing over which she was balked was the thing she must have. There's no affection in her feeling toward me, not even liking. She had only contempt for me, really. And I dislike her heartily."

Lora bit the last speck of meat from a chicken leg and wiped her fingers free of grease. "Since we're being truthful with each other tonight, will you let me ask you something?"

"I know," he said ruefully. "You're thinking of that time in the woods when Jemmy saw us. You want to know why—"

She nodded. "That's the one thing that doesn't fit any pattern I can find for you. You would never have turned away from Virginia."

He made a quick, despairing gesture. "No, I would not," he said. "And yet—"

And yet . . . Lora thought, remembering Adam.

"I'll try to tell you what happened," he said, and there was sudden urgency in his voice. "Do you know that there was a time when I might have married Morgan?"

"I know. And your mother has told me about that day when Morgan struck at her with the curling iron."

He winced. "She is so many things—Morgan. Anything is possible. Just as anything is possible with my mother. Even now I do not know the truth for certain. But Morgan came to me that day in the woods in the quiet, gentle way she sometimes used to adopt as a child and which always appealed to me. She grasped at nothing, asked for nothing, except that

233

I listen. Then she told me that she had never struck my mother that day. Mother had come to upbraid her and threaten her, but though Morgan was angry, she said she did nothing at all but listen."

"What of the burn across your mother's hand?"

"She told me she'd tried to go on curling her hair and had picked up the hot iron when Mother suddenly darted toward her and grasped it with her bare hand. Then Mother screamed for help and when I came she made her accusations against Morgan. And she had a burned hand to prove it."

"But if what Morgan says is true, why didn't she speak up at the time?"

Wade shook his head wearily. "She knew no one would believe her. It was Mother's word against hers, and she had a reputation for doing violent, unpredictable things. I could remember how queerly proud and quiet Morgan was at the time, offering no defense of any kind, but constantly accusing me with her eyes. And I didn't understand."

"She could still be lying," Lora said.

"She had an air of honesty about her. She spoke quietly and simply. In a sense not like herself at all. It seemed to me that she was telling the truth and that we had both been bitterly tricked by my mother. She was crying when she finished telling me, and somehow all of my old feeling for her came back and I held her close to me and kissed her."

He was silent and Lora reached across the table to touch his hand comfortingly.

"But later of course Morgan became her old self again and tried to use that moment to reinstate herself with me. After Virginia's death. I could only feel repelled by her then. By that time I knew that Virginia might well have died because I'd held Morgan in my arms for those few moments. I told Morgan that I wanted nothing more to do with her. Lora, you know that I truly loved Virginia?"

Lora nodded. She knew indeed. "But your mother? If this is true then she did as terrible a thing as she accused Morgan of doing."

"She believed she was saving me from great injury. Perhaps she was. But I knew I had to escape from her after that. My need for escape was one reason for my enlisting. During those months away I promised myself a hundred times that if ever I returned it would be as my own man, owning my own soul."

"You are your own man now," Lora said softly.

He went to the kitchen door and pulled it open, and she

rose and stood beside him. The moon stared palely through a thin veiling of cloud and the April night was mild, with only a touch of sea chill to it. He took her hand and drew her out into the soft gloom.

"Spring!" he whispered. "You can almost hear things growing, getting ready to surprise us in the morning."

"Do you feel that too?" she said, both touched and surprised. She had not dreamed that his thoughts could turn along such lines. How little she knew him really.

He drew a full deep breath that swelled his lungs. "It makes me feel the way I used to as a little boy. As if something mysterious was ahead of me. I can remember a place where the spring sun used to warm a broken wall in the old Hume house. I've gone there sometimes to sit alone and feel myself part of the growing. Part of every living thing."

She leaned her cheek against his arm for just a moment because there were no words to give him. She could love that little boy he had once been just as she could love Jemmy. He traced the curve of her cheek with his fingers and felt the coolness of her skin.

"You're chilled. Enough of this mooning in the back yard. Back to bed with you. Ellie will never get over it if she sees us here."

They laughed together lightly and hurried inside to put things away, conceal all evidence of their repast. If Ellie found some of her chicken gone tomorrow, she could think what she liked, but at least they would leave no betraying signs.

Together they went upstairs, their shadows marching tall beside them in the candlelight. He saw her to the door of her own room and for a moment her breath quickened with the beat of her heart. But he said good night as politely as if he were some swain bringing her home from a ball, and went away to his own room and his own bed.

As she blew out her candle and returned to her rumpled sheets, an unwanted memory forced itself into her mind. The memory of Adam's mouth demanding upon her own—unwelcome, but asking no permission, unafraid of her refusal.

The waxy smell of the snuffed candle pervaded the room as she lay in the dark. She had no wish to think of Adam—yet there the thought of him was, strong and clear as the feel of his mouth had been. And there was no will in her to put the thought away. What would happen if Wade should take her like that—not gently asking her assent, but claiming as a right? She didn't know. She couldn't tell.

The following week saw May blooming full and green across the island. Already forsythia and crocus were gone and dandelion heads were turning white. Along the lane the dogwood blossoms which gave the road its name burst into white magic, and a delicate scent of apple blossom laced through the dark harbor smell that blew across the island.

But now the surging of anticipation, of energy, like sap coursing through green things, had given way to a certain languor, which too was part of spring. For Jemmy it meant doses of sulphur and molasses which he detested and was certain he did not need. For Wade it meant a restlessness that drove him into trips about the island—but whether these were in the interest of the Circle Lora did not know. Sometimes he sat for long hours at the desk in the library, but whether he strove again to write he did not say. And the desk was always carefully locked when he left the room. Not again had there come such a moment of sympathy between them as on the night of Morgan's fire.

Today was so warm that Mother Tyler had asked to be wheeled outdoors. Peter had made a small wooden ramp which he placed against the rear veranda and down this he wheeled her chair. In the garden green sprouts were already piercing the brown earth and Lora had found some satisfaction and release for her own energies in either, working with Ambrose when he came to tend the garden, or alone when he could not come. Morgan's stables were being rebuilt and Ambrose often lent a hand, or a supervisory eye.

This morning Mrs. Tyler sat in the shade of a blossoming apple tree, her hands for once idle in her lap, her eyes observing Lora as she knelt to work with trowel and gloves, digging the scourge of dandelions out of struggling grass.

Rebecca had gone back to work for Morgan a few days before, though somewhat uncertainly and fearfully. And now that Lora had seen in Morgan the transformation of a supposedly poised woman to a tantrum-throwing child, she could understand Rebecca's uneasiness. Lora had seen the girl yesterday and Rebecca had said in her veiled way that everything was fine. Even now she did not accept Lora's interest with complete trust. What had happened about the man she had been seeing, or how important he was in Rebecca's eyes, Lora had no way of knowing. John Ambrose had told her that Morgan had no inkling of that matter and it was better if she did not know about it for the time being. But if Rebecca had to steal away secretly for visits to McKeon Street, her position with Morgan would not be too secure.

Lora dug the point of the trowel into the soft earth and pried up an offending plant, her thoughts coming nearer to home. Only this morning before he had gone to school, Jemmy had looked at her with reproachful eyes.

"I'm not going to get my dog back, am I, Lorie? Papa is never going to let him come home. I know."

She could not promise him outright again. So far Wade had resisted her every effort to bring up the subject. As far as he was concerned the dog could come back if she wanted to take the responsibility with his mother, wanted to work out the whole matter herself. Was she wrong, she wondered, in not taking that easy way out for Jemmy's sake? It was beginning to seem that Wade would never make the step of his own free will. He wanted only to be let alone. When opposing individuals began to put pressure on him his one instinct seemed to be toward escape—not toward fighting the matter out with one or the other.

"You look as if you were talking to yourself," said Mother Tyler suddenly, "—the way you're frowning and pursing your mouth!"

Lora gave a resisting dandelion plant an energetic tug and sat back on the grass, dropping her trowel and stripping off her gloves. "I didn't realize I was giving myself away. But you're right. I was arguing with Wade just then. About Jemmy's dog."

"That matter was settled long ago," Mother Tyler snapped.

"I'm sorry," said Lora quietly, "but it was not. I told Jemmy at the time that I would get his dog back for him. And Wade has given me permission to do so if I manage the whole thing myself." She looked up at the old lady with a challenge in her eyes. "He means that *I* must take all the blame and responsibility when you have an accident or take to your bed again."

The woman in the wheel chair stared in astonishment. "What do you mean? How dare you intimate that—"

"Please," Lora said, looking away from her, "it's too warm a day to get angry. In some ways you are a very honest woman and I admire you. But you aren't honest about this—not even with yourself."

At least the old lady had learned that raging and storming got her nowhere with Lora. She had even begun to give the girl a certain grudging respect because Lora had proved an adversary worthy of her mettle. It was too easy to browbeat everyone else, and sometimes a little tiresome.

"Very well," said Mrs. Tyler tartly, "since I find myself

237

helpless in this chair and unable to escape from the valuable advice offered me by a chit who is scarcely out of swaddling clothes, you may instruct me."

Lora rocked back and forth on the grass, her knees pulled up beneath her chin. "It's not really you I want to be honest about, but Wade. Do you think we could both be honest about him?"

"Since you have known him for a handful of months and I have known him all his life, this promises to be an interesting, if not informative discussion."

"I wonder if you really do know him," Lora said softly.

"Know him? I know his every thought and gesture. I know his waywardness, his refusal to take the advice which would have made a man of him."

"A man in whose pattern?"

"His grandfather's, of course. From the very first I tried to save him from his father's course, tried to hold up to him the ideal that was Jason Cowles. But as a child he would twist in my very hands. And when I managed to extract obedience from him he would fail so miserably that I would wash my hands of him for weeks at a time."

"Do you really think any human being can be turned into something he is not?" Lora asked. "I don't believe Wade could be like Jason Cowles if he lived a hundred years."

"So he became the spineless thing he is!" said Mrs. Tyler, and scorn cut through her voice.

"I don't believe he's in the least spineless. He is trying to go his own way. He wanted your love and admiration very much as a boy. Why didn't you ever seek for something in him to love and admire?"

"As his calf-eyed Virginia did? No, thank you. I see him as he is. For his own good. And now I'll ask you a question— what do *you* see in him to love and admire?"

Lora closed her eyes, rocking again. This was not something she could be entirely truthful about. Mother Tyler had long ago surmised the facts. What the old woman said now was intended to taunt.

She chose her words carefully. "I see the things he could be. I see what is in him to become."

"Pah! Those were the things I tried to see. But he wouldn't grow, or else he could not. He is my son and I have an affection for him, my fine lady, in spite of your accusation."

"I wonder if affection without respect does anyone any good? I wouldn't want such a thing for myself. Why shouldn't he resist an affection like that?"

"You seem to be running in circles," the old lady said. "You won't have me change him, yet you talk about his becoming something else. He gives me nothing to win my respect, yet you talk about love being worthless without respect. Well, enough of this nonsense. Come back and talk to me in twenty years when you've more sense in your silly young head."

Lora straightened and looked at her. "Are you aware that Wade knows the truth about that day when you grasped Morgan's curling iron?"

The old woman was a master at controlling her features. She blinked slowly and started to speak, but Lora went on.

"I know that it's Morgan's word against yours. But this time Wade believes Morgan. So perhaps there is something lacking in what respect he may feel for you."

It was the first time Lora had ever seen Mother Tyler at a complete loss for words. She lay back in her chair and closed her eyes. In the merciless light every line in her face seemed deeply etched.

Lora got up and dusted the bits of earth and grass from her skirts. Then she came over and stood beside the old lady's chair.

"All these things are long in the past and should be forgotten. It is *now* that matters. I want to help Wade. And I want to help you and Jemmy too. Right now, you. Come— take my hands and walk a few steps. Two steps, three, six— no more. You stand every day when you get into that chair. You can learn to walk alone if you try."

She held out her hands while the old woman stared at her in angry resentment.

"Do you think I am pretending this injury? The Lord has seen fit to punish me with this affliction and I can only be resigned to His will."

"I don't believe that," Lora said. "But I do believe He'd help you if you tried to help yourself. You've let your muscles grow too weak to hold you, but there is still muscle control there . . . if we begin to exercise it every day it will increase. Come now—I won't let you fall."

Mother Tyler slapped her hands away and pouted like a child. "I'll do nothing of the kind. Go get me a glass of water, if you please."

"That is changing the subject," said Lora. "I will get your water in a moment. If you know Wade so well, what is it that he wants from life? Tell me that."

239

"To be loved exactly as he is, of course. Just as his blindly devoted Virginia loved him."

Lora nodded. "That's what I've thought too. I suppose that is really what we all want—every one of us. Morgan and Adam Hume and me. And you, too. It would be so easy that way, so pleasant. We'd never have to look our faults in the eye, or do anything about them. But my father never thought that was good for anyone."

At least Mother Tyler was listening now. "Go on," she said wryly. "This is most revealing."

A breeze stirred through the garden and Lora held out her hand to catch the drifting white snow of apple blossoms, then blew them away with a puff.

"I can't go on," she said. "I don't suppose I'm even thinking these things out for myself. I'm remembering my father and the things he told me. But I can't remember enough. I think you're still fighting some sort of battle that was really ended in the past. But you've never found out that the war has long been over and that you can now lay down your arms. You've only friends around you."

"What on earth do you mean by such gibberish?"

"You might even find here in your own house something of what you've been fighting for, all these years."

"May I have that glass of water, or must I scream for Ellie? No one ever brings out my bell when I come into the yard."

"I'll get your water," Lora said, and went quickly off.

She returned with a glass of cool well water, clear and sparkling in the May sunshine, and gave it to the old lady, who drank thirstily. She looked so weary and old that in the merciless light every line in her face seemed more deeply grooved. Lora felt a little guilty. Perhaps she had not been altogether fair or kind.

Mrs. Tyler handed her the glass. "Where *is* that dog?" she asked irritably.

"Why—" Lora hesitated, confused by the unexpectedness of the question. "John Ambrose has him up at Morgan's. He's been there ever since the day Wade had him taken away."

"So that is how his orders are obeyed? But no matter. Get him back. Let the boy have him. I've endured this wrangling and these reproachful looks long enough."

For a moment Lora could only stare in surprise. Then she reached out and touched Mrs. Tyler's shoulder gently.

"Thank you, Mother. But we can't do it that way. Not yet."

"Why not? What do you mean?"

"I—I don't know how to explain it. It's just that I feel this is something Wade must do. He banished the puppy himself to give in to you. Now he should be willing to accept the responsibility of bringing it back—no matter what he thinks you may do. It must be hard for him—or there's no value in it. If you make it easy—"

"You're confusing me. I thought you wanted to see Jemmy happy. And I know what store the boy sets by that dog. I'd already decided to see what I could do about the matter. I can't remember now what I was so angry about. Because you crossed me, I expect. But now *you* are holding back from doing this for the child."

"Jemmy needs love, but not coddling," Lora said. "He's really a very strong little boy when it comes to spirit. I suspect he's like his grandfather Jason. Like you."

The old lady blinked and her mouth creased into a long-unused smile. "What a joke on me—if that proves true. I've always thought him a stubborn child whose will ought to be broken."

"I don't think you can break it," Lora told her. "Any more than anyone could break yours. But Wade is different. Not like his father either, from what I've heard. Like himself. But he has bound himself to a wheel chair in a sense, just as you have, and goodness knows how we're ever going to get either of you to see that you can walk!"

"I don't want to walk!" the old lady said. "Do stop chattering and go back to your dandelions. At least twelve new plants have cropped up while you've been wasting your time!"

Lora laughed and returned to her work. Behind her Mother Tyler closed her eyes and seemed to sleep. But once she opened them and spoke sharply to Lora.

"Think you're a clever one, don't you?" she said.

XXV

ONE AFTERNOON a few days later Ellie came up to Lora's room while she was changing her dress for dinner and announced that Mr. Norwood was calling. He had asked for Mr. Wade, but since he was not in, Mr. Norwood would like to see his wife.

Lora hurried downstairs to the parlor and gave her hand

in greeting to the tall, blond man. They both agreed that it was a lovely day and Mr. Norwood murmured several absent pleasantries.

"I'm sorry Wade is out," Lora said. "But since it's getting late, he should be home at any moment. Won't you wait for him?"

As a rule Murray Norwood was impeccably dressed and unruffled in manner. But today his shoes and gray trousers bore spatterings of mud, as if he had stepped without care into muddy streets. And there was a restless movement to his gaze as it shifted about the room, while his fingers tapped his knee nervously. If she had not been there, Lora suspected, he would have jumped up to pace the room.

"I hope nothing is wrong," she said at length. "You seem to be worried."

He looked at her then, as if realizing her presence for the first time. For a moment he hesitated, as if gauging her, wondering whether or not to speak.

Then he said shortly, "General Burnside has made the most contemptible and ridiculous move of his career. He has had Clement Vallandigham arrested."

Vallandigham—the man whom newspapers referred to familiarly as "Val." The supposed leader of the Copperheads, and perhaps of the Golden Circle. Certainly a leader of the Peace Democrats.

"What has happened?" she asked. "What has he done?"

Mr. Norwood left his chair to move restlessly to a window where Ellie had opened the shutters, and looked out upon the drive as if to see whether Wade were yet in sight.

"He has merely made a speech stating his own beliefs—no more than he has been doing all along."

"I believe Wade said something of an order General Burnside had given—" Lora began.

"Exactly—an order for the arrest of anyone giving voice to seditious utterances. That is a scurvy attempt to muzzle all opposition to the Administration. Then to arrest Val—the man must be insane!"

Lora said nothing, little understanding these matters, and Mr. Norwood, now that he had found release in words, went on.

"This may easily mean civil war within the ranks of the North. I understand that Ohio is up in arms, clamoring for Val's release. Burnside has handed the President a hot potato that he had better get rid of quickly. At least this may serve one good purpose."

He turned from the windows and looked at her triumphantly, as if she had been ready to contradict him.

"This may unite every man in the country who is against this war. It should roll up a tremendous opposition to the draft."

Lora was saved the need for an answer by the sound of the carriage on the drive. "There is Wade now," she said.

Mr. Norwood returned to his chair and attempted an attitude of calm. "Your husband seems very busy these days, Mrs. Tyler."

The remark surprised her. She had supposed that Wade was out on business of the Circle and that this man would know all about his movements.

"He has been away in the army so long," she said carefully. "There are a great many things to catch up with."

"Indeed there must be," said Murray Norwood and bent upon her a look that was more than a little suspicious.

She hurried to the door to open it for Wade. "Vallandigham's been arrested," she whispered as he came in. "Mr. Norwood is here to see you."

He nodded as he turned toward the parlor. "Yes, I know about Val."

She went in with him for a moment, then excused herself. Wade did not seem as anxious to see his visitor as Mr. Norwood was to see him. She felt uneasy about the whole matter as she withdrew, leaving them alone.

Once she heard Mr. Norwood's voice raised angrily, though she did not hear the words. And when he left the house he did so furiously and without any courteous farewells.

At dinner that night Wade seemed preoccupied and sober. He told his mother about General Burnside's order concerning Vallandigham and she nodded emphatic approval.

"About time! Something needs to be done to stop that sort of thing."

"But if the government makes a martyr of him, keeps him in prison," Wade said, "I'm afraid it will only consolidate opposition to the Union."

"I'd begun to think you were part of that opposition," his mother said shrewdly.

Wade shook his head. "I have never opposed the Union. Only the war."

After dinner he shut himself in the library again with the door closed. Lora sat up for a little while in Mrs. Tyler's sitting room and then went up to her own room. It was not yet dark and the clown doll she had brought down from the attic grinned at her from his shadowy place on her dresser. So far her whimsy in bringing him downstairs had led to no inspiration. His presence had provoked no further understanding of old problems which concerned Wade.

Lora herself felt restless tonight, eager for something to do. She didn't want to stay idly in her own room. An idea which had returned to mind several times lately prompted her again and she went quietly down the hall toward Virginia's room.

She opened the door as softly as possible and stepped inside. The mingling odors of dust, long-dried rose leaves and stale air engulfed her and, moved by sudden purpose, she went to the side window and flung it wide. A cool breeze swept in, dispelling the miasma of disuse. She stood in the middle of the room looking about her thoughtfully.

She was startled when Jemmy's voice spoke from the open door behind her.

"Lorie, what are you doing in here?"

She beckoned him into the room. "Tell me, Jemmy, do you ever come in here?"

He shook his head. "Oh, no. Papa said no one was to come in but himself."

Lora went close to him and put a hand upon his shoulder. "Have you ever wanted to come in?"

"Not after the—the beginning," he said bleakly. "I did come in sometimes at first, even though Papa said not to. But she was gone, Lorie. I couldn't get her to come back even when I touched her things and tried to pretend she was here. And it made me feel worse than ever, so I stopped coming."

"That was very wise," Lora said gently. "I know you were angry with me that time when I wore your mama's dress to the party, and I wondered how you'd feel if we packed all these things away in the attic and turned this room into something different."

"What do you mean—different?"

"An upstairs sitting room for you and your father and me," she said. "So we wouldn't have to bother your grandmother when we wanted a place to read and play games in the evening. Or disturb your father, or anyone else who wanted to work in the library. What do you think, Jemmy?"

His hesitation lasted only a moment. Then he nodded solemnly. "I think it would be nice. You know I got over feeling bad about you wearing her dress, don't you?"

"I know," Lora said. "But I'm glad you've told me. And I'm happy that you like the idea of a sitting room."

"What will Papa say?"

"I don't know. Of course we can't do anything unless we have his consent. But perhaps we can bring it up one of these days and start him thinking about it."

Later, while she was undressing for bed, she thought about it further herself. Wade had not gone into the room for a long while, as far as she knew. And after he got over any first feeling of shock perhaps he would begin to see how useful such a room might be to them. Of course she would take care to erase every touch of Virginia. Everything would be changed, new furniture brought in. The room would become truly a family room and if Mother Tyler wanted any part of it, then she could learn to get up here herself!

She was in bed when she heard Wade coming upstairs. His step still halted when he had to climb, but he moved much more competently now and was less dependent on his cane. He might always be left with a limp, but at least it now appeared that he would be able to move about with much greater ease.

He no longer came to her room at night to talk to her when he was troubled, or elated, as he had once done. He had not been here since that night when they had gone down to the kitchen together, and had looked at the moon from the back door, felt the pulsing of spring in the air. She wished he would come in now and tell her something of the reason for Murray Norwood's visit, but she heard his steps retreat toward his door and knew he would not.

She was becoming increasingly disturbed about his secrecy over the matters in which he was involved. And his withdrawal left her with a small ache besides. In the beginning he had clung to her far more than he did now. And though she had wanted him to find independence and had resisted and resented the way he tried to substitute her in his mind for Virginia, she wished now that he might come a little further along the road of friendship that had seemed for a time to be developing between them. She could not help wondering what had happened to stop that growth.

Saturday morning she began to toy with the idea of broaching the subject of the upstairs sitting room to Wade. True, he still seemed preoccupied with his own affairs, and no little worried—as he had been ever since Murray Norwood's visit. He followed the papers eagerly for further word of the Vallandigham affair. The government still held its "hot potato"; and out in Dayton City there had been rioting and a newspaper office had been burned down by rabid Copperheads. Wade was gone from the house on some mysterious mission

245

nearly every day, and often the rest of the time he worked in the library. But still she thought she might try to reach him in this matter.

At breakfast, however, there had been a distracting scene between Wade and his mother. Mrs. Tyler had demanded outright that he tell her what he was doing, what momentous affairs—her tone was sarcastic—he was involved in. Wade had said quietly that she would know in good time. But now he must keep his own counsel.

His mother had plunged to the attack from a new direction. "You've been gaining your strength back rapidly," she said. "You get around with very little trouble now. And obviously you are going over to New York once or twice a week. It is time for you to make up your mind about the bank and let me know at once when you plan to return. Mr. Niles was asking about it only yesterday."

This time Wade did not hesitate. "I am not returning to the bank," he told his mother quietly.

Mrs. Tyler made the familiar choking sound in her throat, but Wade did not move anxiously to her side, and when the old lady caught Lora's interested and expectant gaze upon her, she rallied indignantly.

"So this is the reward of a lifetime's devotion? This is what I receive!"

Wade pushed his chair back from the table, excused himself and left the room.

Mrs. Tyler watched him go in dismay. "All his life I have lived for his good," she said to Lora. "I have lived for him."

"I'm not sure any one of us has the right to live for anyone else," Lora said gently.

"Well, between you, you've spoiled my breakfast," the old lady snapped. "Please get me back to my sitting room at once."

Since there were no longer fires on the hearths, doors stood open and Mrs. Tyler could wheel herself readily where she liked. But Lora signaled to Jemmy and he slipped from the table to push his grandmother's chair into the other room. He did not return to finish his own meal and Lora ate the rest of her breakfast alone in thoughtful silence.

Later in the morning Wade emerged from the library in better spirits than she had seen him for some time and came out to sit in a wooden garden chair in the sun, while Lora hunted dandelions and weeds. His mother sat in the open window and he smiled up at her now and then as though there had been no disagreement between them. It was as though, while he plainly did not mean to withdraw from the stand he had taken, he wanted to smooth over his earlier sharpness.

His mother, however, did not return his smile and there was indignation in every inch of her bearing. Jemmy had disappeared uphill some time before and did not reappear until shortly before lunchtime.

His arrival was dramatic, and somewhat noisy, due to the barking and leaping of the little dog which accompanied him. Jemmy had at last taken matters into his own hands and brought Hamlin home. He was rather pink about the ears, but very determined as he stepped onto the grass directly before his father, trying to restrain Hamlin with one hand.

Lora's heart began to thump and she could not pretend to be interested in anything except the little drama about to be enacted there in the garden.

"I've brought my dog home," Jemmy announced, setting his feet apart as if to brace himself against any explosion which might come.

Wade seemed the more discomfited of the two. "And who has said you might have him back?"

"No one," Jemmy answered stoutly. "But he belongs here. He's lonesome for me and I am for him, too. He lives here, Papa."

"Do you remember that he destroyed an expensive shawl which belonged to your grandmother?" Wade asked.

"He's sorry about that. He won't do it any more. I'll watch him every minute."

Mrs. Tyler spoke sharply from her place by the window. "Oh, let the boy keep the dog, Wade! I've had enough of this!"

Wade threw his mother a look of surprise and relief. "Very well," he said to the boy. "Since your grandmother has revoked her edict, you may keep the dog. But you will have to see that he gets into no further trouble."

The thumping of her heart quieted and Lora could only smile at the bright happiness in Jemmy's eyes. Nevertheless, she was disappointed. Wade, after all, had taken no strong stand, accepted no responsibility himself. Perhaps, in the light of other matters, that no longer counted, but she regretted it anyway.

"Papa," Jemmy said, "do you know Ham's real name?"

"You mean there's more to it than Ham? I'm glad to hear that. I've always regarded it as a singularly unattractive name."

"His name is Hamlin, Papa. I named him after the hero in the book you were writing."

For just a moment Wade was taken aback. "By whose permission did you read my story?"

"No one's. It was there on the desk, Papa," Jemmy said, unabashed. "I thought it was an awfully good story."

Wade looked away from his son. "Apparently I was writing for children and did not realize it."

"Jemmy enjoys Scott and Byron and other grown-up authors," Lora said quickly.

"So a puppy has been named after my hero," Wade said, and stood up. "At least that will give him some chance at fame. But see that the dog keeps out of your grandmother's way, Jemmy."

He went up the back steps into the house and Jemmy stared after him for a moment. Then he went down on his knees and leaned his cheek against Hamlin's sun-warmed fur. No one but Lora saw that where there had been happiness in Jemmy's eyes, there was now a shine of tears.

She spoke quickly, trying to brush aside the emotion of the moment with matter-of-fact words.

"It's nice to have Hamlin back," she told Jemmy. "And I'm sure he's very glad to be home again."

"Come here, boy!" Mrs. Tyler's words startled them both. "Come here to my window where I can look at you."

Jemmy let go of Hamlin's collar, and the dog nosed into the grass on the trail of an interesting beetle. Stiffly the boy went to stand before the window, and there was defiance in his expression.

"Why are you staring at me like that?" his grandmother demanded, staring back.

"I won't let Hamlin go away again," the boy told her, his eyes steady and unflinching.

"Who said he was going away? Didn't you hear me say you could keep him? But it seems that I am to receive no thanks for that."

"Sometimes you change your mind," Jemmy said cautiously.

"I never change my mind about anything!" snapped his grandmother. "Step over here closer, boy. Put your head up!"

248

He obeyed without speaking, stood motionless and waiting while the old woman's eyes searched his face. Then she nodded as if she had come to a conclusion.

"You look like your great-grandfather Jason. The resemblance is growing all the time."

Jemmy gave no inch of ground. "I look like you," he said. "And I don't like it!"

"Hoity-toity!" said his grandmother. "A fine way to talk." But she looked almost pleased.

Hamlin leaped upon Jemmy just then and the boy broke away to chase him around the yard. When Lora looked again at the old woman in the window she saw that she was nodding proudly.

"There'll be no meek bowing of this one's neck," she said. "He won't pretend to go my way and then twist around when I'm not looking. He'll go his own way and never mind the consequences. That's a Cowles trait, Lora."

"Don't forget he has Virginia and Wade in him too," Lora reminded her.

Mrs. Tyler dismissed so unwelcome a truth with a flick of her beringed fingers and changed the subject. "What is my son up to, Lora? What trouble is he involving himself in that he will not confide in me?"

But Lora could only shake her head, having no answer to that herself. In this one thing—their concern over what Wade was doing—she and Mother Tyler were closely allied.

XXVI

THROUGH MAY AND JUNE events seemed to be boiling toward some climax as far as the war was concerned. The lethargy and hopelessness of the winter was past and armies were stirring, moving toward great events.

Clement Vallandigham had been tried by a military court, and sentenced to imprisonment. Indignantly the people of Ohio were offering his name for governor of that state. Lincoln, still wary of holding this unwanted prisoner Burnside had wished on him, commuted Val's sentence to expulsion to the South, with orders that he be rearrested if found behind

Union lines. With the help of Confederate authorities Val had found his way into Canada, and the excitement swirled behind him like the wake of a surging battleship.

Early in June the Peace Democrats held a great mass meeting in New York under the auspices of former Mayor Fernando Wood. The crowd overflowed Cooper Union, shouting for peace and urging Democrats everywhere to denounce and repudiate the war. A resolution was passed denouncing the war as illegal and unconstitutional.

All the while, the day of the intended draft came closer. There were rumors now that Lee intended a march into Union territory and every man was needed. On June 8 instructions were issued for the enrollment of men between the ages of twenty and forty-five, but this was only a preliminary to the actual draft.

Yet June on Staten Island bloomed on as usual, lavish and drowsy. Sunshine warmed the hills and bees hummed through clover, ignoring the mushroom growth of camps which had sprung into being all across the island.

One lazy afternoon somewhat past the middle of June, Lora came outside, crisp and cool in blue muslin, carrying a small parcel wrapped in an old shawl. From the road before the Hume house she glanced hastily in either direction, then ducked beneath shielding branches and ran lightly up the steps that led nowhere. She knew the way very well by now and with a clear sky overhead there were no fingers of fog to intercept or confuse.

She went at once to what had become a favorite nook—a place where broken walls met in a corner and a growth of trees and shrubbery threw patches of dappled shade. Here she spread the shawl upon the grass and settled into her nest. There was quiet here, with only the hum of bees and occasional bird songs to break the hush. All human activity from harbor and lower shore seemed distant, scarcely to be heard. This was a place for thinking, for dreaming.

For a time she tried to follow the course of the story she had brought to read, but her mind wandered and she put the magazine aside to watch the dragonfly darting and swooping nearby. But the dragonfly did not hold her attention either. She curled up on the shawl and placed the small pillow she had brought beneath her head. But she did not nap. Her mind was too busy turning its wheels, worrying its problems.

What dangerous thing might Wade be doing these days? Always he seemed secretive and tense, and he would tell her nothing. She had lost all touch with him lately and lived almost as a stranger in the house as far as he was concerned. He had wakened from his apathy and pain and no longer needed to fool himself. He escaped them all now—his mother, his son, his wife.

Lora turned on her side and sorted out the contents of the bundle she had brought with her. There was the little clown, its pompons shining golden yellow in the sun, and the few copybooks from the attic. She held Jupiter in her hands as if somehow he might take her back into a past she could not know, help her to find the boy who had once played with this toy.

In the beginning she had wanted only to minister to Wade's hurt body, to see the healing of his physical wounds. Later she had been more concerned with the healing of his spirit, feeling guilty because she could not love him when his need for love was great. But now he had hardened into a new pattern and seemed to need her in no way at all. And now she was troubled and confused, not even sure of her own thoughts and emotions.

When she had finally broken through his preoccupation to suggest the transformation of Virginia's room into something more useful, he had been momentarily shocked into awareness of her as a person. But the suggestion seemed not to upset him unduly or to cause any relapse into his previous unhealthy attitude toward the room.

"As you please," he said at length, almost indifferently. But he would take no interest in specific plans. He would not touch the room in any way himself.

She had begun somewhat listlessly to pack Virginia's frocks away, to sort her possessions from bureau drawers and carry things up to the attic. Jemmy too avoided the project and stayed outside or in another part of the house when she worked in his mother's room. Her own interest and enthusiasm for the preparation of the room died for lack of support and the work went slowly. Perhaps next winter when the room was needed more than it was in summertime her interest would return. Now one could be outdoors, or sit on the veranda of an evening.

She felt almost as if she were marking time in some strange way, awaiting an event still in the future—she knew not what. Some turn in the affairs of war perhaps? Certainly the promise of that was constantly in the air these days and on every tongue. If Lee marched into Pennsylvania—if the Confederacy were really as strong as that . . .

She had not seen Morgan since the day of the fire, but according to Ambrose, all appeared quiet in the house on the hill. The new stable and servants' quarters were nearly completed. Rebecca went about her usual tasks and not even Clothilde interfered with her.

Serena was busy as always and the social life of the island had whirled into summer gaiety. Wade could no longer be drawn into the sort of social affair which had once interested him. He was engrossed in his own work now, and had no time for frivolity. Nevertheless, Serena had been able to extract from him a promise to bring Lora to the first beach party of the summer season early in July. Serena pointed out the fact that he was allowing his wife to languish in cruel inactivity, and Lora remembered how Wade had looked at her quickly then, as if he had almost forgotten she was his wife. He had agreed readily enough that some break in the routine of their lives was a good idea.

Since the day of the fire Lora had seen Adam rarely and, to her relief, only when others were around. That day, she had told herself, they'd all been keyed to an intensity out of the normal. When people were both excited and exhausted, almost anything might happen. She still resented his behavior and for a while was fearful lest Morgan Channing try to make something of it by gossiping. But nothing further had happened. When Lora saw Adam she simply avoided his eyes and since he did not seek her out, she did not know what he thought or how he felt. Nor did she care.

She put the doll aside and sat up cross-legged to open one of the copybooks. She had read through two of them completely before this and found a boy's school exercises and essays. But after the first page or so of this book, she realized that it was different. These passages were something Wade had written for himself alone; they were, in fact, the pages of a diary. Familiar names appeared, references to Serena, to Adam, to Morgan and Virginia. In these pages the boy Wade had recorded something of his inner thoughts as well as an account of daily incidents. All this seemed to date back to a time shortly before the incident of the fence.

For a moment Lora hesitated, wondering if she had any right to read what was written here. If she took this book to Wade and asked his permission, would he take it away from her? She had the strange feeling that some key might lie hidden in these pages, something which would better enable her to understand what had gone before and thus help with the present. If she went to Wade he might well refuse her the use of such a key. She read on and the summer day hummed about her, forgotten.

The young Wade had written:

Today Adam boxed Morgan's ears. Adam is not a gentleman but I was glad for what he did. Morgan had teased Virginia because I'd picked her to be on my side, and when Morgan pulled Virginia's hair and made her cry, Adam slapped her hard. Morgan flounced off by herself and wouldn't play any more. She knows Adam is stronger than she is, or she'd try to fight him. I don't know why she has to be so mean to Virginia, who is only a baby, really.

And another entry a few days later:

Morgan is a strange girl. She is very clever and smart. More than people think. If she cared about her studies she could get better marks in school. But she doesn't care about anything except being mean. Everyone says it's too bad that she's not sweet and docile like Virginia. When she hears these things she always gets mad and that makes it all worse than ever. She teases me too—only I don't mind. Because I know what she's like. At least I don't think I mind very much. Sometimes her words sting a little and I'd like to show her I'm better than she thinks. I can be just as brave as Adam if I try.

A month later came a surprising entry:

Morgan can be nice sometimes. Today she brushed her hair and tied it back with a ribbon. She put her mouth into a smile and came out to play in a clean dress without any tears in it. She was kind and gentle and sat beside me while I was getting well from my illness. Today was the first time I could be outdoors. A strange thing happened. I do believe I began to like her a little. I suppose Adam would think me foolish, but I almost had the feeling today that it would be a fine thing to be really liked and admired by Morgan.

The next entry was made the following day:

Of course Morgan was only play-acting. This afternoon I was reading to Virginia up near the pool. I didn't feel like pretending to hunt Indians in the woods the way Morgan and Adam were doing. Morgan came out prettily dressed again, but when we settled down to read and didn't pay any attention to her, she pulled off her ribbon and tied it on a tree branch, and let her hair go scraggly again. She was like a wild thing all morning and teased everyone endlessly. It was as though she wanted *me* to turn on her the way Adam does sometimes. But I won't strike a girl no matter how angry she makes me.

And a week later:

Today a terrible thing happened. Adam was up in the woods howling like a banshee. I was reading about banshees yesterday and I'm sure they must howl like that. Virginia was on the big rock in the pool trying to catch a turtle, and I was helping her, while Morgan sulked on the shore. Virginia and I were very quiet, waiting for a turtle to come out of the water onto the rocks. When one finally did and I was just reaching for it, Morgan got up and threw a stone in the water and of course the turtle plopped back out of sight. I was so angry that I stood up and shouted at Morgan. I told her I'd smack her good if she didn't stop that. I don't suppose I really would because I don't want to be that sort of boy. But she jumped right up and came out on the rock to give me a chance.

Virginia started to cry because fighting frightens her and then . . .

Here Lora found that the page had been torn in half. The record of whatever had happened on that long-ago day must have been destroyed by the writer.

There were only a few pages left in the copybook and they contained nothing of any significance, did not mention Morgan at all. Lora picked up the last of the four books, but here again were only school exercises, with little of the personal revealed. The torn page tantalized her with its unfinished story. What could have happened that day which was so terrible in Wade's eyes that he had torn up all evidence of it? Had he really turned on Morgan at last, as she seemed to desire him to in her perverse way?

The sudden sound of a foot on the stone steps of the old house made her sit up with a start and look across the expanse of grass and clover toward the crumbling wall and doorway. Adam Hume stood in the entrance. His rusty head was bare and he wore his usual jaunty grin that seemed intended to show the world how little he cared for its opinion.

"So this is where you disappeared to?" he said. "I saw you on the road some time ago and kept waiting for you to appear near the path. When you didn't I decided to investigate. Do you mind if I come into your parlor, Mrs. Tyler?"

He waited for no invitation, but jumped down into the space that had once been the interior of a residence and sauntered toward her, his hands in his pockets.

There was no one she wanted less to see, but there was nothing to do about his presence unless she wanted to leave. She knew that a haughty departure would only amuse him, perhaps make her call her a rabbit again. So she stayed where she was, waiting, but his very presence made her uneasy.

He found a sunny spot for himself some distance from her and stretched himself on his stomach in the clover, resting his weight on his arms.

"You haven't forgiven me, have you?" he asked, smiling at her lazily.

"You wish to apologize?" she said.

"For my improper behavior, or for yours? No indeed. I enjoyed it a great deal. And I suppose it makes very little difference whether you are angry with me or not. Since in any event I am planning to go away before long."

She was surprised, and in the same moment strangely relieved, but she gave no sign. "You are going to rejoin your company?"

"To my regret, they will have none of me. No, I'm going west where I can at least get into an active life part of the time. I've a friend who owns a defunct gold mine in Colorado. Between us, who knows what we may stir up? But I wanted to tell you what I planned."

"I wish you good fortune," she said politely.

His grin had a wry quirk. "Thank you, ma'am. I suppose, in order to fulfill the romantic tradition, I should first lay my heart at your feet and announce that I am departing forever because I know you are lost to me."

"You are being ridiculous."

"The other choice would be to beseech you to fly with me. To leave husband, child, home and mother—to sacrifice all in the name of love."

Lora made an impatient sound. "Why are you speaking such nonsense?"

"Because it annoys you. Perhaps this is the one trait I share with Morgan Channing—I like to annoy people." He got up and crossed the patch of clover quickly to drop onto a corner of the shawl beside her. "Don't wriggle away like that. I shan't touch you."

"I have no reason to trust you," she told him, and began to pick up books and pillow, preparing to leave him the field after all.

He reached out and caught her hands to stop her, and now there was no mockery in his eyes. "You have every reason to trust me, though you don't realize it. Because I like you, Lora. Like and admire and respect you. And these are things I have given to few women in my life. Perhaps I could even have fallen in love with you if you had been heartfree. As it is, I will neither ask you to fly with me in the romantic fashion, or promise you my brokenhearted loyalty forever. It is my curious custom to prefer a woman who will love me back. You, in an unaccountable feminine way, are dedicated to loving Wade."

The start she gave was involuntary, as was her manner of denial. She stilled her hands at once and drew them from his grasp. There was no need to deny anything to Adam. What he thought did not matter.

But he had noted with his quick, keen gaze. "You haven't accepted the facts yet, have you? That you are in love with him, I mean. The response you gave me the other day might have led me to a further trial if I hadn't recognized that it was made of the same flimsy stuff as Wade's response to Morgan. But perhaps you didn't understand that yourself?"

She stopped struggling to collect her possessions and looked at him.

"No," he said, "you didn't understand, but now I've put knowledge in your hands. My gift to you in parting. I suppose it will always be a puzzle to my kind of man—what it is a woman sees in Wade's kind. Virginia, Morgan—and now you. Is it the mother in the feminine nature, the need to protect and build up and succor?"

Still she looked at him, saying nothing. Perhaps she could have told him, explained the comparison she was only now beginning to understand. Always Adam would snatch at what he wanted, quickly and without heed, storming towers, flouing conventions. To be loved by him might be briefly exciting and it was even possible that under different circumstances she might have been foolish enough to play moth to his flame. But now—by some whim of kindness—he had indeed put the truth in her hands and she knew well that he would never be what she wanted. There was a richer, gentler love in which a more fulfilling consummation might be possible.

"When are you going away?" she asked, turning uncomfortably from her own strange thoughts.

"In a few weeks. Probably by mid-July."

The copybook in her hands fell open to the torn page and she turned to him suddenly. Adam, at least, had always been one of whom she could ask a direct question.

"Can you remember a time when you were all children," she began, "playing up near the pool? I mean some one occasion when Virginia was out on the big rock trying to get a turtle and Morgan behaved badly?"

"Virginia was always after turtles and Morgan was always behaving badly. What do you mean?"

She went on hurriedly. "This must have been a time when something awful happened. Wade was there too, and you were in the woods nearby. Think back. I need to know."

"Well . . . there was the time when Morgan pushed Virginia into the pool. Could that be what you mean?"

"How terrible!"

"I didn't reach them till it was about over, but I heard Virginia scream and I got most of the story later. Maybe it was an accident, maybe it was a push. But Morgan had gone out on the rocks to see if Wade would really slap her as he had apparently threatened to do. And Virginia, who was little and couldn't swim, fell in. So Morgan jumped up and down and screeched for Wade to jump in and save her. Only Wade had always been babied by his mother, and he couldn't swim either. So Morgan, who could do everything, jumped in herself and pulled her sister out. I got there after it was all over and Morgan was blistering the air with her denunciation of Wade. Is that what you wanted to know?"

"I think so," Lora said. She could understand now why Wade had destroyed his own account of what had happened that day. Rereading it later, he must have been deeply ashamed of his inability to help Virginia, and of Morgan's harsh accusations.

"Morgan was always a fool when it came to Wade," Adam said. "Even while he represented to her the sum total of

257

everything she wanted, she always had to speak her mind rudely. She was forever in conflict with herself over him. I expect she still is. I'd watch her if I were you."

She tugged at the shawl on which he was sitting. "Thank you for telling me, but now please get up so I can pick up my things. I really must be getting home."

He removed books and pillow from her hands and laid them on the grass. Then he took both her hands in his and looked into her eyes.

"Believe me, more than anything I can remember, I want your happiness. Can you understand that? Just this once can you believe, much as you dislike me?"

She looked into his eyes and found honesty there and good will. The impatience went out of her.

"I believe you," she told him. "Thank you, Adam."

He let her hands go. "Now I'll help you back to the house with your load."

"No, please," she said quickly. "I—I'd rather go alone."

The old look returned to his eyes. "Ah? We must avoid the appearance of evil, must we not? Very well, I'll stay here while you go. I can cut up through the woods and come down another way. And thus our dread secret will be safe."

But she would not be riled by him now. She accepted his arrangement gravely, said good-by, and went out the broken doorway and down the steps.

She walked the short distance home slowly. The thing Adam had said—that she loved Wade—would not leave her mind. It hovered, challenging, waiting to be accepted. Was it possible for love to come like this, stealing in unaware, while you went on believing that all was as it had been before and your concern for a man was no more personal than it had been in the beginning? If true, this might be something to fear and regret. She did not want to be hurt any more. She had had enough of pain.

"You look like you're sleep-walking, Lorie," came Jemmy's voice from the veranda.

She looked up and saw that unknowingly she had reached the house. Jemmy put his finger to his lips and ran down the stairs toward her.

"Morgan Le Fay's in there with Grandmother," he whispered. "They've shut the door and won't let me in, though Le Fay has brought down my mother's picture."

"Your mother's picture?" Lora repeated.

"The one that was part of the big painting. She cut it all the way down with a knife, just leaving her own picture in the frame. I suppose that green curtain covers the cut."

So Morgan had done what she had threatened. Well, no matter. It was right that Virginia's picture should be kept for Jemmy. Nevertheless, Morgan's unusual presence in this house was a disturbing thing. Where Morgan came, trouble followed.

Lora started upstairs, having no wish to see the visitor. But before she reached the upper floor, Wade came out of the library and saw her there on the stairs, saw the copybooks and the clown in her hands.

"Where on earth have you been with those things?" he asked, not altogether pleased.

She could feel the betraying warmth rise in her cheeks. With Adam's words in her mind she felt suddenly shy and self-conscious. She could not answer easily and openly as she might have done earlier.

"I've just been sunning myself and thinking in the Hume place," she said. And she ran on up the stairs before he could question her further.

Jemmy was still in the upper hall. "Your birthday's soon, isn't it, Lorie? Don't forget—we're going to have a party."

She smiled absently and went into her own room to put the books away in a drawer. She stood for a moment with the little clown in her hands, then put her cheek against the soft yellow pompons, somehow finding comfort in the gesture. Uneasiness still gripped her, however, and she left the door ajar, listening for Morgan's departure.

She heard Mother Tyler's door open, heard Morgan in the hall speaking to Wade. Five minutes after she had left, Ellie came scuttling upstairs to summon Lora to Mrs. Tyler's sitting room. Uneasiness gave place to certainty of trouble to come.

Mrs. Tyler awaited her alone, so at least Wade was not to be included in this audience.

"Close the door and sit there," said the old lady, pointing. "I want you where you'll be facing the light. I want the truth from you and no subterfuges."

"I believe I have always told you the truth," said Lora with dignity. Morgan had talked. Plainly she had talked about Adam that day of the fire.

She started toward the chair Mrs. Tyler indicated, and

259

then paused, almost stepping upon a strip of canvas which lay spread upon the floor. It was Virginia's picture, one side rudely gashed, where the canvas had been cut in two.

"The woman must be demented to cut up a fine painting," Mrs. Tyler said. "But now I shall have it framed and hung in the house. Perhaps in the front parlor."

Lora sat down, waiting for her to come to the point. The picture, she was sure, was the least of this summons.

Mrs. Tyler went on at once. "Truly, Lora, I am shocked by the facts which have been presented to me today. You have already disappointed me in many ways, but I had not expected betrayal from you. Not betrayal of my son."

"There has been no betrayal," said Lora gently.

"You were seen kissing Adam Hume on the day of the fire. Not only by Morgan, but by the Frenchwoman, Clothilde. Probably by others too. Do you deny it?"

"Of course I do," Lora said spiritedly. "I did not kiss Adam. He kissed me. There is a difference."

"Nonsense. You submitted in any case. And now there is worse. An assignation—one of many, perhaps? In the ruins of the Hume house. Morgan herself saw you there today, holding hands with Adam, speaking of love."

Lora gasped at the unexpectedness of the attack. The mingling of truth with this lie left her helpless for a moment.

"It is plain that you are overcome with guilt," Mrs. Tyler said.

"I am guilty of nothing in the least wrong!" Lora cried.

"But you do not deny that you were there with Adam. Morgan heard voices as she came down the road on her way to bring me this picture. You were so lost in your love-making that you did not hear her, either of you. The moment she understood what was happening she came to me. And for once, I must say, she did the right thing. My son knows nothing of this as yet. I am giving you a chance first."

"Mother, please listen to me," Lora begged. "I went there for an hour or so alone, with books to read. Adam found me and talked to me for a few minutes. It was not what you term an assignation. Nor has it ever happened before."

"A woman in love always lies," said Mrs. Tyler curtly.

"Then it is Morgan who is lying."

"You mean you deny the hand-holding, the talk of love?"

"He held my hands when I wanted to leave. And he told

260

me that I—that I was in love with Wade. Is that what you want to know?"

Mrs. Tyler stared at her a moment. Then she flicked her fingers in a gesture of dismissal, and there was the familiar flash of jewels in the sunlight.

"Go away. Leave me. I can see there is no truth in you. You have brought still greater unhappiness and disgrace upon this house. I must decide now what I shall do."

Lora stood up and the old trembling that had tormented her when first she came to this house ran through her body.

"I have disgraced no one. If unhappiness results from this malicious act of Morgan's, then it will be her fault—and yours." She bent toward the old lady suddenly, looked into the deep-set eyes. "Is this what you have been waiting for all along? Something which would make your son wholly yours again? Or perhaps you want to give him back to Virginia and will have him miserably lost to the world, though once more dependent upon you? Perhaps this is why you want to hang Virginia's picture in the parlor. If these are the things you want, then you have grown old and wicked, Mother Tyler."

For a moment longer she faced the old woman while the trembling ran through her.

Mrs. Tyler sat immobile. She blinked once. That was all. Lora turned and went out of the room. She went straight to the door of the library and rapped on the dark panel. When Wade opened it, she stepped past him into the room, let him close the door behind her.

"I have something to tell you," she said, twining her fingers together to still their trembling. "Morgan has been here talking to your mother."

"I know," Wade said. "She mentioned the picture."

"She mentioned other matters too."

Wade drew a chair near an open window where a breeze stirred the draperies. "You're disturbed about her visit. Sit down, Lora."

She did not take the chair. Somehow she felt stronger, more sure of herself standing, facing him squarely. Her voice did not break or her words falter as she told him of that day at the fire. He leaned against the library table, resting his leg, watching her as she spoke. When she had finished, he glanced away.

"But I already knew this, Lora. Morgan would never have

261

waited this long to be spiteful when she had the opportunity that very day."

"You—knew?" She thought back in confusion. He had waited for her that same day on the steps of Morgan's house —to protect her from the "dragons" in the woods, he had said. And later there had been that little while in the kitchen late at night, when they had seemed close for a time—closer than ever before. Yet he had known of Adam's behavior even then.

"But you put no weight on Morgan's words?" she asked.

"I know Morgan. And I know you." He smiled at her— that flashing smile in which there was a sweetness that was peculiarly his.

"But there's more," she said, and she could not yet return his smile. She told him of Adam finding her hideaway in the Hume place today, and of Morgan spying, reporting to his mother.

"And you are disturbed about all this?" Wade asked when she had finished.

"Naturally. I—I wanted you to know what had been said. I wanted you to know my side, in case there are those who— who might try to prejudice you against me."

He came to her then and put his hands on her shoulders, swung her toward the light. "Look at me, Lora." His hand was beneath her chin, tilting her face toward him. "Do you think I believe in you so little? Mind—I won't blame you if you've lost your heart to Adam. But I trust you completely. I can only feel sorry because I was so blind as to coax you into this poor mockery of a marriage. When I had so little to give, do you think I could blame you if—"

She drew her head away from his touch, unreasonably angry. For a moment she sought futilely for words, then turned and ran out of the room and up the stairs. She shut the door of her own room in a manner that was not entirely ladylike, and then leaned against the panel listening, wondering if he would come after her. But there was only the sound of the closing library door, followed by silence.

She drew the back of her hand across her eyes and went to fumble in the bureau drawer for a handkerchief. Her clumsy fingers went beneath the pile of linen and found a small hard something that she drew out wonderingly—a little sea shell, creamy with brown speckles. Something out of another life—a memory of Martin. For a long moment she stared at it without emotion and then thrust it away again in the drawer. It belonged to another Lora of long ago. She herself could be moved by it only as one might be moved hearing a sad story about another person.

Adam had been right. And she could almost hate him now for the truth he had told her. It was a truth she would rather have kept even from herself. Then she need not have recognized the reason for her vague unhappiness and longing. She blew her nose angrily and dabbed at her eyes. What irony there was in such a situation!—that she must live in this house married to a man whom she had begun to love, but who was as far removed from her, as cool and remote as if they were strangers who had just met.

If he had been hurt just now, or angry, if he had feared that Morgan's accusations might be true... But he had taken his wife calmly for granted as an upright individual who would never deceive him, no matter what she might feel. His own emotions had been in no way involved.

She flung herself across her bed and cried as she had wanted to cry her very first night in this house—and had not. She had been strong then and even in grief sure of her own strength. Now it was as if her position and Wade's had been somehow reversed—though how she was not sure—and she was now the weaker of the two.

XXVII

JUNE DREAMED itself into its last week, and now it seemed sure that the draft was imminent. It might be announced at any moment and the grumblings against it were louder than ever. There was reason enough for some of the dissatisfaction, as Wade explained at the dinner table one night.

New York's quota was inordinately high and there was still further inequity between various sections of the city. The burden would fall heavily on the poor, for a man who could pay the required three hundred dollars to the government might be exempted from draft. Thus the man whose family needed his earnings most was very likely the one who must go to war. The heavy Irish and German population in New York did not help the situation. These people had fled from trouble in their own countries and they had, many of them, not been in America long enough to make its troubles their own. They had no desire to risk their lives in battles for which they had no heart.

In spite of the fact that feeling ran high among certain elements, the papers took a calm view of the matter. After all, they pointed out, the police, aided by the militia, and if necessary the army, would promptly put down any effort at resistance. The grumblers knew this and would be unlikely to risk the more immediate punishment which would befall them if they resisted the draft.

Wade was not sure this sanguine attitude was justified. A few mornings later he bundled up the papers he had been working on for so long in the seclusion of the library and announced that he was going to Washington for a few days. Under no circumstances, he told Lora, was she to let this fact be known.

She ventured anxiously into his room as he packed a bag.

"Tell me, Wade—are you acting on your own, or as an agent for the government, or is this Circle business you're on?"

"Circle business? Hardly. I thought you realized that I gave that up long ago, once I'd had a real taste of what was going on."

"Then—this is evidence of some sort you are taking to Washington?"

"Lora dear," he said gently, "the less you know of what I am doing the better. There are the desperate, the unscrupulous, to be reckoned with. I want you and Mother kept free of all this."

She was silenced for the moment, but she went with him to the door, still anxious. They stood on the veranda waiting as Peter brought the carriage around.

"What has become of the way you used to hate the war?" she asked almost timidly.

"My feelings about that have not changed," he said. "But there are times when a man must do what is necessary for the good of many, instead of a few. For the future good of many."

She brought up the old argument which had always served her before in her own mind. "But these are our brothers we are fighting against, Wade."

"And if our brother behaves in a wayward manner which threatens our home and family, do we stand by and let him destroy the very roof over our heads? Do we lay down our arms and watch him ruin the home that has belonged to us all and which we want to preserve for our children?"

There was somehow a moving quality about him as he spoke. He could be compelling when he was as much in earnest as this.

"Good luck then," she told him as he turned to go. "Come home safely."

He kissed her cheek lightly and went down the steps. As Peter drove away, Wade leaned from the carriage to wave to her reassuringly. When he had gone she sat for a little while on the veranda, thinking of Wade as he had been and as he was now.

She recalled the thought that had come to her mind some months before—that there were only two choices. Either you loved a person as he was and forgave him his faults, or you could not forgive those faults and tried to make him into something else. Neither course had seemed entirely satisfactory to her. Now she was beginning to see that there was still a third. Sometimes a man could change and grow of his own accord when the urge was great enough. He could become his true self in the best possible way.

At length she rose and went back to Mrs. Tyler's sitting room. Wade had not told his mother he was leaving, knowing the storm of questions which would arise, and Lora had promised to meet the torrent and deal with it herself. Since the day of Morgan's visit she had seldom intruded her company upon the old woman. There had been something of an armed truce between them—cold civility, nothing more. Whether Mrs. Tyler had talked to her son about Morgan's visit, or what Wade might have said to her, Lora had no idea. The subject had never been mentioned again.

So now she was not expected in the rear sitting-room, though the door stood ajar. She pushed it open quietly and looked in. The wheel chair was empty and she wondered if Mother Tyler had become ill and been put to bed. There was a sound from the bedroom beyond and she went halfway across the room before she realized what it was. Someone was moving about the bedroom. There was the click of shoes upon the bare floor, then a muffling of the sound as a rag rug was reached, then the click again.

"Is that you, Ellie?" Lora inquired.

There was an instant of complete silence before Mrs. Tyler's voice answered her.

"It is not," said the old woman, and stepped into view in the doorway.

She leaned on Wade's discarded cane, but otherwise stood firmly erect. With careful, unwavering steps she came toward Lora.

"You look very silly with your mouth open like that," she said. "After all, there's no reason to gape."

"But"—Lora was too surprised to find words easily—"but you walk very well. You couldn't just—"

"Of course I couldn't," Mother Tyler snapped. "Not at first. But I've been practicing every day and sometimes at night for quite a while now. I've decided that it was high time I took my proper place as mistress of this house. Everything has gotten too much out of hand."

Lora recovered her power of movement. She ran across the room and put strong young arms about the frail shoulders and hugged them hard.

"You're wonderful!" she cried. "Wade will be so pleased and proud."

"You're throwing me off balance," Mrs. Tyler said, pushing Lora away. But her eyes were bright and for once there was no malice in them.

Lora released her and made no effort to help as she walked to a chair by the window and sat down.

"You wanted to speak to me about something?" she asked Lora.

Swiftly Lora made a decision, feeling with all her instincts that it was the right thing to do. She dropped onto a footstool at the old lady's feet and looked up at her with shining eyes.

"Yes! I came here to tell you that Wade was going to be away for a few days. I was going to give you a story that would have been only partly true about his going away to see about some writing he has been doing. He felt the truth would only distress you and it was better to keep it from you."

"What gibberish is this?"

"Only that I think there is no need to treat you like an invalid or a child, when you are neither."

Quietly she explained about Morgan's involvement with the Golden Circle, and of Murray Norwood's request for Wade's help. She could supply few details herself, since Wade had never wholly confided in her, but she had heard enough from other sources to surmise the rest. Wade had discovered that the movement was not, after all, a peaceful effort to halt hostilities, but a destructive movement which bored at the Union government from within and might, if it was not

266

stopped, cause the entire North to crumble upon itself, defeated by its own inner rot. Wade had apparently written an account of these activities, drawn up his evidence, and was acting on his own initiative in taking the material to Washington.

Mrs. Tyler listened without betraying emotion, except for the gleam in her eyes. When Lora concluded her story, she sat still more erectly in her chair.

"My son has done the right thing. Though I must confess, Lora, that I am surprised. I would not have expected such courageous action from him."

"I think he has never lacked courage, Mother," Lora said. "What chance have you given him to exercise such a quality? You always wanted him to follow a different pattern from his own nature. Virginia shielded him. And I—all I gave him was a shoulder to lean upon. But now he is relying on himself alone and that is the way it should be." She stood up. "Well, I've work to do. I must get to it."

But Mrs. Tyler stopped her. "I have not told Wade what Morgan said. I thought you might like to know that."

"Thank you," said Lora gravely. "But it wouldn't have mattered. I told him myself and he believed me."

She went off then to the task ahead of her. Today would be perfect for readying the upstairs sitting room for final use— the room which had once been Virginia's. And such occupation would keep her busy, shut out the worry concerning Wade which would tug at her until he was home again.

Four days went by before he returned—on the very day that the framed picture of Virginia was delivered to the Tyler house. He arrived, in fact, while Lora was unwrapping the picture in Mother Tyler's sitting room. It was evening, shortly before Jemmy's bedtime, and Jemmy was there too, watching with interest.

When she heard Wade's step in the hallway, Lora ran to greet him and saw at once the discouragement that weighed him down.

"Your mother knows where you've been," she whispered. "It's all right to talk before her."

This assurance obviously did not cheer him.

"Lora shouldn't have told you, Mother," he said. "This is one concern you could have been spared."

"Nonsense. Lora has more sense than you. Tell us quickly, did you get to see the President?"

267

"I didn't expect to go that high," Wade said. "But neither did I expect to be shunted around through so many lesser hands. You'd have thought I was an enemy spy trying to get through the lines. In any event I've been assured that my papers will reach the proper hands and I can only hope they will act upon them."

"That was all you could do?" Lora asked.

Wade shrugged. "It was suggested that I go to Albany with this. But I can imagine how far I'd get with Governor Seymour. Rumor has it he favors the work of the Circle. And he has announced himself as being against the draft."

Jemmy had listened round-eyed, not understanding all this, but now his attention returned to the package Lora had started to open.

"It's Mama's picture that Morgan Le Fay brought down here," he told his father. "Go ahead and open it, Lorie."

Lora glanced at Wade and he nodded, so she took the picture from its wrappings and leaned it against a chair. It was only a fraction of the original size, since the wasted background above the head of the seated figure had been cropped. Because of the ugly gash which had cut through the skirt of Virginia's full dress, it had been necessary to reduce the whole to a head and shoulders portrait, and as such it seemed an entity in itself. Virginia's lips smiled sweetly and her gaze was turned dreamily out of the picture so that three quarters of her face was to be seen.

"It looks better than I expected," Mrs. Tyler said. "But now I'm wondering where to hang it."

Remembering the old lady's previous announcement that the picture was to hang in the parlor, Lora looked at her in surprise. It was not like Mother Tyler to soften like this about a decision once given. Before anyone could make a suggestion, Jemmy picked the picture up almost fiercely.

"It's my mother and I want it for my room."

Wade decided the matter. "You shall have it there if you want it, boy."

"Come along then," said Lora to Jemmy. "Let's go see how it will look." She did not glance again at Wade, afraid to read his reaction to the picture.

Jemmy carried it upstairs at once and Lora hurried after him. While he sat on the bed and watched, she tried the effect for him by holding it up against the wall in various places. After several tries, he decided where he liked it and she marked the place so they could hang it there tomorrow. Then she propped it upon his dresser temporarily and turned to find that his eyes were misted with tears.

"Are you sure you want the picture here, Jemmy?" she asked doubtfully.

He nodded, blinking hard. "Please, Lorie. So I won't ever forget. Sometimes I do forget a little. Then do you know what I do? I go back up the hill to the pool and look at the water until I remember—everything."

She sat beside him on the bed and put an arm about his shoulders. "You mustn't do that, Jemmy. It's not wrong to forget grief. If the picture helps you to remember happy times, then it's fine to have it here. But if it only hurts you, she wouldn't want you to look at it. Think about that, Jemmy. And now suppose I go out so you can get ready for bed. Call me when you're ready and I'll come tuck you in."

The door stood ajar and when she stepped into the hall she found Wade waiting for her. His face was shadowy in the twilight and she could not read his expression. To her surprise he reached for her two hands and raised them to his lips.

"You are very good to my son," he said. "I'm more grateful than you know, my dear."

But she did not need gratitude from him and she was glad for the shadows which hid what she did not want him to read in her own eyes.

"Jemmy has become very dear to me," she said. "Now what about you? If you've had dinner, perhaps I can at least get you a cup of tea."

He did not release her hands but continued to hold them almost awkwardly in his until she drew them gently away.

"Your mother is walking again," she went on. "Do let her know how pleased you are when she shows you. She's like a child about the achievement, she's so proud."

"This is your doing, too, Lora. You've done something for all of us in this house. We can never thank you enough."

Again there was unwanted gratitude in his voice, but before she could make her escape, Jemmy called to her.

"I'm ready, Lorie!"

"Come with me," she said to Wade on sudden impulse, and drew him into Jemmy's bedroom.

The candle on the dresser guttered at a breeze from the window and a moth flew in to circle the flame recklessly.

"We've come to say good night, Jemmy," she said casually.

When she pulled the sheet over him and bent to tuck him in, he reached up suddenly and drew her down, kissed her quickly on the cheek. It was the first time he had made such a gesture and she found that her eyes were moist. She turned to Wade, beseeching him without words. He leaned above the bed and touched the boy's cheek with his fingers.

"I've never told you," he said, "how proud I was to have Hamlin named after the hero of my story. Good night, son. Sleep well."

There was no more than that, yet Lori saw happiness spring up in Jemmy's eyes, and love for his father. She blew out the candle before the moth could make up its mind, and Wade followed her out of the room.

"I'll get you that tea now," she said matter-of-factly. "The upstairs sitting room is ready, so I'll bring it to you there. I know you must be tired."

"That would be fine," he agreed, as impersonal as she.

Lora hurried down to the kitchen and prepared a tray, as she had that night when she had waited for him so late. When she carried it upstairs she saw that the door of the new sitting room was open and a lamp had been lit within.

Wade sat in an old but comfortable chair which Peter had brought down from the attic and he was looking about the room with the air of a stranger who had come into a foreign country and found everything about him unfamiliar. Lora drew up a small table and set the tray upon it.

"Of course the room isn't right yet," she said cheerfully as she filled his cup. "So far I've furnished it with odds and ends, but if it proves a useful place, perhaps we can add some new pieces and make it really comfortable."

He said nothing and she could not tell what he was thinking or feeling.

"Tell me more about your trip," she said. "What is the war news in Washington?"

He stirred his tea thoughtfully. "Since the middle of the month Lee's armies have been on the march. They've crossed the Potomac and moved into Pennsylvania. An attack on Harrisburg is feared, but I gather that Meade's army is being brought in to stop him. All possible men are being sent from this area to Union support."

"Of course we'll stop him," Lora said.

Wade looked grave. "It's terrible to be helpless. Seeing matters as I do now, I know how badly every man is needed. I ought to be in there with my company."

She sat very still in her place by the window, finishing her own cup of tea. The breeze had died out and the heat was growing oppressive. The hot brew made her warmer still and she fanned herself with a handkerchief, wishing she could find words of comfort for Wade. They both knew he could never go back.

"Edgar Lord was home for two days," she told him. "He left to join his men in Pennsylvania yesterday. Serena is terribly afraid he'll be caught in some big battle. But she keeps up wonderfully. She's always planning something to keep us all busy."

"She has cause to be worried," Wade said. But Lora knew that he was regretting his own inability to make a contribution like Edgar's.

A little while later he said good night and went off to bed. When he had gone Lora replaced the tea things on the tray and then stood for a moment looking about the room. All trace of those other days was gone. She had even had a paper hanger in to put up something new in a pleasant yellow-green pattern. There was no longer the faintest scent of rose leaves, and all the mustiness had given way to the fresh odor of the outdoors. But perhaps the memory of Virginia must always haunt this room. There was no way of knowing how Wade felt about it. Where he had once revealed his feelings so easily, he now concealed them and she never knew what he was thinking.

She lay awake for a long time that night, turning restlessly in the humid heat, unable to sleep.

XXVIII

A HUSH SEEMED to lie upon New York those first days of July. 1863 had seen continuous Union defeat, and now somewhere in Pennsylvania a great battle might be raging. Lee had taken Chambersburg and York, and it seemed that Harrisburg might be next in his line of attack. The North held its breath uneasily while rumors and counterrumors alternately afrighted and encouraged.

Soon after daylight on July 4 church bells began to ring. There was the firing of cannon and the explosion of firecrackers announcing a victory for the North. By July 5 fragmentary news began to seep through. The battle had not, after all, reached Harrisburg. Pickett's men had charged the Union line along Cemetery Ridge near a little place called Gettysburg, and it appeared that one of the great, decisive battles of the war had been fought. The victory had been complete and crushing. Lee's army of Northern Virginia was shattered, disorganized, routed.

The crescendo of excitement in the North mounted to delirium. The North's diet had been the bitter bread of defeat for too long. Now people threw restraint aside and gave way to wild rejoicing. Men and women cried and embraced each other in the streets. Surely this ended the rebellion! The South could not fight on! The war would be over in a few weeks! There were wiser heads who were less sure, less hopeful, but who listened to them?

So excited was New York over the battle of Gettysburg that it hardly noticed the surrender of Vicksburg which opened the Mississippi to the North. New York's concern with the fighting in Pennsylvania was understandable, since almost to a man army and militia had been dispatched to stop Lee's army. Only a handful of police remained to protect New York. A sober few of New York's citizens feared the possibility of attack in this undefended moment, but for the most part everyone was too busy shooting off firecrackers and otherwise indulging in emotional release over victory to trouble about such forebodings.

Even Dogwood Lane decided to celebrate in its own modest way. A supper party and beach bonfire was decided upon and Serena Lord was almost feverishly active in working out the plans. Since Edgar had gone off to Pennsylvania, Serena had not heard from him. Lora knew that she was more worried than ever before and that these plans for a celebration party were an effort to keep herself busy and occupied.

Rain spoiled the first date set for the party and it was moved ahead to Monday, the 13th of July. It had been a week since the battle of Gettysburg, a week since Vicksburg, but feeling in the North still ran high. Now, however, most families were beginning to look with dread and anxiety to the return of the soldiers. Who would come, who would be left? By now it was known that the slaughter on both sides had been terrible. If one meant to celebrate victory, perhaps it was well to do so quickly and not wait for the next weekend.

On Saturday, in a surprise move, the Provost Marshal of

New York gave the order which put the draft into effect. Crowds turned out about the draft offices that day, but there was no violence and the tone of the newspapers was optimistic. All would be done in an orderly, lawful fashion, they promised, and on Sunday the good citizens of the town relaxed.

Monday morning Adam Hume stopped by at the Tylers' to see if Wade wanted to go over to New York to witness this historic event and get an idea of how people were taking it. Wade was eager to go. Lora knew he had worried on Saturday when the draft started and that he feared trouble. He and Adam promised to be home in plenty of time for the supper party at the beach.

The party was to consist of a small gathering of those who lived on or near the lane and the children were coming too. That afternoon Ellie packed a hamper with a good lunch and Peter drove Lora, Jemmy and Hamlin out to Serena's favorite stretch of beach on the South Shore. The Lord carriage led the way carrying Serena, Hester Wylie and Serena's two boys. Morgan rode in her own carriage, attended by Rebecca, who was to help prepare and serve the food that evening.

Jemmy had not forgotten that the next day was Lora's birthday and during the drive to the beach he brought the matter up again.

"I reminded Papa last week," he told her, "and he said we could have a special dinner party for just us tomorrow night. You don't think he'll forget, do you?"

Lora smiled. "Thank you, Jemmy, but I don't think this is the time to worry your father about such matters. Grownups don't have to have birthday celebrations."

"You do," Jemmy said. "This is your very first birthday at our house and I've already made you a present."

She squeezed his hand and said they would talk about it later.

They all reached the beach by late afternoon of the gray and muggy day. The place of Serena's choice was a quiet spot, with no bathhouses to mar the stretch of sand sloping down from the beach grass of a high bank, and no other bathers to disturb their privacy. Clean water creamed over the lower reaches of sand and there was driftwood aplenty for the building of a fire.

The three boys undressed in the bushes and got into their striped bathing suits at once. Then, admonished by their elders not to go into deep water, they went splashing in and out of the surf.

"Come with us, Lorie," Jemmy pleaded, so Lora removed her shoes and stockings and ran down to the water's edge to cool her feet in the clear green ripples. Whiskers and Hamlin tore up and down, barking and making wild forays into this interesting wetness. The sun was obscured by a thin haze and the air hung heavy and still with the oppressive heat.

Up on the beach the others had found a sheltered spot beside a grassy hummock where they spread out blankets and hampers, set up camp. Serena, Hester and Lora had worn old dresses without hoops, so they might be comfortable and careless of their clothes. But Morgan, as usual, had gowned herself more stylishly. She too had dispensed with hoops, but she wore flounced white muslin over crinolines and carried a ruffled parasol to shield her complexion from the glare. With the contrast of her dark hair and eyes, white seemed as dramatic on her as black. Lora noted a nervous tension about her today, as if she were keyed to a high pitch.

As Lora stood watching the gulls which soared above the water, Hamlin ran suddenly toward her, shaking himself vigorously, so that water sprayed in every direction. Laughing, Lora dashed for safety, almost bumping into Rebecca, who was coming toward her across the sand.

"How are you, Rebecca?" Lora asked. She had hardly seen the colored girl since she had returned to work for Morgan Channing, though she had inquired about her several times through Ambrose.

For once Rebecca did not quickly veil her dark eyes, but returned Lora's look almost shyly, accepting her friendship.

"I'm fine, Miss Lora," she said. "I've been wanting to say thank you for helping me like you did."

"I helped very little," Lora told her. "But I'm glad everything is turning out well."

Rebecca threw a quick glance over her shoulder at the preoccupied women up the beach, then turned back hurriedly.

"There's a thing I've been wanting to tell you, Miss Lora. I'm hoping to marry Jeb soon as we can work things out."

"That's wonderful!" Lora cried. "I'm very happy for you, Rebecca."

The colored girl threw another quick look in Morgan's direction. "Mrs. Lord sent me down to tell the boys they'd better scoot around now and get driftwood for the fire." Then she added under her breath, "Mrs. Channing—she doesn't know yet. I—I don't rightly know how to tell her, or what she'lll likely do when she hears."

"You're free to do as you please," Lora assured her. "The way things look now, the war should be over soon. And then your mother and sister will be able to come North if they like. And you needn't work for Mrs. Channing one minute more than you want to."

She paused to deliver Serena's message to the boys and they went scampering in three directions, picking up bits of wood as they ran, the dogs leaping after them. Rebecca reached for a stick of wood too, apparently anxious to avoid the appearance of any confidential talk with Lora.

"She'll make trouble for me if I try to leave," she said softly. "I don't know why, but it seems like she wants to keep me working for her no matter what."

Again Lora found herself puzzling over that. Of course it was Morgan's temperament to fight for anything of which she was balked. But there had seemed something more here, something which Rebecca too had sensed.

A sudden neighing came from the road near which the carriages had been left and the horses tethered. There was a sound of jangling harness and the "Whoa!" of a cabby.

"That must be Herbert," Hester Wylie said, getting up to brush sand from the lap of her dress and tidy her wind-blown hair. "He said he'd leave the office early and come out in a cab."

Herbert, Lora knew, worked for the gas company on the island.

"Or it could be Murray," Morgan said, and Lora sensed the uneasiness in her voice. She did not sound as if she were too eager to see Murray Norwood.

The shrubbery which overhung the little-used path to the beach parted and Herbert came through, followed by Adam Hume. When she saw Adam, Lora ran barefooted up the beach in his direction. His appearance was alarming. He wore a shabby, workman's jacket and one sleeve was partly torn from the armhole. Both men looked grave and concerned.

Lora reached Adam out of breath. "Wade? Where is he?"

Adam glanced toward the little camp. "Then he's not here? I thought he might have arrived before I did. No matter—he'll undoubtedly be along later, unless he has gone straight home."

"What has happened?" Lora cried. "Has there been an accident?"

He shook his head and looked at Herbert as if for help. Hester's husband dropped onto the blanket beside his wife.

"The expected trouble over the draft has started," he said.

Morgan leaned toward Herbert, her frivolous parasol shadowing her face. "They're going to stop it, aren't they?"

"I wouldn't go so far as to say that," Herbert told her. "But there are rumors of trouble here on the island. However, Adam's been over in the city—he can tell us much more. There's no use trying to keep this from the ladies, Adam."

Alarm shivered through Lora. "Adam, tell us what has happened!"

"Sit over here, Lora," he said, "and make yourself comfortable. It's a long story, but you needn't look so frightened. Wade and I got separated in the crowd and I couldn't find him again. We went over together this morning, as you know, and took a car uptown until we had to leave it because of the crowds. Rioting had begun around the draft office at Forty-sixth and Third. I heard threats to the effect that the mob meant to burn every draft office in New York. Wade and I hung around on the outskirts for a time without being molested, but tempers were getting ugly and anyone who was decently dressed seemed to be marked for attention."

"Who made up the crowd?" Herbert asked.

"I think it started with the criminal element, which doesn't want to be caught by the draft. But this sort of thing is contagious and it is spreading like wildfire." He glanced at Morgan. "If there was any leadership to start with, it's been lost sight of by now."

"But the police—?" Serena asked.

Adam shrugged. "What can a handful of police do against the thousands who are rioting? Remember, even the militia is still in Pennsylvania. The mob has begun to feel its own power and that's a dangerous thing."

"When I left, shops had begun to close here on the island," Herbert said. "Though I've heard of no real outbreaks as yet."

Serena glanced nervously toward the place where the boys, with the help of Rebecca, Peter, and her own coachman, were piling up wood for the bonfire that was to celebrate Union victory.

"Perhaps we should go home at once," she suggested.

"No need for that," Adam said. "The island is quiet

enough, and no mobs are likely to storm Dogwood Lane. If there is any trouble, we'll be better off traveling after dark."

"But you haven't told us how you lost Wade," Lora pleaded.

"That was this afternoon. By that time fire bells were clanging constantly, though I'm afraid the firemen weren't doing too much toward putting out the fires. In some cases their sympathies are with the rioters. They aren't willing to fight when they are interfered with. We couldn't get a cab or car to head for home, though we saw several horsecars abandoned in their tracks, while the drivers joined the mob that was pulling passengers off and robbing them. There's no law to protect anyone now."

Adam glanced toward Rebecca, who was heaping wood on the rising pile, and lowered his voice.

"Part of the mob's destructive temper is being directed at the unfortunate colored people. The minds of the ignorant have been inflamed against the Negro because of the fear that the cheap labor of freedom will take away their jobs. I'm afraid there may be lynchings before this thing is put down. In fact, that's how Wade and I got involved with the crowd. And that's when we saw Norwood too."

Morgan had been listening intently. Now she put her parasol down with a sharp little click and tossed it aside. But she said nothing.

"There was plenty of drink in the crowd by afternoon and its blood lust was up. Burning buildings wasn't so much fun as finding human quarry. When Wade and I came on this howling pack it was on the heels of a Negro who was running for his life. He'd been caught and beaten, but he'd twisted away and was running straight into our hands. Wade thinks fast and he saw the one spot we could dive for before the crowd was on us—the side door of a warehouse, opening on an alley. We got through it with the colored man between us and shot the bolt before the crowd could decide where we'd disappeared to. By the time they found that door we'd made it to the other side of the building and slipped onto a cross street. A woman saw us from a window and beckoned, so we popped into her house and let the mob howl by."

Adam grimaced wryly and ran a finger around his shabby collar.

"That's when we shed our gentleman's clothes and got ourselves into something less conspicuous. The woman who gave us shelter had worked on the Underground in the old days

277

and she was indignant over what was happening. We left our colored friend hiding in her attic and slipped out through the back door onto another alley. The crowd was out on the street, but it had found a new interest. Luckily I'd found a cap to cover my red hair. We managed to melt into the ranks and allow ourselves to be swept along, waiting for a chance to break away."

"You said you saw Murray," Morgan reminded him.

"That's right. And he did us no good. He was up on a balcony trying to make some sort of speech, and when he saw Wade he began to shout and point. I suppose he was trying to incite the crowd in our direction. However, it looks like this Circle business has backfired on its instigators. Certainly they're not in the lead as they expected to be. There were some boys with pickaxes breaking up a section of pavement so they'd have more ammunition to throw and when they spotted Murray they chucked a few rocks at him and he ducked inside. I expect New York will be too hot for him now and he'll go back to Albany where he came from.

"It was right after this that Wade and I got separated. He couldn't move as fast as I could when Norwood pointed us out. I saw him stumble and fall, but when I tried to get back to him I was carried along without a chance of reaching him. Later I climbed up on a wall where I could see better. He was up again, but he went away from me around a corner, and after that I lost him for good. I hunted for a while, but there was nothing to do but get downtown again where it was quieter and take the ferry home, hoping he'd be here ahead of me."

He wiped his face with a soggy handkerchief and smiled at Lora.

"Don't worry. I think he was out of any real danger by that time."

Lora managed a thin smile, but fear churned inside her. Wade had the disadvantage of his bad leg. If he fell again in a crowd like that he might be trampled. Or he might do something reckless to help some hapless victim of the mob, and be injured himself. She had reason to know how suddenly, how mercilessly death could strike.

Serena's cheerful tones broke the uneasy silence that followed Adam's account. No matter how worried she herself might be, Serena always managed to sound as if she hadn't a care in the world. And her example usually had a healthy effect on others.

"It's getting dark enough for our fire, by now," she announced, and stood up to call the boys. "Get out of those wet suits and into your clothes. We're going to have supper and light the fire."

Everyone broke into nervous activity, but Lora found herself moving in an aura of unreality. It was hard to believe that scenes such as Adam had described were occurring right now in New York.

Only Morgan did nothing. She put Rebecca to work, but sat idly by herself, her white dress ghostly in the fading light. Once Lora stumbled over her extended white slippers and looked down at her impatiently.

"Don't sit there," she said more sharply than she intended. "Do something. If you're worrying about your precious Mr. Norwood you'll be better off if you busy yourself. The rest of us are worried too."

Morgan shook her head. "It's not Murray I'm concerned about. He can take care of himself. You know I'm thinking of Wade."

"Wade can take care of himself too," Lora said, and moved away in quick resentment. Morgan had no right to concern herself, to wear that look in her eyes, to carry her heart on her sleeve for Wade.

As Lora circled the pile of driftwood, Rebecca approached her hesitantly.

"I heard some of what Mr. Adam said. . . . Miss Lora, is it true that we colored people . . ."

"Don't worry," Lora said quickly. "You're with us. Nothing can happen to you."

"It's Jeb I'm thinking of," Rebecca faltered. "And his mother on McKeon Street."

"Mr. Wylie says everything is quiet on the island," Lora assured her. "You mustn't worry." But she knew how futile it was to tell anyone not to worry when her own anxiety would not be subdued.

The three boys were allowed to start the bonfire themselves. Flames began to lick upward through the wood, until the entire pile was a roaring conflagration. Then everyone settled to the business of eating supper, though the celebration was not particularly gay.

Lora hardly knew whether she ate cold chicken or baked ham. The potato salad might as well have been sawdust and she could not eat a bite of chocolate cake. All she wanted

now was to get home and find out whether or not Wade wa
there. She was surprised when Morgan, who was eating little
left her own place and crossed the sand in her direction.

"It's true," Morgan said abruptly, "that Murray is furi
ously angry with Wade. I've done what I could to restrai
him, but if there is real trouble I can't tell what might hap
pen."

"There's nothing we can do when we don't even knov
where Wade is," Lora said stiffly.

Morgan hesitated, as if there was more she wanted to say
She began to speak again, more softly.

"If trouble starts on the island, my house will be safe
Orders will be given to leave it untouched. But other home
—Republican homes—may be threatened. Lora, if there'
trouble, come up to my house and bring everyone with you.

Lora looked at her for a moment. The leaping orang
flames flickered over Morgan's white dress, shone in her eyes
but they did not reveal what she was really thinking.

"Thank you," said Lora, "but I'm not sure Wade woul
want us to accept the protection of the Circle."

Quick anger flashed in Morgan's eyes, but before she coul
speak there was a cry from the direction of the beach. Shield
ing her eyes from the fire glare, Lora could see Rebecca dow
near the water's edge. She was pointing out across the bay.

At first the nearer brilliance was too great for Lora to mak
out what it was Rebecca saw. But when she moved awa
from the fire she could catch the glare of flames here an
there on the opposite Brooklyn shore.

So the trouble had spread out of New York itself.

Up near the road the horses neighed and stamped an
there was the sound of someone coming down through th
brush toward the beach. Lora whirled about in time to se
Wade limp into the aura of light about the fire. For just a
instant she stood staring in mingled shock and relief. He wor
no coat, but only a torn shirt with bloodstains down its front
A purplish bruise made a swelling on one cheekbone an
blood had dried along the edges of a cut upon his forehead

In the instant in which she stood transfixed, Lora lost he
chance to reach him first. Morgan was nearer and Morga
moved at once. Even as Lora recovered herself, the othe
woman flew across the sand toward Wade and flung her arm
unabashedly about his neck.

"I've worried so!" she cried. "Wade, are you all right?

280

She pressed her cheek against his, caring nothing for what the others might think.

An anger sharper than she had ever known flared through Lora, though there was nothing she could say or do.

Wade's reaction was quick and cold and firm. He reached up to break Morgan's hold about his neck, and when she would have clung to him he took her by the shoulders and shook her hard. Then he put her out of his way and turned toward the others.

Serena spoke quickly as if nothing unusual had happened. "We're glad to see you, Wade. Lora has been anxious about you."

But Wade did not pause to look for Lora. "You shouldn't be out here," he told them all. "I stopped at your house, Serena, and when I found you weren't home, I took your pony phaeton and came right out. This trouble has spread to the island by now. There are gangs springing up everywhere and if the smaller groups join forces it may mean something even more serious. We'd better start for home at once."

Morgan went to pick up her parasol and reticule as proudly as though she had not been humiliated before the others, but there was no missing the anger that flashed in her eyes. She fairly snapped at Rebecca, who flew to assist her. As Lora came up behind Wade, he turned to smile at her reassuringly. But the moment when she might have gone to him as naturally and impulsively as Morgan had, was past. She could not even find words to tell him, of her relief. There was nothing to do but busy herself by helping to gather things up and carry them back to the carriages.

The bonfire, much to the regret of the three boys, had to be scattered across the beach and buried in wet sand. There were fires enough tonight, and they were not fires of celebration.

On the way home Serena's carriage took the lead again, with Morgan's immediately following. The Tyler carriage came next and Wade rode with Lora and Jemmy, while Adam took the phaeton to bring up the rear.

They jogged along lonely roads toward the more populated section of the island and nothing happened until they were nearly home. Then Peter, who had a view of the road ahead from his seat, turned to look anxiously at Wade in the open carriage.

"Looks like there's trouble ahead, Mr. Wade. Looks like

281

twenty or more in a gang. They're coming toward us carrying torches."

Lora leaned out her side of the carriage so she could see ahead, keeping a good hold on Jemmy's arm lest he topple into the road in his anxiety to see.

It appeared that the passage of the carriages must certainly be blocked, but as Serena's horses slowed down, the crowd divided to each side of the road and let her carriage through. Morgan's carriage, too, might have been permitted to follow, had not someone held up a torch to illumine the faces of the two women who rode in it—Morgan in the wide carriage seat, and Rebecca riding backwards on a small let-down seat in front.

For an instant the flickering light touched Rebecca's brown skin, shone in her dark eyes, then someone gave a whoop of triumph.

"Here's one now!"

Rough hands caught at the bridles of the frightened horses and Peter had to pull up the Tyler carriage before it crashed into Morgan's. In the weaving torchlight Lora could see that these fellows were hardly more than boys—though big boys in their late teens. One of them reached in and grasped Rebecca by the arm. Lora heard the girl's cry of fear and saw Morgan bring her parasol angrily down upon the boy's head. But the flimsy thing broke in two and Rebecca was being pulled from the carriage, to the delight of the torchbearers.

In the same instant Wade jumped from their carriage and flung himself toward the gang of boys. He struck out with his fist and the fellow who had hold of Rebecca fell back. Adam had already seen what was happening and he leaped from the phaeton to join Wade. But Adam carried a brace of pistols, one in each hand, and even as the gang closed in about Wade and Rebecca, he fired a shot into the air.

The sound of the gunfire had an immediate effect. It was every man for himself as the boys dived for the side of the road, dropping their torches in the wild scramble. Apparently none of them had any stomach for facing real bullets. They might be ready to bully, but they were not eager to risk their necks.

Peter whipped up the Tyler horses and Lora was flung back in the seat beside Jemmy. Wade and Adam jumped into the phaeton and Wade took the reins, while Adam held his pistols cocked and ready. There was an angry muttering, but the fellows who crouched by the roadside made no attempt at pursuit.

The whole thing had happened so quickly that there had hardly been time to be frightened, but now Lora felt limp with reaction. Jemmy, however, was wildly excited.

"Did you see Papa knock that fellow over?" he cried. "And did you see Uncle Adam's guns?"

"Yes, Jemmy, I saw. But it's all right now. We're nearly home."

"Why did they attack us, Lorie? Were they robbers, or what?"

Lora tried to explain calmly to Jemmy what was happening because of the draft. Jemmy was more elated than frightened. This was an adventure, he assured her. Like something out of a story. Would there be more mobs, did she think? And would they come up Dogwood Lane? There was such hopefulness in his tone that she had to smile, even as she tried to quiet him. He seemed disappointed by her assurance that there would be no reason to storm their remote little road.

"Unless because of Rebecca," Jemmy said.

Lora thrust back her uneasiness on that very score. She had no confidence in Morgan's assurance that the Channing place would be safe, no matter what happened elsewhere. Belonging to Morgan Channing had not kept her carriage safe from that mob of boys.

When they reached the lane Morgan signaled her coachman to draw the carriage to the side of the road and wait for the others. When the Tyler carriage drew up, Lora got out and hurried over to speak to Rebecca.

The girl sat limply on the front seat, nursing a bruised arm and betraying more resignation than fear. Lora reached out to pat her hand.

"You'll be all right now, Rebecca. We won't let anyone harm you."

The phaeton had come to a stop beside Morgan's carriage and Wade too came over to inquire about Rebecca. He ignored Morgan, but she broke in upon his words without ceremony. She seemed to have discarded the incident at the beach as if it had never happened.

"You must all come up to my house tonight, Wade. I've enough room to put everyone up, and I'm sure you'll be safer there. I've already suggested it to Lora."

Wade shook his head. "No, thank you. After the taste we had over in town today, I've no belief in Norwood's name carrying any protection, even if he chose to help us. What do you think, Adam?"

"I think we're safer in our own homes," Adam said. "In any event we'd better not lump all our forces in one place and leave our homes to be burned to the ground if trouble arises."

Morgan shrugged with elaborate indifference and drove off up the hill. Adam made a face and rolled his eyes before he followed Serena toward home.

XXIX

LORA SLEPT restlessly that night, though all remained quiet on the lane. More than once she wakened to listen to the night sounds in the garden—the humming of insects, the chirping of tree toads. She wished she could hush their clamor the better to hear other, more stealthy sounds. Rain came late at night and brought some relief from the heat, as well as reassurance. Surely even rioters would not enjoy being wet to the skin.

All the house was breathlessly still. She wished she might go into Wade's room for company, re-establish the old relationship in which each had needed the other. But these days he seemed to avoid being alone with her.

When they'd come into the house after returning from the beach, he had gone at once to bathe his cuts and bruises and change his clothes. Lora had given his mother an account of what had happened in New York before she should be alarmed by her son's appearance. The old lady seemed more indignant than frightened and she scoffed when Lora reported Morgan's suggestion that they all come up to her house. She even gave orders to Peter and got out of her chair to supervise the bringing down of Jack Tyler's guns and pistols from the attic—an event that filled Jemmy with delight. But there was no need for any defense that night and the household retired quietly enough.

Lora awoke the next morning to the somewhat wistful realization that this was her birthday. A remembrance of last year returned unbidden and she winced away from it. This was no time for such youthful doings, and under the circumstances even Jemmy would probably forget. There was very little to celebrate about being a year older when one had accomplished so little, she thought dolefully, and got up to dress.

Jemmy, however, did not forget. He reminded everyone at breakfast that this was Lorie's birthday and they were going to have a party for her at dinner. She would, he said, have to wait for her present till then.

She tried to protest, but Wade sided cheerfully with his son.

"A very good time for a party," he said pointedly, and looked at his mother. "It will help to keep us occupied and entertained, don't you think?"

Lora sensed his unspoken thought—that this was perhaps a way to keep Jemmy's attention off matters that might be altogether too exciting. Mother Tyler apparently understood too, for she gave orders to Ellie to bake a cake, and to set out the silver candelabra and best linen for a party that night.

Later in the morning Mrs. Tyler sent Peter on a reconnoitering expedition to see what had happened on the island during the night and whether the unruliness was now being put down. He came home with a disquieting report. The rioting in the city had begun again in the early morning hours and the mobs were larger and more out of hand than they had been the day before. Beatings, burnings and lynchings were the order of the day and already men had died in the New York area.

Here on Staten Island there had been some trouble during the night, and all storekeepers had cautiously put up their shutters for the day. The ferries were still running, but other transportation had stopped. Negroes were fleeing to the woods, or finding their way over to New Jersey where there was no trouble and they could be safe. Threats were being uttered on every hand—against Black Republicans, against the wealthy, who were being blamed for the war, and against the helpless colored people. The temper of the crowds was ugly and there was no telling what violence might be perpetrated before the uprising was set down.

"Where are the authorities?" Mother Tyler cried, pounding her cane indignantly. "What can they be thinking of?"

Wade shook his head at her fury. "The authorities, as you call them, have about sixty police at their beck and call. And what can such a handful manage against thousands of hoodlums? This is mob rule, Mother, until outside help comes in. All we can do is get up our own citizen groups to protect our homes."

Adam came in during the day with good news from Pennsylvania. Edgar had sent a message through to his wife by telegraph. He had been wounded at Gettysburg, but only superficially. His company was already on the march for home and should be in New York in a few days.

"The town will be all right the minute the army gets back. But until then we'd better have some working plan in case there's trouble up here."

Arrangements were made to send or signal for help if the need arose. But all day long Dogwood Lane dreamed in the muggy July heat and saw no hint of trouble. Night would be the time of greater danger and anxiety, and Lora was glad to see Jemmy thoroughly occupied in his plans for the birthday dinner.

That afternoon Wade called Lora into the library and gave her a sheaf of papers with handwriting across the pages.

"Another book?" she asked. "Or a story?"

"Neither," he said. "I'm trying my hand at articles now, Lora. Some pieces about our own times. About things I know and feel strongly about. Will you read this when you have a chance and tell me what you think?"

She took the pages somewhat doubtfully and he smiled.

"Don't worry. I'm not going to be a sensitive plant this time. Writing is the thing I feel I can do best and I've already had some encouragement from Sidney Howard Gay here on the island. He feels that Horace Greeley, for whom he works, might even want to publish my revision of this piece. I know I have a great deal to learn and I'm willing to work at it."

"I'm very glad," Lora said softly. "I'll read this right away."

She carried his piece to the seclusion of her own room and sat down to read it. She had finished no more than a page before she realized that this time he had found his métier.

Here, set down movingly, compellingly, were the reasons why the Union must fight this war—and win. Yet there was no inciting to hatred in the words. Rather, a cause bigger than North or South was offered—the cause of freedom for every human creature, and of an eventual joining in brotherhood for the sake of a great and useful future.

There were tears in her eyes when she finished. How her father would have loved Wade! He would have approved a cause such as this, no matter how he felt about the war. He would have understood that men were not yet wise enough or good enough to achieve a noble goal nobly. They were still

286

only puny things who must strive foolishly and harm themselves in the striving. But the shining goal stood above and apart, and even the puny might raise eyes of hope and believe in one day being worthy to reach such a goal.

She took the piece back to Wade and put it into his hands. "I'm very proud to be your wife," she said simply, and then turned quickly away.

"Lora—" he began, but she would not stay to hear him. There was too much in her heart for him to see and she did not ever again want gratitude or pity from him.

Shortly before dinner Lora went up to her room to change her dress for the party. Opening the door of her wardrobe, she drew out one gown after another, but somehow nothing seemed exactly suited for the occasion. She wanted no dove gray or pale blue, but some rich and satisfying color.

She found the right dress tucked far back in the closet, shimmering in the dim light of her shuttered room. A feeling of audacity flashed through her, even of triumph. She *would* be beautiful tonight, and she would be unafraid of Mother Tyler or anyone else.

Carefully she drew out the shining garnet dress and held it up. This was the gown she had made so lovingly and which had met with such disapproval the night of Serena's Christmas party. She had never worn it at all. But tonight she did not care what Mother Tyler thought of it. She knew this dress suited her and tonight she would wear it bravely and with confidence.

She made no attempt to set her hair in ringlets, but loosened it a little, so that it waved softly back from her temples. And she clasped her mother's garnets about her throat. Not until she was sure she would be the last one downstairs did she leave her room.

The tall white candles in the candelabra had been lighted and Mother Tyler already sat in her place at the table, while Wade and Jemmy stood waiting for Lora to come in. She swept into the room gaily, confidently, her eyes dancing. Nothing hung in the balance tonight. Tonight her wearing of the dress was only a lark and a distraction. Managing the big hoop gracefully, she went to the chair which Wade had pulled out for her.

Jemmy said, "Whee!" and was quickly reproved by his grandmother. But it was the look which kindled in Wade's eyes as he drew back the chair which made Lora's breath catch in her throat and the color rise warmly in her cheeks.

"You're lovely tonight," he said. "May I compliment you on your choice of a gown?"

She knew he was laughing, but now she did not mind. There was kindness in his laughter—and something more flattering as well.

"Happy birthday," he said, and swept her into her place with a flourish.

Jemmy shouted, "Happy birthday, Lorie! Happy birthday!"

Mother Tyler said surprisingly, "That color becomes you, daughter."

Lora felt tears sting her eyes and she had to blink to hold them back. At her place were three small packages, tied up in paper left from Christmas. There was a paper shortage these days and one used every scrap several times over.

While Ellie brought in the soup Lora opened her gifts happily and exclaimed over each. There was a cigar box, turned by Jemmy into a handkerchief case with suitable pasted-on decorations. A sprig of lavender scented it, combating the odor of tobacco. There was a book of Elizabeth Browning's poetry from Wade, inscribed to his wife. And there was a handsome cameo brooch from Mother Tyler—one of her own treasures.

It was as happy a birthday party as any she could remember and she found herself, like Jemmy, too excited to eat very much. They sat long at the table, telling stories and talking, and for once there was ready laughter in this dining room. Once Lora's eyes sought the place on the wall where the dead game bird had once hung, and which was now graced innocuously by a graceful depiction of fruit dish and grape bunches.

Only now and then did the uneasiness they had thrust into the background intrude itself in some moment of silence, so that they all sat quiet, listening to the evening sounds outside. Then talk would break out again and the sense of disquiet was pushed away. They sat so long at the table that dusk crept over the hill and it was growing dark outside by the time the birthday cake was brought in, its candles twinkling bravely.

Not until they were ready to rise from the table did a sudden knocking sound on the kitchen door. Jemmy dashed from the table without reproof and ran into the kitchen. He was back in a moment, ahead of Ellie.

"It's Rebecca! She wants to see you, Lorie."

Mrs. Tyler raised a finger to stop her when Lora started to rise. "That is the colored girl who works for Morgan? Bring her in here, Ellie."

Ellie opened the door for the girl and she came into the room uncertainly, her glance seeking Lora's reassurance. It was the first time Lora had seen Rebecca without the bright costume in which Morgan chose to dress her. Her black hair, covered by no gaudy turban, was drawn back in a sedate knot on her neck and her dress was a simple one of dark brown. She still wore her mother's gold earrings, but she looked like a young and frightened girl, and no longer mysterious and exotic.

Wade saw her put a hand against the doorjamb to steady herself and he went to bring her a chair. She would not sit in it, however, but stood behind it, leaning upon its back with her hands.

"What is it, Rebecca?" Lora asked. "What has happened?"

The girl threw an uneasy glance at Mrs. Tyler, whose reputation for being a tyrant she undoubtedly knew. The old woman saw the look and gestured toward the chair.

"Please sit down, Rebecca. And stop shaking. You are a friend among friends."

Lora saw recognition spring up in Rebecca's eyes. *A friend among friends*—that was one of the password phrases which had been used in the Underground before the war, when so many in the North were helping slaves to escape to freedom. Lora threw the old lady a quick look of surprise, even as Rebecca slid weakly into the chair.

"You needn't look so startled," Mrs. Tyler told Lora. "This house was once a station on the Underground, though used only occasionally. Now then, Rebecca, tell us what has happened."

Rebecca moistened dry lips with her tongue. "It's Mrs. Channing. She is very angry with me. Jeb came to warn us that an attack may be made on the big house tonight. Everybody knows that Mrs. Channing has me living there."

"Does Mrs. Channing know who Jeb is?" Lora asked.

"That's what made her angry. I had to tell her I was going to marry him. And she said she wasn't going to risk having her house burned down by keeping me there. So she turned me out. She said I'd be all right if I hid in the woods."

"That miserable woman!" Mother Tyler cried.

"Jeb wanted to take me with him. But I knew I'd only

289

make him more trouble. He was going home to get his mother and try to escape to New Jersey. But he had enough on his hands. They'll maybe burn every house on McKeon Street. So I said I'd come down here. I—Miss Lora, I couldn't stay alone up there in the woods. There's—there's that pool and all . . ."

"Of course you couldn't stay there," Lora said. "You did the right thing to come here."

Both Wade and his mother added their reassurances and the girl seemed to take heart a little. Lora took her upstairs to her own room. It would be better to have her out of sight of any curious eyes which might be prying out there in the darkness.

The girl's gratitude was pitiful as Lora insisted that she stretch out on the bed, kick off her shoes and rest herself. She was keyed up and for the first time actually talkative. Lora drew the rocker close to the bed and sat down in it. A candle burned on the dresser and what air stirred in the hot night came in through the slats of the closed shutters. It was best to reveal as few lights as possible while this threat of violence lay over the island.

"I never reckoned it would be like this up North, Miss Lora," Rebecca said. "I was a slave down there and slavery's bad, but I had some friends anyway. And my young Miss Anne was my friend too. She'd never have let anybody hurt me. She cried like anything when I had to be sold to Mr. Channing. But up here Mrs. Channing doesn't know I've got any feelings inside."

Lora listened quietly, recognizing the girl's need for this release into words.

"Miss Virginia was real good to me," Rebecca said softly.

The name "Virginia" seemed to hang there in the room between them, silencing all talk for a moment. Then Rebecca raised herself on one elbow and her eyes were haunted by some inner worry.

"There's something maybe I should tell you, Miss Lora. About Miss Virginia."

"Yes?" Lora asked, startled.

"I never spoke about it before. There isn't so much to tell, rightly. But tonight I had to come down through the woods by myself when it was getting dark. And I had a feeling *she* was there. I had a feeling she couldn't sleep and she had to keep coming back there. I had a feeling it was all my fault and that she couldn't rest because of what I kept secret."

Lora waited in silence. If there was something the girl should tell, then this was not the time for either reassurance or the dismissal of ghosts. But when Rebecca seemed to find it hard to go on, Lora spoke to her gently.

"Do you know something about that day when Virginia was drowned?"

"Not enough." Rebecca closed her eyes and leaned back on the pillow. "That's why I've always kept still. But I reckon Mrs. Channing knows more than she's ever told."

"Why do you think that?"

The story came out then quickly, breathlessly. On the afternoon of Virginia's death, Rebecca had started down the woods path when she met Mrs. Channing running up the hill. Her mistress had been out of breath and looked plainly frightened. When she saw Rebecca she seemed to be glad of someone upon whom she could vent her emotions. She spoke sharply and behaved as though Rebecca had no business being on the path at all, and ordered her back to the house to perform some trumped-up duty.

Later, when news came that Virginia's body had been found, Morgan made no mention of having set foot in the woods near the pool that afternoon. But she had gone about for several days with a queer, set look on her face.

"For a while she used to stare at me sometimes," Rebecca said. "As if she was wondering if I had seen anything, or knew more than I was telling. And a few days after the funeral she began to talk about how I could buy the freedom of my mother and sister if I was a good girl and stayed with her and worked hard."

"So she was actually in the woods that day?" Lora said.

"She was, yes. But I don't know anything about what happened, Miss Lora," Rebecca said quickly. "I didn't see anything. I only know Mrs. Channing seemed upset. If she knew anything about what happened to Miss Virginia, she never told a soul."

Lora shivered in the dim, warm room. Had some monstrous thing happened in the woods that day? Had Morgan perhaps taken matters into her own hands and— But she mustn't let her imagination leap ahead when there was no proof of anything evil. It was just that she could remember Morgan's violence and once or twice her own fear that the woman was capable of doing her physical harm. Then there was that time recorded in Wade's diary when the child, Morgan, had pushed her sister in the pool. True, she had also rescued her that day. No, it wouldn't do to imagine. Rebecca had been right to keep her silence. There was nothing to be told.

Jemmy tapped on the door just then and Lora went to speak to him. He put a finger to his lips and beckoned her, his eyes shining in the light of the candle he held.

"Come quickly, Lora. Come and see!"

She turned back to the girl on the bed. "I'll close the door, Rebecca. Try to sleep. Everything will be all right now."

She followed Jemmy downstairs to the library window, where his father and grandmother stood in the dark, looking out through partly opened shutters.

"Blow out the candle, Jemmy," Wade whispered.

Jemmy blew it out and wriggled in front of his father where he could see out the window. Wade drew Lora into the curve of his arm, so that she could stand between him and his mother.

From this vantage point she could see the shadowy stretch of the lane where it curved downhill toward the harbor. Moving dots of light were approaching up the hill—wavering torches being carried by many hands. The sound of coarse laughter and shouting reached the silent listeners, and it was not a happy sound. There was a deep-toned threat in its depths which made the blood pulse faster in fear.

"Where is Peter?" Mrs. Tyler asked softly of her son.

"I've sent him to put Adam on the alert," Wade said. They heard the click of the back door opening and closing just then. "There he is now, coming back."

Wade left the room to post Peter at a kitchen window overlooking the bolted back door. Then he returned with a pistol in each hand. Now every light in the house was extinguished and it stood shuttered and still. The watchers in the library made no sound, scarcely drawing a deep breath, as if the whisper of their breathing might be heard by the men climbing the hill.

The torches flared brightly as those who carried them drew near, and now the light wavered upon faces alive with angry purpose. These men had not mounted the hill on any idle whim. Nor was this a group of young boys to be easily cowed and driven back. It could only be hoped that the Tyler house was not their goal, though there was always the danger that any house along their way might draw them momentarily from their main target.

Lora gasped as she saw a torchbearer break away from

his companions and start up the drive. But he was hauled back into the ranks almost at once, and as the throng marched by, it became evident that this house at least was not their goal.

"They're going uphill to Morgan Le Fay's," Jemmy whispered. "I know why—they're looking for Rebecca."

Lora put her hand gently on his shoulder. "Rebecca's safe now. They won't know she's here."

She could only hope that would remain true. If this lawless mob started beating the woods for Rebecca and did not find her, it might well be suspected that some family along the lane was hiding her. Especially since the families up here had the reputation of being Black Republicans and supporters of Lincoln.

When the danger was past for the moment, Wade closed the shutters and fastened them. A candle was lighted in the library so that they need not sit in the dark. Peter came in to ask if he should go up through the woods to see how the Channing place was faring. Lora expected Mother Tyler to speak up quickly and give directions as she usually did. But a gradual change was coming over her tonight. She looked to Wade to make the decisions, and oddly enough this did not seem strange.

"Mrs. Channing has her own people to help her," Wade told Peter. "I don't think we'd better take any chances of cutting down our own number even temporarily."

After a while Lora ran upstairs to her own room and opened the door softly to listen. Rebecca's regular breathing told her the girl had fallen asleep, and she was glad that the sound of the rioters had not penetrated her slumbers in this back room.

Nevertheless, the night was not quiet. When a door or window was opened they could hear a distant shouting from the hilltop and could only wonder anxiously what was happening up there.

Before an hour passed, there came a second rapping at the back door and this time Wade went to answer it, with Lora and Jemmy close behind him. Peter, still on watch by the kitchen window, signaled that it was all right to open the door, and Morgan Channing stumbled into the kitchen. John Ambrose was with her and he supported her as she slumped, and helped her to a chair.

Then he wiped his forehead with the back of his hand and looked around at the others. "She's a wildcat, this daughter of mine. She'd have stayed to fight that whole gang if I hadn't made her come away with me. She went right out on the veranda to stop them and they threw stones at her and whistled and shouted for her to give up the Negro girl."

Morgan took the glass of water Lora gave her and drank thirstily. Strands of dark hair hung across her forehead and there was a bramble scratch along one cheek.

"I told them we didn't have Rebecca!" she cried. "I told them they could go hunt the woods for her and that I was on their side. But they wouldn't believe me. I don't think they'd ever heard of Murray or the Golden Circle. They just want to kill and destroy!"

When she paused for breath Ambrose went on with the story. "Some of those fellows pushed right into the house and went through it. By the time I got Morgan out the back door they'd started looting and throwing things out the windows. I had a hard time to keep Morgan from going back when they started a bonfire out on the front lawn with some of those little gold chairs from the drawing room."

"I could have stopped them!" Morgan cried. "I know I could have!"

"You could have got yourself conked in the head," said her father sternly.

For all her keyed-up state, Morgan looked exhausted. "My beautiful house," she went on. "They'll burn it down. And I could have stopped them!"

"What about the servants?" Wade asked Ambrose.

"They couldn't do anything, but they'll be all right. The crowds aren't after the poor. It's the rich man and his possessions they want to destroy. The man they think is to blame for the war."

Mrs. Tyler had come into the kitchen and now, observing Morgan's distraught condition, she turned to Lora. "Perhaps you had better take Mrs. Channing upstairs. She seems extremely upset and it might be as well for her to lie down."

"She can have my room," Jemmy offered. "Rebecca's in Lorie's room."

Morgan stiffened in her chair. "Rebecca is *here?*"

"Why not?" Wade asked. "We are not in the habit of turning out those who need us."

Morgan blinked and something of her normal spirit swept back to brighten her eyes with indignation.

"Don't you know that you may bring that mob down on this house for sheltering her here?"

"If you don't wish to remain in the house with Rebecca," Mrs. Tyler said, "that is for you to choose. But Rebecca stays and we will protect her to the best of our ability. Our concern is not for gilt chairs, but for people."

"Exactly," Wade agreed coldly. "Lora and I feel the same way, Morgan."

Lora, watching the tight, strained look of Morgan's mouth, the burning fury in her eyes, found herself remembering Rebecca's account of that day in the woods when she had seen Morgan returning from the direction of the pool. This might well be the time . . .

She went to Morgan and put a light hand on her shoulder. "I'm sure Jemmy will be happy to have you rest in his room if you wish. Come. I'll take you upstairs."

The fire went out of Morgan, leaving apathy behind. She rose without interest or will and followed Lora from the room. Lora ran ahead of her up the stairs and opened the door of Jemmy's room. She had a plan now. Perhaps it was a cruel plan, but if Morgan knew something about Virginia's death which she had never told, then she deserved no mercy.

XXX

JEMMY WOULD HAVE come too, but Lora sent him back to Wade and led Morgan into the dark room.

"Since the shutters are closed, I can light a candle," she said, groping over Jemmy's dresser. "You'd better take off your hoop so that you can lie down comfortably."

She struck a friction match and held it to the candlewick. Thin light flared through the room, illumining Morgan in her dishevelment. While the other woman attempted to rid herself of her cumbersome hoop, Lora carried a small corner table across the room and set it against one wall. Then she brought the candle and placed it deliberately on the table. The spear of light flickered upon the picture which hung above the table.

As Morgan turned and saw the portrait, Lora could sense her tightening.

"We've had Virginia's picture framed for Jemmy," Lora said casually. "It has turned out very well, don't you think?

Tell me, does it look a great deal like your sister? I never found that your portrait looked very much like you."

Morgan turned away from the picture impatiently. "For heaven's sake, I don't want to stand here fainting on my feet, staring at that silly thing. Do help me with this waistband, Lora. The hooks seem to be caught."

"I will if you'll stop wriggling and stand still," Lora said mildly. "Hoops are such a nuisance, don't you think? I can never get out of mine in a hurry."

Morgan stared at her queerly and jerked away from her hands.

"Put something over that picture!" she cried. "I can't stand the sight of it!"

"Because it reminds you of something?" Lora asked. "Something you'd rather forget?"

Morgan pulled at the band of her hoop, tore it loose, and flung the whole contraption clattering on the floor. Then she slumped down on Jemmy's bed in her voluminous petticoats.

"Do go away and leave me. I don't know what you're talking about, but such chatter hurts my head."

Lora looked at her sternly. "Rebecca was in the woods that day. You haven't forgotten that, have you? She told me about it tonight."

Morgan's shoulders seemed to shrink, as if she waited for some blow to fall, and she sat utterly still.

"You saw something, didn't you?" Lora persisted. "You *were* there that day?"

Something stark looked out of Morgan's eyes. Her lips trembled and she put up her hand as if to steady them with her fingers. But before she could speak, the crashing sound of a shot went reverberating along the hills.

Someone ran through the hall downstairs. Lora and Morgan stared at each other for an instant and then Lora ran out of the room and down the stairs. She heard Morgan following her, but she had no thought of her now. This trouble was more immediate.

The hall was dark, but in the open doorway Lora could see Wade silhouetted against the flare of torches outside. He held his pistols cocked and even as a cry of protest was choked in her throat, he stepped out on the veranda and pulled the door shut behind him. Lora peered anxiously through the glass panel and saw that the veranda was in deep shadow, thanks to the big horse chestnut tree which hid the moon,

Wade had stepped into the shelter of a column and perhaps had not been seen by the mob.

Jemmy came out of the library and bumped into Lora in the dark.

"They've been shouting for Rebecca!" he whispered. "They think she's in our house. Did you hear that shot? It was a signal to Uncle Adam, and it scared those men. They're afraid to come on now."

Jemmy at least had to be kept out of this, Lora thought.

"We need you to do something very important," she told him. "Go upstairs and stay with Rebecca. Go in and lock the door and don't open it except for one of us. Don't let Rebecca be frightened."

Plainly he wanted to stay where the excitement was at its thickest, but the idea that he had an important task to do appealed to him and he ran upstairs, with only a backward look for the front door.

Behind Lora, Morgan spoke in a low, tense voice. "Why don't you give them the girl? Get her out of the house! Do you think she's worth Wade's life?"

"Stop it!" Lora said sharply.

She ran into the library and saw that John Ambrose stood at the partly opened shutters with a gun in his hands, his eyes upon the crowd on the driveway. At that moment Wade revealed himself by calling something to the throng. A stone hurtled past his head and crashed through a parlor window. Immediately there was a shot from the bushes on the right of the house and Lora knew that Adam was there.

The crowd yelled and for a moment it looked as if the brave rioters might break and run. Then a rough voice shouted, "Give up the nigger wench and we'll leave your house stand, mister. If you don't we'll burn it down."

"If you want to stay alive you'd better not set foot across that walk," Wade called from behind his post. "We've got you covered from every window."

There was a muttering among the mob. Those in the rear urged attack, but those in front were more anxious for the safety of their skins. Wade spoke again from his shelter and as the crowd quieted to listen, his voice rang out compellingly.

"You, Billy Barnes!" Wade cried. "You know better than to be out on a job like this. I know your wife and she'll have your hide tomorrow."

There was sudden laughter and then an angry muttering from the rear again.

"And Tom Busby! For shame. I remember you from the days when I was a kid and used to go down to the docks. And O'Reilly—Tim, isn't it? You're an honest man. What bad business is this you're mixed up in? When the police take hold you'll be sorry your name's known."

The muttering began to die sheepishly away. Those on the outer rim began to scatter toward the lane and the crisis might have been over if one of the stone throwers hadn't taken sudden aim and hurled a rock toward Wade's pillar. Lora heard the sickening sound as it struck flesh and bone, and heard Wade grunt in pain. The torchbearers rallied and broke for the steps, but at the same instant shots rang out from several quarters, and this time the aim was not high.

There were yelps and shrieks of pain from the mob, followed by a wild stampede toward the lane.

Lora pulled open the door and rushed onto the veranda. She found Wade leaning against the post, his hand dazedly to his head. Quickly she put an arm about his waist, half supporting him, and brought him inside, slamming the front door shut behind them. Somehow she got him into the library, helped him onto the sofa. All these movements were familiar to her. These were things she was repeating out of the past. But then she had helped a stranger. This was a man she loved.

There was blood on his forehead and he seemed stunned, but the wound looked superficial—there would be more bruise than blood.

Ambrose spoke from the window. "It's over now, I think. Those ruffians have no stomach for gunfire. It's our good fortune they had no guns themselves."

Lora scarcely heard him. All her attention was for Wade, who was coming out of his dazed state.

"I must go see how Adam is faring," he muttered, trying to sit up.

But Adam and Serena's older boy, Eddie, were coming in the back door at that moment, both with guns in their hands. Adam saluted Lora cheerfully.

"So you see, my dear young lady, the ability to fire a gun may come in handy after all. Eddie here helped out our army considerably. How are you, Wade?"

Eddie grinned at Lora, but he remembered that other time in the meadow when she had scolded him. "We didn't kill anybody. We just aimed low at their legs to give them a taste. They're off down the hill now going a mile a minute and dragging the wounded with them."

Hearing voices, Jemmy came out of the bedroom and dashed downstairs to hear what had happened. He regarded Eddie enviously but was somewhat comforted that Temple had been kept at home.

"Rebecca's all right," he told Lora. "She's awake and she's scared, but I told her we wouldn't let anybody hurt her."

Mrs. Tyler came into the room, leaning heavily on her cane and looking both shaken and fierce.

"Where were you, Mother?" Lora asked, but before his mother could answer Wade smiled at her.

"One of those upstairs shots came from you, didn't it? I'd no idea you were a marksman."

"I learned to fire a gun long before you were born," his mother said tartly. "Not that my aim is much good by now. But the Lord helped me pull the trigger and I probably wounded the chestnut tree."

For the first time since danger had engulfed them, Lora thought of Morgan and went to see what had happened to her. She must not leave this house tonight until her full story had been told. She must not be given time to recover herself and invent new lies.

But though Lora looked into the parlor and even into Mother Tyler's sitting room, Morgan was nowhere in evidence. Nor was she anywhere upstairs.

In the kitchen Lora found Ellie making coffee for the besieged party.

"Have you seen Mrs. Channing?" Lora asked.

Ellie pointed to the door. "She popped out there a while ago. Didn't say a word. Just went out like she was seeing ghosts. Guess she was going back uphill to find out what those hoodlums did to her house. Peter says he doesn't think they burned it, or they wouldn't have come down here so fast."

Lora returned to the library for Wade. "Are you feeling better now? Do you think you could come with me to find Morgan? Ellie says she's gone back through the woods, and it's important to go after her quickly."

The earnestness of her manner must have impressed him for he stood up at once.

"I'm all right. Of course I'll come with you."

"And so will I," said John Ambrose from his post by the window.

The three climbed the dark path silently in Indian file, their way lighted only by the mottled moonlight falling through leaves overhead. Not until they reached the pool did the greenish light break into the open, crinkling a path across the water—a metallic path, circled darkly by the rim of trees.

Ambrose reached the clearing first and stopped ahead of Lora. Peering past him, Lora saw Morgan on the far bank. Because of her dark dress she was hardly visible except for the oval of her face, pale in the eerie light.

When Ambrose would have spoken Lora put a hand on his arm. "Let me," she whispered, and went along the bank toward Morgan.

The other woman saw her coming, but she did not move or speak. If she knew of the presence of the two men at the edge of the woods, she gave no sign. She waited for Lora as if in a trance, saying nothing until she was close.

"I'm not as evil as you think," she said in a low voice. "Evil, yes—but not as you think."

"Tell me what happened," Lora said gently. "Tell me so that you may live with yourself again."

Morgan went on dully, without passion. "I was in the woods that day. I saw her here on that rock reaching for a turtle just as she used to do when she was a little girl. She didn't know I was watching her. When her foot slipped and she fell, she didn't know there was anyone near who could have helped her."

"And didn't you help her?"

"I meant to. Truly I meant to. But my hoop would have dragged us both down. I had to loosen the band, to get out of it." For the first time her words faltered. "And I—I couldn't. My hands were shaking and—and—"

"So she drowned while you stood there on the path watching? Is that the way it was?"

Morgan's voice was hardly audible. "Yes."

"And what happened afterwards?"

"I was frightened. I knew I would be blamed—that I was to blame. So I ran back up the path and no one would ever have known I was near the pool that afternoon if it hadn't been for Rebecca."

The pool, the trees, the night were utterly still as if they too listened. Suddenly Morgan moved. She went past Lora to Wade, her hands lifted as if in supplication. But Wade turned sickly away and she let them drop to her sides.

"I'd thought to—to follow Virginia tonight," she said, "but I find I am a woman of little courage."

John Ambrose went to her quietly and took her by the arm. "Come, my daughter," he said. Then he turned back

300

momentarily to Wade and Lora. "I'll be taking her away from the island when things quiet down. Don't concern yourselves."

They did not speak as Morgan went with him listlessly toward the path that led uphill to the great white house. As Lora watched them disappear into shrouding darkness, a lump choked in her throat. Not of pity for Morgan, but of affection for the man who was her father. All this while he had waited nearby, knowing that one day his unruly daughter might have need of him. Now that the moment had come, he would find it in his philosophy to forgive and comfort the living, even while he grieved anew for the dead.

In silence Wade and Lora turned toward home. Not until they reached the lane did Lora speak again.

"You're free now of all blame," she said.

"I'd already wakened from my bad dream," Wade told her. "What we've just learned is deeply saddening, but it makes no real difference."

Back at the Tylers', Adam and Eddie and Jemmy were eating sandwiches informally in the kitchen and Mrs. Tyler was drinking coffee. Wade gave them no more than a brief greeting and went upstairs at once to his room.

"Did you find Morgan?" the old lady asked Lora.

"I'll tell you tomorrow," Lora said with a quick glance at the two boys. Mother Tyler understood and said no more.

Tomorrow, Lora thought, she would tell her all about what had happened in the woods. But now she had no heart for it.

"I'll take a cup of coffee up to Wade," she said, "before he turns in for the night."

A few moments later, when she tapped on his door, there was a pause before he called to her to come in. He had not lighted a lamp, and only a single candle burned on the mantel. He sat on the sill of the open window, looking out into the darkness of the lane.

"I've brought you coffee," Lora said, trying to sound matter-of-fact. "Do you think there'll be any more trouble tonight?"

"I don't believe so," he said. "Those bully boys were looking for someone they could cow with clubs. They've no taste for facing gunfire. By now the army must be sending men to New York's aid and our soldiers will be returning soon from Gettysburg."

He turned to watch her come toward him in the dim light. "How well that dress becomes you, Lora. What was the matter with us all that night of Serena's party?"

She had completely forgotten the dress she was wearing. She glanced down now to find that leaf mold clung to the hem, and some twig had torn a small rent in the skirt. How long ago it seemed that she had dressed for her birthday celebration.

She smiled at Wade. "You wanted me to look like Virginia that night, and I did not. How could you help but be disappointed?"

"How could I not see you as you are?" he said gently. "In the months you've been here, Lora, you've become the very heartbeat of this house. Do you know that?"

She could not tell what he meant, and to hide her confusion she gave him the cup of coffee with so quick a gesture that a little spilled over the brim. He took it from her absently, but did not drink. The strangeness was still in his eyes as he studied her and she felt the need of plunging quickly into words.

"Rebecca is going to stay in my room tonight." Again she tried to sound casual. "So I wondered—"

"Of course," he said quickly. "I'd forgotten about that. You'd like to have my room for tonight, wouldn't you? I can easily sleep on the library sofa."

"If it won't trouble you too much," she said with stiff courtesy. "I'll go and get my things."

But before she had reached the door he set the coffee cup down and came after her. "I'm tired of not knowing the truth. Ever since the night of the fire, after Morgan told me about Adam and you, I've wanted to know what he meant to you. That night when we stood in the yard together listening to the sounds of spring, I knew how dear you had become to me. But I couldn't know how much you might want release from this make-believe marriage I've foisted upon you. I have no wish to hold you against your will."

She looked up at him quickly, searching his face with eyes in which she willingly betrayed her heart.

"But I thought—" she faltered, and the old sense of shyness was upon her again.

He was not like Adam. He would never be like Adam—rough and sudden and compelling. There was both tenderness and gentleness in his arms, though they were strong as

302

they drew her close. There was no need to tell him what she thought because his mouth was warm upon hers and even as her pulses stirred she knew that his kiss meant more than this quick response of the blood. It meant both climax and beginning.

A puff of sea breeze came in the open window, guttered the candle low, then blew it to high flame. It flung the curtains aside and went off in a flurry through the woods. Far up on the hillside the pool stirred, rippling softly at its touch, then slept again, peaceful and untroubled in the summer night.

A NEW DECADE OF
CREST BESTSELLERS